Shy Girls CAN'T DATE Bad Boys

First Published by Halo & Claws Publishing 2023

SHY GIRLS CAN'T DATE BAD BOYS

Shy Girls Sweet Romances – Book 4

For information contact: https://www.hcpbooks.com

Cover Design by Emily Bourne
ISBN: 978-1-925990-36-2

Shy Girls CAN'T DATE Bad Boys

SHY GIRLS SWEET ROMANCES

MILLY ROSE

One

Despite the good I'm doing, nothing prepared me for that encounter. As I near the patient's door, with a copy of 'Wuthering Heights,' the memory hits me like a freight train.

For three weeks, I've volunteered at St. Mark's Hospital in Logan's Point. I spend my time reading to patients and helping the nursing staff with admin tasks. During my last shift, while holding this book, I heard a woman gasping in this room. Adrenaline hurried me to her bedside. She was clutching her chest and choking like something was stuck in her throat.

In shock, I blurted, "Ma'am? Are you okay?"

Her eyes locked onto mine, but swiftly rolled and became vacant. Dark bags hung below her dull eyes, and her skin grew paler by the second.

"Ma'am!" I yelped, tugging the woman's arm.

Her gasps became violent, and as my hand lifted, her body convulsed.

I dashed to the door. "Help! Anyone? She needs help!"

A nurse appeared in the corridor, and I sucked in a much-needed breath.

"In here," I called. "She can't breathe."

The nurse raced into the room, finding the woman struggling for life. She gasped and wheezed, while clutching and scrunching at the bedsheets.

As the machines by the bed beeped frantically, two more nurses rushed into the room. I backed out as Dr. Harris made his way in, steading the stethoscope around his neck.

Dr. Harris got the lowdown from the nurses, and in the chaos, I couldn't keep track of what was said. My eyes stayed locked on the woman as they placed an oxygen mask over her face.

A curtain was drawn around her bed and my knees grew weak. I dragged myself into the hallway, collapsed on the nearest chair, and sat rigid as I stared at the scuffed vinyl floor. My hands were wound in tight fists and my feet bounced against the chair legs.

I jolted when Dr. Harris touched my shoulder.

I stood quickly. "Is she okay?"

"Yes, she is," Dr. Harris said with a smile. He held out my copy of 'Wuthering Heights.'

I took the book, saying, "Oh, thanks. I must've dropped it."

"That was some quick thinking in there," Dr. Harris said. "The nurses said you sounded the alarm."

"It was nothing," I brushed it off. "I was just walking by."

"Don't sell yourself short," he replied. "Some people clam up at the sight of danger. What you did helped save that patient's life."

"I wouldn't call it lifesaving," I insisted. "You and the nurses are the heroes."

Dr. Harris smiled. "I'm glad you're here, Miss Ashworth. You do more good than you realize."

Dr. Harris moved up the hallway, and I took a long breath out.

Now, as I stand by her door, I take another exaggerated exhale. With my hands clasped around my book, my thumb stretches to flick at my bracelet. The fidgety movement helps settle the fizzing nerves inside me.

Okay, Vanessa. Game face on. No one needs to see you get flustered.

I peer into the room and the woman is soundly sleeping in her bed. *Phew.*

I really hate that I'm relieved about not visiting her. It's just I've never seen anyone gasp for breath before. It really rattled me.

I hug the book closer, and move onto the next room. My sparkle comes back as I knock on the open doorframe of my favorite patient.

"Mr. Raymond?" I step into his hospital room. "Would you like some company?"

From his reclined bed, Mr. Raymond's smile spreads and reveals his discolored teeth. His gray, thinning hair and mustache are highlighted against his aged, dark skin. He is a joyous man despite the tough years weathering his appearance.

"Well sure," Mr. Raymond says. "But what's a nice girl like you doing in a place like this?"

I give him my sweetest smile and sit by his bed. "Where else would I be? If I'm not here, I can't see your dazzling eyes."

The old man chuckles, nodding away like he's heard the best joke of his lifetime.

"Aren't you a sweetie-pie," Mr. Raymond replies. "What was your name again?"

"Vanessa."

"That's right. Gosh, my memory keeps slipping. Sorry, dear."

"Don't apologize," I say, resting my hand on his arm. "I've only visited you a few times. It's better you remember the doctors and nurses instead."

"I have rocks in my head if I ever forget your face."

I sit back and lift the book. "Care to hear a chapter from 'Wuthering Heights'?"

"I'd be delighted."

I sit forward on the chair by Mr. Raymond's bed, and he watches the ceiling as I read. I heard one of the nurses say he's living on borrowed time. He is such a lovely man, and I want to do anything to brighten his days. Even if it's just reading aloud a few pages from a classic novel.

Halfway through a chapter, Mr. Raymond drifts to sleep with a happy smile.

"Sweet dreams, Mr. Raymond," I whisper, standing from my chair.

After reading, I make my way back to the nurses' station. A few days ago, I found myself a side project of organizing the stationery cupboard. I get such a thrill from things being orderly and color-coordinated.

Things are in such disarray at the Logan's Point hospital. Or, dare I say, chaotic. Not exactly the vibe you want for a functioning hospital. Although, can you really call this place functioning? It is severely understaffed and in desperate need of new medical gear. There's no emergency department, just one wing that functions as a catch-all for patients.

If people from Logan's Point are lucky, they can travel to Victoria Falls for better treatment. Sadly, most people from this community can't afford that luxury. But they shouldn't need the option. They should be able to seek treatment in their own town.

Contrary to public opinion, I'm not perfect. I have a bad habit of lashing out at people who don't deserve it. After my last transgression, I want to be better. Firstly, I can easily raise funds for this hospital. I come from the wealthiest family in Victoria Falls, and have successfully choreographed many high society events. Secondly, I'm well aware of how red tape creates delays in funds getting to a cause. This is why I chose the instant reward of giving over my time.

My parents prefer I don't get my hands dirty, and work on projects that serve the Ashworth family image. But once I pointed out how this community directly benefits our family, I got their approval. My father's manufacturing plants provide the majority of income in this working class town.

Sadly, I didn't anticipate how my philanthropy would be twisted into a marketing stunt. When benefactors became interested in my venture, a lightbulb shone over my mother's head. Now she's adamant that my friends sign-up to volunteer as well.

My friends are beneficial to my school reputation, but I don't want their vibe in this hospital. Having them here, complaining about the smell of bleach, or a patient's cough, will ruin my soul-cleansing experience.

Thankfully, a sense of ease washes over me from standing in front of the stationery cupboard. As I zone in on the placement of items, making labels, and the overall aesthetic of the shelves, the surrounding noises dull.

"Wow, Vanessa," Nurse Cindy says, mesmerized by the opened cupboard. "You've done a fantastic job. The pens and highlighters look so pretty arranged in jars, and all the paper supplies look so orderly with their labels. Gosh, it's shameful how we had it before."

I close the cupboard and give her a bright smile. "No, it isn't. You need to spend your time looking after the patients. There's only so many hours in a day."

Cindy looks over at the computer and sighs. "I can't wait until you finish organizing the patient files. I know it's taking forever, but it'll be so worth it in the end."

"I'm just sorry I can't spend more time here."

"You haven't graduated high school yet. I'm sure you have much more important and, let's face it, fun things to be doing." Cindy grabs an extra patient file from the desk and moves around the counter. "Thanks for everything you're doing."

"No problem," I say, as she leaves down the hall.

As I sit at the computer and take a sip of water, something grabs my attention. From the corner of my eye, a boy enters the floor. I creep the wheeled desk chair forward and peer over the counter. The boy is tall with scruffy, coffee-colored hair. His broad frame is accentuated by a black leather jacket, commando-style trousers, and large, heavy boots. His head hangs low in an attempt to go unnoticed.

He snoops in rooms and scuffs his way to an unmarked closet.

What is he looking for? Is he hoping to find something worth stealing?

I leave the desk to approach him. If he's here to visit someone, at least I can point him toward the nurses' station where I can look up the patient's room number. He'd appear less suspicious that way.

But he purposefully avoided the desk.

"Excuse me?" I call out as he opens the janitor's closet. "Can I help you find something?"

He has slipped off his leather jacket and let it fall to the floor as he wipes his brow.

Slowly, he closes the door and turns to me. My mouth falls open as I gaze into his dark gray-blue eyes. They remind me of a stormy sea. His tanned complexion softens the angles of his face, and his full lips press into a line.

My heart flutters and I take a step back. I lift my hand, and it trembles in an exciting way. I swiftly lower it, clasping both hands behind my back.

He tilts his head with a questioning stare. He opens his mouth to speak, but then his head slumps forward and then back.

"Whoa," I say, stepping in close. "Are you okay?"

Again, he tries to speak, but this time his shoulders slump forward.

My hands lift toward him, worried he'll fall. "Hey, it's okay," I say. "Let's take a seat."

Before he can respond, his body gives way. I dip my knees, pulling my arms around his waist as he faints.

"Help!" I call out. "Help!"

Behind me, stomps hurry into the hall. Two nurses get on either side of us, lifting him off me.

"Vanessa, are you okay?" Cindy asks.

"Yeah," I say, puffing.

I step aside as Nurse Trisha races a gurney toward us.

"I have no idea what happened," I say, watching them attempt to wake him up. "He tried to speak and then collapsed."

While Dr. Harris paces the hall to reach us, Trisha checks my shoulder and neck.

"Any tension when I touch here?" she asks, pressing on my muscles.

"No. No, I'm fine," I reply. "You should check on him."

"Okay," Trisha says, backing away. "But you tell someone if it becomes painful."

"Will do," I say, standing as they lift the boy onto the gurney.

"Oh no," it tumbles out of Dr. Harris as he examines the boy's arm.

"What is it?" I ask, my heart pounding hard.

Dr. Harris makes eye contact with the nurses and then motions to the boy's lower arm. "You all know what this means. Tread lightly."

My anxiety ruptures and I fling myself by Dr. Harris. "What is it? What's wrong with him?"

"It's okay, Vanessa," he says soothingly. "We don't know yet. We need to get him checked in."

I pan around at the worried nurses' faces and stamp my foot. "What is it?"

Nurse Cindy motions to the inside of his lower arm. "It's this. Do you recognize it?"

My eyes lock onto the scorpion tattoo and I shake my head.

"It's the symbol of a local motorcycle club," Dr. Harris explains. "This is Vic Malone's son, Dax."

"They're thugs," Trisha says less tactfully. "I'd call it a gang, not a club."

"We still have a duty of care," Dr. Harris says to his staff. "No matter who this is, we must treat him with the same level of care we do everyone else."

"We're understaffed," Nurse Cindy counters. "We can't look after everyone."

My eyes grow itchy, threatening to tear up. "But he collapsed. You need to help him."

"Come on," Dr. Harris says. "Let's get him into room one-twelve."

"But that's Mrs. Gibson's room," the nurses protest in unison.

Dr. Harris nods. "Yes, and there's a vacant bed in that room."

The nurses relent and whisk him away on the gurney, leaving me standing motionless and dumbfounded.

Three days ago during my last shift, they aided the choking woman, and praised me for sounding the alarm. Now their contempt is plain to see. They wish I'd let this patient go unnoticed, lying by the janitor's closet.

But how could I do that?

Two

I collect his leather jacket by the closet door and inspect the back. It's emblazoned with a large scorpion, encircled with the words 'Logan's Point Scorpions.'

How is it possible—my bubble is so small—I didn't know there's a motorcycle gang in close proximity to my home?

Fingers crossed, Trisha was exaggerating.

I sling the jacket over my arm and return to the nurses' station. My eyes stay firm on room 1-12. I can't fault Trisha for being wary. My first thought was he was here to steal.

Why didn't it occur to me he could need medical attention?

My mouth runs dry as I edge around the counter, fingers twitching against the laminate. Although I can't fathom what draws me to him, I'm dying for another glimpse.

'Wuthering Heights' sits by the computer keyboard, mocking me. I should move on and keep another patient company, but I'm cemented here.

There was something about his eyes.

Desperation.

Fear.

Resolve.

Have the medical staff been in the room for a millennia, or what? Finally Dr. Harris emerges, focused on his ledger, and disappears down the hallway. Cindy leaves a moment later.

I gain her attention with a questioning stare.

"He's conscious," Cindy calls out as she moves onto another room.

The pounding of my heart softens and I inhale a renewing breath. I don't know this boy, but the relief is exhilarating.

Trisha leaves the room, holding a container of blood vials. "Vanessa, can you please keep an eye on the room?" she asks, passing the counter. "Let me know if Dax Malone tries to leave."

"Excuse me?" I say, taken aback. "How am I supposed to stop him?"

"I'll be right back," Trisha says in a rush. "I just have to get the bloodwork to the lab for Dr. Harris. He needs a tox screen ASAP."

"Okay," I reply weakly.

I fidget by the counter and crane my neck for another hopeful glimpse. Maybe I should go over there and say hi.

Without giving it more thought, I scoop up the leather jacket and march my way across the hall. In the doorway, I falter. All my thoughts vanish when I lock eyes with him.

"Ah… Ah…" I stumble, unable to spit out real words when he's reclining, shirtless, on the hospital bed. There's an IV in his arm, hooked up to a bag of fluids.

Dax's eyebrow raises, watching me grow increasingly awkward in the doorway.

My eyes wander over his defined torso, spotting yellow and purple bruises running along his ribs. They're partly obscured by an eagle tattooed along the base ribcage. My body heat rises when I spy roman numerals tattooed on the right hand side of his chest. I force my eyes away and land on the bed in the corner.

"Hello Mrs. Gibson," I say, stepping into the room. "How are you today?"

"Good, dear," she replies from her bed. "Have you come to read to me?"

"Yes, I… *shoot.*" I left the book behind. Now, there's no cover for my awkward behavior.

The shirtless hunk in the other bed clears his throat, and I turn his way as if he called my name.

He motions at the jacket in my arms. "Is that mine?"

"Umm, yes," I say, pivoting toward his bed. "You dropped it before."

I place the jacket on the table by his bed.

"You were…" His voice is hoarse until he clears his throat again. "In the hall… you caught me?"

A nervous laugh puffs out of me. "I guess you could put it that way."

His expression blankens. "So, what? Am I supposed to thank you?"

I jolt, frowning hard. "Well, no, you don't. I just wanted to help."

"They just took my blood and want to keep me here," he says in a sullen tone. "I was just looking for a quick out."

His building aggression confuses me. Squashing the urge to snap at him, my mother's voice enters my head. *"Poise. Grace. Own the room."*

I clasp my hands in front, and my thumb flicks against my bracelet. With an arched back and steeled nerves, I ask him, "What does a quick out mean?"

"I just needed something to keep me awake," he mutters. "Now I feel more woozy after they drained me. How am I supposed to ride my bike now?"

"You were riding before you collapsed?"

He huffs and looks up at the ceiling with a stony expression. "Why am I talking to you about this? Don't tell me you work here."

"I'm volunteering." I gesture at the IV, attempting to ignore the scorpion tattoo inside his forearm. "At least you're getting fluids. They'll make you feel better."

"Yeah, whatever. I suppose the doc told you about how I blacked out on the bike," he mutters. "It's just lack of sleep, but they take one look at me and think it's booze or drugs."

"And it isn't?" Oops. It just slipped out.

He gives me a heated stare.

I lift my hands in surrender. "Sorry. I didn't mean it."

He smirks, not buying it.

I can't help looking down at his body, zeroing in on the dark bruise over his ribs. I jolt and suck in a ragged breath.

"You right there?"

I wince. "It just looks painful."

He half-smiles. "I'll live."

Beside the bed, a dish holds an ice pack and a damp cloth. I lift the ice pack, offering it to him. "Don't you want to use this?"

He shrugs in response.

I lower the ice pack to his ribs. "May I?"

His head moves, and I take it as a nod, because ignoring his injuries is impossible.

He winces and hisses when the ice hits his skin.

I keep the ice pack steady. "Are you okay?"

"Yeah, just cold. I hate the feeling of ice."

"It'll help, though."

He grunts. "Mmm."

I bite into my lip, peering up at his face. "You're sweating."

"I'm fine."

I settle the ice pack on him and reach for the cloth. "Do you want me to…?"

He flinches. "Want you to do what?"

I hold the cloth closer to his forehead, and he recoils further.

"It's not chloroformed," I joke.

He whispers a laugh and eases on the bed. I seize the relaxed moment, dapping the cloth across his clammy forehead.

His eyes narrow, inspecting me. "Why are you doing this?"

My hand trembles, pulling the cloth back toward me. "I thought it'd make you more comfortable."

His eye contact intensifies. "So?"

I shiver, placing the cloth back in the dish. "Seeing you collapse was really scary."

"That doesn't mean you have to stick around. You could just walk away like the nurses did."

I swallow the building saliva in my mouth. I can't explain why it hurt me so much when Cindy and Trisha didn't want to help him.

"Uhh… I…"

His intensity withers, and he fidgets with the ice pack against his ribs.

With my body flushing with awkwardness, I back my way toward the door. "I should really get back to the desk."

Dax looks to the side of the bed. "Thanks, I guess, for bringing my jacket in."

"That's okay."

Mrs. Gibson pipes up. "Umm, dear. Weren't you reading to me?"

I tuck my hair behind my ears and blow out a shaky breath. "Oh, right. I'll go get my book."

Mrs. Gibson lifts a book from her side table. "I have one here, if you don't mind."

I compose myself and walk over to her bed.

"Trisha was looking through some boxes and found some old

books," Mrs. Gibson says. I take a seat by her bed and she lifts a banged-up version of 'Heidi.' "I loved this book when I was a little girl. Will you read it to me?"

"Of course." I take the book. "My grandmother gave me a copy of this book. I'm Swiss on my mother's side, and it's a tradition for every generation to read 'Heidi.'"

"Oh, that's lovely, dear. Have you ever been to Switzerland?"

I blush. "Yes, recently. I spent a few months over there, living in a chalet with my mother."

"How wonderful." Mrs. Gibson claps with joy. "I'm officially jealous."

I give her a small smile. It's better for her to imagine skiing and sledding, family nights cuddled by a roaring fire, and gazing out the tall windows with sinfully delicious hot cocoa. She doesn't need to know the reality of how heartbreakingly lonely I was over there.

I open the book and wonder if I'll be able to concentrate on the words when there's a gorgeously brooding guy in the next bed.

Mrs. Gibson is four pages in. One of her symptoms is fatigue, and getting this far was probably an effort for her. As I read aloud, my ears prick to the fidgeting and rustling in the adjacent bed. From the corner of my eye, I watch him getting agitated, listening to my voice. My mouth runs dry and I try to quieten so he can't hear me.

"Oh, dear. What was that?" Mrs. Gibson asks, curving a hand around her ear.

I sigh and repeat the line at a louder volume.

As I reach the next chapter, the shifting from the next bed stops.

Maybe he's asleep?

Before I can turn my head to check, Nurse Cindy marches into the room.

"Your blood work will be back soon," Cindy tells the shirtless hunk. "And Dr. Harris wants to organize x-rays."

Dax groans and sits up on the bed. "Nope. No way. I'm outta here."

Cindy leans forward, pushing him back down. "You're not going anywhere. You need to build up your strength."

"I'm fine. I don't need this."

"You fell off a moving motorcycle and hurt your ribs," Cindy says. "We need to identify the extent of the damage."

Dax smirks. "And if I do have broken ribs, what then? Do you wrap a bandage around it?"

"What's the problem here?" Dr. Harris asks, making me jolt as he enters the room.

"He doesn't want the x-rays," Cindy tells the doctor.

Dax gives Dr. Harris a skeptical look. "Can you do anything for broken ribs?"

"Well, no, they mostly heal on their own," Dr. Harris replies. "But if you know the extent of the injury, you can take preventative measures so they heal better and faster."

Dax places a palm on his side and exhales slowly. "I think I'll be fine on my own."

"Even so, you should stay overnight for observation," Dr. Harris replies. "Plus, I'm getting your blood work back and can hopefully identify the cause of your blackouts."

Dax pushes his legs off the bed, woozily sitting up. "I don't need those results. I know there's no drugs in my system besides whatever the nurse gave me."

Dr. Harris sighs and turns to Cindy. "Give us a minute, will you?"

Cindy nods. She turns to me, gesturing for me to leave the room with her. A chill runs over me, and I set the book down on Mrs. Gibson's table. I give her an apologetic smile and hurry out of the room as Dr. Harris pulls a curtain around the Dax's bed.

When I reach the nurses' station with Cindy, concern colors her face. "Everything okay, Vanessa?"

"Oh, umm, I…" I blink hard, taking my attention away from the room. "Yeah, I'm fine. I just feel bad about leaving Mrs. Gibson."

Cindy swats a hand. "Don't worry about that. I need to give her another dose of medication. She'll be out again soon."

Cindy moves onto another patient, and Trisha approaches the desk, writing in a patient's file.

I gesture at room 1-12. "Do you know much about the boy in that room? Do you think he'll be okay?"

She nods, keeping her head down as she continues to write. "Yeah, he'll be fine."

"And you already know him?"

"His name is Dax Malone," she says through gritted teeth. "The Malones run The Scorpions."

"And is it just a club? Or something more sinister?"

"I'd say it's closer to organized crime."

Queasiness grips my stomach. "Oh."

Trisha huffs, looking down at the papers in front of her. "Why in the world did he need to walk in here?"

"But he collapsed," I reply. "He needed help. Didn't he?"

She looks up with consideration. "Those bruises didn't just happen. If he's been having multiple blackouts, I'd suspect he has an illness. We'll know more when the lab results come in."

A weight sits on my chest. "Well I hope whatever he has is treatable."

"This job is taking it out of me." She wipes her brow. "I'm losing my empathy."

"Don't be tough on yourself. It's been a long day."

She winces. "All I see in that bed is a young thug. I don't see the sick boy."

I step away, unsure how to reply.

Trisha hugs the file. "He has something wrong with him, but I'm just terrified of treating him. Part of me wishes he'd stolen medication and left."

My mouth falls open from her words.

She walks away with disdain dampening her posture.

I exhale hard, staring at room 1-12's doorway. I can't imagine trying to steal medication when on the verge of collapse. Even if he's part of a crime-riddled family, he deserves better care than that.

A small voice inside my head begs me to let this go. I stand taller, willing my mother's voice to stay on mute. She'd tell me to pay no attention to this boy. But there's something about him.

Something both exhilarating and terrifying.

Something I can't ignore.

Three

When the nurses coordinate medication rounds, I return to work on the filing system because reading would get in their way. The fact that the nurses' station is in close proximity to room 1-12 is just a coincidence. That's what I tell myself, anyway.

Cindy bustles toward the desk with exasperation.

"Everything okay?" I ask.

"Oh yeah," Cindy says with exhaustion plaguing her tone. "Our new patient in room one-twelve wants to be discharged early. I just need to get the paperwork ready."

"Is that wise?" I ask with heightened concern.

Cindy shrugs, marking the form. "We can't keep him against his will. If he wants to walk out, fine by me."

"You and Trisha are eager to get rid of him."

Cindy frowns. "I wouldn't call him a dream patient. Anyway, you can head off too, if you like. It's getting late."

"Are you sure? I don't mind staying."

Cindy smiles. "Go on. You're young and beautiful. Go have some fun."

I sigh, grinning. "Why does everyone keep telling me to have fun?"

"Maybe because you act like a grown up at eighteen," Cindy jokes. "You can't even imagine the stuff I'd get up to if I were a billionaire's kid."

I laugh and collect my purse from under the desk. "Okay, I'll get going. See you tomorrow."

"Sure thing, Vanessa. Thanks for your help."

I step out of the nurses' station and keep my eyes fixed on room 1-12. I wish I had a good excuse to go back in there. I'd say goodbye to Mrs. Gibson if she weren't already snoozing.

Oh well, perhaps it's for the best. Trisha said his family is dangerous. Shouldn't that be enough to keep me away from him? Why hasn't it sunk in yet?

I pull out my cell phone to call my driver, but before I leave the wing, I notice Dr. Harris approaches the nurses' station. I should keep walking, but my ears prick.

"Does Dax Malone still want to leave?" Dr. Harris asks Cindy.

"Yes, I'm getting the paperwork ready now."

Dr. Harris pauses, frowning at a file in his hands. "I think we should warn against this. I have his full blood count, and the white cell differential has cause for alarm."

I drop my phone and both Dr. Harris and Nurse Cindy turn as I scramble to pick it up. Oh my gosh, that sounded serious. I pull myself together, wave goodbye, and hastily make my way out of the hospital wing.

I leave the building and call for my driver. He won't take long to arrive, and I scroll through my phone to pass the time. I'm so embarrassed, Dr. Harris caught me eavesdropping. Hopefully, he assumes I was glued to my phone and didn't hear a word.

Behind me, the doors burst open, followed by the thud of heavy boots.

I turn around and find Dax Malone walking out of the hospital, thrusting his arms into his leather jacket sleeves. He winces and presses his arm against his ribs.

"Wait," I blurt without forethought.

Dax peers my way with a questioning stare.

"Ah," I stumble on my words. "Sorry. Not to pry, but, should you be leaving the hospital?"

He frowns and I notice the fullness of his lips. "Why?"

My eyes fall on the hand gripping his side. "You're in pain."

He smirks. "Nothing I can't deal with."

Dax steps away from me, fumbling inside his jacket pocket. He pulls out a pack of cigarettes and places one between his lips.

When he flicks on a lighter, "You smoke?" tumbles out my mouth before I can catch it.

Dax takes a puff and pulls the cigarette from his lips. Smoky haze covers half his face.

I use my most apologetic smile. "I'm sorry. I didn't mean to blurt that out."

"You got a problem with me smoking?" he asks and returns the cigarette to his lips. It's then I notice a red rose tattooed below his thumb and running down the length of his hand.

"Don't you?" I question. "It's well documented they're bad for your health."

He laughs and takes another drag. He blows the smoke out the side of his mouth and holds the cigarette behind him. "Sweetheart, I got bigger problems than cigarettes."

My jaw clenches and I fold my arms across my chest. "My name's not Sweetheart."

He trudges my way, smiling. "Oh yeah. What's the name, then?"

I look him up and down. He's like no one I've ever met. Every shift at St. Mark's Hospital, I meet people from the community. No one has struck a cord like this guy.

"Cat got your tongue?" he jokes, flicking cigarette ash on the cracked pavement. He coughs, grunts, and presses firmly against his ribs. "What are you doing here anyway? You look dressed for Snob Falls."

I frown hard. "I look like a snob?"

"No, you twisted my words." He nods at the hospital, and asks, "What are you doing wasting a Friday at a hospital?"

"I'm here to serve the community."

"Who said you rich kids don't know how to live?"

Irritation gets the better of me. "Would it be better to let the nurses' go without any help?"

Dax replies with an eyebrow raise, and takes another puff of his cigarette.

As the repulsion filters through me, Roger pulls up at the curb in the shiny black sedan. I've given him strict instructions to never bring a limousine into Logan's Point. Turning up to a low socioeconomic area in a stretch is in very poor taste.

"Let me guess," Dax says, "your ride?"

"Correct," I say as Roger walks around to the rear passenger door.

"Miss Ashworth," Roger says, standing by the open door.

"Coming," I reply.

"Goodbye, Miss Ashworth," Dax replies in a teasing tone.

I walk to the door and thank Roger. He nods and walks back to the driver's seat. I take a step into the car, and then pull back.

I turn around and meet Dax's stare.

"How are you getting home?" I ask.

His jaw rocks. "What do you mean?"

I nod at the hospital. "Weren't you in an accident? Is your bike damaged?"

He scratches his head, further messing up his scruffy hair. "Ah, it'll need a bit of work, but it got me here. I can ride it home."

"With broken ribs?" I question. "Why don't we take you home? Is it close?"

He takes another drag and coughs while inhaling. He grimaces as he holds his side.

"Okay, get in," I say, stepping aside and holding the door wide open. "You can't walk or ride home in this condition."

"A little cough is nothing new," he argues.

"The cough is just a symptom of broken ribs."

"They probably only bruised."

"Probably?"

He shrugs. "They wanted to take x-rays, but I don't have that much time to waste. Plus the doc said they'll heal."

"There could be complications."

"It's not that bad. I'm positive they're just bruised."

"Oh, yeah? Where did you go to med school?"

Dax laughs, pressing onto his side. "You're a sassy one, aren't you?"

The description takes me off guard. "Sassy?"

"Yeah."

"No one has ever called me sassy."

"Well, you're giving me sass."

"Maybe because I've never met anyone like you."

"What, charming and adventurous?"

"Argumentative and trouble."

"Okay, I'll agree that I argue, but trouble? What have I done to cause you trouble? You're the one who started this conversation."

"I saw your leather jacket and tattoo."

"Am I branded a criminal because you saw a scorpion?"

I fold my arms, suddenly feeling cold. "I didn't know about The Scorpions before today, but apparently your gang has quite a reputation."

He smirks. "But not a big enough rep to get across to Snob Falls? We can't be that bad then."

I lower my guard. "Maybe not."

"Those scaredy-cat nurses like to exaggerate. You shouldn't believe everything you hear."

"I'm capable of forming my own opinions."

"Oh, I'm sure you are, Sassy."

I roll my eyes and find myself smiling. "It's Vanessa."

"What is?"

I sigh, shaking my head. "My name. It's Vanessa."

"Sassy suits you better."

"Ugh. You're impossible."

He grins. "No, I'm Dax."

"Can you stop being a clown and get in? Is it really so hard for you to accept help?"

With another trademark eyebrow raise, I gather his answer is yes.

He drops the cigarette to the ground and stomps on it with his boot. When he strolls toward me, I feel miniscule. Am I really letting a total stranger into the car? Not to mention, a stranger with an incredibly bad reputation.

"I'll take the bike home," he says flatly. "But thanks for the offer, Miss Ashworth."

Dax backs away and I notice his unbalanced steps as he approaches his motorcycle. I slowly enter the sedan, keeping a watchful eye as he hoists a leg over his bike.

"Roger," I call. "Can you follow him on his motorcycle? He's passed out twice today, and I want to make sure he gets home safe."

"As you wish, Miss Ashworth."

Roger takes off a few car lengths behind the motorcycle. Dax weaves around cars and takes corners sharply. My mind replays his slight limp and the way he held his side. I swallow hard, dreading the idea of him skidding off the moving motorcycle.

Is it an image I want to see in real life? I don't know this boy. I shouldn't want to know this boy. I should forget this boy, go home, and get ready for dinner at the country club. But I can't get Dax out of my head. Something deep inside me desires to know more about him.

But this is crazy. If my parents knew I was venturing further into Logan's Point, they'd be livid. I just won't get out of the car. I'll check Dax gets home okay, and then leave. Hmm. Maybe I'll also check out his home. And maybe see that smirk one more time.

As we breeze by the main street of Logan's Point, the houses outside my window become smaller and decrepit. The car jolts along potholes and cracks in the road. Unsupervised children gather by the road, and Roger is forced to brake hard when one chases after a wayward basketball. Unkempt plant life grows in the cracked sidewalk and disappears into abandoned homes. At least, I hope no one lives in them.

As the houses worsen, my stomach quivers when a thought hits me. How bad must Dax's home be? As the car slows where the motorcycle turned off, I gulp anxiously and unbuckle my seatbelt.

The car idles outside of a ranch-style tavern. Above the windows and below the guttering, an aged sign reads, 'Scorpions.'

"Miss, I don't think it's a good idea for you to get out of the car," Roger says, turning in the driver's seat.

I press a hand against my window, searching for Dax. "Do you think he got inside okay?"

"Yes, Miss. I really must be getting you back to Ashworth Estate."

As I look at the rundown building across the street, my blood runs cold. The front yard is cemented, but in true Logan's Point fashion, it's cracked and littered with overgrown grass and weeds. A few motorcycles are parked out front, accompanied by abandoned engine parts and other junk.

I assumed Dax was going home, but this must be where the motorcycle club meets up.

Despite it being a bad idea, I open my passenger door. "I'll be right back."

"Miss Ashworth, please…"

I don't let him continue. "Don't follow me. I'll be quick."

I leave the car and walk across the street. A damaged chain link fence surrounds the uninviting property. A knot ties between my shoulder blades and my jaw clenches. I don't understand what is drawing me in, but the need is hefty.

I take a deep breath and open the flimsy gate. The tall, deadened grass itches against my legs and the oily, garbage smell wafting from the abandoned junk agitates my nose. I look up at the beaten and torn screen door, and move along the side of the building.

Four motorcycles are parked along the driveway. Further down is an opened garage and I spy Dax's motorcycle parked inside.

I sigh out. *"Phew."*

Okay, Vanessa, that's enough. You've seen the bike and have confirmed he's home. Now, back away. No good can come from going any further.

Disobeying my inner voice of reason, I edge further down the side of the building.

"Where the hell have you been?" a garbled, mocking voice bellows from within.

I raise on tippy toes to view through the dusty window. Three burly men sit along a bar, which is cluttered with beer bottles and glasses of whisky. Standing against the bar is a leaner man with a muscular physique. He straightens up in order to grab Dax by his leather jacket.

Dax exhales hard when the man drags him closer.

"Huh?" the man says loudly by Dax's ear. "I asked you a question, pip-squeak."

Dax shoves him off and straightens his jacket. "Lay off, would ya."

The man appears to be twenty-five, and he laughs in a taunting way. "Come on, man. Can't a guy be concerned about his baby bro?"

Dax grumbles, walking away from the bar. "Why would you start now?"

The man and the burly crew at the bar cackle together as Dax disappears into the darkened rear area.

I lower onto my heels and turn back toward the road.

"Well, well," a husky voice says behind me. "Who do we have here?"

My breath hitches in my throat and I spin around to see an older, grease-stained man, grinning at me under a handlebar mustache.

"Hello, princess," he says, bearing a set of yellow teeth. "Looking for a bit of fun?"

I suck in a shallow breath, tripping over my feet as I back away from him.

The man chuckles, stepping toward me. "Don't be frightened, girly. I won't bite. *Hard.*"

Instinctively, I clutch my side where my purse usually hangs. My heart sinks, thinking about my bag sitting on the backseat, my cell phone resting inside. I want nothing more than to call for Roger's help. If I yelled out his name would he hear? Or would the moment I open my mouth enrage this man into hurting me?

The man steps forward, but is distracted by movement behind him. He turns around, and I spy Dax moving our way from the garage. He notices me and hastens his pace.

"Whoa. What are you doing here?" Dax asks, blinking hard at me.

The man sniggers. "You know this chick?"

"I know she shouldn't be around the likes of you," Dax says, stepping up to the hulking man. "Go back inside, McCoy. This doesn't have to be a thing."

"Give me a break," McCoy says, growing stern. "I saw her first."

I back against the wall, shivering as Dax shoves McCoy away from me. When Dax steps toward me, McCoy powers a fist into Dax's side.

My hands rush to my mouth as a gasp wooshes out. Dax's lips press together, muffling a moan. He then cracks a fist and smacks a bent elbow into McCoy's chest. Dax then swivels and punches him in the chest.

Dax shoves McCoy away, kicking dirt behind him as he yells at him to get inside.

McCoy straightens up and spits onto the ground. He roughly wipes his mouth, staring hard at Dax. "Only because I know it's not worth roughing up Malone's kid."

McCoy goes inside, and I place a trembling hand over my chest, desperate to slow my anxiety. But when Dax locks onto me, any hope of calm vanishes.

On his approach, my back fixes to the wall, and there's only a slither of air between us. His forearm raises over my head and rests against the wall. His eyes glue to mine in a way that makes blinking impossible. His breath hits the side of my face and I wince at the lingering cigarette scent. If fear hadn't paralyzed me, I'm sure my knees would knock.

"Hmm?" he says in a gravelly tone. "What are you doing here?"

I swallow hard. "I... I..."

His eyebrows knit together, and he frowns in confusion. "How did you get here?"

I shiver against the wall, trying to form a sentence. "I thought... You were... I didn't know if you'd make it home."

Dax removes his arm from the wall and steps back. "You followed me here?"

I gulp and nod.

"Why would you do that? Are you so bored you go looking for trouble?"

I try to catch my breath. "I couldn't... I didn't want..."

His head tilts and he moves in close again. "Were you spying on me? What exactly did you hope to get out of that?"

"I wanted to check..." I pant, searching for a solid breath. "Are you okay?"

Dax groans in frustration. "Just let it go. I don't need help." His hand fishes inside his jacket and presses onto his side. "You need to go home. You shouldn't be here."

My arms prickle with goosebumps. "Should you?"

He drops his tattooed hand, deadpanning at me. "This is my home."

We stare at each other for a long moment. All I hear is my heavy breathing, until the smashing of glass bottles and raucous laughter explodes from within the building. The reality of where I'm standing sends a shockwave of fear through me. I jolt off the wall and knock into Dax, who grasps my upper arms.

My mouth falls open as I look up at him. He releases one of my arms to slowly lift a pointed index finger over his lips.

I shudder against him, ready to keel over.

His veiny hand cups my wrist, pressing my bracelet into my flesh, while his other hand lowers to press on my middle back.

"I've got you," he whispers.

Footsteps hurry down the driveway. "Miss Ashworth." Roger's voice comes out panicked between labored breaths.

With an accelerated heart rate, I rip my hand from Dax's clutches.

"Come with me," Roger says, beckoning me toward him. "This isn't safe."

"I'm okay," I reply, attempting to placate him.

Roger's eyes don't blink as he pans between me and Dax. Color drains from Roger's face, and he swallows hard, determined to do anything in his power to remove me from this place.

"Please, miss," Roger says with hearty desperation. "They'll be expecting you at the country club."

When more loud crashes and voices come from within the building, Dax moves toward the side door.

"Well, what are you waiting for?" Dax says in a cold tone. "Get out of here."

Unexplainably, my shoulders slump, like I'm hurt he wants me to leave.

Before I can respond, Roger grasps my arm. "Miss Ashworth, we must go."

He releases me immediately, and I give him an agreeable nod. Pacing, we make it back to the car. Roger pulls the car onto the road before my seatbelt clicks.

As we leave Logan's Point, I move my thumb against my wrist, but don't feel my bracelet.

My heart drops to the pit of my stomach.

It's gone.

I scrunch my eyes closed, remembering how hard Dax held my wrist. I open my eyes, seeing the indentation from the chain.

My gut quivers and I swallow hard.

Did he intentionally steal it?

Four

"Not a word about this to my father," I warn Roger when he parks the car outside the three-story mansion I call my home.

"Yes, miss," Roger replies diligently.

I thank him and exit the car. As I approach the heavy front doors, they open and Murphy, our butler, stands in wait.

"Welcome home, Miss Ashworth," Murphy says with a cheery smile. "Hope everything went well during your hospital shift."

"Yes, thank you," I say, passing him in the foyer.

"Can I get you anything, miss?" he asks, closing the doors.

I wave him off. "No, I just need to take a shower and get ready for dinner at the club."

"Of course, miss."

I move through the hallway, barely glancing at the priceless art and antique furniture decorating the space. On my approach to the staircase, I overhear my brother, and there's heat in his voice. This can only be the result of one thing.

Our parents.

Ash bursts out of a side door, almost knocking me over.

"*Ness*," he yelps, reaching out and propping me up. "Sorry. I didn't know anyone was around."

"Your voice was muffled by the door, but I could hear the intensity. What's up?"

Ash flips his phone upward. "Just on the phone with our mother."

I hiss like I'm in pain. "That can't have been fun."

"I don't understand why she's constantly making things difficult," Ash complains. "It's been months since she left. Can't she just come home already?"

I bite into my lip. "Ash, Mom's not coming home."

Ash groans. "Why do you always have to be like that? Just because she didn't come back with you, doesn't mean she's staying over there forever."

"Even if she comes back to Victoria Falls, it won't mean she'll return to Ashworth Estate," I reply. "And if she did, I doubt she and dad will be back together."

"But none of this is certain."

"You didn't hear how she spoke in Switzerland."

Ash rolls his eyes. "Dad was cold while you were gone. But it didn't mean he didn't want you both back home."

"He was in denial." I pause for a beat before adding, "Just like you."

"Why are you being such a cow?"

"I just want you to get your head out of the clouds."

"I'm not delusional. There's nothing wrong with holding out hope."

"I can see what'll happen if Mom comes home," I say, sorrow drooping my expression. "I don't want you to be disappointed."

Ash's frown hardens as he stares me down. "How about you stop telling me how to feel?"

A lightning bolt of pain causes a splitting headache behind my forehead. I clutch it, rubbing a tight circle with my thumb, and turn away from my brother. I move toward the staircase and hear someone descending. I lower my hand and view my father tightening his cufflinks as he takes the last few steps.

"Oh, Dad," I say as he strides toward us. "I didn't know you'd be home. Are you joining me at the club?"

"Hi honey," Dad says, kissing my cheek. "No, afraid not. Two gents from Clifford and Garricks are in town so we're taking them to The Steakhouse."

I follow behind him as he marches toward the front door. "We?"

Ash's footsteps sound behind me. Over my shoulder, I watch him pull on a blazer.

I slow my pace, gawking at him. "You're going with Dad?"

Ash mutters, "You're so lucky you don't get dragged along to these things."

Yeah. I'm so lucky my younger brother gets included in the family business and I've been excluded my entire life. I exhale hard, derailing the negative thoughts, and catch up to Dad.

With my hands clasped in front, I ask, "Are you sure you don't want to wine and dine them at the country club?"

"I'm sure. They are guys' guys. They like a good pound of prime rib and a quart of scotch in them." Dad throws an arm around me. "They're not the type of men I want in the same vicinity as my little lady."

"I can hold my own. Plus, I can change my plans and join you at The Steakhouse."

Dad lets me go, chuckling. "No, darling, that's not something I see happening."

I pout. "I don't have to be kept on the shelf."

Dad cups my chin. "Of course you don't. You'll venture into the world and do amazing things. I don't need to watch over you because you're a good girl."

I smile despite the heavy weight of defeat. "Okay, Dad."

Dad moves over to Murphy, who holds out his coat.

My apathetic brother stops by me. "This'll be fun. Sitting around while they get liquored up and I've got four years until I'm allowed to drink with them."

I narrow my eyes. "Would you really want to get drunk with these guys?"

Ash shrugs. "It'd probably help the night go faster. And it'd help me forget all the vile things you've said to me."

I grimace. "Ugh. You wouldn't hide your problems with cocktails like our parents, would you?"

Ash smirks. "I know you've got the good and pure act going on, but wait until you get a taste of the real world."

I scoff in dispute. "And, what? Because Dad doesn't take me on business trips, I don't know what the real world is like?"

Ash pats my shoulder, wearing a teasing smile. "You just stick to planning social events."

"Ready to go, Ash?" Dad asks, walking out the front door.

"No, but I'm coming," Ash jokes, following Dad outside.

While Murphy closes the front door, I take the stairs, needing more than ever to wash this day away. Upstairs, I move through the halls to my wing. A swell of relief fills me on the approach to my bathroom. And then the doorknob turns.

Huh?

The door opens and Christie, my brother's girlfriend, emerges.

"Oh, hi, Vanessa," she says, almost startled. "How was your time at the hospital?"

I stop dead, unimpressed. "It was fine, thanks."

Christie's shoulders slump forward with guilt. "Oh, sorry about using your bathroom. It's just closer to my bedroom, and I didn't know you were home."

I force myself not to scowl. "It's fine. Although, it shouldn't matter if I'm home or not."

Christie raises her hands, palms facing me. "It won't happen again. I promise."

I rub my head, wanting this exchange over and done with. "It's no problem. I've just had a long day."

"Did you have a difficult shift?"

"It's a shock to the system, seeing so many people in distress."

"I bet. I think it's amazing what you're doing over there."

"Thanks." I move over to the bathroom and grip the doorknob. "What are your plans for this evening?"

"Movie night with my parents," she says, upbeat. "We'll be in the third floor family room. I'll see you later?"

I wave her off. "Probably not."

Before I enter the bathroom, our housekeeper Claudia enters the wing, passing Christie on her way out.

"Hello Miss Ashworth," Claudia says with a cheery smile. "How are you this evening?"

"Well, thank you. Although, I'm dying for a shower."

Claudia tilts her head with mild concern. "You look exhausted. How about I run you a bath with essential oils?"

Just the mention of it fills me with calm. "Would you mind?"

Claudia makes her way into my bathroom. "For you, I never mind."

"Thank you," I whisper, and wander into my bedroom.

I plonk on the edge of my bed and flop backwards on the quilted comforter. I stare at the vaulted ceiling as water hitting porcelain echoes throughout the hallway. Flashes of Dax and McCoy's scuffle replay in my mind. I shudder, frightened at how close I came to physical danger.

What the heck was I thinking? How did following Dax home seem like a good idea?

I press my hands against the sides of my head and scrunch my eyes closed. *Stop thinking about it. Stop thinking about it. Stop thinking about it.*

"Miss Ashworth," Claudia calls. "Your tub is ready."

I pull myself up despite my head feeling like an anvil. I drag myself into the hall and toward the bathroom. Mentally exhausted, I embrace Claudia for one of her cozy, warm hugs. Like magic, my head feels substantially lighter.

In the bathroom, I grin at my sparkling white, oval-shaped soaking tub. The scent of jasmine and lavender wafts from the bubbles and steam. I shed my clothes and submerge into the water.

"Ahhh."

I sink to the bottom of the tub and let my body float. My head rests on the ergonomic pillow, water seeps over my chin, and the scented fumes renew my energy.

Maybe I won't go to the country club tonight. Spending an hour in the tub and then heading to bed would be delightful. Murphy could organize a serving of pasta primavera to be sent from the club restaurant. I could eat in my bath robe while wearing a clay face mask.

Ah, sounds like heaven. If only my friends' mothers wouldn't be at the country club. When they notice my absence, it'll circulate its way back to my mother.

I'm already hearing her lecture. *"Being seen is everything, Vanessa. Every time you're in one of your peers' stories, it reminds their parents of the importance our family has in their lives. Your role is paramount in keeping those cogs moving. We can't afford any slip ups."*

And just like that, my serenity is destroyed. Any thought of my mother tips me over the edge. Despite the fact she left town, she insistently rules my life, as well as those in our circle. Sometimes, her instructions are so overbearing, they cause me to lash out.

And it's never at her.

Innocent bystanders take the brunt of my aggression. Hence the importance of volunteering at the St. Mark's Hospital. I have some serious karma cleansing to do.

As I gather a wad of bubbles, Dax Malone pops into my head again. Dang, I'd just gotten rid of him. What is it about this boy that makes him stick? He's an agitating, scruffy smoker, who's possibly in trouble with the law.

I exhale hard and focus on the heat of the water. *Snap out of it, Vanessa. He hasn't made your heart flutter. You're mistaking that feeling for repulsion. He's not worthy of being in your brain.*

Stop thinking about him.

Five

Before dressing, I slip into a bathrobe and apply my makeup on the fluffy stool in front of my vanity mirror. Claudia stands behind me, fanning a blow-dryer over my hair to create some volume. She gives me two braids atop my head, letting the rest of my hair sweep past my shoulders in carefully created waves.

Claudia then chooses three outfits from my closet, and I pick a white dress with a dusty pink and fuchsia floral design. The perfect early spring dress. It has a sweetheart neckline, but the decolletage is covered by a thin, netted lace. A jeweled brooch sits above the pointed toe of my dusty pink heels, and Claudia selects a matching purse, readying me for the country club.

On the drive into town, I keep my head down, pointed at my uninteresting phone. Not that Roger and I usually talk, but this trip feels especially prickly. He's the only person who knows I went to The Scorpions Motorcycle Clubhouse. He must think I'm such a fool. Or, at the very least, be wondering where my lack of judgment came from.

I'd also like to know.

When we pull up outside the country club, I wait for Roger to leave his seat and walk around to my passenger door. I give him a courteous smile as he moves to let me out.

"Any idea of what time you'll finish dinner, miss?" Roger asks.

I shake my head. "No, sorry. Sometimes the girls like to go into town for ice cream afterwards."

Roger's smile grows, endeared by the innocent act. "Very well, miss. Have a lovely evening."

"Thank you, Roger."

My heels click as I make my way toward the front glass doors. The doorman tips his hat, opening the door for me. I discreetly pull a bill from my purse and hand it to him on my way through.

"Good evening, Miss Ashworth," Gregory, the front of house manager, greets me with open arms. "So lovely to see you again."

I lean in and kiss his cheek. "Thank you, and you too."

"Your table is ready," Gregory says, leading me to the dining room. "Your two guests are already seated."

Gregory has a server escort me to my table. Despite the string quartet playing, tension stretches through my body. Chatter buzzes around the room, and like a reflex, a fake smile plasters on my face.

Hope and Sylvie sit across from each other at our usual table. A yellow and white flower arrangement nestles in a golden vase on the beige linen, surrounded by tall water glasses and perfectly polished silverware.

"Hi Ness," Hope and Sylvie say in unison with eager waves.

I tuck a wave of blonde hair behind my ear, sitting as the server pushes in my seat from behind. "Hi ladies."

The server fills my glass with sparkling mineral water, and I thank him with a tip.

"How was your shift at the hospital?" Sylvie asks, swirling her water glass. "I don't know how you stand it."

"I'm telling you girls, it's so rewarding to see the patients' happy faces after I read to them." Even though I don't want to ask them, my mother's voice is in my head. "Would either of you be interested in volunteering?"

Nervous laughter sizzles out of them.

Sylvie hunches, finding my eyes. "Wait. You're serious?"

I swallow hard and force a smile. "Mm-hmm. It could be a fantastic way to help drive donations."

Hope winces. "Maybe. It just makes me squeamish."

Sylvie nods. "Agreed. Being around all that sickness is one thing, but the place is so rundown. Makes me want a tetanus shot just thinking about it."

Hope smirks. "Maybe if we raise enough money, and they spruce up the place, I'll make time to go down there."

Sylvie takes a sip from her glass and sets it on the table. "You know we're in when it comes to fundraising. I can't wait for the black tie gala."

I sit back in my chair. "Me too because the planning is overwhelming."

"Don't stress, you have us," Hope says, patting my wrist. "I've heard buzz from my parents about the amount of redevelopment happening in that town. Plus, I think Victoria Falls residents will be happy to fundraise so Logan's Point people can find care in their own town."

My nose wrinkles as I avoid frowning. She may as well suggest we nail 'Keep Out' over the 'Welcome to Victoria Falls' sign. I know the girls think I'm crazy for spending my time in Logan's Point, but at least things are unexpected over there. Here, I can predict every single thing that will happen.

"Hello, Vanessa," a voice says from behind me. "Now my day feels complete at the sight of you."

I don't need to peer over my shoulder. I know exactly who belongs to the voice, and I'm already tired by his lingering presence.

"Oh, hey, LJ," I reply with a flat sigh.

Everyone wants me matched with Landon Prescott Junior, or LJ, especially my parents. His father is vice president of my father's plastics division. If LJ and I were a couple, it would mutually benefit our families.

LJ is a typical preppy boy who thinks he's God's gift. He's tall and slender with white blonde hair and aqua eyes. He's not Mr. Popular, but he's at all the right parties and is never on the wrong end of a conversation. On paper, he's the right boy for me to date.

If only I had one shred of romantic feelings toward him.

LJ slides a dining chair over from a nearby table, and sits himself between me and Sylvie. "How was your day?"

Sylvie rolls her eyes and scoots her chair to the right for some breathing room.

Before I answer LJ, I gesture at Sylvie. "Are you okay?"

"Now I am," Sylvie jokes, eyeing LJ. "I didn't want your suitor leaning over me to chat you up."

LJ chuckles. "Suitor? Are Vanessa and I in a Victorian era courtship?"

I place my hands in my lap, knowing LJ is two slimy sentences away from grasping my hand. "LJ, we're not courting in any era."

"Come on, Ness," Hope says with a mischievous grin. "You two are adorable together. You're like, picture-perfect couple goals."

An air of surprise puffs out of me. "Hope, you're the one who has an adoring boyfriend. LJ and I are not a couple."

"Vanessa's right," LJ says, turning to my friends. "Despite all the social events and charity balls I've escorted her to, she's hesitant to commit."

My eyes go up and to the right, but I'm careful not to let them roll.

I want to roughly huff my exasperation, but only a faint whisper glides from my tight mouth.

Sylvie plucks her glass and lifts it to her neckline as a teasing smile graces her lips. "Maybe you'll escort Vanessa to the upcoming gala we're planning."

LJ turns to me with an eager grin. "Color me intrigued. What's the new cause?"

"Ness's pet project," Hope cuts in. "St. Mark's Hospital in Logan's Point."

LJ settles in his seat, folding his arms across his middle. "Logan's Point has become a new fascination. Seems everyone wants to buy up some part of that town."

"I don't want to buy the hospital," I say dryly.

LJ smirks. "Of course not. You want to buy them a new x-ray machine or a batch of defibrillators?"

"They're running on a shoestring budget," I reply. "I think it'll take more than one event to raise all the funds they need. For a start, they're understaffed, so signing up volunteers is step one."

Hope and Sylvie shift in their seats, averting their eyes so I don't put extra pressure on them.

LJ turns toward me in his seat, hanging a crooked arm on the back of his chair. "So, you ladies would make up the candy striper initiative?"

Could he be any more condescending and sexist? I don't give him the courtesy of eye contact when I reply, "They don't have candy stripers at St. Mark's."

LJ sniggers. "Isn't that why you want to sign-up volunteers?"

Instinctively, my hand presses on my chest, and my palm massages a burrowing ache. "What I'm doing at St. Mark's means something. It's not just a way to pass the time because I'm a girl."

"Oh, Vanessa," LJ says in a softer tone. In a sweeping movement, he takes my hand from my chest and envelopes it in his hands. "Of course it's meaningful. Anything you do has merit."

The girls awe at his gesture, yet my back seizes. I want to yank my hand from his grip, however, the unkind gesture would make it back to my mother. Even though she's on another continent, she knows more about what's happening in Victoria Falls than I do.

I clear my throat and send my hand limp in his. He releases me, and I take the opportunity to focus on the girls. With my mother's voice still in my head, I double-down on the volunteering. As soon as Hope's eyes meet mine, I strike. "So, can I expect you to officially sign-up to volunteer your time at St. Mark's?"

Hope audibly gulps and her complexion slightly pales. I hold her stare, forcing her answer, "Oh, yeah, sure. Of course."

I smile and turn to Sylvie. "You too?"

Sylvie chokes on a mouthful of mineral water. She lowers the glass and clears her throat. With reddening cheeks, she coughs and nods. "Umm, yeah, totally."

"I just have too much work at the moment," Hope says, refolding her linen napkin on her lap. "You know, juggling school assignments and planning committee duties."

"Oh yeah," Sylvie is quick to pile on. "Me too. There's just not enough hours in the day."

Hope feigns laughter. "Yeah, you know what our mothers are like."

Yeah, a cake walk compared to mine.

LJ leans close to me. I know he'll reject the suggestion, but his smugness is irritating me.

"You know, it's not just girls who can sign-up."

LJ smirks, throwing a thumb at himself. "Are you suggesting I volunteer too? I can just imagine my father's reaction. You know he wants me at the company as much as possible before I pack up for college."

You mean *my* father's company? The words want to fly out my mouth, but what good would it do?

He stands, and my stomach squirms in anticipation of what's about to happen.

"I have to get back to my table." LJ lifts my hand and bends over to kiss it. "I'll catch up with you later, sweetheart."

My insides revolt from his touch, mocked by the squeals of delight from my friends.

Sylvie moans when LJ leaves. "Oh my gosh, I miss having a guy around."

I grin at her. "You use guys as playthings. No wonder you can't keep one around."

"I used to be able to call up Beau Stevenson to take me out," Sylvie says with a devilish smirk. "Gosh, my parents absolutely hated that. Ah, I loved it. But, no. Now he has to be a doting boyfriend to his mousy girlfriend."

Hope smirks, nudging me. "Even you had your eye on Beau for a moment or two."

I tap the side of my water glass and sigh. "I'd like someone to look at me the way he does his girlfriend."

Hope and Sylvie share a look and then burst into laughter.

Hope grabs my hand and locks eyes with me. "Ness, honey, every guy looks at you like that."

I frown and pull my hand away. "No, they don't. All they think about is my last name and dollar signs."

"Oh, stop being so miserable," Sylvie orders. "You're gorgeous with or without the heiress title. You can have any guy you want. It's beyond me why you haven't made it happen yet."

I shrug. "I haven't met anyone I could see a future with."

Hope splutters a laugh and motions at LJ's table. "You have a real-life Prince Charming waiting to put a ring on your finger."

My tongue sticks to the roof of my mouth, almost gagging on the thought. "There's nothing charming about LJ's game."

"Just get over it," Hope says. "I can already see the multi-page magazine spread about you and LJ, your fabulous life, and all your children."

"Whoa." I scoff. "How far in the future do you daydream?"

Hope snaps her fingers at me. "We can all see a future for you and LJ. Why can't you?"

I sit back on my seat, as our server asks for our meal orders. Unfortunately, I'm not surprised by my friends' attitudes. Even when they have boyfriends of their own, they constantly remind me about their jealousy. How they'd die for an LJ-type to vie for their attention. They're convinced I'm playing a big game, waiting for LJ to promise me more for our future.

I wish, just once, someone would believe I'm not interested in that future. I've seen where it leads. My parents rarely speak to each other, and when they do, it's on a video call in the middle of the night that's ninety-percent arguments.

Halfway through dinner, the conversation turns from school gossip, back to me.

Hope clears her throat, leaning in. "Is the reason you're pushing LJ away because you're still hung up on your tutor?"

I drop my fork, letting it clank against the china plate.

Sylvie giggles. "Look at her. Oh my gosh, Ness, you're going red."

From anger, not from embarrassment.

"Aww," Hope coos. "She misses him."

I pick up my fork, muttering, "Just drop it."

"All I wanted to say," Hope whispers, "is that I get why you're standoffish. You're hung up on a guy you can't be with. Your mother didn't approve, right?"

My back tightens and I keep my focus on my dinner plate. "I don't want to talk about it."

A hush falls over the table, and the sound of chewing takes over the airspace. Soon, Sylvie and Hope steer the conversation back to school gossip, but I'm checked out. I don't even remember where this silly rumor about me and my tutor started. But compared to what really happened while I was in Switzerland, it's better I don't deny their speculation.

Six

Before I explode from the onslaught of gossip, I excuse myself from the table. Ensuring the girls don't follow, I tell them I'm leaving to speak with Mrs. Haverford about her upcoming local council re-election campaign.

I just need air before I can finish my evening with them.

As I make my way to the foyer, my ears prick to my name being called. My shoulders slump and I mutter a groan.

LJ catches up to me, slinging an arm around my shoulders. "Where are you going, sweetheart?"

Gosh, I hate it when he calls me sweetheart. It's a Stepford Wife training name.

"I just need some air, LJ." I lift his forearm from my shoulder. "Can I have a minute alone?"

"What kind of gentleman would I be if I didn't escort you outside?"

"You really don't have to," I say as the doorman opens the front glass door.

LJ walks me out. "Don't be silly. It's my pleasure to be by your side."

Sickening. Must he lay it on this thick? I swear, everything in my life is a rehearsed show. I bet conversations went down like this between my parents when they met in college.

"You seem down tonight," LJ remarks. "Something's wrong?"

I shrug it off. "Just feeling a little off."

LJ stays close. "Why don't you tell me about it?"

I step back. "It's nothing, really."

He gives me a skeptical look. "Ness?"

I sigh, turning away from the front entrance. "I just want people to think better of me."

"How could anyone not see you as the best?"

"Ever since I left for Switzerland, rumors have circulated about me."

LJ sniggers. "And after you got back. The girls talk a lot about my competition; your hunky tutor. Apparently, when you were abroad, you spent all your time with him."

I flick my hair off my shoulder and keep my eyes downcast. "I'm well aware of what's been said."

"Should I be worried?"

I lift my eyes and blanken my expression. "LJ, we're not a couple."

"There's no guy at Ashworth Academy who's closer to you than me."

"That doesn't mean anything. I'm not dating anyone from school."

"So there is someone outside of our circle?"

I sigh, shaking my head. "There's no someone in my life."

"Then why are you making things so difficult for us? High school would've been the perfect time to get all the dating out of the way. We'd be engaged during college, and married by the time I'm a junior executive of plastics."

A soft retch hitches in my throat. "It's all so easy to figure out, isn't it."

LJ leans in close. "We're lucky, Ness. Most people don't come from such influential families with mutual benefits."

"I don't want to be a benefit," I say in a feeble tone. "I want to be more than a commodity that helps someone step up the corporate ladder."

LJ laughs. "Sweetheart, this is the real world. Why don't you relax and join me in it?"

An indignant huff rushes out of me. With a stamp of the foot, I spin on my heels and march away from him.

"Vanessa," he whines, following me. "Come back here."

He reaches for my arm and I flail to get him off.

"Vanessa. Would you stop?"

"No!" I snap. "Let me go."

"Not until you calm down."

"Stop telling me how I should feel."

"How would your mother feel about you acting this way?"

My chin drops and my mouth hangs open. Did he really just go there?

He releases my arm and I wobble on my heels, fighting to stay upright. From behind, LJ's hands cup my waist, keeping me balanced.

I swallow roughly, taking a step forward, but his hands don't leave me.

"I'm fine," I mutter. "You can let me go."

His hands fall off my waist, leaving prickles under the material of my dress. I fight the urge to shudder.

"Let's go back inside," LJ says in a low voice, "before we make more of a scene out here."

"Can you just give me a minute? I need some air."

"I don't think that's a good idea."

I fold my arms, keeping my back to him. "LJ, please."

"Fine. Don't be too long."

LJ's footsteps back away, and I finally let out a breath of relief. As the swing of the front doors sounds LJ's exit, a new sound snatches my attention. A rev that makes my heart skip a beat.

My stomach twists as I turn toward the parking lot. I freeze when I see him. Dax Malone, straddling his humming motorcycle.

What the heck is he doing here? Is this an intimidation tactic? Does he want to berate me some more?

Dax leans forward and rests his arms on the handlebars.

Is he seriously just staying here?

I tilt my head, waiting for him to ride away. But he doesn't. He continues to sit there, taunting me.

I eye the doorman and notice his growing suspicions of Dax. The last thing I need is him confronting Dax, who then tells him he's on the property grounds because of me.

That's it. He has to go.

I click my heels down the path towards the running motorcycle.

"Hi there," he says with a cheesy grin.

"Umm. What are you doing here?" I ask, feeling shaky on my approach.

A teasing smirk tugs at his lips. "What? Don't you like when people turn up to your place unannounced?"

"You're here because I followed you home?"

His expression grows serious. "I want to know why you were there. There has to be an angle."

I shiver from his intent gaze. "There was no ulterior motive. I just wanted to know you were safe."

Dax rolls his eyes with a laugh. "What a load."

A hurt gasp shoots out of me. "I was."

"What is this?" Dax says, gesturing at the front facade of the club. "Is this how you rich kids pass the time? Find some charity case to snoop on until you get bored and look for the next?"

I place a trembling hand over my chest. "I didn't call you a charity case. I just didn't think you were well enough to ride your motorcycle. I wanted to make sure you didn't have another accident."

He tilts his head, looking me dead in the eyes. "And why would you care?"

"Because I saw you collapse at the hospital and it scared me," I reply. "I tried to hold you up when you were out cold."

"No one else in that hospital cared about me," he says in a low voice. "Why would you?"

I cross my arms and turn away from him. "Look, I just didn't want someone seriously injured or worse on my conscience. It's no big deal. Can we just drop it now?"

"Can you understand why it was so weird to have an Ashworth at the clubhouse?"

I turn to view him over my shoulder.

He gives a slight nod. "I know all about your family. If any of those guys knew who you were, you wouldn't have made it out of there."

I suck in a sharp breath. "Is that a threat?"

He shakes his head and I turn my body toward him. "It's a warning. I don't want to see you back there ever again. It's not safe for someone like you."

"I saw your bruises. Is it even safe for you?"

Dax pushes off the handlebars and reaches for his helmet, which sits behind him. "Maybe you should get back inside. Your boyfriend looked super pissed you didn't follow him in."

I scoff. "He's not my boyfriend."

Dax wriggles his eyebrows, intrigued. "Then who is he?"

"He's none of your business."

Dax laughs. "So he is your date?"

I click my tongue, looking up at the twinkling stars to calm my frustrations.

Dax taps the helmet sitting on his lap. "Oh. He's someone you want to get away from?"

I look back at Dax, hoping it's not written all over my face.

He snaps his fingers. "Okay, got you." He lifts the helmet, offering it to me. "You want an out, then?"

"I thought you just said being around your place wasn't safe?"

Dax sniggers. "I wouldn't take you there. I'll just get you away from here before Mr. Preppy comes strolling out, looking for you."

I shift my weight between my feet, and clutch the strap of my purse before it slips off my shoulder.

Dax hikes a leg over the motorcycle and moves to the rear. He lifts the lid of the small locker trunk anchored to the bike. "You can chuck your bag in here, if you want."

I grip the strap of my purse tighter, feeling cemented to the footpath.

Dax digs into a pocket of his leather jacket. "Oh, before I forget. I found this on the clubhouse driveway."

My mouth falls open as I stare at my bracelet in his hand.

His eyebrow raises. "Do you want it back?"

My hand trembles as I reach for it. "You didn't steal it?"

Dax snorts. "*Nice*. No, you ripped your hand away from me so fast, I guess the clasp opened." Dax tilts his head, looking at the slim chain in his hand. "I mean, I thought about keeping it. Looks like it's worth a pretty penny, but I thought you might be missing it."

I take the bracelet and clasp it around my wrist. "I was. I feel like I'm missing a limb when it's gone."

"Bit dramatic."

"I just wear it every day, that's all."

Dax gestures at the motorcycle. "So you coming or what?"

I look back at the clubhouse, thinking about my friends and everyone else who expects me to go inside.

Dax smirks, waiting for my response. "Make a decision, Sassy."

This is something I'd never expect to happen. Yet, here it is, playing out before me. If I say no, I walk back inside the club. I'll listen to more gossip, order coffees, and then move on to the ice-creamery where the girls will text their crushes and I'll feign interest.

If I say yes, I have absolutely no idea what will happen.

My thumb flicks against my bracelet, and I smile. I hold out my purse, letting Dax take it. I pick up the helmet and lift it over my head. "Does this just slide on?"

"Yeah," Dax says, closing the locker trunk. "It has a strap underneath the chin."

The helmet fits loosely around my head and I fiddle with the strap until it tightens. Dax closes in and swivels the helmet by my ears.

He taps the sides, saying, "Just checking it's snug."

"I guess it's a little loose," I reply. "But it's safer, right?"

Dax throws a leg over the motorcycle. "Sure."

"Where's your helmet?"

"You're wearing it."

"Oh. You'll be driving without one?"

Dax chuckles, motioning to the space behind him. "Relax. This isn't my first rodeo. Now, hop on."

Ignoring my reservations, I lift the skirt of my dress and climb on behind Dax. I snuggle in close to him and hook my arms around his middle.

Dax revs the engine. "Get ready."

Before there's a moment to back out, I squeal as the motorcycle takes off. He glides by the parking lot and out the main property gates. The bike swerves around street corners and weaves through traffic as we flee the country club. I press myself against the dip between Dax's shoulder blades. We live in a lush mountain area, and the motorcycle makes me feel the incline and dip of every hill.

Dax avoids the main streets, skirting the motorcycle through neighborhoods until he reaches the edge of town. My arms brace around him like they're made of steel. My jaw clenches and my mind whirs. Why would this boy track me down? He shouldn't want anything to do with me. I don't even know where we're going. What if he takes me toward his home?

As the neighborhoods I'm familiar with zoom past us, I realize we're headed in the direction of Logan's Point. The pressure in my mouth builds as I grit my teeth harder. He made a point of letting me know he knew about my family. How could I be so stupid and get on this motorcycle? This was a setup. A trap. He lured me to follow him so The Scorpions could kidnap me and ask my father for a hefty ransom.

My arms tighten around his waist. "Stop. Stop."

Dax groans. "Geez. You wanna loosen your grip?"

My hands clench together and I push them into his stomach. "Stop! Stop the bike."

Dax slows the motorcycle and veers to the side of the road, and a muted scream rushes out of me. Once parked, I whip a leg off the bike and back away with urgency. I rip off the helmet and chuck it to the ground.

"Whoa. What's up with you?" Dax asks, getting off the bike and stepping toward me.

I lift my hands in defense. "Stay back!"

Dax halts, arching an eyebrow in curiosity. "What happened? You seemed pretty eager to jump on the back at your fancy country club."

"Tell me that wasn't all planned," I say in a rush.

Dax sniggers. "What? That I knew when you'd walk out and that you'd agree to ride with me? I wasn't even planning on asking you."

I slam a hand on my chest. "You know who I am?"

The fun in Dax's expression drops. He stares at me, dumbfounded. "What was that?"

"You said the men at your clubhouse would trap me if they knew I was an Ashworth." Jitters run throughout my body and my heart pounds. "Did you tell them who I was? Did they make you find me?"

Dax huffs, running a hand over his face. His jacket sleeve rides up, exposing part of the scorpion underneath. "Are you asking if I'm kidnapping you?"

I hug my middle and my stomach drops. "Yes."

Dax shakes his head, retrieving a pack of cigarettes from the inside pocket of his leather jacket. "You're unbelievable."

My teeth chatter. "That's not an answer."

"Why would I have told you to leave when you were at the clubhouse?" Dax asks, perplexed. "Why would I waste my time like that? I could've let McCoy take you right then and there."

The thought sends me into a shiver.

He looks me dead in the eyes. "I told you being there wasn't safe. I'm not taking you back."

I rub my goosebump-riddled arms, trembling at the honesty in his words. "Can you understand why I jumped to that conclusion?"

Dax smirks. "Sure. Why should you believe someone like me?"

He digs a cigarette out of the pack, along with a lighter.

"Wait!" I shout, lifting a hand like a stop sign.

He pauses with the cigarette and lighter fixed between his fingers in mid-air.

"Don't light up." I look around our surroundings for an excuse. "Can we go somewhere else?"

He lowers the cigarette and joy sparks within me.

"Why?" he asks skeptically. "You just accused me of kidnapping you. Why would you want to get back on the bike?"

I shrug. "It was just a little panic attack."

"Forget that," Dax says gruffly. "Why would *I* want to take you anywhere? I should just leave you here on the side of the road."

Fear bubbles inside me and I hurry closer to him. "I'm sorry I accused you of something so ugly. Please don't ditch me here."

He tilts his head and his grin verges on sinister. "Why? Afraid you don't have cell service to call your driver?"

I frown, powerless.

Dax chuckles, putting the cigarette pack inside his jacket pocket. He leans against the motorcycle, lighting the cigarette which sits between his lips. He exhales smoke from the corner of his mouth and grins at me. "No, I got it. Little Miss Precious doesn't want to call her driver and explain why she's stranded alone on the side of the road. Is that right? Afraid it'll get back to Mommy and Daddy?"

I fold my arms and my facial muscles contract as I sigh. He's so irritating I forgot to conceal my frustration.

Dax lifts the cigarette, inspecting it. "Wait. Is it this? Were you trying to stop me from lighting up?"

"You have to admit, it's a vile habit."

He takes another drag of the cigarette, gradually exhaling the smoke. "You called your little outburst a panic attack. I'd call it having a good day." He lifts the cigarette and his shoulders slump forward. "These things keep me from spiraling. I'm leveled out when I have one."

I bite my lip, contemplating his words.

He takes another drag, perching against the bike. "It's better than getting loaded on booze everyday."

Is it? "Hmm. I guess."

After another puff, Dax stands, drops the cigarette, and stomps on it with his heavy boot. Clutching his side with one hand, he dips to retrieve the helmet I chucked on the ground.

"Do you really want me to take you somewhere?" he asks.

I gesture to his side. "Are you okay to go somewhere?"

He shrugs. "I'll be riding around regardless."

"I don't want to go back to the country club," I admit. "And I'm not ready to go home. Other than those two places, I have no idea where I want to go."

Dax offers the helmet. "I have a place in mind. That is, if you won't freak out again mid-ride."

I take the helmet. "Where are we going?"

"Nowhere near the clubhouse."

I slide on the helmet. "Okay."

He slides off his leather jacket. "Here, take this. You've been shaking this whole time."

I take a step backwards. "No, it's okay."

He pushes his tattooed arm out further. "Just take it."

Inadvertently, I shiver again. I grasp the jacket and murmur a thank you, somewhat exhilarated by the fact I have no idea where I'm going.

Dax throws a leg over the motorcycle and revs the engine in preparation. I slide my arms into his jacket. I could fit another set of arms in the sleeves and the waist could wrap around me one and a half times. Trying not to inhale lingering cigarette fumes, I zip up the jacket and then climb on behind him.

When I hug my arms around him, he remarks, "Try not to cut off my air supply this time."

A nervous chuckle hiccups out of me. "Sorry about that."

Dax revs the motor again and takes off from the side of the road.

Seven

Dax rides further out of town, hugging the edges of Mountains Road, which is notorious for sharp bends and winding curves. I keep my helmeted face planted against Dax's back, barely opening my eyes. However, they're forced open when I feel the bike descending.

"Huh?" I mumble, as the bike skids down a dirt track.

I hug Dax tighter and he wheezes in response. I want to apologize and loosen my arms, but fear keeps me locked. I only relax once the motorcycle comes to a stop.

Dax turns off the engine and pats my hands, which are still intertwined around his gut.

"You can let go," he teases.

I squeak and unlatch my hands. I yank off the helmet and slide off the motorcycle, giving him room to move.

When he gets off, he takes one look at his bulky jacket bulging around me and sniggers. "Looking good, Sassy."

I sigh and unzip the jacket. "You can have it back."

He lifts a hand, shrugging. "No, you keep it. It gets pretty chilly out here at night."

Dax moves to the rear of the motorcycle and retrieves my purse from the trunk. He hangs it on the handlebars, because I'm mesmerized by the view. He has brought us off the road and closer to the ravine. There are no street lights or headlights to brighten the area, instead leaving the job to the bright moon and magical stardust above. They highlight the striking mountain edges, casting shadows in navy, gray, and forest green. Further into the ravine, the lake reflects the spectacular view.

"Wow," it breathes out of me. "I haven't admired a view like this in such a long time."

Dax takes a seat on a clump of rocks. "This is my favorite place in all of the mountains."

I smile, but it quickly fades when Dax habitually checks for his pocket.

He looks at me and beckons me over. "Hand me a cigarette, would ya?"

I wince, not budging. "Must you?"

"Must you give me a hard time? You've already complained twice when I've lit up. Do we need to do this a third time?"

I cross my arms, feeling the cigarette pack press against my ribs. "I just don't know how you can do it when they're proven to kill people."

Dax leans forward, resting his forearm on his bent knee. "Maybe if I lived in a mansion and was swimming in enough cash to have anything I wanted, I'd make better choices."

"I'd feel this way about cigarettes whether my family had money or not."

"But they do," he says bluntly. "And that gives you access to things

I don't have."

I step forward and point at his scorpion tattoo. "So, because you're part of that gang, that means you have to smoke? I'm not buying it."

"First of all, it's a club, not a gang." Dax stands, dusting off his trousers. "Second of all, don't pretend to know anything about my life."

He steps toward me, reaching for the jacket zip. I gasp, jolting in place as the zip lowers down my body. I seize up when he reaches inside and retrieves the pack.

Dax moves back to the clump of rocks, plonks down, and pulls out a cigarette. His eyes move up and down my body, and I hastily pull the jacket zipper higher.

He smiles. "Are you comfy in that?"

I frown, yanking at the collar of the jacket. "Actually, no. It smells of ash and smoke."

He twirls the cigarette between his index and middle finger. "If you'd prefer to freeze, I won't be offended."

I can't take his attitude any longer, and a groan thunders out of me. I unzip the jacket and let it fall off my shoulders and hit the ground.

I step away from the jacket. "I wouldn't call this temperature freezing."

He blankly stares at the rejected jacket. "Aren't you going to pick that up and give it to me?" His gaze lifts to me. "I thought you rich kids were taught manners."

My gut squeezes. Ordinarily, I'd never discard someone's personal property like that. But this is no ordinary situation. Dax Malone is pushing all the buttons no one in my community does. I'm usually twelve steps ahead of everyone I meet. But with this guy, I have no idea what will happen next.

I look down at the jacket, and then back at him. "What will happen if I don't pick it up?"

Dax stares at me for a long beat. Nervousness squirms inside me. I'm about to cave and pick it up, when Dax startles me with a sizzle of laughter.

"Nothing," he says, shaking his head as the laughter dissipates. "Nothing will happen if you leave it there."

My eyebrows knit together. My teeth graze my bottom lip, curiosity getting the better of me. "And what if I pick it up? Will something happen then?"

The unlit cigarette twirls between his fingers. "No. I'm not planning to do anything either way."

With no clue what that means, I pivot between Dax and the jacket. I lower and scoop up the jacket, asking, "Any chance I can use it as a seat cushion?"

Dax runs a hand over his scruffy hair and shuffles along his rocky seat. "Sure. Take a load off."

I move toward him and place the jacket on the bumpy surface. "Thanks."

He shrugs a response.

I motion at the view. "So, you come here often?"

A murmured laugh puffs out of Dax. "Sounds like a pick-up line."

A hot blush attacks my cheeks, and I duck my head, covering my face with my hand. "Oh my gosh. I totally didn't mean it like that."

Dax's body language softens beside me. "Relax, I'm teasing you. Anyway, yeah. I come here anytime I get away from the clubhouse without someone giving me a job to do."

"What kind of jobs do they give you?"

Dax shuffles further back on the rocky seat. "Mmm. Never mind that."

I turn my face away from him. "Sorry. Didn't mean to pry."

"It's not that," Dax says. "You just wouldn't want to know."

I rest my hands in my lap and kick my feet out, letting them dangle below. "It couldn't be as mind-numbing as the tasks my family have me doing. Planning parties is all I'm good for."

"You're not a party person?"

"I just don't want to be doing it for my whole life."

"Does that mean you won't be taking over the family business one day?"

I scoff indignantly. "Like I have a choice. I'm the first born, but I was born the wrong gender."

Dax rears back. "What does that mean?"

I take a moment before admitting what I'm not supposed to say aloud. "My dad has no interest in taking me under his wing because I'm a girl."

"Geez, what is this, the stone age?"

"My mom had a little bit to do with it too," I say with a shrug. "She wants me as her pet and to continue her legacy. Either way, I don't have a choice in my own future."

"So, your brother will get taught the business stuff?"

"My brother tells me I'm lucky not to be included," I reply. "He's so uninterested in the family business. But at least he has options."

"Well, you could have it a lot worse than planning parties," Dax says, hiking a leg up and resting his elbow on his knee. "You wouldn't want to be a woman in my neighborhood."

"Why? Are girls not allowed to ride motorcycles?" I tease.

Dax's expression grows stony. "No, they can ride. They're also used as punching bags."

Breath hitches in my throat, turning my voice raspy. "What?"

Dax gives a slight nod, running his fingers over the pendant hanging from his neck. "That's why I wanted you to leave the clubhouse right away. It's no place for women."

I pick at my manicure, thinking about the bruises I saw on Dax at the hospital. "They treat women worse than they treat the men?"

Dax shifts uncomfortably, anger heating his face. "Women are treated like they're worthless."

My heart aches. This sounds personal.

"Did..." I stammer. "Did someone close to you...?"

Dax huffs, kicking his leg down. "It's nothing."

He lifts his cigarette to his mouth, and flicks on the lighter.

"Don't," I blurt, placing my hand over his. My fingertips touch the red rose running below his thumb.

He sighs, taking the cigarette from his lips. "Vanessa."

"Can't you go a little longer before lighting it?" I ask, swallowing the bulge of my leaping heart.

When he looks me in the eyes, there's a softness in his gaze. "You don't quit, do you?"

"I overheard Dr. Harris talking with the nursing staff," I say with a timid rattle to my tone. "Your body's not as strong as you might think." I gesture at the cigarette pack. "These things aren't helping you."

"I'm not stupid," he says bluntly. "I realize they're bad for me. But I have nothing else."

I sit back. "What does that mean?"

"It's not like I fell off my bike today and that's when my life became crappy," he replies. "I've had years of crap to get through."

I wince at the cigarette still in his hand. "And you've been smoking those for years?"

"If you found something that made the days easier to get through," he says in a gravelly tone, "wouldn't you take it?"

"But there are other things that can help you," I say with urgency. "Dr. Harris can identify what's wrong with you and prescribe medication or other treatment." I leave the rock and reach for my purse. I retrieve my phone and open a search browser. "I'll look up what I remember him saying about your chart."

"Forget it, Vanessa," he says with irritation. "I don't need medical treatment."

"You don't know that," I say, sitting beside him, continuing to search the web. "Dr. Harris sounded serious when he talked about your white blood cells."

"My what now?"

I scroll through a promising article and tilt my phone toward him. "See, there are options to fix a low blood cell count. It'd take away your fatigue and dizziness. It's safer than…"

He interrupts me with a groan. "*Vanessa.*"

"No, Dax," I insist. "You need to look into this stuff."

"Will you stop?"

I lean closer with the phone. "No, you stop. Why are you ignoring the issue?"

"I don't want to deal with it."

"But I can…"

I can't finish my sentence because Dax rushes forward. In a sweeping movement, his lips press against mine. His pressure is hard, completely muting me. My thoughts blanken as his head tilts, using his mouth to keep me quiet.

With a jolt, my thoughts come back and I push on his chest. I reef my head back and let out a faint squeal.

"What are you doing?" I yelp, getting off the rock and backing away.

Dax wipes his mouth with the back of his hand, smirking. "What's the big deal?"

I gasp, horror-stricken by his casualness. "You can't just kiss me!"

"Oh please," Dax splutters. "Would you calm down?"

I press a hand on my chest above my thumping heart. "No, I won't." My eyes water with an itchy sensation. "How could you just do that?"

"It was easy." He leans forward with a glint in his eye. "Want me to show you again?"

"Ugh. No!"

He pulls back, mumbling a laugh. "Why are you freaking out so much? I just did it to shut you up."

My mouth hangs open, as the magnitude of someone's lips on mine swells inside my head. "It's the fact that you just did it." I squeeze my eyes closed, and gasp when they reopen. "No one just does that. That's why I've never..."

"You've never what?"

I gulp. "...Been kissed."

Dax blinks at me. His forehead creases, unable to comprehend my words. "What? You're joking."

I click my tongue, avoiding his gaze. "Don't look at me like that. I was just waiting for the right time. It was supposed to be special."

"It's just a kiss."

"It might be no big deal to you, but it means something to me."

Dax rolls his eyes. "I just wanted you to stop blabbing about medical stuff."

"I just wanted you to see your options."

Dax stands and his broadness makes me quiver. "And why do you think you can control what I do with my life?"

I clutch my elbows, feeling two feet tall. "That's not what I was doing."

Dax scuffs his boot across the ground. "Look, you were helpful in the hospital. I couldn't stop thinking about you with the washcloth and the ice pack." He blows out a hard breath. "I mean, man, no one's done anything like that for me before."

I wipe under my eye. "Well, that's a little sad."

He chews his lip. "So you get why I wanted to see you again?"

Tingles run down my spine.

"But, when it comes to treatment, or whatever, can you agree to drop it?"

My stomach flips with unease. "Okay."

Dax scratches his head, making his hair messier. "You were kidding, though, right?"

"Huh?"

"That wasn't your first kiss," Dax says with a hint of embarrassment. "I mean, there's no way. Look at you."

An indignant gasp shoots out of me. "What are you saying? I look like a girl who gives it away?"

He lets out a nervous snort. "No. You look like a girl who's asked on a lot of dates. I'd assume those dates end with kisses."

"Well, mine don't," I reply, standing taller. "I've never been on a date with a guy who was worthy of a kiss. The closest they've ever gotten was the cheek. I always wanted to wait for a perfect first kiss." My gut sinks. "And then you just took it, and I had absolutely no control over it."

"Maybe that's been your problem," Dax says. "You've been trying to control it, when it should be spontaneous. I mean, who ever heard of a great, passionate kiss that was planned and controlled? It doesn't exist."

My frown stiffens. "I wouldn't call what you did great or passionate."

Dax rubs under his chin, stepping closer to me. "You want to try it again?"

I recoil in disgust. "*Eww*, no."

Dax laughs. "*Eww*? Did you really just *eww* me?"

I look up and into his eyes as we stand a foot apart. There's nothing about this unruly and reckless boy that should charm me. But my heart throbs, and my intuition doesn't tell me to run.

"I didn't like the proposition," I say with a dry mouth. "It's not exactly spontaneous."

Dax nods, smiling. "You want me to wait for the right moment?"

I bite into my lip, hesitation freezing me from within. I clear my throat, and reply, "I wouldn't say you have the greenlight."

As I clutch my elbows, Dax's hand grazes the goosebumpy flesh of my upper arm. "Are you cold?"

His dry, calloused knuckles leave lingering warmth on my skin. "Maybe," I whisper. "Could I put your jacket back on?"

Dax walks back to the motorcycle. "I have another option." He opens the locker at the back of the bike and pulls out a gray blanket. "I've spent so many nights out here that now I'm always prepared."

He beckons me back over to the rock formation. I sit beside him, again using his jacket as a cushion, and he drapes the blanket across my shoulders.

My teeth chatter as I process his words. "Do you sleep out here? All night?"

He nods, putting the excess blanket in the space between us. "Sometimes it's better than going home."

"Oh my gosh," I murmur. "I couldn't imagine."

Dax sighs. "Not that I really have a home anymore."

I grip the inside of the blanket, pulling it tighter. "What does that mean?"

He rubs the back of his head. "Nothing. Just that I mostly live at the clubhouse."

"Oh."

"It's where my brother is, and he wants me around all the time."

My hands curl into fists, remembering someone inside the clubhouse who called him 'baby bro.' I swallow hard and admit, "I saw him."

"Huh?"

"Your brother," I clarify. "When I was at the clubhouse, I saw how your brother treated you."

Dax laughs. "That was him being nice."

I look down, filled with shame for not listening when he said his life was hard.

Dax nudges me. "Is your brother nice to you?"

"Mostly," I reply. "We disagree about our parents, but mostly our relationship is good."

"What's happening with your parents? Are they not buying you enough ponies?"

My head hangs low. At this point, why be coy about the truth?

"They're splitting up," I say matter-of-factly. "Or they have already. Ugh, it's complicated. They live on different continents and play mind games instead of talking about anything directly. My brother wants them to get back together, but I know they never will."

"You're sure about that?"

I nod, feeling the weight of the truth dragging me down. "My mom is having an affair."

Dax lets out a low whistle. "That's heavy."

I swallow the sick feeling rising from my stomach. "There are loads of rumors swirling that I spent my time in Switzerland, making out with my tutor. I didn't correct them to save my family from embarrassment. The truth is, my mother's the one spending all her time with my tutor."

Dax slaps his thigh. "Whoa. You've got one ballsy mother."

I lift my head and stare at the twinkling stars overhead. "I never should've left with her. It was a decision made out of guilt. All she did was use me as a pawn in her games with Dad. Even when she's nowhere near this town, she still makes my life miserable."

"Do you think she'll come back?"

Anger tears through me. "She couldn't be bothered to show at Christmas, why would she now?"

"I'm sorry."

"Don't be. It is what it is."

"I don't have my mom around either."

I look at him and find a mixture of melancholy and peace I don't quite understand. "Can I ask what happened?"

Dax meets my eyes and he smiles. "She got out."

I stay quiet, wanting him to elaborate.

He kicks out a boot, scuffing the dirt below. He sighs at the view ahead and rests his arms behind him. "There was an opportunity for her to escape her crappy life, and she took it."

I lean closer to him. "Did you know she was leaving?"

He nods, breathing heavier. "I was supposed to go with her."

My heart crushes. "Oh, Dax. What happened?"

He lets out a weighted exhale and turns to me with a crooked smile.

"It is what it is."

I hold his gaze for a long moment. The moonlight reflects the silhouettes of trees in his dark gray eyes, and as my fear sheds, my grip releases on the blanket.

There's nothing scary about the boy sitting next to me. He's a guy who was dealt a really bad hand. There's something so pure and dejected in his face.

I move my hand out from the blanket and rest it on his. "It's one thing for me to accept my future as a socialite with no career prospects. It's another for you to accept abuse as normal. I can give you what you need to get out. You can find your…"

"No I can't," he interrupts, pressing a hand over the pendant dangling in front of his t-shirt. "I don't know where she is."

My confidence plummets.

His thumb rubs against the side of my hand. "It's better I don't know where she is. I don't want someone else finding her first."

My blood runs cold. "Someone like who?"

Dax tilts his hand to glimpse his rose tattoo at a better angle. "You know, I got this one for her," he murmurs. "She always liked roses."

I swallow the saliva pooling in my mouth. "That's cute."

"And this chain is from her," he says, letting the pendant swing. "She got me and my brother these St. Christopher pendants when we were old enough to start riding. She gave them to us for protection." His index finger rubs over the rose tattoo. "I got this after deciding to stay in order to protect her."

The open space around us closes in. While he holds my hand, clamminess coats his palm.

I clear my throat, and whisper. "Doesn't your brother want to help you look for her?"

His jawline flexes. "My brother is the reason I didn't leave with her. If I didn't stay behind and cause a diversion, he'd have found her. I knew he'd treat her worse than he would me."

A mixture of terror and squeamishness swirls inside me. "Is your dad in the picture?"

Dax fidgets in his position. He removes his hand from mine and runs it around the collar of his t-shirt. "I don't want to get into it."

I swallow and exhale slowly. "Okay."

My eyes fix on the surrounding nature cast in dark shadows. We sit in silence, and a nervous part of me waits for him to suggest we leave. Or worse, he'll leave me here alone.

Dax stretches beside me and then hunches with a cough. He presses on his side and shivers.

I stand, cloaked in the blanket, and retrieve his jacket from beneath me. "Here."

He winces, still clutching his ribs. "Nah, I'm good."

"Just take it," I urge. "I'm warm enough, and you look cold."

Dax stands and gingerly pulls on the leather jacket. He lowers, but instead of sitting on the rock, he moves to the ground, closer to the ravine. I watch him lie back and gaze up at the stars.

"This is the way to do it," he says.

I smile and lower to the ground next to him. I tug the blanket loose, whipping part of it across his body too. When my arm releases the blanket, Dax catches my wrist, inspecting my bracelet.

"And what about this?" Dax asks, running a finger over my bracelet. "Does it have a story?"

I smile at the dainty chain. "I own so much jewelry, but I wear this piece everyday. It feels like I'm missing something whenever I don't wear it."

Dax touches his pendant. "I get that."

"It's basically a security blanket at this point. Whenever I'm nervous or intimidated, I flick my thumb against it, and something deep inside says everything will be okay." I giggle and shrug. "Eventually, that is."

"Well, I'm glad I got it back to you then."

"Me too."

Dax lets my wrist slip away and returns to the starry scene above. I follow his lead, looking up at the wondrous display. Pieces of what he's told me replay in my mind. I have no idea why he opened up like that. All I know for sure is, I want to know more about him.

I turn my head and admire his rugged side profile. A girl like me should never have met a guy like him. My heart flutters with dangerous excitement. What must my friends be thinking? I left the table and never returned. And what if it gets back to my parents? They'll want to know who I left with.

I turn my head back to the sky above, and a gleeful grin stretches across my face.

Eight

"I never do this," I whisper, gazing at the stars.

"What?" he whispers back. "Disappear on a motorcycle with a total stranger?"

I mumble a laugh. "Well, yes, that." I gesture at the sky. "I just meant this. I never take the time just to appreciate nature. I always have to be doing something. Although, I guess I slowed down a bit in Switzerland."

"Why did you tell me all that stuff?"

I fidget with the blanket, fighting my nerves. "What stuff?"

Dax grunts and shifts in place. "About your family."

"You just pushed my buttons in a way no one else does. Conversations with my friends always circle around the same superficial stuff. I dunno. It's just different with you." I look out into the ravine and sigh. "Before leaving for Switzerland, I had this perfectly curated life. I lived up to all the expectations, and had the good girl image down to a T."

Dax snorts. "Do you think you're some kind of bad girl? Sweetheart, I've got news for you..."

"Don't call me that." I cut him off with a groan. "I've just done some really stupid things since I first suspected my mom was cheating. And that was before we went overseas. All I wanted to do was hurt her, but I ended up hurting everyone else."

Dax turns his head, looking at me for the first time in what feels like forever. "But you don't hurt her because you feel some kind of loyalty, right?"

I nod solemnly. "Yeah. But my illusions were shattered, and now every single thing in my life feels completely fake. I just don't want to do this anymore. I'm sick of predicting what everyone around me will say and do." My chest constricts as I exhale shallowly. "Does it ever feel like that with your family? That, no matter the situation, they have high expectations of you?"

Dax grimaces, turning away.

I sit up, looking down at his sour disposition. "Why did you tell me stuff about your family?"

Dax sits, pulling the blanket as he drags himself further forward. I stare at his back, emblazoned with the scorpion logo.

"You're the only one who's ever given a damn enough to ask."

"That's all it took?" I whisper. "I showed you some kindness at the hospital and now I'm the only person who has shown they care?"

His back hunches as he replies with silence.

I push the rest of the blanket off my legs and stand up.

Dax turns around, concerned. "What are you doing?"

I retrieve my phone from the rock and open the group chat with my friends. It's littered with unread messages, wondering where I went.

"Just texting my friends that I'm not dead," I say, busily tapping the screen. "I don't want alarm bells ringing and a search party coming after me. I'd rather give you my undivided attention."

Surprise puffs out of him. "Seriously?"

I look up from the screen. "Yes. If you need someone to open up to, I'm here for you."

His grin sends me giddy, and I finish my text messages. I make up an excuse that my family needed me home for a conference call with my mother. Hope and Sylvie will buy that. I then text Roger, telling him I'll be at Sylvie's house and won't need him again tonight.

I toss the phone in my purse and sit next to Dax. "All taken care of."

"What did you tell your family?"

I swat my hand. "Oh, they're the only ones I didn't text. They won't be expecting me home, so I'm in no rush."

"Wow," Dax murmurs. "You're actually smiling."

I touch my cheeks, noticing the stretch happiness has caused. As I lower my hand, there's a flutter in my chest. "Oh."

"It's the happiest I've seen you since we met," he remarks. "What's changed?"

My face flushes, and I look down. "I feel silly saying this, but I feel free."

Dax tilts his head, intrigued. "How so?"

"When I'm with my friends, I can predict everything that'll happen," I explain. "When I'm with my family, I have certain expectations to uphold. Right now, I have no idea what will happen. I don't know what you'll say or do. Anything could happen, and it's thrilling. It's the first time I truly feel alive in this town."

A hesitancy comes over Dax. "And you feel like that because you're with me?"

I shrug, biting my lip as I nod.

Dax lifts the blanket and I scooch closer to him and snuggle underneath. As he wraps the blanket around us, he anchors an arm behind me, and ensures I'm warm.

My veins fizz with energy. Before his hand lifts off the blanket, I grasp it. I want to keep him close. The urge is overwhelming and uncontrollable, and I'm lost in lust.

I have to have it. I crave it.

I'm going for it.

I hold onto his arm and push myself forward until my face meets his. I press my lips onto his and pour myself into the kiss. I devour the fullness of his bottom lip, and press my hand against the side of his face. His prickly stubble digs into my palm, until I shift my hand.

Dax's arms hug around my middle, and I enjoy the way his hand presses into my back. Usually, this kind of touch would freeze me up. All I'd want to do is push the foolish boy off me. But this is different. Dax's hand feels natural. It doesn't feel like he's pawing at me, or attempting to use me. This feels valuable and unrestrained.

When Dax kisses me back, it sends a hunger through me. My heart pounds with lust and I need him more. Every time his lips move, mine work harder. My hand moves from his cheek to the back of his head. I run my hand into his thick, scruffy hair and plant it there. Not only do I want to experience an awesome kiss, I want it to be amazing for him too.

We only break apart when I need to come up for air.

"Whoa," he says, almost breathless. "That was something else."

I cup a hand over my mouth, the pink hue burning in my cheeks. "Sorry, something just took over me."

Dax grins. "Don't be sorry. That was amazing. This is one area where I love you taking control."

My hand trembles, lowering it from my face. "Really?"

He leans in and pecks my lips. "Really."

"Good. Because I like how much I wanted to kiss you. I've never had this feeling before. It was overpowering and I just had to do it."

Dax wiggles his eyebrows. "I'm that irresistible, huh?"

I laugh and nudge his arm. "Oh, stop."

Dax runs a finger down my cheek. "I love how much you blush."

I lower my head with a muted gasp. "Ah, I hate that. I'm supposed to have more confidence than letting stupid nerves get to me."

Dax moves his finger below my chin, gently lifting my head. "Who said? Your mother?"

My heart sinks as I stare into his eyes.

"Remember when you felt free?" he says softly. "Where'd that happy girl go?"

I breathe out, feeling my shoulders relax as a hint of a smile returns to my face.

Dax's hand leaves my chin and he smiles back at me. "There she is."

I take his hand in mine. "Thank you."

Dax intertwines our fingers, and when the moonlight highlights his grease-stained nails, he sighs and releases my hand.

"But this can't happen."

My hand stays raised, hoping to touch his again. "What can't?"

He motions between us. "Us. It's never going to happen."

I choke. "Excuse me?"

"We can't be together." He shifts away from me. "It's not safe for you."

"I can hold my own."

His gaze is intently serious. "Did I not explain the dangers of bringing a girl into my world?"

I clutch my bracelet and gulp.

He grunts and shakes his head. "I didn't mean to scare you. Look, you're gorgeous, but that's not enough to risk you getting hurt."

"Do you expect me to walk away while you continue to get hurt? I'm not an idiot, Dax. I know those bruises came from the guys at the motorcycle club."

"Exactly why you shouldn't get messed up with me. After seeing what my mom went through, I won't do it. I should've just returned your bracelet and rode away."

I grab his shirt front. "But you didn't, and now I'm not willing to give you up."

He sighs. "Sassy."

"You didn't just return my bracelet because you think I'm pretty. Admit it."

His Adam's apple bobs.

"Dax?"

He huffs, looking away. "No. I couldn't stop picturing you with that wash cloth. You're special."

"So, you admit there's something here between us?"

"It's not enough, Sass. Being with me will be the biggest mistake you ever make."

"But who said I had to step foot in the clubhouse to be with you?"

"You don't expect me to hang around your country club, do you?"

I side-eye him. "You don't exactly fit the dress code."

He smirks. "Are you suggesting we meet up under the stars every night?"

I clutch my chest and sigh. "That actually sounds like magic."

He shakes his head. "You'll want more than that."

"I'm surrounded by guys who say they can give me anything. If I wanted that, I wouldn't be sitting here with you."

"You don't back down, do you?"

I wiggle my eyebrows. "You should just give in now."

He wraps an arm around me. "You're too much."

I look out at the view and then back at him. "I know you want to be with me, or you wouldn't have brought me out to your favorite spot."

"Well, you needed to get away, and I wanted to see what a girl like you is like out of her element."

"Apparently, she loves it."

With urgency, we lean in at the same time, sharing a short, soft kiss. This time, I take in something that my heart made me block out last time.

I pull away, turning green.

"Hey, what is it?" he asks with concern.

I wince. "The cigarettes. I can taste them when I kiss you."

"Oops. Maybe I need some gum."

"Or chug some mouthwash."

Dax grins, silently chuckling. "Noted."

"So, are you willing to give us a chance?" I cross my fingers. "I've never spoken so candidly with someone, and this was raw for you too. Like you said, this is special."

He plays with a curl. "No, I said you're special."

I blush. "Regardless, we can't walk away from this."

"Walking away would be the smart thing to do."

I shake my head. "I don't want to go back to my predictable life."

"It won't be better with me."

I grasp the collar of his leather jacket. "Tell that to the flutters of my heart."

"This will only work if you promise me one thing. You'll never go near my clubhouse." His voice is low with seriousness. "You're safe in the main center of Logan's Point, near the hospital, but you don't venture further. Today was your one and only time. Understood?"

My lips press together and I nod hurriedly.

His hand grasps my jaw. "Tell me you understand."

I suck in a breath and utter, "I do. I understand."

He smirks. "Good, because I want to see you again."

My pulse intensifies. "Really?"

"Yeah, even though I'm sure you'll wake up tomorrow morning and come to your senses."

"Dax, I've never thought more clearly."

He sniggers, running his hand down my neck and resting it on my shoulder. "We'll see about that, Sassy."

We huddle together, silently looking out at the ravine. If he's worried about my life being worse with him, I want to change his mindset. I want him to think life could be better with me.

Our closeness brings back memories of earlier conversations that didn't end well.

"I know you don't want me to go there again, but I have to ask." I pause, ready for the possibility of pushing him away. "Will you reconsider taking your health more seriously?"

Dax exhales hard, looking away from me. "Going to the hospital was a mistake."

I clutch his upper arm. "Not fully," I say with a hint of mischief. "If you didn't walk in there today, we never would've met."

Dax smirks, turning back at me. "That must've been why it felt much more necessary to see a doctor."

My gut tightens, amplifying my concern. "This necessity won't go away."

Dax slumps beside me, sighing. "I don't want to think about it right now."

Hope lights inside me. "But you will, eventually?"

Dax throws his head back with a laugh. "You really don't quit. Okay, sure, I will." He looks at me with an easy smile. "It's weird having someone stick by me."

"I saw your brother asking where you were today." My mouth runs dry. "Although, I wouldn't say it seemed compassionate."

Dax shrugs it off. "It's just part of his power-trip."

"What do you mean?"

"He's taken over the club since Dad's been out of the picture."

"Oh." It's all I can think to say, busying myself with pulling the blanket higher on both of us.

Dax tilts his head as if trying to get a read on me. "You really haven't heard about this?"

I shrink beside him. "Heard about what?"

"What happened with my dad?"

I grit my teeth, forcing them not to chatter out of trepidation. "Why would I have? I didn't even know your club existed until today."

Dax's eyebrows raise, and he exhales with a soft laugh. "Okay then. Just, usually, the people I run into look at me like they know my whole life story."

I nod. "Like the nursing staff today."

"Exactly. Anyway, long story short, my dad's in jail."

I suck in a breath, wincing. "Oh, Dax, I'm sorry."

A smile lingers from his quiet laughter. "Don't be. He put himself there. Or, actually, my mom put him there."

"What does that mean?"

"I told you my mom found a way out," Dax replies. "She was an informant with the sheriff's department. She knew when everything was going down, and planned to leave town that day. I was the only one she told about it."

"Whoa. That's a tough position to be in."

Dax shakes his head. "Not really. I wanted out too."

My heart breaks. "Dang. And you're still in."

Dax slumps against his bent elbows, gazing up at the starry sky.

"When did you get the scorpion tattoo?" I ask. "Did you have to get it to officially be in the club?"

Dax pushes up the sleeve of his jacket and smirks at the tattoo inside his forearm. "Do you see how crappy this thing looks? I didn't choose to get this."

"What do you mean?"

He sits up to show off the tattoo better. "I got held down and forced to get it. Not only was it a bad job back then, but I was ten, so it's stretched."

The air is whacked out of my lungs. I tap my chest and cough hard. "They forced it on you at ten-years-old?"

His brow crooks as he nods at me.

"That's horrible." I'm breathless. "I can't believe they'd do that to a child. What did your parents say?"

"My dad made my mom shut up, and he told the guys to hold me down."

I swallow hard, feeling violently ill.

He caresses my cheek and whispers, "Sorry to turn you green."

I blow out a shaky breath. "I'm just sorry for you."

He shrugs, smiling. "I chose to get the other tattoos."

I take his hand from my cheek. "The rose for your mom. What do the other tattoos mean?"

He laughs, looking away. "They're so dumb."

I bite into my lip, smiling. "Tell me."

He draws a finger over the right hand side of his chest. "I was feeling really down one day, like I'd never get it together, and always be under someone's thumb. I just had this sinking feeling like I'd never be free. But then something made me feel lighter. I thought, maybe, when I'm eighty I'd be free. So I walked into the tattoo parlor and got roman numerals of the year when I'll turn eighty-years-old."

The randomness of the tattoo makes me giggle. "And the thought of being eighty makes you feel happy?"

He rubs the side of his head and laughs. "I guess so."

I squeeze his shoulder. "I'm sure you'll be free long before you're eighty."

"It's a backup plan at least," he jokes.

"What about the eagle tattoo?" I ask. "I saw it at the hospital."

He wiggles his eyebrows. "I saw you checking me out."

I blush hard.

"That one's just purely dumb." He laughs. "I got it on a whim. It has absolutely no meaning."

"Oh my gosh. I couldn't get something inked into my skin if it didn't have a meaning."

He looks at me with intrigue. "But you would get a tattoo?"

I bite my lip. "That's not exactly what I was saying."

"I think you'd look good with some ink, Sassy."

"Maybe one day."

Dax rubs his forearm where the scorpion lies. "I dunno. It feels like some kind of control to get tattoos that I choose after how I got my first one."

"It's sickening how that happened."

"At least my dad isn't around anymore."

I can't help myself. "So, what is your dad in for?"

For a moment, confusion contorts Dax's expression. "I don't know."

"Huh?" I'm dumbfounded. "How can that be? Didn't you know as much as your mother did?"

A pensive look crosses his face. "Well, I got told once he was in, that he got charged with burglary. But that doesn't make any sense because he was the boss. He didn't do the jobs, he sent the guys out. But no one else got arrested. So I don't really know what the truth is."

"Oh, that is confusing."

"I also heard they're stringing him along. That his court case won't be for a long time, making him rot in jail." Dax huffs. "Maybe it's so they can connect him to more stuff? I've got no idea."

"How often do you visit him?"

Dax looks me dead in the eyes. "I never have."

"Oh."

"Even my brother, Lance, doesn't visit. He has, once or twice, but he prefers not to so he can run things his way." Dax winces and grabs his side. "The older guys, like Boscoe and McCoy, visit on occasion. They're more loyal and I can tell they're peeved that my brother is giving them orders."

"Has the club always been run by your family?" I ask. "Or can anyone be in charge?"

"Anyone can be in charge. My brother just got there first."

"Do you think he knew what was going down with your dad?"

He shakes his head solemnly. "No. He's just an opportunist."

As Dax shifts uncomfortably, still massaging his wounded ribs, I nestle closer to him. "You really should get that checked out."

He grunts. "It's not from the fall. It happened earlier. It'll heal."

I run my fingers along his jawline and sigh. "I'm sorry you feel like no one has stuck by you. But I'd like to, if you'd let me."

Dax pulls an arm around me, cuddling me close.

"So, I guess, none of them are wondering where you are right now?"

Dax snorts. "It only matters when I show up again. No one comes looking." He rubs his hand down my arm. "What about you? Your family must be going nuts. Don't you want to call them?"

"Nope. I've hit my limit on being ignored. Maybe it'll scare Dad so much that he takes me on his next business trip instead of my brother."

"Be careful how you play it. Does your home have a tower they can lock you up in?" Dax jokes.

I click my tongue. "My life isn't that much of a fairytale."

"It mustn't be," Dax replies. "Otherwise you'd be sitting here with Prince Charming."

"I've met Prince Charming," I say dryly. "He's a disappointment."

Dax laughs, holding his ribs. "Maybe you were supposed to kiss him. You know, like the frog."

I giggle. "I didn't take you for a guy who was well-versed in fairytale lore."

Dax shrugs, sporting a boyish grin. "I went to preschool."

My heart swells, and I'm overly eager to know so much more about this unorthodox but ruggedly handsome boy.

I rest my chin on Dax's shoulder and sigh. "I just want my dad to see me as more than a party-planning socialite. Maybe giving him a scare will be the jumpstart we need."

"Like an electric shock."

"Yeah, just slightly less painful."

Dax's fingers play at my hair. "So, is there a party you're currently planning?"

"It's a little bit more high-end than a party, but yes. I want to raise funds for the Logan's Point hospital, and we're making it a black tie gala."

Dax lets out a long whistle. "Whoa. *Classy*. Isn't black tie too fancy for Logan's Point?"

I shake my head. "Not if we want the right people with big wallets to attend."

"Sounds like it'll cost a lot."

"Our society events committee has a funds account for the actual event."

"Don't you think you should just donate that? Why blow so much money on a party to get more money?"

For a moment, my brain malfunctions.

Dax rubs my arm again, laughing. "Sorry. I didn't mean to make fun of your whole deal."

My back tenses as I lean against him. "No, it's fine." I tuck my hair behind my ears, taking a moment to let my body temperature cool down. "It's just, those who usually donate won't just do it without us bringing it to their attention. And we bring it to their attention by hosting events."

Dax shrugs, continuing to run his calloused hand against my skin. "It's all good, Vanessa. I don't get it, but it's not for me to get. I'm not someone who's buying a ticket or getting invited."

I mumble a laugh, letting my mind wander. "Oh my gosh, I can hardly imagine my family's faces if I brought you along as my date."

Dax sniggers. "Maybe that's the jumpstart your dad needs."

I lift my hand, softly dragging it over my bottom lip and chewing on my thumbnail. "Hmm. That's an idea."

Dax squirms against me. "I wasn't being serious."

I bat my lashes. "I bet you'd look great in a tux."

Dax grimaces, shifting away. "Hell would have to freeze over."

I run a hand down the front of his leather jacket. "You could arrive in this, but I don't think you'd get past the front doors. I mean, I have pull, but maybe not that much."

Dax laughs. "Okay, you're joking. I thought you were. You are, right?"

"I guess, as per usual, I'll be escorted by LJ to keep the peace."

"And who's LJ?"

"The guy you thought was my boyfriend."

Dax smirks. "Oh, the guy you kept flinging off you? Does he always grab you like that?"

"Pretty much. But I always see it coming."

"I know I kissed you without warning, but I don't like the thought of any guy touching you whenever he wants. He's not also Prince Charming, is he?"

"One in the same." I sigh. "It'd be beneficial to my family if I married him one day. That's the level of romance I deal with when it comes to LJ."

"Yikes." Dax's hand finds mine. "I can tell how much you hate the guy. I'd wear a tuxedo everyday if it kept you away from him."

The image makes me laugh. "That would be a sight."

He holds my hand tighter. "I mean it, though. You shouldn't have to be with some guy just to make your parents happy."

I lift my head. "Wait. Would you actually go to the gala?"

Dax caresses my cheek. "There's that smile again. You only look happy in brief moments. If being at the gala will make you smile like this, I'll be there, right beside you."

I fall into him, wrapping my arms around him. "Oh my gosh, Dax. I have no idea how that would play out, and it's exhilarating."

<h1 style="text-align:center">Nine</h1>

Why is it so cold? As soon as the thought hits my brain, my limbs spasm with shivers. My flesh is bumpy, and while my eyes are half-closed with sleep, I vigorously run my hands over my arms and legs.

Ugh. Why do I feel coarse, sandy dirt?

"*Ahh!*" it screams out of me as I jolt to sit up.

My heart jumps out of my dress as the surrounding view is highlighted in a warm glow from the emerging sunrise.

A groggy moan sounds beside me, and Dax rises with a yawn and a stretch.

"Not a morning person, princess?" he asks with a smirk.

I plant a hand on my chest and exhale hard. "I forgot where I was. I didn't realize I'd fallen asleep."

Dax yawns again, running a hand over his mess of coffee-colored hair. "Yeah, me neither. All that talking last night took a toll."

"Bored you?"

Dax chuckles. "No. It was intense."

"Oh." I smooth my hand over my hair and instantly blush. What must I look like?

As I feverishly comb my fingers through my hair, Dax gently touches my hand.

"Don't panic," he whispers. "You still look beautiful."

"Oh." I smile nervously as my blush intensifies. I run my hands down the skirt of my dress, noticing the dirt marks on the white material.

"I'm guessing this is the first time you've slept on the ground."

"A lunch date on a picnic rug is as close as I've come to lying on the ground," I reply. "And that's usually on the grounds of Ashworth Estate. Speaking of which, I should probably get back home."

"Ready for the wrath of daddy dearest?" Dax jokes.

I suck in a breath and can't help grinning. "He'll think I was being reckless. I have no idea what he'll do about it."

Dax's eyes narrow. "And you're happy about this?"

I bite into my lip, knowing I shouldn't be. "I haven't felt this alive in a long time."

Dax pats my knee and gets up. He holds out a hand, saying, "Okay, let's get you home for the showdown of a lifetime."

I stand with him, smooth down my dress, and wipe off excess dirt. Oh my gosh, if my parents saw me like this they'd be appalled.

Dax bundles up the gray blanket, and I remember it was mostly on me last night. "Did you wake up cold?"

Dax wipes his brow. "Actually I was sweating."

It takes me by surprise. "Oh."

Dax places the blanket in the bike's locker trunk and leaves it open for my purse. He then picks up the helmet and hands it to me with a devilishly gorgeous smile.

"So, when can I see you again?"

Before I take the helmet, I dig out my phone. "What's your number?"

With a smile, he places the helmet on the motorcycle seat and pulls out his phone from his leather jacket's pocket.

We swap phones to input our numbers, and I grimace. His phone screen is cracked and the edges are smashed like it's been dropped from a considerable height.

"Does this thing even work?" I ask.

Dax laughs. "Yeah, it does the job."

"You know, I can replace this for you."

Dax shakes his head. "Don't bother. It'll only get smashed like the others."

I suck in a hesitant breath, and type my number into his phone. "Okay, here," I say, returning the phone. I take mine from him and drop it back into my bag.

With my purse dumped back inside the bike's locker, I climb on behind Dax with the helmet strapped on. Dax asks for directions to Ashworth Estate, and it's hard work calling out turns over the motorcycle's engine. My throat already feels rough and inflamed due to a night out in the cool air.

On the approach to my home, my stomach flips. My back stiffens and an ache burrows between my eyebrows.

This is really happening. I spent all night out with a stranger, didn't call home, and now I'm facing the consequences. Oh my gosh, how did I think this was a good idea?

The motorcycle slows down at the wrought-iron gates, and I lean across to the speaker monitor and press a button.

After a few moments, Murphy's voice answers. "Ashworth Residence."

"Hi, Murphy. It's me, Vanessa. Can you let me in?"

"Certainly, miss," he responds, and the gates open.

Dax whistles. "*Sheesh*. That was easy."

"No, he works for me," I reply, trying to hide my dread. "I'm sure he's now alerting my father."

"Do you want me to stay while your dad confronts you?"

I chew on my lip, thinking about it. "No, that'll only make things explosive. Could you drop me off by the manor and then drive back out?"

"Sure. Only if you promise to meet up again with me."

I hug my arms around him. "Deal."

Dax takes us into the estate and toward the manor. The motorcycle glides by the topiary garden and slows by the front steps. When we come to a stop, I reef off the helmet and slide off the motorcycle.

I hand the helmet to Dax and impulsively press my lips onto his. He kisses me back with urgency and I wish my father's footsteps weren't already sounding in my head.

I pull out of the kiss and rush to the locker for my purse. I pull it over my shoulder and return to Dax for one final kiss.

Breathlessly, I whisper, "Okay, you'd better go."

Dax grins, pecking my lips one last time. "Good luck."

The motorcycle takes off, and I shiver, watching him disappear.

Okay. This is it.

I turn toward the steps and spy the front doors peeling open.

Move it, Vanessa.

I walk up the steps with purpose, and Murphy emerges into view. I keep myself poised, waiting for my father to follow suit. Two more steps, and he still hasn't appeared.

I meet Murphy at the entrance, and can't see my father anywhere.

Is he so angry he can't even look at me?

"Good morning, Miss Ashworth," Murphy says, stepping to the side. "Another late evening at Miss Sylvie's?"

"Huh?" I double-take at Murphy, and mumble, "Oh, umm, yeah."

"Can I get you anything?" Murphy asks, noting my attire. "Hot cup of tea? A dressing gown? Claudia to run a bath?"

I step inside the foyer and slip off my heels. "Where's my father?"

"He's on his way to the helipad, miss."

I double-take at Murphy. "He's leaving?"

"Yes, miss. He wanted to get to the office to start on contracts after his dinner last night." Murphy closes the doors behind us. "Seems the meeting went quite well."

I tuck my hair behind my ears and stretch my neck to rid the cramping pain. "Did he ask about me last night?"

"In regards to what, miss?"

I throw my hands up, exhausted. "When he got home, did he ask where I was?"

"No, miss," Murphy says matter-of-factly. "He had me bring coffee into his study and got to work until the early morning hours. I presume he got, at most, two hours sleep before leaving for the office."

He was awake all that time and never wondered where I was?

I narrow my focus at the nearest staircase. "And he's already left the manor?"

"Yes, miss," Murphy replies. He follows me into the hallway. "Perhaps you should go upstairs and freshen up."

My dad left and hasn't thought about me.

Even if I told my driver I'd be at a friend's house, checking if I'm okay shouldn't be the very last thing on my father's mind.

"Don't follow me, Murphy," I say, storming toward the staircase.

Is this really all the attention I get? I was out all night for goodness' sake!

I make my way into my wing and huff my frustration all the way to my bedroom.

Claudia moves from the opposite direction, holding a bundle of towels. "Good morning, Miss Ashworth."

"Mm-hmm," I mumble, keeping my head down.

Claudia places the towels on a side table, taking a keener interest in me. "Is everything okay, miss?"

Unable to control myself, I let out a shrill squeal. Angry knots cramp inside me, and I have trouble turning my bedroom door handle.

Claudia closes in on me. "Miss, what's the matter?"

I turn and slump against the door. When I see the concern etched into her face, my shoulders sag. Is it so bad I expected a tenth of this concern from my father this morning?

"I'm okay," I tell her softly. "Just disappointed."

"Oh, I'm sorry, Miss Ashworth," Claudia says with a pout. "Is there anything I can get for you?"

My heart sinks. "I think I'll just go to bed."

"You look haggard," Claudia says, placing a hand on my shoulder. "Why don't I ask Murphy to call your masseuse? You look like you need it."

I pull myself up. "Okay, thank you. That would be lovely."

After a piping hot shower, scrubbing away the hurt from my father's obliviousness, my masseuse sets up in my bedroom. New age music is playing, and the scent of the essential oils is pleasantly calming.

Tonya, my masseuse, welcomes me in, asking me to lie down on the massage bed.

"How's the pressure, Miss Ashworth?" Tonya asks as she melts her palms into my back.

"It's perfect," I murmur, closing my eyes.

I let the hardening of my muscles tell her how hard she'll need to work. I can't stop thinking about my father. I took such a risk last night, and none of it paid off.

For a brief moment, my muscles loosen.

It wasn't a total waste. Kisses with Dax flood my mind. What a wonderfully unexpected experience.

Miserably, my mother forces her way into my mind. I don't want to imagine what she'd do if she found out about my time with Dax.

"You feel tense," Tonya says softly. "Do any muscles hurt?"

Does my heart count?

"No, I'm okay," I whisper.

A headache builds from the collision of warring thoughts. I've angered my brother by pointing out our parents are doomed to stay separated. But I can't live in make-believe with him.

Dad is mad at me for disappearing on that plane with Mom. We gave him zero notice, and Mom made it worse by limiting the time I could speak with him on the phone.

But what good will come from acting like I'm still away from home?

Tonya digs her hands into my back, and every muscle resists. My teeth grit hard, as my body seizes.

"Honey, you need to relax," Tonya whispers.

My hands curl into fists and I scrunch my eyelids closed. Nothing in this house will change. I've felt nothing but pain since I arrived back. When Dax fills my mind, a sliver of peace runs through me. Nothing has felt more invigorating than being with him.

I lift myself up and gather the sheet around me.

Tonya steps back with her palms lifted. "Everything okay?"

I shake my head. "Not really. I don't need this. You can pack up your things."

Tonya's face drops. "Oh, Miss Ashworth, I'm sorry if I…"

"It's not you," I cut her off. "I just know I need something else right now. Will you excuse me?"

Tonya backs away and leaves my bedroom. I slide off the massage bed and move toward my phone. I open up a text message and add Dax.

"I need to see you again."

I've never texted anyone in such a hurry. Adrenaline has my heart pounding furiously.

"I knew you couldn't get enough."

When I get his reply, my body finally relaxes. Who knew a nicotine-scented boy would win against an essential oils massage?

Ten

A frustrated huff pours out of me. "Mom, this really isn't a good time." She has called me during the drive into Logan's Point.

Mom smirks through my phone screen. "You don't have five minutes to talk with your mother?"

When are our talks only five minutes long? "Okay. What do you need to talk about?"

"You have a prep meeting tonight."

Ugh. Don't remind me. "Yep, that's right."

"And you will control the room," my mother says commandingly.

I bite inside my cheek to stop the annoyance showing on my face. "It won't be hard," I reply. "You know they all fall into line when an Ashworth enters the room."

"But you know how Naomi Fisher feels about the society event meetings," Mom says, narrowing her stare. "We need to keep her in check. She's gunning to take my place."

"She didn't succeed when I was in Switzerland with you," I reply. "As far as I can tell, you still have full control."

"You said she was undermining you at the last meeting."

I sigh, wishing I'd never opened my mouth about that. Mom called me after the last meeting, and I was so wrecked I did something completely foolish. I vented to my mother.

"No, it wasn't that bad," I say, feigning confidence. "I'd had a long day at the hospital and it was playing on my mind. I promise, I'll be on my A-game. I won't let you down."

Mom smiles. "Good girl. I know you'll handle this. It's our legacy, but it's your future. You won't mess this up, will you?"

"No, Mother," I say, sporting a fake grin yet avoiding direct eye contact with the camera lens. "I got this. I just need to go because I'm approaching the hospital."

"And how's the volunteer work going?"

I nod happily. "Well, thanks."

"And how many others have signed up?"

My happiness sinks into a glum frown.

"Vanessa?" she presses.

I try a tactful response. "You only just asked me to get others to sign-up. It'll take some time."

Mom's disappointment comes through the phone screen clearly. "You should've made it a priority as soon as you first approached the hospital."

I bite my tongue. How on earth do I explain to my mother I'm not volunteering as a PR stunt to further the Ashworth family brand. It's a non-self-serving exercise.

"Vanessa, you'll get a list of volunteers at tonight's meeting. Won't you."

My back stiffens from her tone. It was a statement, not a question.

I clear my throat and nod. "Yes, Mother."

She smiles. "Okay, I'll let you get ready for your shift. Talk soon."

"Yes," I reply as the call abruptly ends.

I lower the phone and sigh. "Love you too, Mom."

I swipe my thumb across my phone and spot the notifications blowing up from my group chat with the girls. I open up the app to a bombardment of unread text messages.

"Seriously! Tell us what happened last night."

"Ness, you left with LJ and then vanished. What is up?"

"Are you mad at LJ?"

"OMG. Are you mad at us?!?"

How am I supposed to respond? *Hey girls, I'm sick of predicting what everyone will say and do so I jumped on the back of the first motorcycle I could find.*

Somehow, I don't think that will fly.

Roger slows the sedan to a stop in front of St. Mark's Hospital. As he walks around to open my passenger door, the perfect way to end the incessant texts comes to mind.

I reply with, *"How about you all join me for a volunteer shift at the hospital?"*

The texts run cold, with feeble excuses of other plans they have for the day. If I had suggested a day at the spa for facials and manicures, I'm sure it'd be a different story.

Do I know my friends, or what?

Before I leave Roger, I tell him I won't be needing him for the rest of the day.

"Are you sure, miss?"

I give him a bright smile. "Yes. Have a wonderful day off."

Roger smiles and nods. "Thank you, Miss Ashworth."

I wave him off and make my way into the hospital. My brown leather ankle boots have a small heel, which clip-clop on my way in. The primary objective today is seeing Dax. This led to me choosing pants over a skirt, in hopes of getting back on his motorcycle. My pants and shirt are navy, which I layered with my brown tweed blazer. My arms got so cold last night as the wind whipped past while we rode. This outfit is still chic enough to keep up my image without arousing suspicion.

"Oh, Vanessa," Nurse Trisha says, standing near the front desk. "I wasn't expecting you."

I smile and wave on my approach. "I have some plans for later in the day and didn't want to leave you in the lurch. Thought I'd clock in my volunteer hours now."

Trisha smiles and bats a hand. "Honey, you didn't need to come in. You're allowed to have a life. You're only eighteen once."

I slip into the nurses' station. "It's no problem. I enjoy coming here."

"Well, you know I'm always glad to see you here." She gestures to a stack of files. "And you know how much I hate data entry."

I sit on the desk chair, collect the files, and scoot toward the computer. "Consider it done."

"You're a lifesaver," Trisha says playfully.

Guilt swirls in my stomach, and I swallow hard in an attempt to rid it. "Oh, before you go," I say. "How's the woman who had the breathing issues?"

"Much better," Trisha replies. "I'm sure she'd love a visit from you."

I nod, stepping away from the desk. "I'll see her first."

Trisha leaves to see a different patient, and I leave my purse by the computer. After I texted Dax to meet up, I opened the search tab from last night when I googled Dax's illness. Even though it's wrong, I just need to know what Dr. Harris found out about Dax. I hate admitting my sole purpose coming here today was to look up Dax's file.

My fingers twitch as I take a second glance at the computer.

No, Vanessa. Visit the woman first. Do at least one selfless thing today before snooping through the hospital's patient files.

I leave the nurses' station and make my way to the woman's room. I walk past Mr. Raymond's room and smile. He's lying on his back, sound asleep. I step into the doorway of the next room and knock on the doorframe.

"Yes?" the woman asks, reclined in her bed.

I step into the room, giving her a friendly wave. "Hi there. My name's Vanessa. I just wanted to check in and see how you were feeling."

She sits up in bed. "Oh, you're the girl who sounded the alarm." She places a hand on her chest. "Boy, am I grateful for you. Thank you so much."

"I'm glad you're doing better," I say, stopping by her bed. "But honestly, I didn't do that much. It was all the medical staff."

"Either way, thank you," she says with a hearty smile. "I hear you're the one trying to make this hospital better."

"I'm just organizing a fundraiser."

"That's amazing. If it means more staff, then maybe it won't be up to the girl who reads to find a woman struggling to breathe."

My stomach wobbles from a feeling I don't exactly understand. I give her a kind smile and turn toward the door. "I'll let you get back to resting."

She waves me off. "Come back and say hi anytime."

I leave the room with an unsettling feeling. I don't feel worthy of her praise. All I'm doing is organizing a gala that has more political and social advantages for my mother. Sure, I help the nurses with their paperwork, but I'm also just a real-life audiobook for patients.

I make my way back to the nurses' station, plonk down on the desk chair, and perch my fingers above the keyboard. Ugh. This is so wrong. But then Dax's face fills my mind. Memories of cuddling up with him under the stars collide with the memory of him collapsing in this very place.

That's it.

I open the database.

I have to know more.

I need to help him get better.

I search: *Malone, Dax*. Dax's file appears on screen. His notes from yesterday were entered by Cindy, and my gut cramps as I read them. Apparently, the blood tests showed Dax's white blood cell count is high.

I sneak out my phone from my clutch purse to search what this means. The first result suggests his body is fighting off infection. Hmm, that doesn't seem so bad. Physical labor and injuries also make the list. And then my body chills when I read that smoking can be a cause.

Panic courses through my veins as I read the symptoms. Fever, night sweats, weight loss, easy bruising and bleeding, and fatigue. My head grows woozy and I swallow hard. Dax told me he sweated throughout the night. Oh my gosh. Does having more symptoms mean his prognosis could be much worse?

What if he's immunocompromised?

I put down my phone and look back at the file on the computer screen. Dr. Harris has suggested emotional stress or anxiety could also be a cause. Even though I'm already crossing a major line, I push it further by taking a photo of Dax's file on my phone.

I slip the phone back into my purse and exhale hard. What am I doing? I'm supposed to have left this sneaky, conniving girl in the past.

I stand from the desk and tuck my hair behind my ears. I straighten the chain strap of my purse over my shoulder, and walk out of the nurses' station.

Nurse Cindy approaches the desk, surprised. "Oh, hi, honey," she says with a wave. "I didn't know you were in."

"I'm sorry but my family just called. I'm needed back home. I won't be able to do my shift today."

Cindy smiles and shrugs. "No biggy. You gotta do what you gotta do."

Guilt spasms inside me, but I hold it together like my mother taught me. "Thanks. I hope you have a good day."

She waves me off. "You too."

I leave the hospital and walk past the small legal-aid office. I take out my phone and stare at Dax's file in my camera roll. Now, if he doesn't believe that he needs medical treatment, at least I have photographic proof.

I move past an employment agency, and inhale deeply as I enter the pharmacy. It's narrow inside, housing an array of shelved items. I hug my purse close as I make my way to the rear counter. The pharmacist, wearing a long white coat, greets me with a warm smile.

"Good morning," she says. "How can I help you today?"

"Hello, there." I place my bag on the counter and avoid direct eye contact. "I'm after something a little unusual today."

"I'm sure I can help with whatever it is."

I clear my throat and feel the heat brightening my cheeks. "I need nicotine patches."

Her voice lilts with surprise. "Oh."

"It's for a friend," I say, instantly regretting it. "Ah, I mean patient. I just think of him as a friend. I'm a volunteer at St. Mark's."

The pharmacist's face lifts with recognition. "Oh my goodness. You're Vanessa Ashworth."

I smile hesitantly. "Guilty as charged."

"Well, I think it's wonderful what you're doing. Are you planning a fundraiser?"

"Yes, of course. But right now, I'm just volunteering my time."

"Excellent." The pharmacist, Penny, her name tag reads, gestures to the boxes of nicotine patches. "And you're getting these for a patient there?"

"Yes, he's an older gentleman named Mr. Raymond," I lie with a sweet smile. "He's such a kind man and wants to get his health back on track. I had no idea how expensive these things were. If it's one small thing I can do to help him, I'm glad to do it."

"That's so gracious of you, Vanessa," Penny replies. "I'm sure you're making such a difference over there."

Oh my gosh, I feel sick. I came back to Victoria Falls to be better than a liar.

"So, what strength do you need?" Penny asks, tapping a box of patches.

"I have no idea. He's smoked for years and it'll be his first time quitting."

Penny takes a box from the shelf. "I'd suggest these ones then."

She places the box in a small white bag, and I hand over cash. This isn't exactly something I want on my credit card statement. I thank Penny, and leave the pharmacy.

My grip on the small white bag causes my palms to sweat. I walk further into the center of Logan's Point, nearing a mechanics workshop. It's the location where Dax suggested we meet when I texted him earlier.

Giddy nervousness sizzles down my spine as I spy him leaning against his motorcycle. He has on his same heavy, dirt-stained boots and thick commando-style trousers. Under his Scorpions leather jacket is a tight-fitting gray T-shirt, which makes it easy to spy the pendant on the silver chain around his neck.

"I was surprised you wanted to see me again so soon," Dax says, looking me up and down. "To be honest, I thought I'd never see you again."

"Why's that?"

Dax smirks. "I figured one night of rebellion would've filled your rich girl quota."

My mood sinks. "You really think I was just using you?"

Dax's body language eases. "No. I just still don't understand why you want anything to do with me." He pulls himself off the bike. "You do realize you're too good for me, right?"

A twinge of nerves jabs me. "No, I don't. All I've had is the *right* guys in my life, and they've always felt wrong."

Dax steps closer, causing me to look up and into his eyes. "And you think the bad boy is gonna make everything right?"

I smile as butterflies turn my insides to goo. "Labels aren't everything."

"Oh, that I'm learning, Sassy."

I clasp my hands in front, feeling a swirl of excitement. I lift onto the balls of my feet and lean my body toward him. Dax's smile doesn't wane, and he scratches the underside of his chin. As the silence brews between us, a surge of electricity pulses through me.

Dax pulls a silver flask from the inside pocket of his jacket. The sight of it makes me freeze. He unscrews the cap and chugs the contents. He smiles at me with ballooned cheeks and then turns to the side and spits green liquid.

Something sour lines the back of my throat, causing me to grimace.

He wipes his mouth with the back of his hand and leans in with puckered lips.

I raise my hands and step backwards, repulsed. "*Eww*. What do you think you're doing?"

Dax laughs, pulling back. "What?" He lifts the flask. "I thought I'd freshen my breath so you weren't tasting cigarettes."

I wince. "So you thought you'd spit in front of me?"

Dax blows out a breath and rolls his eyes. "Oh man, lighten up. I was trying to do something nice for you."

I frown, suppressing the need to gag.

"Nice." He smirks. "You look completely grossed out."

I shrug, mumbling, "Can you blame me?"

Dax laughs. "Okay, maybe I'm not what you'd call tactful."

"Not in the slightest. I mean, you could've used mouthwash before we met up. Was it that hard not to smoke right before you saw me?"

Dax shrugs, leaning against his bike and wearing that devilish grin. "What can I say? You got me nervous, Sassy."

My mind ticks back to the note Dr. Harris wrote in Dax's file about emotional stress being a possible cause for his condition.

"Do you often smoke because you're nervous?" I ask sheepishly.

Dax crosses his arms and shifts his weight. "Yeah, you're making me want to light up again."

I place a hand on one of his folded arms. "I'm sorry. I didn't mean to come off as harsh or judgmental. It's just been a rough morning."

Dax unfolds his arms, standing taller. "Oh, right, your dad. How'd that go down?"

I shrug. "It didn't. He left for the office because he didn't notice I wasn't at home."

Dax's jaw drops. "Are you serious? Look at you. How could anyone not notice you were missing?"

I shrug again, exhausted. "I'm not really a priority for my dad."

He blows out a breath. "*Geez.* Guess your plan to get his attention really bombed."

I try to smile. "That's an understatement."

Dax motions to the direction I came from. "I thought your driver would've dropped you off."

"He did. I just needed to go to the hospital first."

"Such a goody-goody," Dax teases.

"It was just a quick visit. Then I needed to buy something."

His brow raises. "What were you buying in Logan's Point?"

Queasiness ripples through me and I tuck the bag behind me. "Never mind. It's not important."

"No, seriously, what did you get? There can't be anything worth you walking this strip alone."

I sigh and lift the small white bag. I open it and reveal the contents. "Just to prove how pushy I am, I bought you nicotine patches."

Dax rubs his face, laughing. "Good lord, Sassy, you really want me to quit."

"Do you hate me for doing this?"

He lowers his hand, his laughter simmering. "Hate you? No, this is the reason I want to keep seeing you. No one's in my corner like you are."

I pull the box out of the bag. "Do you want to try one?"

"Maybe later. Right now, I have something else in mind."

"What's that?"

"Any chance you're still in the mood to shop?"

It takes me by surprise. "What do you mean?"

Dax slings an arm over my shoulders. "Well, you texted me saying you want to get back on the bike, right?"

I look up into his eyes, nodding as my heart pounds with anticipation.

Dax grins and playfully knocks on the side of my head. "Then we need to get something to protect your head. My helmet did the job last night, but, really, it's too big for you."

My teeth graze my bottom lip. "You want to buy me a helmet?"

He kisses my forehead. "Yep."

I raise my purse. "Well, I've got enough cash to…"

He presses down on my hand so I lower the bag. "Don't go flashing your cash around here. You shouldn't even be carrying around a purse like that." Dax leads me to the back of the motorcycle and opens the locker. "Stash it inside here. I got this covered."

"You can take the money out of it," I offer.

He shakes his head. "Keep it in here."

I do as told, and Dax closes the locker.

Eleven

With his arm around me, Dax walks me into a store, rich in the scents of dust, oil, and leather. The sensations assault my nose and scratch my throat.

Old antique-style tin signs hang from the ceiling, advertising motorcycle brands, gas stations, and cigarette companies. Overall, the merchandising is haphazard, with clothing, engine oil, valves, fittings, boots, and tools intermingling.

"Malone, how ya doin'?" says a man in his mid-thirties. He has a scraggly beard, his hair tied into a top knot, and wears a sleeveless denim jacket over a gray tank top and heavy chain necklaces. He leaves the front desk with heavy boots, and the same thick commando-style trousers Dax wears.

"Hey man," Dax says, grabbing the man's hand in a friendly

greeting. "Just looking for a helmet."

The man laughs as they unlatch their hands. "You crack yours again?"

Dax throws a thumb over his shoulder in my direction. "No. I need something for the lady."

The man peers over at me and a sly whistle draws out of him. "Who's this? Sure she's not lost?"

Dax laughs off the comment. "Just show me a helmet that'll fit her."

The man turns and walks toward an array of helmets. Dax beckons me to follow, but my feet don't budge.

Dax gives me a sympathetic smile and steps closer to me. "Pay no attention to Hugo. He's just never seen a pretty girl before."

I look around at the disarranged shelves and the particular style everyone dresses in. The sight of cobwebs hanging from the cornices, light shade, and shelves, makes me feel dirty.

I shake my head, muttering, "I don't belong here."

Dax clutches my hand and gives it a gentle tug. "All we're doing is getting some gear, and then we're out. We're not staying."

I give him an uneasy look. "It won't take long?"

Dax smiles and swoops in to kiss my cheek. "No. I promise."

I squeeze Dax's hand, signaling I'm ready to move forward. I walk with him toward Hugo, who's holding a helmet in each hand.

"This one's an RTX," Hugo tells Dax, motioning with the black helmet on his right hand. "And this one's an Aria. Not as good a brand, but a smaller fit. So it might not bob around as much."

Dax inspects the helmets for himself. From the bottom, he stretches them out, feeling for how easily they bounce back. He then presses inside, inspecting the padding, before knocking on the hard outer shell.

"Okay, try this one," he says, holding out the Aria helmet to me.

"You don't look impressed," I say, taking the open-faced white helmet.

He holds up the black, full-face RTX helmet. "You'll try this one next."

I pull on the white helmet, and it's almost too snug. It pops on, molding around my ears and down the back of my head.

Dax places his hands on the sides of the helmet, trying to jostle it. "How does it feel?"

"Snug."

Dax gives a half-impressed nod as he slides down the opaque visor sitting atop the helmet. "Not bad for a scooter helmet."

"It feels good," I say. "Do you still want me to try the other helmet?"

He nods, picking up the RTX helmet he left on a shelf. "Yeah. It's a better helmet, I just think it'll be too big."

It's an effort to pull off the white helmet, and my hair rises with it. Dax laughs and smooths the shaggy mess down for me. We exchange helmets, and I happily pull on the black, full-face helmet to hide my hair.

The helmet slips over my head much easier than the white helmet. Similar to how Dax's helmet felt last night. Dax grabs the piece that covers my mouth and chin, yanking it and swiveling it, left to right.

"Hey!" I squeak.

Dax laughs. "Sorry. Yeah, I thought this one would be no good."

"It's the smallest size I have in RTX," Hugo comments.

Dax pats the top of the helmet. "Guess we're going with the Aria then."

I pull off the helmet and when Dax takes it from me, I hurriedly fix my hair back in place.

Hugo places the black helmet back on the shelf and takes the white helmet to the front desk.

Dax slides a hand across the side of my face and into my hair. "Don't worry, Sassy. You're still looking good."

I blush hard. "Thanks."

"Dax?" a female voice calls out from the back of the store.

Dax turns, finding the person belonging to the voice.

"Hey," says a tall, pretty girl with long jet-black hair, overlined eyes, and dark maroon lips. "Haven't seen you in a while."

She notices me, giving me a once-over while I do the same to her. Her sheer black T-shirt is torn, her leather pants are skin-tight, and her boots have a tall, chunky heel.

Dax shrugs. "I haven't needed anything new in a while."

The girl's eyebrow arches and she nudges her shoulder my way. "Looks like you're into something new at the moment."

Dax motions to me. "This is Sasha." He gives me a smile, and then introduces the girl. "Sasha, this is Stella."

I hold the confusion from my expression, and instead, give Stella a friendly smile.

"Hi," Stella says with a wave. "New to town?"

The sarcasm lies thick on her tongue, so my mouth stays tight as I respond. "I live close enough."

She chews her fingernail, and her eyes move from me to Dax. "Snob Falls, huh?"

I sigh hard. "Does everyone around here call it that?"

Stella sniggers. "Just a little inside joke between me and Dax."

My skin crawls. Inside joke? Just how close are these two?

Dax turns away, joining Hugo at the front desk. "We'll just grab the helmet and go."

I follow him to the desk as he slides cash across to Hugo. He scoops up the white helmet and stashes it under his arm. He holds out his other arm, welcoming me in.

Giddiness bubbles inside me, and with a faint squeal I return to my rightful place, under his arm. As we leave the store, I feel two overlined eyes burning holes into my back.

Walking back to his motorcycle, I can't help the pettiness raging through me. "So, how do you know that girl?"

"Who, Stella?" Dax asks, pulling his key from his pocket and inserting into the ignition barrel.

"Yeah. Her."

Dax shrugs. "We grew up together. You know how it is. She's just a person in my life."

"A person?" I hate this green-eyed version of myself. "Not an ex-girlfriend?"

Dax laughs, sitting my helmet on the bike's seat. "I was as close to dating Stella as you were to dating LJ."

"Oh," I say, relieved. "And, why did you introduce me with the wrong name?"

Dax sighs, looking off to the side. "Remember how I told you it wouldn't be safe if anyone at the clubhouse found out you were an Ashworth?"

I shiver with icy fear. "Those two were dangerous?"

Dax meets my eyes and shakes his head. "No, they're cool. Just, some of the guys go into that store, and Hugo goes into the clubhouse for beers. I didn't want to risk anyone talking about you."

My chest deflates. "Oh, okay."

"Plus, Stella follows a lot of you rich girls on social media."

I snigger. "Really? She seemed like she was dissing me."

Dax shrugs. "She got a little obsessed when a girl she knew moved to Victoria Falls after her mom married some rich guy."

"Oh. So, Stella keeps you in the loop with what she's up to?"

Dax crooks a finger under my chin, lifting my face. "Are you jealous, Sassy?"

"I... I..."

Dax runs a hand down my back, and whispers, "I don't know if I've made this clear, but I'm not interested in any other girls."

A shiver runs down my spine. The good kind. "I've never felt about someone how I feel about you."

Dax smiles, keeping a hold of my chin. He leans in, giving me a perfectly soft kiss. I lift onto the balls of my feet and kiss him back, letting a moan escape.

I mumble a nervous laugh and cup a hand over my face. "Is it crazy to feel like this when we've just met?"

Dax traces my jawline and then scoops his hand into my hair. His lips press onto my forehead, and the gentle touch spreads tingles across my head. I smile at my reflection in his stormy gray eyes, completely relaxed in his presence.

"Do you still want to go to the gala with me?" I murmur, bracing for a no.

He rubs the back of his neck. "You still want me to go?"

I run my hand down his T-shirt front, biting my lip. "I'd love you to."

"Then, yes. Absolutely."

"I have a meeting this evening with the society ladies to discuss planning details," I say. "Would you be interested in going for a tux fitting tomorrow?"

His eyebrow cocks. "A fitting?"

I nod, grinning. "You'd look so dashing in the right fit."

He eyes me suspiciously. "This is a necessity for the gala?"

"Yes, it's a strict dress code."

"Okay, but if I have to get fitted for a monkey suit, you have to do something too."

"What's that?"

"When we go for a fitting you need to dress basic. Jeans and a tee."

I puff out a laugh. "No way. The tailor is part of the strip mall. People I know will see me."

Dax folds his arms and a smug smile tugs at his lips. "So?"

I smooth down my tweed blazer. "I've already tried dressing down."

Dax laughs, letting his arms fall to his sides. "Everything about you looks expensive." He gestures in the direction of the motorcycle store. "You stood out like a sore thumb. A very pretty thumb, but still."

"Basic isn't really something I'm *allowed* to have in my wardrobe."

"Maybe you'll have to find it at the mall?"

I click my tongue, fighting off my smile. This boy is too darn irresistible. "Okay. I'll find something."

Dax stifles a laugh. "No matter how you dress, I bet you'd never blend into where I'm from. And that would be a good thing."

I flick my index finger over my eyelashes. "Maybe I would if I wore some heavy eyeliner."

Dax twists his lips. "Hmm. Not your style."

"Neither are jeans and a tee."

"Nah. You'll look super cute." He caresses my cheek. "Your big brown eyes are just too pretty to be ruined by thick black lines."

I blush under his gaze. "Oh. Well, thanks."

He plants a soft kiss on my lips. "You're welcome."

"I think you'll look ridiculously handsome in a tux."

Dax laughs. "I dunno. Sounds like a bit of a stretch."

I grab onto the front of his leather jacket and lean into him. "Guess I'll have to wait and see tomorrow."

"I guess so." He wraps his arms around me. "So, you want to go riding again?"

I nod eagerly. "Take me somewhere where it's just us."

We both slip on our helmets, and I climb onto the bike behind Dax.

"Ready, Sassy?" Dax calls over the rev of the engine.

I hug my arms around his middle. "Ready, broody."

Dax laughs at my pet name attempt, pulling the motorcycle off the curb. It doesn't take long for us to gain speed, and I plant my helmet against his leather-covered shoulder blade. Soon we're out of the town center, and headed toward Mountains Road.

As the township disappears and the motorcycle opens up, my body stays relaxed. Something I couldn't experience during my massage earlier. An uncontainable smile brightens my helmet-framed face. I can't imagine any scenario where being with Dax will cause me undue stress. Being at home with my absent-minded father, bickering with my moody brother, or video chatting with my control-freak mother, are all confirmed ways I'll rip out every strand of hair on my head.

Being with Dax is the closest to peace I've ever felt.

Twelve

On our ascent up the mountains, we approach a spot loaded with parked cars and people huddled in groups. It's called Dead Left Cliff. It's a steep cliff-edge where kids from school like to party and hangout. I've gone a few times when my friends haven't had better suggestions of how to spend our free time. I always thought the view was exceptional, but it's nothing compared to the place Dax took me last night.

Dax's shoulder bounces with a snigger. He motions to the people gathered by the side of the road. "Bunch of posers," he yells over the air zipping past us.

"Isn't it dangerous?" I yell back.

"More like a tourist attraction," he says, laughing it off.

I tug my clasped hands into his stomach. "You're not taking me somewhere more dangerous, are you?"

He coughs. "Take it easy with my gut, would ya?"

"Oops, sorry!"

"Anyway, don't panic. Just a little further, then I'll pull over."

The motorcycle swerves around a few more curves, and slows by a parking area which overlooks an embankment. At a complete stop, Dax pats my clasped hands, asking, "You good, Sassy?"

I break my hands apart and peel myself off his back. "Super good."

He chuckles. "That's what I like to hear."

I slide off the bike and take in the view. "Is this another one of your favorite spots?"

Dax throws a leg over the bike, reefing off his helmet. He smooths a hand over his scruffy mop of hair, and shakes his head. "Nope. It just seems like a good spot for you to take over."

"What?" I yelp.

He laughs, patting the handlebars. "Come on, admit it. You want to take the lead and drive me around."

My heart leaps into my throat, and I remove my helmet. "Umm, no. That's crazy."

Dax takes my helmet, hanging it on the opposite end of the handlebars. He then digs into his jacket pocket, sliding out his pack of cigarettes.

"Wait," I say in a wounded tone. "What about the patches?"

He winces, lowering the cigarette pack. "I dunno. You just kinda threw those at me. I need to work up to the idea."

I frown, edging toward the motorcycle locker. "Won't you just try one? They'll still give you a nicotine hit."

Dax frowns, eyeing the pack in his hand. "Not exactly the same, though, is it?"

"Please?" I tap my fingers against the top of the locker. "Won't you try?"

Dax huffs, shoving the packet back in his pocket.

"Yay!" I squeal, clapping my hands.

Dax lifts a hand, halting my joy. "Not so fast. I want to make a deal."

I swallow hard. "What kind of deal?"

He wiggles his eyebrows, smirking. "I'll put on a patch if you take the bike for a spin."

"What kind of deal is that?" I protest. "The patches are an attempt at saving your life. What you're offering could end mine."

Dax splutters a laugh. "Don't be so dramatic. I'll be right behind you."

"Isn't it enough that I ride with you?" I counter. "Believe me, it's the most daredevil thing I've ever done."

Dax leans an elbow on the handlebars, with one leg crossed behind the other in an irresistible James Dean kinda way. "I'm just asking you to up the ante. Can you understand why it's difficult for me not to light up? I just don't think a patch will be enough."

"But it could be?"

Dax smiles in the most delicious way. "And you might just freaking love steering the bike."

I look up at the sky, letting out a groan. "Okay, I'll try."

I look down as Dax pushes off the motorcycle and steps toward me. His arms wrap around me. "That's my girl."

My body shivers again in the good way. I cuddle my arms around him, soaking up his radiating warmth. I exhale a shaky breath, and find myself smiling. "I trust you."

We pull out of the hug and Dax reaches to grab my helmet. When it's in his hand, my nerves frazzle and I grab onto his arm. "No, not yet."

He puts the helmet back and then cups my face. "What's wrong?"

"I... I can't."

Dax's smile is adorably cute as he holds the sides of my face. "Ness, I won't leave you. I'll sit right behind you, holding the handlebars with you. You'll be safe, I promise. I wouldn't do anything that puts you in harm. You trust me, right?"

I shiver, not in the good way. "Yes, I do."

"Then *we've* got this. Okay?"

I nod, not fully committed. "Okay."

Dax doesn't reach for the helmet again, instead he moves to the locker. He slides off his jacket, flopping it onto the seat. "First, I need to show you that I'm in this with you."

When he takes out the box of nicotine patches, I'm quick to say, "If you think I'm being too pushy, you don't have to try them. I don't want you to do it just because I said so."

He opens up the box, pulls out a patch and unpeels the sticky side. He slaps it onto his upper arm and winks.

I latch onto his hand and give it a gentle squeeze. "You're okay with this?"

"Do you want me to throw my cigarettes off the edge of this cliff to prove it?"

"That would be a dramatic gesture. But, no, don't litter."

Dax's shoulders relax and he leans in close, meeting my lips with a kiss. I caress his cheek, molding my lips against his supple bottom lip, enjoying the taste of a smokeless kiss.

"Mmm," Dax moans, pulling out of the kiss. "I think I could handle withdrawals without the patches if I have you around twenty-four-seven to kiss."

My face flushes with hot pink. "Umm, ahh, well... Umm, I don't think I can promise that level of commitment."

Dax feigns heartache, clutching his chest and wincing. "Ugh. That cuts me deep."

I fan my face. "Sorry. I got embarrassed."

He rubs his neck, his eyes sparkling at me. "That's too darn cute."

I exhale hurriedly, looking away with extra nervousness.

"Okay, so what do you say, Vanessa?" he says, redirecting our conversation. "Ready for your first lesson?"

I twirl a piece of hair around my finger, smiling bashfully. "It feels weird when you call me Vanessa.”

“Why? It’s your name, isn’t it?”

“Yeah, but I’m used to you calling me a ridiculous nickname.”

Dax laughs. “Then why are you complaining if you don’t like being called sassy?”

“Because it reminds me that every other guy is boring and predictable. Every reckless and unpredictable thing you do makes my heart flutter.”

He hooks his thumb under my chin, lowering his voice to a gravelly tone. “Then I’d better keep driving you nuts, shouldn’t I?”

I bite into my lip, nodding as his head tilts and eyes fall shut. His stubble grazes my cheek, making my blood pump hard in my veins. When his lips find a sensitive spot below my earlobe, my knees weaken. My hands slide up the material of his T-shirt, and my breathing cuts short when I feel the physique underneath.

I catch my breath, resting a hand on his broad shoulder. “Okay, I think I’m ready.”

He mumbles a laugh, tickling my neck with his warm breath. “Have your nerves gone?”

“Well and truly.”

Dax grabs his jacket and pats the motorcycle seat. “Hop on the driver’s seat.”

I throw a leg over the motorcycle as Dax pulls his leather jacket on. He hands me my helmet, and I slide it on as he snuggles behind me. As I grip the handlebars, my veins light with electricity. Being in front feels a million times different to being on the back.

“It feels heavy,” I say timidly.

He laughs, planting his hands by mine. “You’ll be okay. I’m right here with you.”

“You’re not wearing your helmet.”

“It’s okay. You’ll hear me better without it. Besides, I don’t think we’ll be getting any speed behind us today.”

My stomach flips as he talks me through where the clutch, the brake, and the gears are located. My helmeted head feels as heavy as a bowling ball and I'm certain it'll roll off my neck any second now.

"Did you get that?" Dax asks in a light-hearted tone.

I shake my head, overdoing it to counteract the fictional weight I'm carrying.

"Whoa. Watch out. You'll knock me out doing that. Then you really will have to drive us home."

I take my hands off the handlebars. "This was a mistake. I shouldn't be doing this."

"Hey, hey. Don't panic," he says gently, his hands staying fixed to the handlebars. "I promise you'll be fine. If you just see what it's like to move the bike, I think you'll be much more confident riding with me. Maybe you'll stop squeezing the life out of me."

"I'm sorry," I squeak, raising my shoulders to my helmeted ears. "That's been really annoying you?"

He takes a hand off the handlebars and uses it to turn my face toward his. "Nothing you do is annoying. You're adorable. I just want you to feel more comfortable when you're with me. Will you just try it? Just move six feet?"

I relax my shoulders. "How could I say no to that face?"

He gives me a cheesy grin. "Handsome, ain't it."

I turn my head to face front and grip the handlebars once more. "Just six feet?"

"That'll do it."

"Okay. How do I do it?"

"On your left, that's the clutch. Give it a squeeze and pull it in."

I do as instructed and Dax pulls his arm around me to reach the center console and turns the ignition key.

"See that green light," he points out. "That tells you the bike is on and in neutral. See the little red button on the right?"

I reach my thumb out to hover over by it. "This one?"

"Yeah. Press it and that'll get the ignition going."

I'm too scared to let go of the handle, and stretch my thumb to press the button.

A breathy laugh pours out of Dax. "You can loosen up a bit, you know."

"Mmm, no I can't."

He taps his right hand over my hand. "This hand is on the throttle. You'll want to give it a little turn as you ease off the clutch."

I suck in a hesitant breath as the sweat builds under my clutch squeezing hand. "I have to do both at once."

"Only a little bit. You don't want to completely let go of the clutch as you take off, and you only want to give it a little bit of gas."

"*Eep*. I don't think I can."

"Hey, I'm right here. I won't take my hands away."

I swallow some of my fear. "Okay."

I very slightly lift my fingers off the clutch, and very gradually turn the throttle. The motorcycle creeps forward inches.

"Yeah, that's it," Dax cheers.

I give it a little more gas and then completely take my hands off the clutch. The motorcycle lurches forward and then jerks back, stopping dead.

Dax pushes into my back and my chest hits the center console. He laughs, keeping one hand on the handlebars as he uses his other to scoop me up.

As I lean back on him, he says, "You stalled it."

"How did I do that?"

"You let go of the clutch. I said to ease it off."

"I thought I did. It had started moving."

He chuckles again. "Okay, my bad. It takes a while to fully ease off. You need some speed behind you. How about you try it again? This time don't let go."

I rub my sweaty palms on my thighs and place them back on the handlebars. Dax kicks the kickstand back down and turns the ignition key again. He tells me to hit the red button and then he kicks the stand back up.

"I can go?" I ask.

An easy laugh plays out of him like music. "Yes, Sassy. Go for it."

With some renewed confidence, I ease off the clutch, and give it a little gas. We edge forward, wobbling a little until Dax realigns the handlebars for me.

"Nice work. Now, do the opposite to bring us to a stop."

"Here goes nothing."

I try bringing the clutch back in, but when I hit the throttle, I turn it too hard, revving us forward again with a jerk.

"Whoa."

Dax slides his hand over mine, regaining control of the motorcycle and helping me slow it down.

He snorts, kicking out the kickstand. "Almost."

"What do you mean, *almost*. It stopped."

He rubs my arm. "It stalled."

"Ugh."

"I love that you care about getting this right."

My heart flutters. "I like doing things correctly."

He leans around me, grinning with pride. "You'll be a motorcycle rider in no time."

I take my hands off the handlebars and shake out my arms. "It's hard work, though. Will I have to do weight training for it to feel less heavy?"

"A different bike would help with that. It's kinda like muscle memory. Once you get used to riding, you don't even think about it anymore."

I lean back against him. "Thanks for teaching me. I'd like to try it again, but maybe you should take me back into town. My meeting will be starting soon."

He turns the key to the off position and then hugs his arms around my middle. "Deal."

Thirteen

Dax slows his motorcycle by the country club parking lot. I climb off the back and pull off my helmet. When Dax frees his head from his helmet, I'm quick to peck his lips.

"You aren't afraid of people seeing me drop you off?" he asks, smiling from the kiss.

I move to the back locker and swap my helmet for my purse. "More like I'm afraid of leaving your side and entering a room full of my mom's frenemies."

"Wow, you make it sound so fun," Dax jokes.

"Thinking about hanging out with you tomorrow will get me through."

"I can't wait either."

I swipe my fingers through his wayward hair. "What are you doing tonight?"

"Just going back to the clubhouse. I think my brother is out tonight, so maybe I'll get some sleep."

My chest constricts. "Will you be okay?"

Dax clutches my hand and kisses it gently. "Yeah. I'll be thinking about you."

A confusing mix of worry and giddiness bubbles inside me. I stumble on the right words to say as Dax lowers my hand.

"Vanessa?" Sylvie's voice makes me jolt and I lose grip of Dax.

I turn and find her and Hope walking towards us. Sylvie has an excited, curious look on her face. Her open-mouth smile shows how badly she wants to bombard me with questions. Hope, on the other hand, has bewilderment plastered all over her. Her eyes narrow and her head shakes like she can't believe I'd let someone like Dax be in my presence.

"Ah, hello?" Sylvie says, salivating for a response. "Care to make some introductions?"

I swipe at my forehead, catching the forming sweat beads. "Ah, yeah. This is Dax. Dax, these are my friends, Hope and Sylvie."

Still sitting on his motorcycle, Dax lifts his hand off his knee and barely forms a wave. "Hi."

"*Soooo*," Sylvie drags out the word, leaning in as she waves her hand between Dax and me. "How did this happen? Where did you two meet? Why are you here together?"

I turn Sylvie around by the shoulders. "He just gave me a ride back from Logan's Point."

With a gasp, Sylvie digs her heels into the pavement. "Oh my gosh. You came here on his motorcycle?"

Dax smirks. "She even took over the handlebars."

This time it's Hope who gasps. "Ness, you didn't."

I shrug. "I trust him. That's why I asked him to be my date to the gala."

"*What?*" both girls exclaim at once.

Dax sniggers from the bike, while regret slivers through my nervous system. Telling these two gossip queens was probably not the smartest idea.

Sylvie beams at Dax. "I need to know everything."

"Hold up." Hope's hand raises like a stop sign. "What about LJ?"

Dax taps his helmet like a drum. "What about him?"

Hope scoffs in response.

Sylvie links arms with me. "Seriously, who is this?"

I give Dax an apologetic smile. "Thanks for the ride. I'll see you tomorrow?"

Dax smirks and puts his helmet back on. "Yeah, you will."

When the motorcycle revs, both girls gasp by my side. Hope plants a hand on her chest. The horrified look on her face might be etched into her skin forever.

"*Ness*." Sylvie gasps, grabbing my shoulders. "How long have you been keeping him a secret?" We watch him ride away, and Sylvie sighs. "I mean, I totally get it. Like, super, *super* get it."

I slide her hands off me. "There's nothing to tell."

"Oh, come on," Sylvie pries. "You just said he's your date to the gala. Plus, I saw him do the whole Prince Charming move by kissing your hand."

An uncontainable smile grows on my reddening face, and my insides melt to goo.

Hope grabs my wrist with a shocking amount of force. "He's not your Prince Charming."

"What?" It's all I can manage to get out.

Sylvie raises her palms and takes a few steps away from us.

I pry her hand from around my wrist. "What are you saying?"

"Why don't you want the fairytale with LJ?"

I double-take at her, wondering what planet she's on. "Why does it matter so much to you?"

"I just think…" Hope bites her tongue, thinking better of her words.

But the scowl on her face sends my blood boiling. "Just say it, Hope. What do you think?"

Hope groans at the evening sky. She then looks back at me with a sigh. "Don't you think, maybe, you're being just the teeny-tiny bit ungrateful?"

A laugh sputters out of me. "Ungrateful? How so?"

"You have this whole life set up for you," Hope replies. "You have the family money, a future laid out for you, and the dream guy who'll keep everything afloat. Don't you think the rest of us want something like that?"

My gaze narrows. "No. I assumed everyone wanted to make their own decisions in life."

"Well, sometimes it's too hard to think about the future. I mean, my mother is still climbing the freaking social ladder. I feel doomed in her shadow." She takes my hand, squeezing it hard as urgency floods her expression. "Ness, I care about you. I don't want you throwing away your future because you're having family problems. It'll pass. You'll be sorry if you don't make it work with LJ."

I snatch my hand from her grip. "Don't pretend to know what's going on with my family."

She raises her hands in defense. "I'm not. I just know it's been hard for you and Ash having your mother away."

"And you think that's why I don't want to be with LJ?"

She nods with sincerity brightening her eyes. "It's obviously a cry for attention. I'm just letting you know I'm here for you. Please don't forget that."

I blow out a breath, lowering my guard. "Okay. I understand your concern, but it's not necessary. What I need is for you to back off and stop pushing me toward LJ."

"I just don't want you to blow it."

My heart sinks. She doesn't get it.

"Are you two coming or what?" Sylvie asks, hands on hips as she taps a foot on the sidewalk.

I look at Hope, unable to force a smile. "Just give me a minute, will you?"

Hope nods. "My mother and sister are inside waiting, anyway. If I keep them waiting any longer, my mother will start breathing fire."

She walks past Sylvie, making her way toward the building.

"Is she giving you a hard time about rolling up with Mr. Tall-dark-and-handsome?" Sylvie jokes.

"You could say that." I shrug. "Let's just ignore it. I need all my strength to get through this meeting."

Sylvie motions to the front entrance. "I suspect Hope's mom is still gunning for you."

"She thinks she can push me around because my mom's not here," I reply. "But my mother is constantly calling me about not letting that happen."

Sylvie sniggers. "I bet a phone call from *your* mother is a lot scarier than a snarky remark from Hope's mom."

"It's pretty obvious my mother's unwilling to give up her hold on this town. Mrs. Fisher needs to wave the white flag already."

"Like that'll happen," Sylvie replies. "Both women are too stubborn for their own good."

"Never a truer word spoken." I click my tongue. "Speaking of which, my mother asked me about volunteer sign-ups this morning. Any chance you could sign-up so I can get her off my back?"

A sour grimace twists Sylvie's lips. "I thought we went through this last night."

"Oh, I know," I say softly. "It's just…"

She pats my arm. "If I had the time, I would."

The only word to correctly describe her smile would be condescending.

I nod, not in the mood for defeat. "Sure, I understand. Just know, I'll be asking again inside. It'd be nice if a friend stood by me."

Sylvie looks around the foyer as we enter the country club. "Yeah, sure. Why does your mom even care? Wasn't volunteering just your idea?"

"You know what my mother is like," I say dryly as we make our way into the meeting room. "It's not impressive if I do something on my own. I have to be the driving force behind an entire team. And if I fail, she sees it as her failure."

"Excuse me, ladies," Mrs. Fisher calls from the front of the meeting room. "Will you be joining us? Or will I need to start the meeting without you?"

My stomach flips, but I don't dare show it on my face. "No, I'm here to start the meeting."

I make my way to the front where all the chairs face. Mrs. Fisher gives me a curt smile and takes a seat at the front next to her daughters, Hope and Meghan.

"Good evening, everyone," I say at the impeccably well-styled audience of women. "Thanks for coming together again as we get ready for the upcoming gala. We'll cover everyone's roles again in the second half of the meeting. First, I just wanted to speak to you all about the current state of St. Mark's Hospital and what I've witnessed first-hand." I pause for effect. "I watched a woman gasping for breath, alone in her hospital bed." The room responds in gasps. "The hospital is so understaffed that I had to sound the alarm for help. If I hadn't been there, who knows what would've happened."

Mrs. Fisher elbows Hope in the ribs. "You should be there."

"Ugh. I don't want to see a dying woman," Hope complains.

Mrs. Fisher fake laughs, turning to the group. "She was just kidding, of course."

"Thank you, Mrs. Fisher," I say, returning attention back to me. "Yes, if we did have more volunteers, it would help ease the burden in the short term."

Mrs. Saxon raises her hand, and I nod, letting her speak. "But what about the long term? How will we guarantee that the money we raise will help with the staff shortages?"

I clasp my hands in front, taking a scan of the hesitant faces before me. "It's been proven that a well equipped hospital entices more staff to the area. When we upgrade the equipment or, let's face it, provide it in the first place, I do believe more medical staff will come to Logan's Point."

Sylvie's mother, Mrs. Grant, joins the meeting with a martini in hand. She snorts as she takes her seat. "And you think doctors and nurses will want to move into those dilapidated homes?"

Mrs. Fisher turns behind her to Mrs. Grant. "Redevelopment is happening in that town." She clears her throat, sitting taller. "And there's more confidence in the town's renewal since my husband took on several projects."

"Give me a break," Mrs. Grant mutters over her martini.

The room hums with mutterings and mumbles, growing in volume. Ladies shuffle in their seats with mini debates breaking out.

My mother's voice echoes within my head. *"Control the room."*

I lift my hands as I speak. "We all know the Logan's Point economy won't decline because of my father's manufacturing plants." The room quietens as if they've remembered an Ashworth stands before them. "The only reason that town functions is because of the industry my family established there. I really believe there's no cause for concern. The staff will come, and eventually, Logan's Point will thrive."

The meeting moves along, and I open the floor for others to discuss their tasks leading up to the gala. I take a seat at the front, leaving a seat spare between me and Mrs. Fisher. I know I should be paying attention, but I just can't help opening my purse and checking my phone.

There's a text from Dax. *"Did I leave fast enough for you?"*

"I'm so sorry about my friends. I just didn't want them ruining what a fun day I had with you."

"Did they ask you a million questions?"

"More like they had a million assumptions. Tomorrow can't come fast enough."

"You're already craving more time with me?"

"Yes, badly."

When the meeting concludes, I'm quick to make my way to Sylvie. "You drove, right?"

Sylvie nods and throws a thumb back in the direction of her martini-swigging mother. "Yes, thank goodness. I don't want to have to wait around for her to finish with her drinks."

"Feel like taking a detour to Ashworth Estate?"

"No driver tonight?"

"I gave him the day off."

Sylvie wiggles her eyebrows. "So you could spend the day on the back of Mr. Leather-jacket's motorcycle?"

I stifle a giggle. "Can you drive me home or not?"

"Sure. Let's go to the valet."

As we leave, someone catches my eye. I turn to spot the bright red hair and infectious smile of Hope's younger sister, Meghan. I tell Sylvie I'll catch up to her, and pivot my direction.

I smile and wave. "Hey Meghan."

"Are you leaving?" she asks.

"Yeah. I have an early start tomorrow."

"Well, I'm so glad to have seen you again."

"I was surprised to see you. Is your Mom letting you help with the gala prep?"

Meghan giggles and shakes her head. "No. I just complained so much about being bored and home alone, she caved and let me tag along."

"This was better than being home and watching a rom-com?"

Meghan throws her palms upward and jokes, "That's how boring my life is."

For a moment a weight of sadness drags me down. "Are you doing okay? How's the new medication?"

Her eyes stay as bright as ever and a rosy glow highlights her freckled cheeks. "I'm doing amazing. The new research and treatment seems on the right track."

"That's amazing. I'm so happy for you." Something Dax said pops into my mind, and I can't help asking someone who might know the right answer. "Were you happy that we threw a benefit to raise money for your treatment?"

Confusion creases Meghan's chipper exterior. "Yeah. Why wouldn't I be?"

"I was just wondering, would it've been better if we donated all the money to the cause instead of spending a big chunk on the event?"

Meghan pouts. "Oh, I never thought of it like that. Are you mad at how much money the committee spent on my benefit?"

"No, it's not that," I rush.

Her bottom lip quivers. "Because I really enjoyed that party. I'm stuck at home all the time, and it was the first time I saw all my friends and felt normal again."

I clutch her hands and look her square in the eyes. "It's okay, Meg. I just wanted to know if you were happy it happened. Clearly you were, and that's amazing. I mean it." I let her hands go, scared I'm squeezing the feeling out of them. "It's just that someone asked me why we don't donate all the money instead of hosting an event."

Meghan scrunches her nose. "*Eww*. Does this person not like parties?"

I giggle. "I don't know, actually."

She shakes her head. "Doesn't sound like our type of person."

I shrug. "He's okay."

Her eyes sparkle with excitement. "He?"

I cup a hand over my smile. "Don't look at me like that."

She grabs a hold of my upper arms. "Oh, come on, Ness. You know I'm a diehard romantic. Let me live vicariously through you."

She releases me and I can't help smiling. "The next time I see you, if there's something to tell, I'll spill my guts."

Meghan holds out her pinky. "You swear?"

I hook my pinky around hers. "I swear."

Once Sylvie and I are in her car and on our way to Ashworth Estate, it doesn't take long for our conversation to circle back to our arrival at the country club.

"Don't worry about Hope," Sylvie says, turning the car around a corner. "She's just jealous."

"It would make sense if she wanted LJ," I reply. "But she's angry that I *don't* want to be with him."

"It's probably because LJ's parents want him to be with you, and Hope's parents haven't been able to gain their attention."

"Can't she just be happy she has a boyfriend and leave my love life alone?"

"Oh my gosh, I know. *Hello.* I don't have a boyfriend and I'm not as crazy as her."

I turn to her with a sigh. "Thank you for not taking it out on me too."

She shrugs with a happy smile. "It's no problem. I've never had trouble finding a date I wanted. The only problem is that my goal is to piss off my parents."

When she winks at me, I recoil. "That's not what I'm doing."

She gives me a doubtful look. "Who are you talking to?"

I flick my thumb against my bracelet and stare out the window. "Just drive me home."

"Hey, I'm not Roger. You can't just bark orders at me."

I glance back her way with a small smile. "It was worth a shot."

Fourteen

"Wow. You found a pair of jeans," Dax jokes, clapping his hands.

It's the next day and my driver has dropped me at the strip mall, where Dax is ready and waiting. My jaw almost hits the floor when he's out of his usual uniform.

"Where's the leather jacket?" I ask, stopping by his motorcycle.

He laughs, perched against the motorcycle in ripped black skinny jeans that only serve to make his legs look more muscular. The white T-shirt he wears serves as the perfect canvas to highlight the pendant hanging from his neck.

Dax pats the denim jacket hung over the handlebars. "I thought this was less of a walking advertisement." He looks me up and down and whistles. "How do you still look like a million bucks in regular clothes?"

I had Claudia snoop through Christie's wardrobe for something I could wear. The blue jeans are a great fit, the lilac T-shirt has a nice cut although loose fitting. I even managed to snag a pair of white sneakers, and didn't bring a purse. Instead, I only have my phone which sits in my back pocket.

"I borrowed them from my brother's girlfriend," I admit. "We're not allowed to dress casually at home, but Christie's parents aren't as strict. Unfortunately, their nurturing vibe hasn't rubbed off on my dad."

"Are they over at your place a lot?"

I nod, twisting my bracelet around my wrist. "Yeah, they live in the manor with us."

Dax's eyebrows raise and surprise releases in his laugh. "Wow. Your brother has his girlfriend under the same roof? Bet you don't see a lot of them."

"Dad made him move into another wing, but yes, they're inseparable."

Dax tilts his head, gauging my emotions. "Are you jealous of them?"

I look down pensively and shake my head. "No. I'm just surprised my brother started dating. He was never the type. It was a shock when I came back from Switzerland. We used to stick together through all the family drama, but now he has her to lean on."

"Aww." Dax throws an arm around my shoulders. "Well, I don't mind if you lean on me."

I rest my head on his chest. "Thanks."

"Okay, should we get this tux fitting out of the way?"

I lift my head and tug on Dax's hand. "Yes! Come with me."

"Wow. You're way too excited."

I giggle, leading this gorgeous hunk inside the building. I made an appointment with Ralph, the best tailor in the mountains' area. He greets us with his trademark slight nod and barely visible smile. His gray hair is slicked back, and his eyes are framed with oversized, black-framed glasses. He wears a maroon velvet suit with a navy dress shirt and a polka dotted tie.

"Vanessa Ashworth." Ralph's arms glide into the air. "Lovely to see you again, my dear."

I kiss his cheek. "You too. Dax, this is Ralph. He makes all my father and brother's suits."

Ralph kisses my hand. "It's always a pleasure doing business with the Ashworth family." He then turns to Dax and shakes his hand. "Looks like this is your first tailor fitting."

Dax looks Ralph up and down. "What gave you that impression?"

I place my hand on Dax's upper arm. "Yes, Ralph, it's his first fitting. Plus, we need your top shelf materials because he's escorting me to the upcoming gala for St. Mark's Hospital."

Ralph flings a measuring tape over his shoulder and turns on his heels. "Let's not waste another moment then."

Before entering the fitting area, Ralph gives Dax a pair of dress pants to try on for size. He then frowns, remarking, "I see you're already wearing an undershirt."

I cup a hand over my mouth, muffling my laugh as Dax pulls at his white T-shirt.

"This is my best shirt," Dax mutters. "See, no stains or rips."

I pat his arm. "Just get into the pants."

After Dax changes trousers, I follow into his fitting area where Ralph has Dax stand on the podium in front of the three-way mirror. Ralph cuffs the bottom hem of the dress pants and takes the rest of his measurements. He then measures around Dax's waist, chest, shoulders, and arms. Afterwards, he pins together shaped materials over Dax's shoulders and down his back, showing me some different options.

When I greenlight the materials for Ralph, he gives Dax a dress shirt to try on.

Dax buttons down the crisp white shirt, and Ralph frowns, looking at him sideways.

"Hmm. Wrong size," Ralph mutters.

I shrug. "It looks good on him."

I catch Dax's reflection grinning at me.

Ralphs turns on his heels. "No, I shall find a better size."

With Ralph gone, Dax leans closer to the mirror and lightly plays at his hair. I catch him smiling and have to ask what he's thinking. He turns to me with nervous enthusiasm.

"Do you know anyone who could fix my hair?"

I step closer to him. "What do you mean?"

"For the gala," he says, angling his head in the mirror. "Might be a good idea if I got this mop actually styled."

"I didn't think you'd care about that."

He shrugs. "It might be nice. Especially when I'm on the arm of the most beautiful girl in town."

I blush. "I don't know about that."

He reaches for my hand, and then recoils, inspecting his fingernails. "I should probably get rid of the grease under these."

I place a hand over his. "I have a good manicurist."

He laughs. "Why not do this right?"

"Are you really into this?"

He shrugs, unable to hide his smile. "Maybe this is my glow up moment?"

"Does that mean you'll stay styled after the gala?"

"I doubt it. I spend too much time riding and tinkering with the bike."

I lift on my toes and peck his lips. "Good, because I like you just the way you are."

As I run my hands down Dax's shirt front, the good feelings bubble inside me. That is, until a voice sounds behind me.

"Vanessa, darling, I didn't expect to see you here." .

His voice cuts through me like shards of glass. Tension seizes my back as I turn, knowing who belongs to the voice.

My teeth grit as I fake a smile. "LJ, hi."

"Wait," Dax lingers on the word before LJ has a chance to respond. "This is LJ?"

A cheesy grin stretches LJ's mouth. "Aww. You've been talking about me, sweetheart?"

Dax shifts beside me, uncomfortable at hearing LJ's pet name for me.

I blow out a tired breath. "LJ, what are you doing here?"

"Well, when we discussed the gala at dinner on Friday night, I thought it made sense to get my new tux ready," LJ says, straightening the cuffs of his shirt. "Have you started looking for a dress, sweetheart?"

"LJ, I never said we were going together," I say, hating having these two guys standing off in front of me.

LJ puffs a laugh. "Oh, darling, I'm used to getting your last minute invitation. Heck, it happened at the last school dance."

"So, what?" Dax cuts in. "You just sit around waiting for the phone to ring?"

I rub my lips together, hiding the laugh busting to escape.

As Dax fiddles with the collar of his shirt, LJ fixates on Dax's hand tattoo. I can only imagine the assumptions running through LJ's mind. I also hope he notices the veins on the back of Dax's hand, which show how powerful it becomes as a fist. Knowing LJ, he'll mouth off something snarky. And I really don't want Dax getting into trouble in a place my dad and brother come to often.

Ralph returns with another crisp dress shirt for Dax to try on. "This will be a better fit."

Dax hesitates. "I think I'm good."

Superiority flashes in Ralph's eyes. "Trust me. You're not."

"Just try it," I gently suggest to Dax.

Dax's eyes slide in LJ's direction. From the side of his mouth, he mutters, "Are you okay being here?"

"Mm-hmm."

When Ralph places the hanger on a nearby hook, Dax undoes the buttons on his shirt and tugs it off. As if he's locked on target mode, LJ zeroes in on the scorpion tattoo. Thank goodness the undershirt hides Dax's other tattoos, or LJ's eye might pop out of his skull.

I'm relieved when Dax tries on the new shirt.

"Ralph," I say, straightening my posture. "You can move on to helping LJ if you like. We can wait until he leaves."

"I'm happy to wait," LJ interjects.

Ralph brushes his hands over Dax's shoulders. "No. I never stop midway through a fitting. Besides, Felipe is working with Mr. Prescott."

"Oh," I say, scanning the room for Felipe.

LJ smirks. "He's out back looking for a higher grade material for the lining of my jacket."

"Well, we won't keep you," I say, nudging my head in the direction of the other fitting area.

"Trying to get rid of me, sweetheart?"

Dax looks over his shoulder, glaring at LJ. "You gotta stop calling her that."

LJ folds his arms, sporting a smug smile. "Is that so?"

"Yes. She hates it."

LJ smirks. "I think I know what Vanessa likes a little more than you do."

"You really are deluded," Dax says as Ralph folds his collar, which I can only imagine is steaming right now.

LJ sees red. "Excuse me?"

Ralph steps back, admiring Dax's frame, seemingly oblivious to the fight about to break out in the fitting area. "Ah, see, I told you it'd be a better fit." He then pats down his shirt front, looking for his measuring tape. He excuses himself to find it, leaving the three of us to stew in the awkwardness.

LJ gives me a shrewd look. "What's really going on here?"

I recoil. "What do you mean?"

"I got a panicked text from Hope…"

I cut him off. "You what?"

"She's worried about you. I thought for sure she was lying when she said you had a new date for the gala."

My eyes narrow with confusion. "So, if you knew I had a date, what is this all about?"

"My concern over you will never vanish." LJ turns to Dax with contempt. "This is obviously a cry for help."

Ugh. He's using Hope's exact wording.

Dax's knuckles crack and he steps forward. "You'd better watch your mouth."

My heart squeezes. There's the mouthing off I predicted. I push between them, hoping to lower the testosterone-fueled rage.

Dax wraps an arm around me, and I gladly lean against him.

"I don't know what kind of charity scheme you're running here, Vanessa," LJ says, motioning at Dax, "but it won't last long. You know it only makes sense to be with me."

"Why don't you let her make up her mind," Dax says, "instead of telling her how to think."

"Oh, look who thinks he's so progressive," LJ says, thick with sarcasm. "Learn that on the streets, did you?"

I pull away from Dax and step forward, forcing LJ to step backward. "LJ, give it a rest. He hasn't done anything to you."

LJ grimaces. "He offends me by standing next to you."

"Then get ready to hurl," Dax blurts, clutching my hand and giving it a gentle swing.

LJ stares at our hands and then his eyes wander upward to meet mine. "Is this really how you want to be seen? What happened to what we talked about?"

I give him an incredulous look. "There's no we."

LJ looks at me pointedly, lowering his voice. "You always told me how your reputation is your number one priority. Do you really want this getting out? Do you really want to ruin everything you've worked for?

What your family has…"

"All right, LJ!" I snap, dropping Dax's hand as I stomp my foot. "Just cool it, will you? It's no big deal."

"Hope promised not to tell anyone else about this." LJ glances at Dax before sending his attention back at me. "We're hoping you come to your senses, and that's when I'll get your call."

LJ walks away, and I let my frustration billow out like a steaming kettle.

"Are you okay?" Dax asks, stepping away from me.

I sigh, smoothing a hand over my hair. "Yeah. I tried not to let him get to me, but I just broke."

"You dropped my hand pretty quick."

I lift my head, and his mood is down. "Are you okay?"

"He was right, wasn't he?" Dax asks, avoiding my eyes. "You'd stop seeing me to save your reputation."

"What? No!" I step forward and place my hands on his forearms. "I want to be with you. I'm so excited to walk into the gala with you."

"And after we do that and piss off your parents, then what?"

My gut tenses. "I don't know."

"That'll be the end of this. Won't it?"

I run my hands up until I reach his jawline. I move his head so his eyes meet mine. "I don't want this to be over. I'm alive when I'm with you."

"But what about your…"

I shake my head. "None of it matters. I'm in this."

A tentative smile dashes his lips. "Really?"

"As long as you'll have me."

"Well, that's a no-brainer." His smile springs to life. "I'm totally hooked on you."

Fifteen

When we get back onto the strip mall footpath, I ask Dax, "Do you feel like getting a smoothie?"

He snorts. "I don't think anyone has ever asked me that." When I give him a confused look, he adds, "And I don't think I've ever had one."

I throw my palms upward. "How is that possible?"

He mumbles a laugh. "I don't really hang around anyone who'd get a smoothie. They're more into soda or beer."

I wince. "You drink beer?"

"Rarely," he admits. "I'm just saying, smoothies are never an option."

"Do you want one anyway?"

He hangs an arm around my shoulders. "When in Rome."

I clutch his hand hanging over my shoulder and lead him down the footpath. "Good, because the Raspberry Rush is calling my name."

"Is that the name of the smoothie bar?"

"No, it's the smoothie I want."

His arm tenses around me. "Is this one of those ultra-colorful places with all the wacky drink names?"

My grin grows, loving his awkward reservations. "Oh, so you have been there before?"

He sighs out. "Oh, geez."

I take Dax into the smoothie bar and it's so hard to fight off the fit of giggles exploding within me. He seriously looked more at ease during his tux fitting than he does standing here. With his hands stuffed into his jean pockets, his jaw flexes while his gaze wanders over the rainbow decals on the walls. It's like his brain almost malfunctions when he spots the tall list of selections written on the wall in fun cursive chalk.

"Hey, how are you guys doing today?" says the chilled-out server. Behind the counter, he wears a green apron with a name tag saying, Chad.

"Hi Chad, we're well," I reply. "I'll have a tall Raspberry Rush. Dax, what do you want?"

With statuesque posture, Dax stares at the overwhelming list of items on the chalkboard.

I look back at Chad and smile. "It's his first time here. Too many choices."

"I hear that," Chad replies with a cheesy grin.

Dax points to a selection. "Citrus Got Real," he chooses. "I need to know if I've been drinking fake orange juice."

I raise an eyebrow at him. "I thought you only drank soda or beer."

He shrugs. "My mom sometimes had OJ in the house. It wasn't often."

Chad rings up our order, and I tap my phone to pay.

When we get our drinks, I watch Dax take his first sip and there's a glint of surprise in his eyes.

He lowers the straw and nods. "Not bad."

"Does it make your former OJ feel fake?"

"Yeah. Come to think of it, what Mom bought probably wasn't real orange juice. It didn't have that real orangey smell. This tastes thicker."

I take a sip of mine and smile. "Well, I'm glad you like it."

"How's yours?"

"Scrumptious as always."

Dax grins. "Sounds like a winner."

We wander out of the store and hit the pavement. I clutch his hand and give it a gentle swing. "What do you want to do today?"

"Anything, as long as I get to spend time with you."

I lift onto my toes and nuzzle my nose against his. "Aww, so sappy."

He looks away and chuckles. "Sorry, it's just how I feel."

"I'm glad the tux fitting didn't scare you off."

"Ralph was a bit much," Dax replies. "But LJ was nothing. I deal with a lot worse at home. I'm just sorry you have to deal with him."

"He was about to explode when you told him not to call me sweetheart."

"Hearing him say it makes me sick that I ever used it. No wonder you can't stand it."

I chew my fingernail, smirking. "Sassy is a much cuter nickname."

"Well, today hasn't turned me off." He holds up his thumb and index finger an inch apart. "The smoothie store was cutting it close, though."

Foolishly giddy, I lead him further along the path. "Well, let me see how far I can push you. There's a department store ahead."

"Yikes. Are you trying to make me run?"

I tug harder on his arm. "Come on. It'll be fun."

"Is shopping a hobby for you, or something?"

"Hey, you taught me how to start a motorcycle. I'll teach you how to navigate a department store."

He laughs, moving his pace in line with mine. "Okay, Sassy. Teach me your ways."

When we enter the department store, Dax's grunt cuts through the pop music playing from the overhead speakers. His eyes dart around the aisles, trying to spot the rear of the store.

"This place is too big," he mutters.

"At least it's not covered in cobwebs like the store you took me to."

"Hey, we got what we needed from that place."

"Well, right now, we don't need anything." I lead him further into the store. "We're just here to look around and have fun."

"How in the world is hanging out here supposed to be fun?"

I motion at the array of aisles. "How can it not be? We have so much to see. Clothes, shoes, housewares, skincare, handbags…"

"Hold up." He cuts me off with a raised palm. "Giving me the rundown will only turn me off. I'll just follow you around."

"Okay, maybe I'm being too much," I concede. "I come here with my girlfriends, who get a little overexcited about all this stuff. I don't do the whole dating thing, so I've not seen this from a male perspective."

He grins. "Is that what this is? A date?"

I shrug, keeping my shoulders bunched high as nerves fizzle and pop inside me. "Isn't it?"

Dax runs his hands over my shoulders, helping them lower to their rightful position. He smooths back my hair, and when his mouth slightly opens, I gently close my eyes and feel his lips press against mine.

Electric tingles of joy obliterate my nervousness. I hold onto his T-shirt front, conscious of the fact my weakened knees might buckle. The raspberry on my lips mingles sweetly with the taste of citrus in his kiss. A soft moan purrs out of me, and his smile grows as I suck on his bottom lip.

When our lips break apart, I can't help spying the area over his shoulder. Even though no one was watching us, my face still flushes with an awful mix of bashfulness and shame. I'm not supposed to be making out with a ruggedly handsome guy in the middle of the department store.

His thumb grazes my cheek. "Are you okay?"

I clear my throat, turning away. "Yeah, sorry."

"Don't be. You almost blew my socks off with that kiss."

I slurp a large mouthful of my smoothie through the straw to help lower my body temperature. The icy goodness takes my mind away from the expectations of others.

Dax takes my hand again, and we make our way through the aisles. In the housewares section, we smell a wide selection of candles. I can't get enough of a coconut and lime candle, and Dax deems the vanilla bean his favorite.

We move onto the book section, and Dax waits by my side as I read a few back covers.

I place a book back on the shelf, and ask, "Have you ever read a book that made you feel things you hadn't felt in real life?"

"No. I don't read books."

"I read a lot of classics," I tell him. "Especially ones where the female lead leaves home to go on an adventure."

"Did it inspire you to go to Switzerland?"

I frown, tapping my fingers across the book spines. "No. I left to follow my mother. It was a dumb idea."

"Oh, sorry."

"Don't be. Spending time with you in Logan's Point is an adventure away from home." My lips curve upward as my mind wanders. "I used to be obsessed with romance books. I wanted to feel sparks and tingles I'd never found in real life." I meet his eyes and my stomach instantly flutters. "And now I know it was nothing compared to the real thing."

Without needing to say a word, Dax leans in. This time when our lips connect, I'm zapped with an electric shock. The spark takes us both off guard, but only for half a second. We magnetize again, dumping our smoothies on the bookshelves so we can wrap up in each other's arms. When I think about someone I know seeing us, I bump it out of my mind.

Nothing will stop me from soaking up this moment. My back arches as Dax cradles me in the kiss. The faint smell of motor oil lingers from his hands, and I can't get enough of it. He's like no one I've ever met, and I couldn't be more glad.

When we unravel, I'm flushed by passion and longing. I snatch my smoothing cup from the shelf and place it against my forehead to cool off.

Dax bites his lip, smirking. "That good, huh?"

I put the cup back on the shelf. "Exceptional."

We stumble across the accessories section, and I tell Dax, "We need to avoid the section on the right. It's the shoes, and you'll never get me out of there."

"Noted." Dax leads me over to the rack of sunglasses. He pulls out a pair of aviators. "I used to have a pair like these. I can't remember if I broke them or lost them."

"Put them on," I encourage. "Let's see."

He puts them on and they're made for him.

"Okay, you have to get them," I gush, placing my hands on my chest.

He slides the glasses down his nose and winks. "They work?"

My heart flutters. "Mm-hmm."

Dax takes off the glasses and thumbs through the rack. "Which pair should you try?"

"I don't know if any are my style. I only own oversized black pairs."

"So that you're always prepared for a funeral?"

I click my tongue. "*No*. They go with everything. They're *chic*."

Dax mumbles a laugh, searching through the rack. "Aww, these would look cute on you."

He slides a pair of pale pink heart-shaped sunglasses.

I wince, flaring my nostrils. "I don't think so."

He holds them out to me. "Oh, go on."

Again, how can I say no to that face? I chew on my lip to counteract the dorky smile springing from the corners of my mouth. "Okay."

I take the glasses and put them on. I comb my fingers through my hair and pose in front of the tiny mirror.

"Okay, maybe you were right to reject them," Dax teases.

I playfully nudge him. "Hey!"

I take off the glasses as Dax picks out another pair.

Dax slides on a pair of gold star-shaped glasses and the wind is knocked out of me. I collapse forward, struggling for breath as I spurt out laughter.

Dax holds onto my jiggling shoulders while I fail to compose myself. I manage an inhale of air, but when I lift my head, it rushes back out of me. One look at him has me falling apart. Dax struggles to hold back his laughter, sucking in his lips and squinting behind the ridiculous sunglasses.

He sighs out, planting a hand firmly on his chest as his laughter drifts away. "Man. It's been so long since I laughed like that."

I nod, catching my breath. "Me too."

He takes off the sunglasses and wipes under his eyes. He smiles like he's on the edge of laughing again. "It's good to have a minute where everything doesn't feel so serious."

"When was the last time you felt like that?"

His eyebrows raise, searching for a memory. "Ages ago. I remember one time my mom and I were messing around at a gas station. There were some weird novelty hats and she made us try on every single one." He looks away, smiling. "Even Lance had fun that day."

"Lance? That's your brother?"

"Yeah."

"Was your dad there too?"

He shakes his head, and some of his happiness disappears. "No. I don't really have any fun memories with my dad."

I frown as the sorrow hits my gut. "I'm sorry."

"Don't be. It was my mom's department."

"You really want to see her again, don't you?"

He fiddles with the glasses in his hands, looking down as he nods.

I touch his arm, lowering my voice. "You know, I could help you do that. I could hire someone to track her down."

When he looks up, fear saturates his eyes. "No. You can't do that."

I take my hand off him. "It was only a suggestion."

"I want to find her, but I can't risk it. I can't have anyone asking questions and tipping off Lance as to where she might be."

I nod hurriedly. "Okay. I won't do anything."

He shoves the sunglasses back on the rack and wraps his arms around me. "I know you only said it to help.'" His face buries in the nape of my neck, and I lift onto my toes, hugging him back. "I just can't do anything to jeopardize her safety."

"I get it," I murmur. "But there's a guy on my dad's staff. He's discreet."

He hugs me with more urgency. "No, don't have anyone look into this."

I swallow hard and croak, "Okay."

He unravels his arms from around me, and I feel him shiver.

"Baby," I whisper, keeping my hands on his arms. "Are you okay?"

He blows out a long breath and forces himself to nod. "Yeah. Thinking about her just got my heart pumping."

"Sorry."

An easy smile brightens his face, and he hooks a finger under my chin. "Don't be. I'd be feeling a million times worse if I didn't have you with me."

"Do you think about your mom often?"

His head tilts to the side. "Sometimes. Like if something reminds me of her. Or when I look at her stuff I saved."

"She didn't take it with her?"

"She took what she could, but she had to travel light."

"And what happened to the rest of her stuff?"

"Lance got angry and torched it."

My heart crushes. "Oh, I'm sorry."

"There's some things I wish I still had, but I like the stuff I got to keep." He pauses, stroking the pendant on his chain. "Plus, I have this."

"Does it help you feel close to her?"

"Yeah. At least Lance lets me wear it."

"You expected him to stop you?"

"Well, I had to hide Mom's things that I kept."

Intrigue gets the better of me. "Where do you have them?"

He smiles, shaking his head. "It's such a dumb idea, but they're still at the house."

"The clubhouse?"

"No, our old house."

"As in where your family lived?"

He nods. "It's still empty."

"Oh."

"Sometimes I hang out there, but I have to be sneaky about it. As soon as Mom left and Dad was locked up, Lance wanted me to stay with him full-time at the clubhouse."

"I don't get why you can't have a home too."

Dax shrugs. "He just wants power. I guess I'm the easiest person for him to control."

I frown as my shoulders droop. "I get that."

"I don't know why I still care about that place. It's falling to bits."

I place my hand on the space over his heart. "It's your home."

He rubs his hand over mine and the drumming of his heart enlivens.

"If it's special to you, I'd love to see it."

Dax's smile twitches. "No way. You wouldn't want to see it."

"It's your home."

"It's no palace," he warns. "Actually, it's the total opposite of a palace. It might be a dungeon."

"I wasn't expecting anything Buckingham-level."

He hesitates. "You really want to see it?"

"Would it be okay? I don't want to make your brother mad."

"None of the crew have been there in months. It would be just the two of us."

I grin. "Well you know how much I enjoy it when it's just us alone somewhere."

Dax laughs and takes my hand. "You're serious about this?"

"I'm dying to know more about you. If you're willing to share it with me, I'd love to see it."

Sixteen

On the way to the registers to buy the aviator sunglasses, Dax grabs a sweatshirt because my arms get notoriously cold on the back of his motorcycle. It's pale pink and says, 'Dream Girl' in white stitching. Ordinarily, I wouldn't wear it in public. It's more suited for a Tuesday night at the manor; when I'm wearing an avocado face mask and watching a trashy reality show. But Dax says I look cute in it, so I wear it with pride.

At this point, the ride from Victoria Falls to Logan's Point on the motorcycle feels natural. Who knew I could get used to this mode of transport so quickly? But that's where the comfort ends. When we reach Dax's family home, my stomach tosses about like a rickety old ship in the middle of a bad storm.

Dax parks the motorcycle by the side of the house. The exterior siding is damaged, large chunks of paint have stripped away, and long, prickly grass grows into the cracks in the wall.

I pick up my jaw before I slip off the motorcycle.

Dax pulls off his helmet and winks. "Home, sweet home."

"I'm excited to see where you grew up." It's not a lie. I want to know more about him. Everything about him. And this deteriorating home is part of his story.

Dax leads me into the house. The front patio is spongy, and I imagine myself falling through. Dax barges his shoulder into the front door, forcing it open. The hinges squeak and the door thuds against the interior wall.

Dax sucks in a breath, gritting his teeth as he holds his ribs.

"Oh my gosh, you're hurt," I panic.

He sucks in another breath, removing his hand as he stands upright. "No, I'm good. I just forgot to use my other side."

"You know, you can still get those x-rays."

He looks at me with dismay. "Don't start that again."

I raise my hands in surrender. "Fine. How about you give me the grand tour?"

Dax steps to the side. "Right this way, my lady."

I use every trick my mother ever taught me about keeping a happy disposition on the exterior, masking all the emotions inside. It's not the fact the house is small that's tripping me out, it's how dark it is. There's some shabby curtains covering one window, but the other three are bordered up.

Dax closes the front door and steps ahead of me. "Don't go in the kitchen," he says, motioning to the left. "There's so much mold, and the drain is clogged, giving it a really funky smell."

I grimace as my mouth pools with saliva. "*Eww*."

"Plus the fridge died a long time ago," he adds. "It's so gross."

I cross my fingers and ask, "Are you telling me this so everything else will seem better?"

Dax sniggers. "Just getting the warnings out ahead of time."

"Well, I don't cook at my own home, so I wasn't planning to go into your kitchen."

We walk through the living room, which I assume is now home to spiders. Cobwebs fill the ceiling corners, dead bugs litter the light fixtures, and dust cakes the table and chairs.

Dax points out the bathroom, but after the kitchen warnings, I don't dare peer inside. Dax moves ahead and stops in a doorway.

"This is where I hang out when I come here," he says.

He moves aside and I enter the space. There's a chest against the wall with one out of three drawers missing, and a double bed with a beige sheet covering the mattress.

"This would be better than sleeping outside," I say, inspecting the bed.

"Sometimes," Dax says, moving into the room. "But it's easier to hide outside. Lance knows I like it here."

"Does he come here looking for you?"

Dax sits on the edge of the bed. "Not in a long time because I stopped coming here. Now he thinks I avoid this place."

"Which makes it easier to hide?"

"Yep. I just can't come too often or he'll work it out again." Dax pats the space beside him, and I sit down. "So, what do you think?"

I don't answer because the dust is playing havoc with my nostrils. I finally sneeze, making Dax laugh.

"Maybe we needed to buy that vanilla candle you liked," I tease. "Give this place some ambiance."

"You mean, give it a better smell?"

I throw a palm upward. "I was trying to be nice."

"I told you it wasn't a palace."

"To be totally fair, the smell isn't that bad. It's just musty."

"Yeah, I haven't done any upkeep. If I tried to fix anything it'd be a big red flag to my brother."

"He'd prefer to see this place waste away?"

"Mm-hmm. Just like how he thinks about our family."

I rub a circle on his back. "I'm sorry."

He smiles. "It is what it is."

"We can change that, though."

"You have money to change your life. I'm more stuck than you."

I rest my chin on his shoulder. "I have money that can change *both* of our lives."

Dax scoots backward and lies on his back, looking up at the discolored ceiling. "This isn't something you can just throw money at and fix. Doesn't this place show you just how different our lives are?"

I crawl up the bed and lie by his side. "I wasn't trying to change or fix you."

Dax turns on his side, nestling an arm around my waist. "I've seen your home. Don't you think we're too different?"

"I'm here aren't I? Who cares where we're from? I loved my night under the stars with you, and I loved being goofy at the mall."

Dax plants a kiss on my forehead and sighs. "I've never met anyone like you. I can't imagine not having you in my life."

I hug my arm around him. "You never have to."

In our embrace, Dax pushes me back onto the bed, leaning the top half of his body over me. "I'm sorry this isn't the most romantic setting."

I shrug, sinking into the mattress. "I kinda like how quiet it is. And I love that no one would guess I'm here."

"In that case." His gravelly tone comes out to play as his hands wander my waistline. "Perhaps we should get more comfortable."

As I lie beneath him on the bed, wondering how on earth we could get more comfortable, his kisses accelerate with heat and force. His lips begin to miss mine, and wet warmth sticks to the spot above my chin.

The sweatshirt bunches around me, allowing Dax's hands to roam. My hand runs the length of his neck and plants on his shoulder. I give it a squeeze, catching my breath. When his hand snakes up my shirt and touches my torso, I flinch. With more zeal, his hands cup around my chest.

In panic, I shove the hand inside my shirt, and scamper to the other side of the bed.

"What happened?" he asks, hovering above where I was lying.

I sit up, noting the flush in my chest and face. I pull my T-shirt down as the sweatshirt unravels from above my ribs.

He scoots beside me, placing a hand on my upper arm. "Hey. You okay?"

"It's just... I... You're... You're the first person I've kissed. This is all just moving really fast for me."

He takes his hand off me. "I'm sorry. I didn't mean to freak you out."

I hug my arms around my middle, shying away from him. "You're obviously more experienced than me."

"I don't know if that's true." He lets out a nervous laugh. "You just bring out a need in me. I want to be with you as much as I can."

"I told you I like waiting for moments that feel special." Pouting, I pan around the derelict room. "This doesn't exactly feel special."

He sits back, combing a hand through his hair. "You just told me you liked it here. How am I supposed to know if you're telling the truth or not?"

I place a hand on my chest. "I wasn't lying. I just needed to slow down."

Dax leans back on his arm. "That's fine. I just want to be with you. We can stay at opposite ends of the room for all I care."

I can't help feeling sensitive and inexperienced as I turn away from him. "You have done a lot more with other girls, though. Haven't you?"

"Why are you asking that?"

I bundle my hands inside the sweatshirt sleeves, keeping my head low. "You and Stella... You seemed close. Like, in jokes and history."

"How much more obvious do I need to be about how much I like you?"

His words make me turn to face him.

He leans forward with purposeful eye contact. "There's no other girls on my mind."

It keeps gnawing at me. "But are you hiding how close you and Stella are?"

Dax's jaw flexes as he breaks eye contact. "Is that why you recoiled when I touched you?"

Like a reflex, I pull my shirt down again. "No, but..."

"Vanessa," he says softly. "I don't want to rush you, and I don't want to be with anyone else. There's never been anyone else. I'm sorry I got handsy. I won't do it again until you tell me you're ready."

My heart leaps into my throat. "Really?"

His sincere smile eliminates the tension seizing the room. "Of course. I got caught up, and that's on me. I won't do it again. Really. I'm sorry."

I hug my middle, unsure of how to act. "I didn't mean to make you feel bad or anything."

He shrugs. "You're just setting boundaries. I can respect that."

I loosen my arms and edge closer to him. "I'm sorry for getting obsessive about the other girl."

He caresses the side of my face. "Look, I've hung out with her over the years, but there's nothing there. I never felt a spark before I met you."

I bite my lip, leaning into him. "Really?"

"I remember seeing you before I collapsed," he admits. "Everything was going white, but I saw you. There was all this light around you, like an angel. Part of me thought I was dying."

I nuzzle my face against his. "I'm so glad I was there to get you help."

Dax pulls away from me, his face stony as it turns toward the doorway. My hand lies on his chest, feeling the thumps of his heart. As if seeing his ears prick, I hear it too. The rev of motorcycles coming to a stop outside the house.

Dax moves to the end of the bed, listening intently to the outside noises. When a louder engine roars, Dax jolts.

He looks back at me with heightened concern. "That's my brother's bike."

I sit up, blood draining from my body. "What do we do?"

"They must've seen my bike," Dax says, standing. He holds out a hand to me. "You'll need to hide."

"What about you?" I say, standing with him.

"I'll get them out of here."

My heart thuds against my ribs. "Them?"

He nods, eyes fixed on the doorway. "I heard two other bikes with him."

Dax moves around the bed, pulling the rickety chest of drawers off the wall and closer to the bed. He takes me by the hand, silently directing me to crouch behind it. Here, I'll be further away from the doorway.

When he turns away, I squeeze his hand, begging him to stay.

He gives me a sympathetic look and leans down to kiss my forehead. "It'll be okay," he whispers. "Just stay here. No matter what."

I tremble from the implication of his words.

He frees his hand and walks away. From this crouched position, I can see past the doorway and into the next room. Dax flexes his hands and cracks his knuckles.

Loud voices boom their way inside. I cringe as heavy footsteps quake their way into the decaying home. My eyes stay on Dax. His stance broadens, watching the newcomers enter. With their backs turned to me, I have a clear view of three Scorpion leather jackets. My heart squeezes and, for a moment, I forget how to breathe.

"Hi, baby bro," Dax's brother says with a menacing undertone. "What are you doing?"

Dax swallows hard, watching the three men loom closer.

Lance shoves Dax hard. "Answer me."

Dax leans forward, rubbing his chest and coughing hard. He wipes his mouth with the back of his hand. "Lance, I…"

Lance holds Dax up by the collar of his T-shirt. "What have I told you about coming here?"

Dax grunts. "Don't."

Lance smirks, letting him go. "Correct. So, why don't you listen?"

Dax stumbles to keep his balance. I rise on my knees, ready to step forward and help him, but he subtly lifts his palm, signaling for me to stay put.

"Boscoe and Stitch noticed your bike," Lance says, nodding at the two other men. "You have them to thank for the drop-in."

"We saw an extra helmet on the handlebars," says the older, more rotund man with a long graying beard. "You got someone here with you?"

When Dax stays silent, Lance shoves him again. "Boscoe asked you a question."

Dax winces, leaning to one side. I hug myself, assuming they hit his bruises.

Lance dominantly leans over Dax. From this angle, I glimpse the large tattoo across his neck. "Hugo told us you were with some pretty little thing from Victoria Falls."

The third man, Stitch, who's bald and skinny, grunts and spits on the ground. "Yeah. What's a dog like you doing with someone like that?"

"Unless." Lance stands tall, stepping back from Dax. "Are you doing some recon for us, Dax? Is she worth something?"

"What? No." Dax forces himself upright. "I'm not with some rich girl. How would that even happen?"

"Then who's here with you?"

"Who else would I be with?" Dax says it like the answer should be obvious. "Stella's only a few houses up, and here we can get some privacy. Well, that is until you all showed up."

"You want me to believe Hugo would let his niece ride around with some baby's-first-scooter helmet?"

"It was just something she had with her. She's not even here anymore. She's gone back home. Guys, you ruined the mood."

Lance rushes at Dax, pinning him against the wall. Dax groans, grabbing his side.

"No," Lance says authoritatively. "How about you be straight with me?"

Dax grunts, sucking in a breath to get through the pain. "About what?"

"About the bust up you had with McCoy." Lance broadens his stance as he looms over his brother. "That was over some girl, wasn't it?"

"Why do you care?" Dax asks through gritted teeth.

"You've been MIA," Boscoe says, crossing his arms like a sheriff waiting for a crook's confession. "And when you do come back to the clubhouse, you make another excuse to leave."

Stitch sniggers, bobbing his head up and down. "Probably out, licking his wounds."

Lance steps away from Dax. "No, he took care of McCoy. Bro, I've seen the look in your eyes."

A scowl crosses Dax's face. "What look?"

Lance closes in on Dax, tapping his open palm against his cheek. "You're being secretive with me." Lance pulls back, letting out a throaty chuckle. "Although, I guess that's what you do. Isn't it, baby bro? You keep secrets from me."

Holding his ribs, Dax pulls himself off the wall. "I'm still with you, aren't I?"

Lance stomps a foot forward and whacks Dax in the gut. As Dax doubles over, Lance holds him up, growling, "You've never been with me."

I shudder in my crouched position. A bead of sweat runs from my hairline, and drops between my eyebrows.

"You want to know what look you give me?" Lance's menacing tone freezes my blood. "It's betrayal. Just like when you helped Mom take off."

Lance holds Dax by the scruff of his hair. When his fist winds up, everything plays out in slow motion. I blink hard, unwilling to see Dax get hurt again.

"Don't!" I scream, springing up in plain sight.

Lance turns to me and drops Dax, who stumbles forward.

"Well, well," Lance says with a vile grin. "Look who came out to play."

With my heart pounding to an aching beat, I move toward the doorway, very aware of every eyeball following my movements.

Dax puffs out air, forcing himself to stand. "Stay away from her."

"What's that?" Lance says, whipping around to his brother. He plants his hand under Dax's chin, pressing his thumb and fingers into Dax's cheeks. "Leave who alone? Or has Stella had an upgrade?"

"I'm sorry, it was my idea to hide," I say in a shaky voice. "I'm not supposed to leave my house. I'm grounded."

Lance releases Dax as he, Boscoe, and Stitch throw their heads back in laughter.

Adrenaline races through my body, ignoring the men and keeping my sights on the only person I care about. Dax stares at me with mournful eyes. I know he wishes I'd stayed hidden, but how could I let the abuse continue?

Boscoe folds his arms over his round belly. "So, who are you? Miss Hide-and-go-seek?"

"I met Stella and Hugo yesterday," I admit. "I'm Sasha. I just didn't want to be seen in town because my parents are way too strict."

Boscoe holds his round belly, which jiggles while he laughs. "Look at that. Dax did get himself a pretty little thing. What's the plan? Trying to corrupt the good girl?"

"I'm not trying to be bad," I yammer as my knees knock. "Can you just let us go so Dax can take me home?"

Lance grins at me, tilting his head. "And where's home?"

"Give it up." Dax groans. "She's not one of those rich kids. She lives in Victoria Falls but is barely middle class."

Lance's muscular arm tenses as he grabs Dax's neck. "Bro, you need to pipe down."

I gasp, shooting my hands over my mouth. Shivering, I let out a muffled, "Let him go."

Stitch moves toward me, grabbing my shoulders and tugging me forward. I squeak, tripping over my feet, and repulsed by his touch.

Lance releases Dax, narrowing his eyes at Stitch.

"Want me to deal with her, boss?" Stitch asks, his boney fingers digging into my shoulders.

"Since when do I want you to deal with anything?" Lance says bluntly. "Let her go. In what world would someone important lie for my brother? She's just another little girl wanting daddy's attention."

Stitch grunts, shoving me away. I gasp, falling to my knees.

Lance grabs the scruff of Dax's hair again. "You get out of this house. You hear me? If I find you here again, I'll burn it to the ground."

Lance steps away, whistling at the other two men. "Move it. We've got things to do."

The three men stomp out of the house. Each step ripples the floorboard with aftershocks.

Dax slides down the wall and I scramble to my feet in an effort to get to him.

I skid on the floor and crouch in front of him. "Dax! Are you okay?"

He coughs, winces, and holds his side. "Yeah. Just gimme a minute."

"I'll call my driver to take you to the hospital."

"No. No way," he says adamantly. "No hospital."

"But you're hurt."

"There's nothing for them to fix," he argues. "I just keep getting hit in the same spot. It'll heal."

"But Dax, your health issues are more than just bruises."

His eyes fill with pain as he whispers, "Please don't go there."

I bite my lip as despair washes through me. "Okay. Well, we need to get you out of this place."

"I have to go back to the clubhouse," he says regretfully. "It's my only option besides sleeping outside somewhere."

I caress the side of his face, and shut my eyes with a sigh. "No, it isn't. You'll come back to Ashworth Estate with me. I'll take care of you."

Dax pulls away, but I hold the sides of his face, bringing him back to me. "Your father won't want me there."

I stare into his disillusioned eyes. "No, it'll be fine. I'll explain that you're hurt and have no place else to go." I exhale slowly, running the back of my hand against his cheek. "More importantly, I'll tell my father how much you mean to me. You're amazing, and there's no way he can turn you away."

Dax's smile curves to the side. "Someone's feeling optimistic."

I take my hand from his cheek and gently touch the space around his ribs. "How are you feeling? Will you be okay to stand? Are you breathing okay?"

He winces, scooting his legs closer to sit up. "Yeah, I'll be fine. Been through worse."

My heart hurts, watching him take his time to stand. I get up with him, keeping my hands on his sides.

He laughs quietly. "It's okay. I won't break."

I let out a nervous laugh, instinctively running a finger under my eye, and it catches something wet. I sniff back a tear and force another laugh. "Yeah, I know. You're Mr. Tough-guy."

Dax takes my hand and kisses the tear-stained finger. "I'll be okay because I have you."

Trepidation spirals in my gut. When Dax releases my hand, I

swallow hard and reach for my bracelet.

My mouth falls open, when all I feel is skin.

"Oh my gosh, where is it?"

Dax narrows his eyes. "What?"

I look around the space. "My bracelet. I don't have it. They couldn't have taken it, could they?"

Dax leans against the wall craning his neck. "If it's not here, maybe you dropped it at the mall?"

"No, I remember touching it when we were on the bed together." I swallow hard, feeling every jerk in my stomach. "Crap. I can't have lost it."

He squeezes my shoulder. "Don't panic. We'll find it."

I shove him off me, pacing across the room. "Oh my gosh, where is it?"

"It's over there."

I turn back, finding Dax holding his ribs and pointing at a spot two feet away from me.

I spy the shiny gold chain on the dusty ground and sigh. "Oh, thank goodness." I bend down and collect it. "Sorry for getting so anxious."

Dax shrugs. "It's okay. It's your favorite."

"It must've come off when Stitch grabbed me."

"That guy is gonna pay for laying a hand on you."

I clasp the bracelet around my wrist and make it back to Dax. "He didn't hurt me."

Dax's jaw flexes and his knuckle crack. "Still didn't give him the right to touch you."

"At least they're gone." I pan over his hunched position against the wall. "Will you be able to ride back to Victoria Falls? Ashworth Estate is another twenty minutes past town."

He frowns, shaking his head. "Nope. You'll have to take us there."

I choke. "What?"

He cracks a smile and throws an arm around my neck. He tousles my hair and then kisses the top of my head. "I'm just playing. Your face was priceless."

I slide his hand off my head. "It's bad enough what the helmet does to my hair. Don't you wreck it too."

He laughs. "You seriously need to chill. I don't think there's a scenario where you'd actually look bad."

"You don't need to keep flattering me," I tease. "I already said you could move in with me."

Seventeen

The ride back to Ashworth Estate was excruciating. All I could think about was my first time meeting Dax after he'd fallen off his motorcycle. Now, the abuse from his brother mixed with his fatigue has me terrified he'll fall unconscious again.

Before getting on the motorcycle, he changed into his leather jacket for extra protection against the elements. While we ride, there's noticeable pressure between his shoulder blades. I think he senses my fear, and is doing everything he can to remain alert. His speed slows every now and then, and I call out that it's okay to pull over.

Stubbornness got us here. Dax didn't stop the motorcycle, and soon I'm hitting the intercom buzzer outside Ashworth Estate.

After Murphy answers, I reply with, "It's me, Vanessa."

The gates open, and Dax starts the motorcycle again. His loud exhale cuts through his facade. His fatigue takes over, and this last stretch is the most agonizing of the entire journey.

He parks the motorcycle by the front stone steps of the manor. I'm quick to get off so I can get him inside. When Dax gets off the bike, I notice a shakiness in his legs.

"Oh my gosh. Are you okay?"

He pulls off his helmet and rubs the heel of his palm against his temple. "Yeah. Just a little dizzy."

"You shouldn't have ridden all the way. I should've called a driver."

Dax hangs his helmet on the handlebars. "Don't do that to yourself. I wasn't leaving the bike behind no matter what you said."

I clutch his hand, leading him up the steps. "Let's just get you inside. You can finally get some rest."

Dax rocks his jaw and dawdles behind me. "Are you sure this will be okay?"

"It'll be fine," I say to myself as much as him. When he's still doubtful, I gesture at the manor. "It's not like we don't have the room."

Dax's nerves diminish, taking in the grandeur of my home. "I guess that's true."

The front doors burst open, and I assume it'll be Murphy. The wind is knocked out of me when my father races toward us.

"Get away from my daughter!" he yells at Dax.

Dax drops my hand, but I don't unravel from his arm. I've never seen such fury in my father's eyes.

A chill runs down my spine. "Dad, why are you yelling?"

"Why are you with this boy?"

I gulp, feeling like I've committed a crime. "We're friends." It comes out in a feeble tone. "Dad, he needs help. He's not well."

"Then I'll have a driver take him to a hospital," Dad says gruffly.

"No, he can stay with us," I insist. "Just like Christie's family does."

"No, that's ridiculous. He's leaving now."

"I knew you'd do this!" I cry. "You let Ash's girlfriend stay here, but you won't take in someone special to me."

"This isn't even close to being the same thing. I let an employee and his family stay here."

"And you let Ash and Christie be together." I choke on a sob. "Admit it. You love Ash more than me."

Deep lines crease my father's forehead. "Why would you say that?"

I step in front of Dax. "Because you'd never tell one of Ash's friends to leave. Why are you being like this?"

"Because I know where he's from." Dad shoves Dax away from me. "You need to leave. Now!"

I gasp as Dax stumbles backward. "No, he needs to come in."

"Murphy!" Dad calls. "Call the police!"

My jaw drops in disbelief. "The police? He hasn't done anything wrong."

Dad points a finger at Dax. "I'll give you ten seconds to get off my property, or I'll make sure they lock you up."

"*Dad*!" I yell as Dax gets back on his bike. "He needs our help. He'll…"

"Murphy!" Dad cuts me off.

My vision blurs with the sting of tears and I turn my back on my father. I dash to Dax's motorcycle and pull on my helmet. "Let's get out of here."

He stares at me for half a second, making sure I'm certain. When my expression turns pleading, the motorcycle revs. My shoulders jolt as we take off.

I imagine my dad is calling after me, but all I can hear is my racing heart and the buzz of the engine. I tap Dax's shoulder and point to the left before the front gates. The motorcycle swerves, cutting the corner and weaving behind the tall hedges. We are down on a slope, and if anyone heard the bike, they'd easily assume we were out on the road.

I direct Dax toward the staff quarters, and when the motorcycle slows, I lean around his side and tell him where to park in the rear maintenance shed.

I jump off the bike and stay close as he does the same.

"The bike will be fine here," I say, breathlessly. "We have staff who are very loyal to me and won't breathe a word."

"Where are we going? Your dad…"

"It's a big property," I blurt. "I'll keep you safe."

I lead the way out of the maintenance shed. After sighting the coast is clear, I beckon him to follow.

Behind me, Dax mumbles something. When I turn and ask him to repeat it, his eyes glaze over.

"*Dax!*" I cry, lunging for him as his body slumps. With all my muscles working overtime, I barely prop him up. "Dax! Dax, wake up."

He mumbles something again, slouching against my body.

I jostle him the best I can, repeating his name and willing him back to me. Crouching, I lower him to the ground. He's too heavy to move off me, so I just hug him and plead for him to wake up.

With another mumble and a pain-stricken groan, his eyes gradually blink open.

"Dax," I whisper in relief. "Oh, thank goodness."

He groans again, cupping his head as he sits up.

I clutch his shoulder. "Take your time. Don't rush."

"What happened?"

"You fell." My voice quivers, causing him to look at me with concern. "I tried to wake you up."

He caresses the side of my face. "Don't be sad. I'm okay."

I swallow the urge to sob and shake my head. "No, you're not."

Doubling down on his stubbornness, he gets himself up. I slowly follow, keeping my eyes glued to his unstable legs. He holds a hand out to me, and I feel foolish taking it. He's the one who just blacked out. He shouldn't be tending to me.

"How's your head?" I ask, leading him to the rear of the manor.

"It's thumping, but I'll live."

My vision blurs and I don't say anything because it'll only unleash a torrent of sobs.

I lead Dax towards the pool and walk him past the cabana lounges. I wipe my eyes dry as we enter the pool house.

"Oh boy, this place is huge," Dax says.

Even though the day is drawing into evening, the pool house is light and airy. Another stark reminder of the difference between mine and Dax's lives. But none of that matters. I lead Dax by the hand into the bedroom, because nothing and no one will stop me from looking after this boy.

I help Dax onto the bed and he shifts against the mountain of pillows covering the headboard.

"Dax." My voice shakes as I sit beside him. "You need a doctor."

"I'll be fine. It's not the first time I've blacked out. I'll just get some sleep and then get going."

I rub my sweating palms against my thighs. "Dax, I saw your file at the hospital."

"You did what?"

"I needed to know what was wrong with you."

"Since when is it your business?"

I slap a hand against my chest. "Since I care about you. You weren't going back to the hospital, and I overheard Dr. Harris talking about you."

Slouched against the pillows, his jaw flexes. "What'd he say?"

"Something about your white blood cells. Your file said they're too high."

"So there is something wrong with me?"

"You need to follow up with the doctor about these tests."

He swallows hard, shifting away from me. "No. No way."

"*Please.*" It comes out more wounded than I intended. "I can't do this anymore. I can't watch you in pain and wonder when you'll fall unconscious again.”

He watches me intently, and his bottom lip twitches with undecided words.

I take his hands and rub my thumb over the rose etched into his skin. “You mean so much to me, Dax. I just want you to be okay.”

He wipes sweat from his brow, growing pale as he whispers, “I’m scared. I don’t know what they’ll find, or what it’ll mean.”

“It’ll most likely mean you get put on medication,” I say as calmly as I can manage. “From what I read online, your condition can be managed with a better diet, regular exercise, and quitting smoking.”

Dax chews his lip, and his eyes have trouble settling on one spot. “But what if it doesn’t work. I don’t want to find out if something way worse is wrong with me.”

I hold his hands tighter and pull him toward me. I rest my forehead against his, feeling the clamminess, and exhale slowly. He tries timing his breath with mine, but his anxiety spikes, sending his nerves haywire.

“I got you,” I whisper, briskly rubbing my hands along his arms. His skin is cold and prickly. I search his chest, finding his heartbeat, which races like a thoroughbred. “Oh, babe, this is the biggest problem. Your poor heart. This anxiety is plummeting your health.”

Panic rushes over his face. “I don’t know what that means.”

I sit up taller, and take another long breath in and out with him. He follows along, shakily.

“I don’t want you to worry,” I whisper, holding the sides of his face steady. “It’s not your fault you were dealt a crummy hand in life. You’ve dealt with it the best way you could. But it can get better from here.”

He shakes his head, choking on an inhale of air, and then coughing it out.

“Hey, hey,” I coo. “It’s okay.”

“I don’t want to drag you down,” he says in a hoarse voice, tapping a fist on his chest. “I don’t want to give you my problems.”

“But I don’t want to leave you alone with your problems.”

His eyes still and some color comes back to his face. His shoulders relax and he leans forward, kissing me like I'm his life preserver. "Dang. How'd I get so lucky to have you?"

"So, is it a yes?" I gently kiss the nape of his neck, tracing my finger along his collarbone. "Will you see a doctor?"

He catches my hand with his. "Only if you come with me."

I give the sensitive spot another butterfly kiss. "Of course, baby."

In my back pocket, my phone buzzes. Keeping a hand firmly on the back of Dax's neck, I pull out my phone. When I see it's my dad calling, I immediately cancel the call.

"Maybe you should answer it," Dax murmurs.

I put the phone down on the bed and nuzzle my nose against Dax's jaw. The phone buzzes again, but I don't budge.

"Vanessa?"

I squeeze my eyes shut. "I'm not talking to him."

The buzzing stops, and a moment later, starts again.

Dax motions to my phone. "He keeps calling. You should answer it."

"No. I don't care what he has to say."

"Make things right with your dad," he urges. "Don't let it get worse. I'm not worth it."

"Don't say that." My voice becomes raspy with desperation. "Of course you're worth it."

He shakes his head. "I'm not worth ignoring your family. You're taken care of here. You can't risk that."

"But it doesn't make me happy." I scoop his hand in mine and rest them against my chest. "You make me happy."

Sadness dulls his blue-gray eyes. "Don't put it on me. I don't want to get between you and your family."

I lift his hand and kiss it. "I'll talk to my dad purely because I hate seeing you sad."

A hint of a smile twitches the corners of his mouth. "Thanks."

I move off the bed and leave the bedroom. As I move down the hallway, I grip the phone so tight it might snap in two. When I reach the living area, I hit answer and lift the phone to my ear.

"Dad?"

"Vanessa." He's breathless. "Where are you? I'll send a car. I need you back home."

"I didn't leave the grounds."

Surprise litters his tone. "You didn't?"

I nod against the phone. "I'm still at Ashworth Estate. I just need some time to myself."

"As long as you're not with that boy, we can talk about this."

I huff, raking a hand through my hair. "Meaning the alternative would be, if you saw me with him, you'd ignore me?"

Dad pauses, and I can almost hear his nostrils flaring. "No, honey. I just want you at home and safe."

I spent a whole night out of the house with him and you didn't even notice. Even though it's on the tip of my tongue, I dare not say it.

"You don't even know him. He's not dangerous."

"LJ told me about his tattoos."

"Wait," it hisses out of me as anger injects into my veins. "LJ went running to you and that's why you flipped out when you saw me with Dax?"

"Do you have any idea what that scorpion tattoo means?"

I huff and throw my hand up. "It's a motorcycle club."

"It's more than that." Frustration gets the better of him, and his tone grows urgent. "You shouldn't know about these things."

A deep scowl embeds in my face. "Why? Because I'm just a simple girl?"

"Yes, you're my little girl."

I retch. "Don't demean me. I'm more than just your daughter."

Dad sighs. "I'm trying to protect you."

"You haven't been protecting me. You've been shutting me out."

"Vanessa." His voice turns stern. "Don't be like this."

"Why shouldn't I? I'm not the child you want to talk with."

"You need to stop acting like this. I've never played favorites with you and Ash."

A laugh erupts out of me before I can catch it.

"What has happened to you?" Dad says in a low tone. "You've never acted this way before."

"Because I'm finally saying what's on my mind. I'm not being your good girl who solely goes to the country club and plans parties."

"Vanessa, I know you do more than that."

"Do you? Because you've never taken me to work with you."

"I didn't think you were suited to it."

"No, it's because I'm not your son."

Tears fill my eyes and I quickly wipe them away, because this is too stupid to cry over.

"Maybe I should've taken you to the office," Dad murmurs.

My heart pounds. "What was that?"

"Then maybe you'd know more about The Scorpions."

"What does that mean?"

"They've disrupted work at our manufacturing plants in Logan's Point," Dad replies. "They're menaces."

"This is why you want me to stay away from Dax? Because you lost some efficiency in your factories?"

"No. I want you away from him because he's a gang member. If you spend time with him, he'll corrupt you."

I groan, pinching the bridge of my nose. "You don't know what you're talking about."

"Vanessa, come to my study. We'll discuss this in person."

"No, I can't. I can't be around you tonight."

"It's non-negotiable. I need to see you in the next ten minutes."

"No." I stomp my foot as my clammy hand squeezes the phone. "There's countless bedrooms in this manor. I'll find the one furthest from your wing and camp there. Just leave me alone.”

I end the call before he can get in another demand. I pant heavily, staring at my phone, and my body fuels with adrenaline.

Holy cow. I just told off my dad.

I wipe the back of my hand over my forehead, collecting beads of sweat.

I trudge back to the bedroom and find Dax sprawled out on the bed. His forearm covers his eyes, until his ears prick to my footsteps.

He lowers his arm and sits up. “How’d it go?”

I shrug and sit on the edge of the bed. “It doesn’t matter.”

He slides his hand over mine, and his warmth calms my nerves. “Yes, it does.”

I exhale and focus on the thumping of my heart. “He knows about The Scorpions because they’ve caused havoc at his factories. LJ saw your tattoo while we were at the tailor’s and tipped off my dad about us.”

“I get why your dad’s worried about you. He probably never expected to see his daughter on the back of a motorcycle.”

“That’s the problem. He has too many expectations for me.”

“He just wants to protect you.”

“But he won’t listen. If he did, he’d know I don’t need protection from you.”

“Yeah, but he thinks I’m like my dad.”

“If he saw what I witnessed today, he’d want to take you in and keep you safe.” I sniff hard, choking up. “That’s all I want.”

Dax scoots forward and pulls me into his arms. I rest my chin on his shoulder, fighting the urge to cry, as his strong hands rub my back.

Eighteen

When Dax falls asleep, I leave the pool house to get him a fresh change of clothes. If Claudia will snoop through Christie's wardrobe for me, it's not much of a stretch to ask her to do the same in my brother's room.

As I meander through the first floor, I near Dad's study. The door is ajar and light streams across the hardwood floors. I press my hand firmly into my queasy gut, and step forward. This is a mistake, but I push the door open anyway.

"Dad?"

Dad's focus lifts from his work and a pleasant smile brightens his face. "Vanessa."

"I just wanted to show my face before going upstairs."

"I'm not happy about the way you spoke to me." Disappointment sharpens his stare. "But I'm glad you're back."

"I told you, I never left."

"But you got on the motorcycle with *that boy*."

"You only cared about me being around Dax once LJ brought him up." Heat rises in my voice. "You don't care about how long I've actually been seeing him."

Red morphs from underneath his shirt collar and rises up his neck. "How long has this been going on?"

"It could be a day, a week, or a year. It wouldn't matter," I argue. "I won't stop seeing him."

"Yes, you will," Dad replies, stealing some resolve. "That boy isn't good enough for you. Not for my daughter."

I click my tongue and pat the space over my heart. "You don't even know him. Can't you try understanding why he's in my life?"

"How could I possibly understand?"

"How about by listening to me for once?"

Dad sighs, standing from his chair. "This conversation is going in circles. Just promise me you won't see him again."

"That's like asking me to stay chained to this house. Is that what you want?"

He walks toward me. "That's never what I've wanted for you. I want you out in the world, making a difference. And you have exceptional skills to do so." He pauses and brushes back a lock of my hair. "But when you came back from Switzerland, I promised myself I'd never lose you again. I never want anything to get between us because those months were far too difficult."

I let my guard down and lower my voice. "You're afraid of losing me?"

He smiles and his eyes grow glossy.

Tears prick the corners of my eyes and I suck in a shaky breath. "I didn't know you felt that way."

Dad pulls me into a hug, and silence fills the room. My breathing is quick and shallow as thoughts collide in my head. How will I ever have a proper relationship with my dad if I can't talk to him about my boyfriend? And is he really afraid of not having me in his life if he's ordering me to stay away from Dax?

This won't work.

"I've missed this," Dad whispers, rubbing a circle on my back. "I've been so happy to have you home, but I've been walking on eggshells. There's been such awkwardness between us. Am I right in thinking it's because you're still siding with your mother?"

I gasp and pull out of the hug so I can look Dad in the eye. "I never sided with her."

"But you left."

I nod, swallowing hard. "Because she asked me to."

Dad smiles. "Ash said the same thing about you."

"It's true. If you had asked me to stay, I would have."

"I would've asked if I knew anyone was leaving. I didn't realize how hard I needed to fight to keep my family together."

I bite into my cheek to distract myself from the breaking of my heart. "Is that what you want? Your family back together?"

He rubs my arm. "I just want my kids home and safe. That's my number one priority."

I give him a small smile and nod. I'm glad his priority doesn't include Mom, because unfortunately, I know he isn't part of her plans.

I sniff back my tears. "You know, about that boy…"

Sternness creases his face. "I don't want to hear about you spending another second with him."

"Dad's he's not…"

"You don't know what he is."

"Yes, I do."

"Vanessa, you've been sheltered from the harshness of this world."

My hands ball into fists. "You have no idea what I've seen. If only you'd been there today."

"Why? What did he do to you?"

I groan and move to the doorway. "One day you need to start listening to me. Dax will never hurt me."

"If you go near him again, hurt is all you'll get."

"You won't be seeing me at dinner," I say, leaving the room.

"Vanessa, tell me you heard me."

I turn back into the room. "Sure, Dad. I'm your good girl, aren't I?"

Leaving him staring at the doorway, I fly up the nearest staircase and hurry to Ash's suite. I knock on his door and there's no answer. I push the door open and walk inside. There's a change of clothes tossed on the end of the bed, but the rest of the room is neat thanks to Claudia. She obviously hasn't been here since Ash got home and changed his clothes for dinner. I head straight for the chest of drawers by his closet. Still with shop tags, I find sweatpants, a T-shirt, and a hoodie, and bundle them together.

Keeping my head down, I move back down to the first floor. With everyone on their way to the dining room, I make it to the pool house undetected. I move into the bedroom and plonk the clothes down on the bed by Dax. He shifts on the bed, groggily opening his eyes.

"Hey. What are you doing?" he mumbles.

"I got you a change of clothes."

"Oh, thanks." He yawns and sits up. "Are they your brother's?"

"He won't miss them."

Dax gives his T-shirt a whiff. "Maybe I should take a shower."

I throw a thumb over my shoulder. "Bathroom's right over there."

On his way out, Dax pulls his T-shirt over his head. It's painful to watch the way he hunches and grimaces.

"We should think about organizing a doctor's visit."

He walks into the bathroom. "Right now?"

"I can arrange for a doctor to come here to the manor."

"No. I don't want to tip off your dad and get you into trouble."

"I can handle myself. Besides, Murphy won't say anything about it. Like I told you, I have loyal staff."

His jaw flexes and he shakes his head. "It was off-putting hanging at the mall in Victoria Falls. I don't think I could handle a swanky doctor. Maybe I should just go back and see the doc at Logan's Point."

"I can call Dr. Harris and arrange a time for us to see him in private."

His eyes light up. "You'll really go with me?"

"Of course. I said I would." I pull my phone from my back pocket. "I'll give him a call now."

Dax closes himself in the bathroom, and I wander down the hallway, waiting out the rings until someone answers. It's Nurse Cindy.

"Oh, hi, Vanessa," Cindy replies. "Are you coming in? Like every Sunday, we're swamped."

Guilt clamps down on my stomach. "Ah, no, I'm sorry. I was wondering if Dr. Harris is available?"

"Not at the moment, sorry. Do you want me to leave him a message?"

"I was just wanting to arrange a time to see him in person." I fidget with my bracelet. "In private."

I hear the clicking of keys. "Hmm. He's in surgery tomorrow morning. I don't think he'll be done until early afternoon. And then he'll need to be around for post-op care. Is it about the fundraiser?"

"No, it's medical, I mean private. Are you able to book me time with him?"

"How about tomorrow afternoon at four?" Cindy suggests. "It's the first time I can semi-guarantee availability. You won't need to see him for longer than thirty minutes, will you?"

I glance at the bathroom door. "Umm, I dunno. Maybe not."

"Maybe if he needs to see a patient, you can wait for him to come back into your meeting?"

"Yeah, maybe," I reply. "Thank you for booking that in, Cindy."

"No problem. If you have any spare time to spend with us, we'd love to have you back."

Another whack of guilt. "Mm-hmm. Yep. I'll see you."

I end the phone call and exhale heavily. I plonk on the edge of the bed and rest my forehead in my palms. Listening to the shower's running water, I try to focus on the boy who needs me, instead of spiraling with heavy thoughts.

When the water turns off, I force myself to breathe slower, but it only causes me to sweat. The more I try to compose myself, the more worked up I get.

"Are you okay?" Dax asks, entering the room in the new T-shirt and sweatpants.

I force a smile. "You're booked in tomorrow at four p.m."

Dax tilts his head. "You don't look happy about it."

"No, I'm okay. The nurses just sounded like they needed help."

"Do you want to go over there?"

Sadness droops my shoulders. "No. I want to stay here and make sure you're okay."

Dax bends at the knees and scoops me into his arms. "You're feeling guilty."

"My mother would be so disappointed in me. I can hear her voice in my head, telling me I'm dishonoring my commitments."

"Hey, hey," he whispers, stroking my hair. "Your mother left her family commitments behind. She's not exactly a role model."

I lay my head on his chest and a weight slips off me. "Thanks. I needed to hear that."

"I saw those nurses praising you," Dax says. "They also told you to make the most out of your free time. Yes, they appreciate all you do for them, but they also want you to have fun."

"Fun isn't a priority."

Dax playfully knocks on my head. "Hello? Vanessa's mother, get out of her head."

I giggle and hug my arms around his waist. "At least the hospital has been a good cover to get my friends off my back. The little white lie has allowed me to be with you instead."

"Hmm. Maybe you are a bad girl," Dax jokes.

"I can't help that you're my addiction."

Nineteen

Just like last night when Murphy organized our dinner, I called him again this morning for a pool house breakfast delivery. I didn't say either time who the second plate was for, and he's too good at his job to ask. Staff have clear instructions to leave the dishes in the living area and not enter further into the house.

Last night was rough. Dax tossed and turned, and moaned in his sleep. It was hard to tell if it was pain or bad dreams. I guessed both. I'd stroke his forehead and kiss his cheek until he settled. Because I couldn't tell if he was okay, I barely slept.

I let him sleep late, and the midday arrival of crispy bacon, fried tomatoes, and poached eggs stirs him awake.

"Hungry?" I ask, smiling at his scrunched expression as he stretches his arms out.

He blinks a few times, waking up. "Is that food?"

"Yes. Do you want me to bring it in here?"

He shakes his head, sitting up. "No, we can go out there. I haven't even seen the pool in the daylight."

"There's a nice view of it from the comfy couches in the living room."

"Is your family still here?"

"No. Ash will be at school, and Dad will be at work."

"Okay, good. I'm not in the mood to look over my shoulder all morning."

"You don't have to worry. Let's go eat."

I lead Dax into the living area and watch the smile grow on his face.

"I didn't notice how nice this place was before," he says, looking around the airy space. "And this isn't even your main home."

"It's probably so nice because it hardly gets used," I joke.

"You don't use the pool?"

At the coffee table, I pull the cloches off our plates. "I do, sometimes. It's a good stress reliever. We could go for a swim later, if you like?"

Dax sits beside me. "Yeah, maybe."

We eat breakfast in silence. Dax continues to look around at the plush furniture and beachy aesthetic. He told me the mall made him uncomfortable, so I hope he's not feeling out of place here.

When our plates are cleared, we sit back on the couch, cuddled together.

"We have some time to kill before your appointment this afternoon," I say, stroking his coffee-colored hair. "Do you want to rest?"

"I should probably swing by the clubhouse."

My gut tenses. "Why would you do that?"

"So no one has a reason to look for me."

"Dax, yesterday your brother hit you so hard you blacked out."

"He just hit me where I was already bruised."

"Baby, you need to stop making excuses for him. This situation is not okay."

Dax rubs his palm across his chest. "Just stop."

I put my hand over his. "I'm sorry. I didn't mean to make you feel worse."

"All I need to do is walk in there for five minutes."

"And what if he has a job for you to do?"

"I'll tell him I'll do it."

"Will Boscoe or McCoy follow you?"

Dax frowns, rolling his shoulders forward. "You're doing it again. You're making me tense up."

"I'm just scared," I whisper. "I don't want you to get hurt again."

He lifts my hand and kisses it. "And I don't want them finding me again when I'm with you. If I go to them, everything will stay the same. It's safer."

"When will you go over there?"

"I'll go before the doctor's appointment. You can have your driver take you to the hospital. Just tell your family you're going for a volunteer shift."

I suck in my bottom lip, and it trembles when I let it go. "Okay."

He rubs my arms, searching deep into my eyes. "Trust me. It's what I have to do."

My eyes prick with tears. "I don't understand why you can't just stay here. You're safe here."

"I'm hiding here."

"My father will come around."

"Ness, I'm still staying here with you. I just have to show my face at the clubhouse. That's all."

I nod, my frown immovable.

He kisses my forehead. "It'll be okay."

"Okay. I don't understand, but I trust you."

He smiles. "Thank you."

I reach for a glass of water from the coffee table and take a sip. "If you want to get out of here for a little bit, I could give you a tour of the manor."

Dax gets off the couch, moving toward the glass sliding doors to view the manor. "It looks like it'll take all day to move around that place."

"I'll only show you the important rooms. There's a few wings I haven't been in for years."

Dax laughs. "I don't get why your family needs to live in such a massive place."

I smirk, walking over to him. "Because this is Ashworth Estate and we're the Ashworth family."

Dax slaps his forehead, playfully. "How could I be so dumb?"

"I need to change anyway," I say, looking down at the T-shirt and shorts I slept in. "I can't have anyone see me walk around in this during the day."

"I think you look cute," he says, taking my hand. "You look so relaxed. You're not even wearing makeup."

I look away with embarrassment. "Don't make fun of me."

He holds onto my hand tighter. "I'm not. Honestly, you look great."

I cup my cheek, feeling it grow hotter. "Anyway, it doesn't matter. I'm not dressed appropriately."

Dax chuckles. "I thought I told your mother to get out of your head."

"It's not just my family. The staff will look at me funny too."

As we walk toward the manor, Dax asks, "Do you need to go to school today?"

"Going to school for me and my brother is mostly for image sake," I reply. "When the school is named after our family, we kinda get away with not attending. Besides there's three ivy league colleges competing for me, so my future isn't dependent on high school."

"Do you know what college you want to go to?"

"I haven't thought about it because it's not my decision."

Dax sighs. "I see why you want to feel free."

"My problems are nothing compared to yours."

His thumb rubs against the back of my hand. "But they're your problems, and they matter."

I lean into him, appreciatively.

Before we reach the manor, Dax asks, "Are you sure my bike is okay in that shed?"

"Yeah, it's fine. When I spoke to Murphy earlier, he said the groundskeeping staff had asked about it, but I had him instruct them to ignore it."

"It's that easy?"

I grin. "Yep."

"So where does your driver park his car?" he asks. "Or does he take it home with him?"

"We have a garage for the limousines and town cars," I explain. "Roger and the other drivers park their personal cars by the staff quarters on the back of the property."

Instinctively, Dax looks over his shoulder. "Just how far back does this property go?"

I giggle. "Yeah, we own a lot of land. We passed the staff quarters on the way into the maintenance shed. There's a service entrance down there where you can make a smooth getaway."

"Sweet. So the garage with your father's car isn't near that?"

"No, his garage is closer to the main house. The service cars have one section, and the main area is for the sports cars." When Dax's eyes light up, I ask, "Do you want to start the tour there?"

"We won't get caught?"

"Like I said, my dad and brother are out. Plus, Dad always chooses to travel by helicopter. I don't even remember the last time I saw him drive. I think the cars are just trophies at this point."

"Okay, I gotta see."

With his excitement sending waves of happiness through me, I lead Dax to the garage. It's warehouse size with polished cement floors and crisp studio lighting.

Dax whistles, taking it all in. "Wow. There's an insane amount of money in this room."

We walk between the sleek and shiny cars. Dax awes at the exteriors, scrutinizes the interiors, and checks out a few of the engines.

"So which ones have you taken for a spin?" he asks, tapping fingers along the hood of a Mercedes roadster.

I blush. "None."

"Oh, come on." He moves over to the Dodge Viper. "Don't you rich kids ever rebel?"

"Sometimes peer pressure gets the better of my brother, and he'll take a car out." My eyes wander to the Porsche 911, my favorite car. "But it's not that rebellious. There's trackers in all of them, so we're watched wherever we go."

"Is that why you haven't taken one out?"

"To be honest, I haven't thought about it. Despite having my driver's license, Dad told us not to drive ourselves. Plus, I'm used to having a driver on call."

He tugs on my hand. "Come on, show me the rest of your digs."

I lift a pointed finger. "Before we do, I need to give you something."

I take Dax into the service car garage and over to a lockbox. I punch in a code and pull out a swipe card.

"This will open the service entrance at the back of the property. Only staff have these, and my family won't notice if it's used or not."

Dax takes the swipe card. "Is it really okay that I have this?"

My heart bounces happily. "I just want you to be able to come and go without my dad screaming at you. This is the easiest option."

Dax grins, pocketing the swipe card. "Okay, then. Thanks."

When we enter the manor, we wander around the great room, which is stuffed with antique furniture and centuries old artworks.

Dax's eyes wander up the stairs. "So, where do you sleep?"

Nervousness ripples through me. "You want to see my bedroom?"

He smirks. "We've slept next to each other twice, and you're tripping out over me seeing your bedroom?"

"Oh gosh. I still can't believe how whirlwind meeting you has been. I wouldn't even let a boy kiss me, and now I can't imagine spending a day without you."

"I know. I'm irresistible."

I snigger and lead him to the stairs. "There's a few wings to pass before we get to mine."

"Of course this place is a freaking maze."

I lead him toward my bedroom, navigating the different hallways. "This is my wing. It's nicknamed the kids' wing. Any time our cousins or friends stay with us, they always have a bedroom in this hallway."

"Is it just you and your brother now?"

"My brother moved into a suite in a different wing. His girlfriend's bedroom is right there, and next door was my brother's room. Once our parents found out they were a couple, they made him move."

"Is it better having space away from your brother?"

"No. I wish Christie was the one who moved."

"Oh, that sucks."

"It was just unsettling to come back home and find my brother's bedroom wasn't a few doors away, but a few hallways away."

"And you don't get along with his girlfriend?"

"I don't dislike her." I mistakenly wince, and then force myself to hide the emotion. "I guess, I get jealous of her. Her parents are so sweet and affectionate, and mine use me as a pawn in their marriage wars. Even little things, like Christie and her mom were on the planning committee, but they decided they wanted some time off. My mother allowed it, like it was no big deal. Yet, she uses me as a microphone while she's overseas. It's just hard watching someone's life and thinking it's a lot easier than yours."

"I guess I can understand that."

I laugh at myself. "Well, sure. You look at mine and it's way easier than yours. Ugh. I need to stop complaining."

"Hey," he coos, clutching my hand. "Don't do that. There's so much control in your life. No wonder you want to snap like a rubber band."

I thank him and lead him into my bedroom. He whistles, looking up at the vaulted ceiling and hanging light fixtures.

"You've got some fancy furniture in here," he says, strolling through the room.

"They're all antique. That armoire over there was my great grandmothers. She had it shipped over from France."

"And this bed is massive. You could have six people in here."

I chuckle at the ridiculousness.

He grins. "Makes the pool house bed look tiny, is all I'm saying."

"Miss Ashworth?" Claudia calls, stepping into the room. She jolts back, surprised by Dax. "Oh, I'm sorry. I didn't know you had company."

"It's okay," I say, clasping Dax's hand. "Dax, this is Claudia. She's one of the most special people in my life."

Dax waves. "Hey."

"Claudia, this is Dax." I pause for a beat, blushing. "My boyfriend."

Dax grins and gives a slight nod, approving the official title.

Claudia gasps and lets out a chuckle. "Miss Ashworth, why didn't you tell me you had a boyfriend?"

Dax nudges me. "Yeah, Miss Ashworth, why didn't you tell her?"

My blush is in overdrive. "Claudia, it's on the down-low. I don't want my father finding out Dax is here."

"Oh." She nods knowingly. "Well, it was lovely to meet you. Mister?"

Dax bats a hand. "Just Dax is fine."

I wink at Claudia. "It's Mr. Malone."

Claudia grins brightly, and I tug Dax out of the bedroom. "We'll get out of your hair."

Dax waves, following me out. "Bye."

"Come on, I'll show you the other side of the house, and then you should get more rest."

"Believe me, I'm fine. I got more sleep last night than I have in a long time."

"You seemed pretty restless."

"Well, I feel better than I have in ages."

I hold his hand, smiling. "I'm glad."

When we get back downstairs, I get a jolt of excitement from a nearby room. I veer him closer to the double herringbone doors.

"This is one of the rooms the housekeepers hate the most," I say, opening the door. "They complain there's too many windows and it's too hard to reach the chandeliers, even with tall ladders."

"Wow, this looks like a ballroom," Dax says, walking across the high-shine herringbone floors and marveling at the exceptionally high ceiling, which boasts three five-tier chandeliers. "Why don't you have your gala here?"

"We host some events here," I reply. "But they're mostly dinners with executives from my father's companies."

"You make it sound like this place is low tier."

"It just depends on the function. Some events aren't appropriate to have on the estate."

"If you say so. The only parties I've ever seen are a bunch of guys getting loaded at the clubhouse bar."

"Well, our parties are a little more upscale," I tease.

"No doubt." Dax pulls me into his arms. "So what kind of stuff happens at a black tie gala?"

"Oh, it's a riot," I say sarcastically. "Old men talk about stocks and bonds, older women drink too many martinis, and my friends rate everyone's outfits on the harshest scale."

"Wow. How have I never been before?"

"Wait, how could I forget. There's also dancing."

His jaw clenches. "Dancing?"

I stifle a laugh. "Have you ever waltzed?"

His eyebrow raises and he gestures at himself. "What kind of question is that?"

I giggle and lift my arms into waltz position. "Wanna try?"

He backs away from me. "You're not serious."

With my arms still in position, I wave him over. "Come on. Go for a twirl with me."

"I don't twirl."

"If you don't learn to waltz, I'll be forced to dance with LJ."

Without a word, he steps in close to me.

My heart flutters. "That was quick."

He puts his hands on my waist. "That guy's not laying a hand on you."

I pluck his hands off my waist. "Well, right now, your hands are wrong." I reposition his hand under my shoulder blade, and lift his left hand to hold mine. "That's better."

"This feels awkward."

"Do your ribs hurt?"

"No. It's just holding you like this feels wrong."

"It's not wrong, it's elegant."

He rolls his eyes, which makes me laugh. I then instruct him on the correct steps. The fact he gets to lead entices him, but the monotony of the box step has him tensing up.

When his feet fail to come together, I whisper, "Relax your body."

"This doesn't exactly feel natural."

"But if you have these basic moves down, you'll fit in on the dancefloor."

Before I can instruct him on the steps again, I squeal as he lifts me into the air. Wrapping his arms around my middle, he hugs me close and spins me around.

I squeal again as we stop spinning and he lowers me to the ground.

As our chests heave, he smooths back my hair. "Maybe I don't want to fit in on the dancefloor," he whispers.

Tingles electrify my body and I grin at him. "Oh boy, I can't wait to take you to the gala."

His arms unravel from me and I instantly clutch his hand. The burst of happiness has me skipping as I tug him out of the room.

He laughs, following behind. "Where are we going now?"

"I want to show you the view from the parlor." My cheeks hurt from the stretch of my smile. "It's one of my favorite places in the manor. That is, when we're not hosting society meetings there."

"Okay, if it's got you this giddy, I gotta see it."

At that, I halt, and Dax bumps into me from the abruptness. I send my hands up to the sides of his face and lock onto his eyes. "It's you. You have me giddy. I just want to share everything with you."

Dax's hands caress mine and I lower my intensity. "I love how excited you are, but you can slow down. I'm planning on sticking around."

It's like my limbs are filled with helium. I'm so weightless and ballooned with joy.

I sigh, lowering my hands. "How'd I get so lucky? I truly believed I'd never find my person."

Dax smirks. "I never expected to fall for someone like you."

I bite my lip. "You're falling for me?"

He brushes back my hair. "Isn't it obvious?"

I sigh again and lift onto my toes. As I toss my arms around his neck, his arms pull around my lower back. Our lips connect as our chests collide. His kiss sends fireworks of ecstasy over my lips. I almost lose balance as my toes curl. Feeling me wobble against him, Dax holds me tighter.

I kiss him back harder, sending my hands down between his shoulder blades. As I let my hands explore, my ears prick to movement behind me.

"What the hell?" my brother's voice cuts through.

Dax and I break apart. I spin around to gawk at my brother.

"Ash?" I clear my throat, hoping my cheeks aren't bright pink. "You're home early."

Ash's eyes pan from me, to Dax, and then back to me. "Yeah," he drags out the word. "Classes were boring and Christie's busy with an art project, so I decided to skip out. What exactly am I looking at?"

The flush in my cheeks radiates across my face. "Umm, I'm… We're…" I turn to Dax, and clamminess sits on the back of my neck. "This is my brother, Ash."

"Hang on." Dax's eyebrow arches. "Ash Ashworth?"

"Ash is his nickname," I clarify. I glance at my brother, stifling a laugh. "He's Little Ash."

Ash groans and rolls his eyes. "Oh, shut it. I haven't been *little* in a long time."

I ignore my brother's complaint and tell Dax, "He's the third Thomas Ashworth. A nickname was needed for the baby."

"Okay," Ash says, waving his hands in front. "Can someone please explain what's going on? Since when do you have guys around the manor?"

I shrug coyly. "It's never been plural. It's just one guy."

"*Ness*?" He drags out my name, waiting for a real answer.

"This is Dax," I concede. "Can you please promise you won't tell Dad you saw him?"

Ash's eyebrows knit together. "Has Dad met him?"

My jaw clenches. "More like he tried to kick Dax off the property."

Ash folds his arms and narrows his focus at Dax. "Why? What'd he do?"

Dax broadens his stance. "Why are you looking at me like I'll hurt your sister?"

"Because I don't know you," Ash replies.

I step in front of Dax. "He'd never hurt me. He just needs somewhere to lay low while he gets better."

Ash tilts his head, nodding at Dax. "You're hurt?"

"I'll live," Dax mutters.

"Look, it doesn't matter what's going on with him," I say to Ash. "Just, please, don't say anything to Dad."

Ash huffs, unfolding his arms. "When have I ever ratted you out?"

I move forward and wrap him in a hug. "Thank you, Ash."

When I turn back to Dax, he shifts awkwardly. "I should probably get going."

My heart sinks. "Are you sure?"

He nods. "I'll just check in with the others, and then I'll meet up with you later. You'll have your driver take you there?"

"Mm-hmm."

Dax pecks my cheek and squeezes my hand. I then show him the hallway that will lead to the rear of the manor.

"Remember to take the service entrance on your way out."

Dax lifts his hand in a wave and disappears down the hallway.

I exhale hard, and hear my brother's fingers tapping against his arm.

His tone is dry. "The service entrance?"

"It's no big deal."

"Why are you hiding him?"

"It's complicated."

"How? Because he's not part of our circle?"

"For starters."

Ash lips twist with indecision. "I just hope he's worth it."

My chest constricts. "You're not thinking about saying something?"

He touches my shoulder. "I said I wouldn't."

"*Phew*. Thank you."

When Ash and I move along the hallway, more footsteps enter the space. Ahead, Murphy and two groundskeeping staff march towards us with different sized luggage. My heart seizes when I recognize the set.

"Murphy?" my voice trembles. "What's going on?"

"Darling, you sound positively frightened," my mother's voice echoes up the hall. "I thought you'd be excited about my return."

Ash's jaw drops. "Mom?"

Our mother comes into view with her arms stretched out. "Hello my darlings. Come and give Mommy a hug."

My gut twists in on itself.

My heart hammers against my ribcage.

My skin grows pale with an icy chill.

Ash, on the other hand, pushes past me and rushes to our mother.

He hugs her, asking, "Why didn't you tell us you were coming home?"

Mom rubs a circle on his back. "Don't you love the surprise?"

Ash pulls out of the hug. "Of course, I do. Does Dad know you're home?"

Mom smooths down her blazer where it meets the hem of her pencil skirt. "I thought I'd surprise everyone. Vanessa, come over here."

I oblige and meet them in the hallway. She opens her arms, but I remain stiff. Not wanting to make a scene, Mom leans in and kisses my cheek.

"I'm so happy to see you again, darling," Mom says, squeezing my shoulder.

"We just spoke on the phone," I say bluntly. "Why didn't you tell me you were planning to come home?"

My mother huffs. "I've never heard you sound more ungrateful."

"We're just surprised," Ash cuts in. "You never gave us a clue when you'd be back."

Mom smiles at him, stroking the side of his face. "You've become much more handsome than when I left. The video chats haven't done you justice.”

“I’ll ask Murphy to arrange the helicopter to bring Dad home,” Ash suggests eagerly.

Mom touches his arm, and her smile twitches. “No, don’t do that. I have to get going again.”

His nostrils flare and outrage fires in his eyes. “You’re leaving?”

Mom chuckles. “Just for a meeting. Don’t worry, darling. I don’t plan on leaving Victoria Falls any time soon.”

Tension leaves Ash’s shoulders and he exhales gradually.

My skepticism radar pings, and I stare down Mom. “So this means *someone* knew you were coming home.”

Mom taps her index finger against her painted lips. “Not exactly.”

“What does that mean?”

“I’m not done with my surprises,” she replies. “I’ve emailed the society ladies about a menu tasting at the country club. Chef Renaldo wants their opinions, and I can’t wait to see the looks on his and the ladies’ faces when I’m there in person.”

Keeping them behind my back, my hands ball into fists. “You want to have a catering meeting? Today?”

A sparkle glints in her eye. “This mother and daughter team is back together at last.”

“What if I’m unavailable today?”

Mom pats her pinned hair, looking down her nose at me. “Considering your only task for the immediate future is planning the gala, I’d say whatever’s on your schedule can be moved around this.”

I suck in a breath to steal some composure. “Even a volunteer shift at the hospital?”

“I’m sure one of your peers can take your shift. You did have a number of them sign-up, didn’t you?”

I look away before she sees the lies in my eyes. “Fine, I’ll move things around. Is the menu tasting soon?”

“Yes. I expect you to get ready.” She then smiles at my brother. “I need to freshen up, dear. I'll see you at dinner, okay?"

Ash hugs our mother. "I still can't believe you're home."

She smooths a hand down the back of his head. "I'm so sorry I left you for so long. But it was for the best. I hope you know that."

He doesn't reply. Instead, leaves the hug with a smile and disappears down the hallway.

"Okay, Vanessa, get changed," Mom orders. "I need you well-styled for my debut back on the Victoria Falls social scene."

My jaw clenches, hiding my dismay. "Yes, mother."

Twenty

My mother babbles for the entire drive to the country club. I take as much notice as when she was on the phone, because I know she doesn't want my input. Knot twists in my back with every mile closer to our destination. I can't believe she's back and organized a meeting for the moment she returned.

I should be biding my time to meet up with Dax at the hospital. I have no idea how I'll escape my mother's plans and get back to my own.

Roger slows the car in front of the country club, and we exit after he opens the door for us.

From the foyer, I spy Sylvie and Hope standing off to the side, whispering.

My mother speaks first. "Good afternoon, girls. You're both looking as lovely as ever."

They both reply with toothy grins. "Hello Mrs. Ashworth. Welcome back."

I motion to my friends and tell my mother. "I'll meet you inside."

Mom nods. "Very well."

Phew. I move over to my friends, needing a breather.

Sylvie deadpans at me. "So, your mother comes home and now we need *another* meeting? What could've changed since Saturday?"

"The menu, apparently," I reply. "We're doing a tasting."

Sylvie's eyes light up. "Talk about burying the lead. The food at the cafeteria today was a disaster. I could do with something actually tasty."

Hope flicks her chestnut hair over her shoulder. "Not that Vanessa would know. Where were you today?"

I avoid her gaze. "Since when is it surprising that an Ashworth doesn't go to school?"

Sylvie nudges me. "We just miss you. You know that."

I smile. "Thanks."

Sylvie covers her mouth, sniggering. "Hope's just being aggressive because her mother's in a panic."

Hope clicks her tongue, turning her shoulders away as her arms cross.

"Believe me," I say to Hope, "I'm not exactly thrilled to have my mother back."

"It would've been nice to have a head's up," Hope grumbles.

"Agreed," I reply. "It was a surprise to me too."

Hope's scowl deepens. "Sure it was."

I back up, unnerved by her hostility.

Sylvie steps between us. "Hope, chill."

Frustration coats Hope's tone. "Whatever. My mother puts her all into these events. Yet, your mother still believes she controls everything. In reality, she couldn't do anything from her ivory throne in Switzerland."

"Well, she's back now," I mutter, dumbfounded. "Besides, I was here to…"

Hope huffs so violently, it cuts me off. "Yes, Vanessa, you were here to undermine my mother too."

I clutch my chest, hurt by the cruelty of her words. "I was just doing what my mother asked. You don't think I want to be anywhere else instead of these meetings?"

Sylvie slings an arm around me. "We're all just here as our mothers' puppets."

Hope cackles. "Oh, yes, Sylvie darling. Your martini-addicted mother is such a dictator."

Sylvie drops her arm from around me and turns her back on us. "Why am I even trying to help?"

"Sylvie," I call, but she walks toward the dining room.

"Look, you know this is nothing personal," Hope says. "Your family takes up so much space in this town. My family is just trying to take a piece."

"And you expect my mother to back down? You know better than that. It'll never happen."

Hope shrugs. "We'll see."

Pain spasms inside my head as Hope walks toward the dining room.

I check the time on my phone. It's an hour until Dax's appointment. My stomach churns and my headache compounds. I know how these meetings go, and my mother will want to dominate the room. How will I ever get out of here in time?

The back of my hand swipes over my piping hot forehead. This whole situation is making me physically sick. Perhaps I can leverage it as an excuse to leave early. Entering the dining room, I press my hand into my stomach and taste every sour note washing over my tongue.

"Vanessa, darling," my mother calls, standing at the head of the table. "Are you all right?"

I frown at her and give a slight head shake.

She beckons me over and I exaggerate the wobble in my walk. Mom puts an arm around me and feels my forehead.

"What's wrong?" she asks in a low voice.

"I feel sick," I whisper discreetly. "I have a headache, and my stomach is so fragile."

Mom pats my back and motions to the nearby chair. "You'll sit next to me. You don't have to taste everything." She snaps her fingers at a server. "Get my daughter a glass of ginger ale."

The server nods. "Right away, Mrs. Ashworth."

I clear my throat and lean in closer to my mother's ear. "Perhaps I should go home."

Mom stifles a laugh. "Don't be ridiculous."

A server pulls out my chair, and another places the ginger ale in front of my setting. With defeat, I plonk down on the dining chair as everyone takes their seats.

"Hello ladies," my mother greets everyone, still standing. "It's so good to once again see you all in person."

Breathy laughter and smiles beam back at her from around the table.

"Hilda," Mrs. Fisher addresses my mother, standing from her seat. "We are so happy to have you back, but the jetlag must be draining. I'm happy to continue steering these meetings until you're back on your feet."

I watch the condescension twitching at the corners of my mother's smile. "It won't be necessary for you to start doing that, Naomi." Mom gestures to me. "We're all aware my daughter has been running everything smoothly in my absence."

It rocks Mrs. Fisher, cracking her smug expression. She lowers in her seat, mumbling, "Yes, of course."

I catch Hope's nostrils flare as her mother retreats beside her.

Chef Renaldo joins us in the dining room. Demure applause welcomes him from the table, and he and my mother kiss each other on both cheeks.

"Thank you all for coming and tasting the wonderful menu I've put together for you," Renaldo says in his slight French accent. "I'm so honored to help such a wonderful cause, brought to our attention by Vanessa Ashworth."

Mom leads the table in a heftier round of applause.

I lift a hand in a humble response.

Chef Renaldo introduces the first dish; an entrée of pan-seared scallops with arugula pesto. It's hard to feign illness when something so exceptional is placed before you. I only eat one of three on my plate, giving my mother a saddened look about not being able to finish the rest.

When entrées are cleared, my eyes dart to the clock on the wall. Oh my gosh, it's getting dangerously close to Dax's appointment time. I promised to be there with him, which is what made him agree to it. What will he do if I'm not there?

When I scheduled the meeting with Cindy, I didn't even mention Dax. But surely Dr. Harris will meet with him. He's the one who discovered the issue with Dax's white blood cell count.

Maybe if I text Dax I'll be late, he can tell Dr. Harris I arranged the appointment for him. I can confirm everything when I get there. Dax just needs the heads up.

There's a tremor in my hand as I pull out my phone. I exhale shallowly and open my text chain with Dax. As I start the message, my mother shifts beside me.

Mom places her hand over my phone. "What on earth could be so important?"

My fingers cramp and my heart stops for a millisecond. She's not going to ask who I'm texting, is she?

"Put it away," she scolds. "This meeting is the only important thing in your life."

Mom lifts her hand and I quickly lock the phone. "Sorry," I mutter, tucking the phone back into my pocket.

Servers place two alternate mains on the table. A classic Beef Bourguignon, and a crispy roast salmon, with smashed potatoes and split peas. As I taste the salmon, delight bursts within me. I wonder if there's any way I can get this packaged up and take it to Dax?

When the tiramisu is served for dessert, I lean close to Mom and keep my voice low. "I really should make a call."

Mom huffs and doesn't make eye contact. "Exactly what is so important?"

"I told you earlier," I whisper. "I had a volunteer shift at the hospital."

Mom turns to me with a perplexed expression. "I thought you said you'd taken care of that."

I shrink in my chair. "What?"

"I told you to get someone to cover your shift. Did you not do that?" Mom then turns to the rest of the table, clearing her throat to gain everyone's attention. "Excuse me, which girl is supposed to be at St. Mark's right now?"

All the girls avert their eyes and shuffle in their seats.

Mom's expression colors with stern disappointment. "Well?"

Saliva surges in my mouth as I wait for them to stop squirming. I hug my middle, bracing for the moment my mother's dissatisfaction crashes onto me.

Mom nudges me. "Who did you ask to cover your shift?"

"I... I..." I swallow hard. "Umm, no one here."

Mom's eyebrow raises higher than I thought her botox would allow. "Why not?"

My mouth opens, but I can't push a single syllable out.

"The other girls have signed-up, haven't they?" Mom's stare lingers on me, and then slowly pans across the rest of the table. "Raise your hand if you're currently volunteering at St. Mark's Hospital."

There's no movement at the silent table. After an excruciating long moment, Sylvie gradually raises her hand. My pulse blares in my ears as my mother's head tilts with interest.

"Umm." Sylvie's voice breaks. "It's not that we aren't *going* to sign-up. It's just that school is so busy and…"

"So it's a no?" my mother interrupts.

Sylvie's hand drops to her lap, and she looks at her mother for an appropriate response.

Mrs. Grant responds with a large gulp of her olive-stained martini.

Mrs. Fisher straightens in her seat. "We determined volunteering wasn't the best use of the girls' time."

Mom's lips twitch with pleasure. "Oh, you did, did you?"

"It's senior year and they need to concentrate on their grades," Mrs. Fisher replies. "When they're here, their attention needs to be focused on the gala. That's priority number one."

"And you don't think community outreach is a branch of that priority?" Mom asks calmly. "We all know the clubs and volunteer groups they join at school contribute to them graduating from high school. How did you not think their charity acts would reflect positively on the gala? When benefactors learn about the young women in our community helping those less fortunate, it helps lend the cause authenticity and increases their desire to monetarily support."

Mrs. Fisher looks at Mrs. Grant and then back at my mother.

"I mean, really, I would have thought this was obvious," my mother says, leaning into the pleasure of talking down to her peers.

Mrs. Fisher dabs her linen napkin across her brow. "Maybe I didn't consider all the options." She lowers the napkin to her lap. "When Hope told me she didn't want to do it, I started thinking about how…"

Mom cuts Hope in half with a penetrating glare. "Oh, you didn't want to volunteer, Hope?"

Hope smooths her hair with trembling fingers. "It's not that I didn't want to."

Mom turns to me. "You couldn't convince them?"

Again, my mouth opens but nothing comes out.

"Shouldn't your suggestion be enough to get a handful of yeses?" Mom presses.

I look away, unable to respond because she won't like the answer.

I didn't force the issue because I don't want girls from school swarming the hospital floor. Three weeks ago, when I approached the nurses about helping, my goal was to reform. To make up for every time I used my influence for personal gain, and in turn, negatively affected others.

I only encouraged my friends to volunteer because my mother saw it as an opportunity. How do I tell her the truth? She wants to know why I didn't use my position to coerce my friends.

Mom looks back at the table. "The gala will be here before we know it. I need you all clocking at least fifteen volunteer hours before then. Is that clear?"

A fearful unison of yeses responds back to her.

Mom smiles with satisfaction, and everyone returns to eating their tiramisu in eerie silence.

After everyone approves Chef Renaldo's menu, the meeting concludes with idle small talk. The women mingle about my mother, asking her to delight them in cozy stories from her time away.

I make my way to Sylvie and grab onto her arms "You gotta get me out of here. Can you drive me to Logan's Point?"

"Yeah, but will your mother let you out of her sight?"

I look over my shoulder at Mom deep in conversation with Mrs. Saxon. I turn back to Sylvie and nod. "We'll say we're going so I can introduce you to the nurses. She'll buy that."

Sylvie groans. "Yuck."

I nudge her. "They're good people."

"I believe you. I just don't want to step foot in the hospital. Even a good one freaks me out."

"When you volunteer, all you do is sit and read."

"When my English teacher can't get me to do that, how do you think a nurse will make me?"

"Because it's neither," I reply. "It's my mother making you."

Sylvie's eyes widen. "Yikes, you're right. Let's get going."

We approach my mother. "Sorry to interrupt Mrs. Saxon. Uh, Mother, we have to get going."

Mom shakes her head. "Not yet."

"I'm taking Sylvie to St. Mark's to introduce her to the nursing staff."

Mom brushes me off. "You can do that another time."

"I guess I could stay and we could share stories from our time in Switzerland," I reply. "Did you continue that little entanglement you started before I left?"

Mom's expression tightens. "It's nothing we need to discuss here. You're free to leave, and we'll talk about it back at the manor."

I keep my smile small to hide how big a victory I just won.

I link arms with Sylvie. "Okay. Let's go."

Sylvie leans into me. "What was that about?"

I let a giggle of happiness escape me. "Never mind. Let's just go before she changes her mind."

Twenty-One

"Do you want me to stay so you have a ride home?" Sylvie asks when she parks her car outside St. Mark's Hospital.

I unbuckle my seatbelt. "No, it's fine. I'll go back home with him."

Sylvie smiles mischievously. "On his motorcycle?"

"Goodbye, Sylvie," I say, exiting the car. "Thank you for the lift."

"Oh, wait," Sylvie calls, and I lean back into the car. "Can you do me a favor?"

"You got me away from my mother, so, of course."

"Can you talk to Mr. Riley for me?"

"Your English teacher?"

She nods eagerly. "I'm totally not getting the dumb poetry he has us reading. Can you do something to get him to lay off?"

I flick at my bracelet. "What do you want me to do?"

"I dunno; the usual thing you do to make teachers back off. *Please*, Ness. I've been struggling with this class for weeks."

I nod, stepping back from the car. "I'll see what I can do."

She claps. "*Eep*. Thank you."

I close the door and wave her off. As I turn into St. Mark's, my stomach churns. I clamp my hands together, hoping with all my might Dax is seeking treatment. At least it'll explain why I haven't heard from him. I called three times on the drive over with no answer.

I swallow hard. He'd have no clue why I was late. I just hope he knows I was getting here as fast as I could. My stomach twists again. Oh gosh, why didn't he answer the phone? Oh, please, be inside with Dr. Harris.

I make my way to the nurses' station and find Trisha walking my way.

She waves. "I didn't know we'd be seeing you today."

"Really?" The hairs on the back of my neck stand on end. "I had an appointment with Dr. Harris. Cindy scheduled it."

Trisha runs a hand over her brow. "Oh, perhaps she did. I've been running around so much, I haven't kept track of Dr. Harris's schedule."

I view the hallway. "Umm. Is he around? I'm really late and couldn't call ahead."

"I think he was getting a patient's test results back."

My head gets woozy. "Erhm. By any chance, umm, did Dax Malone come in today?"

Trisha's posture jolts straight. "What? Why?"

I clear my throat, hoping to rid the shakiness in my voice. "Is that a no?"

"I haven't seen him," Trisha says, scanning the surrounding area. "He's not coming back here, is he? I thought we were done with him."

"So there's no chance Dr. Harris saw him?"

Trisha's jaw clenches and she shakes her head. "I wouldn't miss that guy walking back in here. Any of those Scorpions send my blood ice cold."

My heart thuds to a melancholy beat and I back away. "I have to go. Can you please apologize to Dr. Harris for me?"

With a mixture of confusion and fear in her expression, Trisha nods.

I'm nauseous as I hit the cracked pavement outside St. Mark's Hospital.

Dax never went in.

Did he ever arrive? Did he black out somewhere and that's why I haven't heard from him?

Oh my gosh, he was meeting up with his brother. What if he got an even worse beating and couldn't make it here?

If only I wasn't stuck in that stupid meeting with my mother. If I'd been here, I could've known he was in trouble earlier. I could've found him and gotten help.

I pull out my phone and call him again. Every time it rings out, I hit redial. With the phone fixed to my ear, I pace from the hospital and in the direction of the clubhouse.

My fingers vibrate around the phone.

Sweat builds in my palm.

I hug my free arm around my middle.

I could hurl right here on the sidewalk, but I suppress it. I need to get to Dax. I won't forgive myself if something's happened to him.

Finally, he answers. "Yeah?"

"Dax, thank goodness. Where are you?"

"Why?"

"I'm at the hospital and they said you never went in." Panic courses through my veins. "I've started walking toward the clubhouse to find you."

"What? Stop."

"But I…"

He huffs into the phone. "Where are you now?"

"I'm not too far away from the hospital."

"Just stay there. Don't go any closer to the clubhouse."

I reply with, "Okay," as the phone line goes dead.

It feels like an eternity as I shiver on the footpath, waiting for Dax to appear. He stops a few feet ahead, and I'm breathless as I race toward him. "Oh my gosh, what happened to you?"

Dax pulls off his helmet and his face is stony.

I skid to a stop, my heart pulsing in my throat. "Dax? Are you okay?"

He shrugs. "I'm fine."

I point behind me, and my chest heaves from an oversupply of adrenaline. "You didn't go inside? You didn't see Dr. Harris?"

He rests his helmet on his thigh, tapping his fingers on the hard plastic. "I was waiting for you."

Sweat dampens my hairline. "But you left?"

"You didn't show up."

"I tried. I mean, I got here as soon as I could."

"You told me you'd be here with me. I knew you'd come to your senses."

My back knots. "What are you saying?"

"That I'm another pet project, but I'm not actually good enough for you."

"That's not true! I was stuck at the club, but I'm here now."

He snorts. "The club? That snob-hub was more important than being here?"

"Of course not! My mother wouldn't let me leave."

He rolls his eyes. "Good lord. Just hang up on her when she calls."

"I can't hang up when she's standing right in front of me."

Dax loses grip on his helmet and it falls onto the ground. "She's here?"

I swallow hard and nod.

He blinks hard, wincing. "Wait. Your mom came home? Today?"

I tug at my bracelet. "I'm so sorry. I couldn't get away from her."

His eyes dart from left to right as he comprehends the new information. "You had no idea she was coming home, right?"

"None. If I'd known, I would've left the manor with you." I pinch the bridge of my nose. "Every time I tried to leave, she had another reason for me to stay. It's sickening how easily she had me under her control."

Dax sighs. "Whoa. This is big."

I look into his stormy gray eyes and my vision blurs. "If I could've contacted you, I would've. You have to believe me."

Dax lifts his hands onto my shoulders and smooths them down my arms. "She was already living rent free in your head. I get that her return had you spooked."

"Shell-shocked, more like it," I reply bluntly.

Dax gets off the motorcycle and pulls me into his arms.

I bury my face against his shoulder and mumble, "All I want to do is spend another night under the stars with you."

"If you think I'll go back to sleeping outside after the pool house mattress, you're crazy" Dax jokes.

"So you'll come home with me?"

"Will your mom be on your case? I don't want to make things more complicated."

"All I want is you."

He nods, holding me tighter. "I just want to be with you too."

I motion in the direction of the hospital. "We could still meet up with Dr. Harris before we leave."

Dax's Adam's apple bobs and a frown stretches his lips. "No, I'm done."

My heart squeezes. "What?"

"No hospital. I don't need a doctor."

"But, Dax…"

His eyes flare with determination. "I've made up my mind, Vanessa. Don't push me on this."

My heart shatters. "Okay."

I left him alone with his thoughts, and he decided not to prioritize his health.

He's not magically better. I know he still needs treatment.

And it's my fault he's not getting it.

"We can't leave," I murmur.

He runs his hand over my hair. "What do you mean?"

"I wasn't here, but that's no reason not to see a doctor."

Dax's shoulders slump. "Ness, I just said…"

"But you already agreed."

"And you promised to be here."

"I know, but I couldn't help it."

Dax shrugs. "And that's how things go."

"This isn't the time to be stubborn."

His stare cuts through me. "I told you, quit trying to control me."

I clutch my elbows, dejected.

He grabs my shoulders and exhales hard. "Let's just go. Okay?"

I nod at his muddy boots.

He tilts my chin until I give him eye contact. "I'm not mad at you. Just let this go."

"I'm worried about you."

"Don't be."

"This is it? We just go?"

He nods. "Grab your helmet."

"But I need to fix this."

"No, you don't."

I don't push because I want to be with him. Especially with the return of my menacing mother. Zipping my lips, I get my helmet from the locker trunk.

With the engine running, Dax turns to me and pulls his jacket off his shoulders.

"What are you doing?" I ask.

"You don't have a jacket. You'll be cold."

"I'll be fine. You keep it."

He pulls the jacket down further. "Just take it."

"No, I don't want it," I argue. "You keep it on."

His expression is masked by his helmet visor, but I sense irritability as he pulls his jacket over his shoulders.

I don't care if I've annoyed him. He's not well, and I don't want him riding unprotected.

During the ride across Mountains Road, I hate every second I hold onto him. Why couldn't I convince him to enter the hospital? Why did I let him walk away from help?

Ugh. I'm so stupid!

Dax takes us onto Ashworth Estate via the service entrance and parks in the maintenance shed. I watch every step he makes toward the pool house.

"Go inside," I tell him as we near the pool. "I need to change and get my laptop."

My mood has plummeted as I enter the manor. I'm so grateful to have Dax here, but what does this mean for his health?

I remind myself, I don't own him.

After I snagged clothes from Christie's closet, I asked Claudia to dig out casual outfits from storage. It's where my out-of-season items go before donation drives. Neatly folded in my drawer is a super comfy black and pink tracksuit. I change into it, quickly brush my hair, and carry my laptop out of my bedroom.

Unwilling to waste another moment away from Dax, I jog down the stairs, which lead to the rear of the manor.

"Vanessa," my mother's voice calls before I can escape down the hall. Her stilettos clip-clop on her approach. "Where are you going?"

With my feet in sandals, she towers over me. "Out."

She looks me up and down. "I hardly think so."

"Did you want something, Mother?"

"What was that crack at the country club?"

I trip over my feet to get some space between us. "Huh?"

"The *entanglement*."

I steady my footing. "You know exactly what I was talking about."

"How on earth did you figure it was appropriate to say it in front of company?"

My insides quiver. "How did you think I felt seeing it in person?"

Mom glances away. "You know you weren't meant to see anything."

"But I did," I hiss. "And I haven't said a word."

With a grateful smile, Mom strokes my hair. "Oh, my good girl."

I jerk my head away. "Dad deserves to know."

"I'm not here to have that discussion."

"Then why are you here?"

"For my children."

I choke on my breath, stunned by her answer.

"Why aren't you dressed for dinner?"

I hitch the laptop under my arm. "I'm not eating with the family."

Her hands slam on her hips. "You aren't serious. It's my welcome home dinner."

"Does Dad even know you're home?"

"Why are you being so insolent? I'm here, as well as your brother, and the Klein family." She snaps her fingers. "You are joining us."

"You didn't give Dad a head's up? He would've left the office and flown the chopper back if you'd called."

"That wasn't my priority. Seeing you and Ash is."

I hug the laptop against my body. "Besides doing a menu tasting with the society ladies. You could've sent Dad an email in between messages with Chef Renaldo."

Mom sighs. "Would you put the laptop down and change into something more appropriate? Why have you started dressing so casually?"

"I can't join you tonight," I persist. "You took up all my time this afternoon, and I need to contact a teacher. Plus I need to send volunteering instructions to the girls."

"If you hadn't neglected signing up volunteers, there'd be no rush to contact them now."

I back away. "Look, you didn't give me any notice about your return. I'm just honoring my commitments, like you taught me."

"Your family is one of your commitments."

I halt, lowering my laptop. "I guess I could stay and talk about what I saw in Switzerland."

Mom's chin drops and astonishment rounds her eyes.

Cradling the laptop, I raise my chin. "Your choice."

Mom bats her hand. "Fine, get going. I can't stand your constant arguments."

Before she changes her mind, I dash down the hallway and exit the manor.

"I'm here," I call out, hurrying into the pool house.

Dax leans out the bedroom doorway. "I was just going to lie down. Is that okay?"

"Of course," I say, moving up the hall to meet him. He's pulled off his jacket and is in a tank undershirt.

I place the laptop on the nightstand, and sit beside him as he flops on the bed like a starfish.

"How are you feeling?" I ask, placing a hand on his forehead.

His eyes drift upward. "You don't have to play doctor."

I remove my hand. "I was just wondering if the ride took some of your strength."

"I've been riding as long as I've been walking. You don't have to worry about me on the bike."

I frown at him. "You've blacked out on your feet and on the bike."

He huffs at the ceiling. "*Sassy.*"

"I'm sorry, I'm not trying to go on about this." I scoot closer to him.

"There has to be a way for me to make this better."

Dax grunts as his chest rises with frustrated breath.

I curl my arm around his. "Let me fix this."

"It's fine," he mutters. "I didn't want to see the doctor. I only agreed to make you happy."

"That's not entirely true. I know it."

Dax shrugs. "Sure, I got scared yesterday, but I'm fine now. I can take care of myself."

"I know you can, but you don't have to. I'm here."

"I'm not your project."

I release his arm. "I just care about you. I want your life to be easier."

He traces my jaw and whispers, "It is. Just being with you is enough."

"I can do more," I insist. "It doesn't have to be medical. I'll do anything, and I promise to see it through this time."

"Sassy, it's fine. You don't have to…"

"I know I don't," I blurt. "But I want to. I was serious about my father's private investigator. No one would know he's on your mother's trail."

Dax's complexion dulls and fear amplifies the gray in his eyes. "Don't do that."

"Are you sure? He's the best in the business."

"I said no!"

I sit back, arching my shoulders high as my heart thumps to break free.

Dax runs a hand over his face. "I'm sorry. I didn't mean to snap. I just don't want to risk Lance finding her."

I sit up as the dread rolls off my back. "It's okay, I won't do anything. I don't want you to be mad at me."

"I'm not. You just need to cool it."

I lower myself beside him. "Easier said than done."

His arms sweep around me, and he pulls me on top of him. I melt into him, worried I'll inflame his bruises, but he keeps a hold of me. He mumbles a soft moan in our kiss, and the friction between us deepens. I plant my hands on his chest, my fingers playing with the pendant on his chain.

I move my kiss down to his chin, his neck, and along his collarbone. As my hands move across his chest, they slip under the low collar of his tank. I smile as my fingers trace the roman numerals tattooed into his skin. MMLXXXV.

I mumble a laugh. "When you're eighty, huh?"

He smiles and sinks into the pillow. "It's funny. Being alone with you is the closest to freedom I could ever imagine."

I lower my lips to his and comb my hands through his hair, taking in his earthy scent. His hands press into my back and wander down my spine. As everything blurs around us, his heart pulsates toward mine, and its rhythm lulls me into nirvana.

His hands rise along my back, one camping between my shoulder blades, the other tucking hair behind my ear. As we kiss, I catch his hand and clutch it hard as I seize the burning cravings inside me.

Our spell breaks as a muffled banging sounds in the living room.

Dax's lips slide away from mine and his head turns toward the wall. "What was that?"

I slide my hand on his cheek, turning him back to me. "It's a staff member dropping off food. I already organized it with Murphy."

My lips devour his again, enjoying the taste like it's the first time.

"Well, this is interesting," my mother's voice interrupts from the doorway.

I slide off Dax and choke as I stare at my mother.

"Is this the important work, which stops you from having dinner with your family?" Mom asks, folding her arms.

Dax sits up, shifting his legs off the bed, ready to bolt. His hands ground into the bed cover, and in an effort to keep him by my side, I plant a hand over his.

Mom takes two steps further into the room. "Won't you introduce us?"

I dig my fingers between Dax's, and when his hand jerks, I clamp down on it.

Mom releases a throaty chuckle. "You do know his name, don't you?"

"This…" The tremble in my voice makes me pause. "This is Dax."

"Hello there," Mom says, looking him up and down. "I'm Vanessa's mother, Hilda Ashworth."

Dax shifts again, not saying a word.

Mom smiles at me. "I'm guessing your father doesn't know about this."

I criss-cross my legs and arch my back. "Are you going to tell him?"

"I don't know what there is to tell," she responds. "*Yet.*"

I glance at Dax and then back at my mother. "What do you need to know?"

"Nothing really," Mom says, tilting her head. "I can tell by his appearance he's not part of our circle. Far from it."

"You can forget I was here," Dax says, moving off the bed. "I'm not here to get Vanessa into trouble."

Mom lifts a hand, making Dax stop in place. "You might not realize how many boys are after my daughter. She hasn't taken an interest in any of them. Yet, young man, she's clearly infatuated with you."

"Mom." My heart cautiously beats. "What are you saying?"

"If this is something you don't want your father to know." Her eyes run over Dax. "Then I won't say anything."

I swallow hard. "Why would you do that?"

"Because I also have something I'd prefer didn't get back to your father."

I bite inside my lip. "It's blackmail."

Mom mumbles a laugh. "You'd know all about that, considering how you spoke to me earlier."

When will I learn I'll never get the upper hand on my mother?

She smiles with calculating eyes. "We both have secrets we wish to keep, darling. It'll be in your best interest to listen to me."

Twenty-Two

Again, I barely slept. Hearing Dax asleep made me so thankful, but I could've done without my mother's voice causing havoc to my body. Her internal rants had me contorting in the sheets.

Just like Dax halted our conversation about doctors, I didn't let him push me into talking about my mother. But, perhaps if I vented I wouldn't have lied awake all night.

Doubt it. There's no stopping my mother's voice, even when imagined.

I leave the bed before Dax wakes. He's in a deep sleep, and I'm too restless. I take my laptop into the living room to write an email to Sylvie's English teacher, because I put it off last night.

On my school portal dashboard, I have Sylvie and Hope's log-ins as options. From time to time, I go in and fix things on their behalf. I contemplate writing to Mr. Riley from Sylvie's email, but instead, log back into mine.

An email from me will be actioned. Mr. Riley will only tell Sylvie to work harder. We already know that won't happen.

As I contemplate the appropriate wording, Marcella from the kitchen enters with our breakfast. I glance up at her, smiling with my eyes, and she leaves discreetly.

Not long after, I press send on my email and Dax emerges from the bedroom. He walks into the living room in sweatpants and a tank, smoothing a nicotine patch over his upper arm. His eyes are bright with energy and his smile is adorably cute.

"Thought I'd kick the cravings," he says.

"You look like you're in a good mood today."

He sits beside me, greeting me with a kiss. "I had the best sleep last night. Plus, who wouldn't jump out of bed when they have this beauty to see."

Nervous laughter simmers out of me. "Sorry I left the bed early. I didn't want to disturb you."

"It's fine." He reclines back on the couch, resting his arm over the backrest. "Did you wake up early?"

I wince. "I kinda didn't sleep at all."

A frown droops his sunny disposition. "Oh, I'm sorry."

I clutch his hand. "Don't be. I was glad you were getting some good sleep."

"Was it your mom keeping you awake?"

I nod and huff. "I can't believe she's back. And worse, her arrival got between us."

"But we're together now. We don't need to rehash everything."

I stare into his gray-blue eyes and the whites are so much brighter. "You look really good today."

"I *feel* really good today. All I needed was some sleep."

"I remember in the hospital you kept blaming sleep deprivation."

"I was running on empty because I was either working for my brother, or staying out all night to avoid him."

My heart swells with optimism. "So, you really knew you'd get better?"

He grins and winks. "All I needed was a pretty girl to give me kisses and a place to crash."

I cuddle into him. "Well, that I'm happy to keep doing."

I sigh out with happiness as he presses a kiss on my forehead. Maybe he really is okay. Dr. Harris wrote in Dax's file that stress could be a factor. Perhaps being with me has dialed down his stress levels, so he is indeed getting better.

I touch my cheek, feeling the stretch from my grin. Oh my gosh, I truly hope it's the case. I mean, why else would Dax keep insisting he's better when medical treatment is an easy option? Who would know his body better than he does?

Breaking our happy bubble, the glass door slides open.

"Good, you're up," my mother says, standing with perfect posture.

Tension seizes my back as I sit up on the couch. "Morning, mother."

She glances at her wristwatch. "Don't you think you should be dressed by now."

"No. I didn't sleep well last night."

Mom glances at Dax. "Because you had company?"

"No, because of your surprise."

"Why aren't you happy I'm home?"

"Because I'm waiting for your true agenda to come out."

Mom sighs, averting her gaze. "I'm not playing these games with you. Besides, we have a big day ahead of us."

"Us? You planned my day again?"

Mom glares at me, unimpressed. "Since when is that a surprise? I've always given you a schedule for upcoming events. Now, get dressed."

"I already told you, I've made plans for this week. If you'd given me notice, I could've moved things around. I'll look rude if I cancel at the last-minute."

"You should know better than to argue with me, Vanessa." She turns toward the door. "You've got one hour to meet me in the car."

When she leaves the pool house, I stay glued to my seat.

Why did she need to come home now? This is the first time I've ever been interested in a guy, and she's ruining it.

"Shouldn't she be jetlagged or something?" Dax mutters.

"That would show weakness," I say dryly. "That's not a trait my mother allows anyone to see. Besides, we get a bed, a shower, and butler service during our flights. It's not hard to feel refreshed afterwards."

Dax smirks. "Of course."

"I'm sorry she's dragging me away again. Will you hang out here?"

"Are you kidding? Hanging by a billionaire's pool all day sounds like heaven."

I grin and kiss his cheek. "I'm glad you're so relaxed. It's all I've wanted for you."

He wraps an arm around me. "Having you by my side would make today perfect, but I can wait. If you don't play nice with your mom, I can't stay here anymore."

"Ugh. I hate that she has this leverage over us."

"I still can't believe she's cool with me being here. She really doesn't want her secret getting out."

"And somehow she still wins." I sigh and stand from the couch. "I better get back to the manor and glam up."

He smiles. "Just remember you don't need all that stuff. You're more beautiful when you're natural."

I blush like a fool and slink away, mumbling a giddy, "Thank you."

I hold onto the good vibes while Claudia does my hair and I apply my makeup. But by the time I'm dressed, and in the car with Mom, they've completely faded. When she says she's taking me to a dress fitting, my mild protest is firmly squashed.

"We have lots to do today," Mom says, leading me into a boutique. "I want to finalize the floral arrangements and redo the seating charts. But first, you'll have a dress fitting."

"We already have ladies working on floral arrangements, and Mrs. Fisher is in charge of the seating chart."

"They were doing a fine job, but now I can make it better."

"Do you really think it's a good idea to ruffle feathers the minute you get home?"

"Don't be silly. They'll be glad to finally have my help."

Inside the boutique, racks of formalwear surround us.

"I don't need to pick a dress," I complain. "I'll just wait for the designers to send me something. It's what I've done for the past three events."

"It's different now. It's been months since we've spent time together."

"It's not my fault you didn't come home with me."

"Be serious, Vanessa," she chastises. "Even when you were overseas, you didn't spend time with me."

I shrug. "Did you want me to?"

Mom thumbs through a few items on a rack. "If you spend this time with me, then I'll let you spend more time with your boy toy."

"Boy toy?" Is she really comparing what I have with Dax to the torrid affair she had with my tutor? "You might want to give him more respect. He'll be my date for the gala."

Mom chokes on her surprise. "Is he now? What happened to LJ?"

"There's never been anything with LJ."

"Well, there you go. That's what I was getting at with this new boyfriend. You do want to spend time with him, don't you?"

"Well, yes, but…"

"Then let's stop squabbling and pick a few dresses. Shall we?"

I swallow the urge to groan and move to another rack. The sales assistant, Ramona, greets my mother with a kiss on each cheek, and recommends dresses from Antonia Balletti's latest collection.

Happy not to dig through the racks myself, I fall into the fitting room where Mom and Ramona discuss the gowns while I play a life-like mannequin.

Ramona helps me into a beaded, baby blue, princess cut dress. The hem swims to the floor and the straps fall off the shoulder. It feels a little Cinderella on the way to the ball, and I'm not loving the vibe. Yet, Ramona gushes about how it was made for me.

Mom grins. "She looks like she's worth more than Ashworth Estate."

I pull out the tulle covering the skirt. "I'm not loving how big it feels."

"Oh, please," Mom replies. "No one will be able to take their eyes off you. This gala is happening because of you, after all."

Ramona claps. "Oh, Miss Ashworth, that's wonderful."

My mother beams. "Yes, Vanessa single-handedly reached out to St. Mark's Hospital and discovered how much help they needed. She's quite the philanthropist."

Ramona clutches her chest. "You must be so proud, Mrs. Ashworth."

Mom gives a dignified nod, happily taking credit for my achievements.

At least she's not wallowing in my failure.

I view myself in the three-way mirror and wince. "Can I see something else?"

"Fine." Mom huffs and gestures at Ramona. "Get her another dress."

Ramona helps me out of the dress, sensing the change in my mother's mood. She then helps me into a dusty pink, floor length gown. It has an A-line cut, gathered fabric, and spaghetti straps.

"This is gorgeous," I gush at the mirror.

"*See*," Mom blurts. "Doesn't Mommy know best? I knew you'd enjoy coming here."

Calm down. I like the dress, but could live without the outing.

As Ramona sits the bottom of the dress in a more flattering position, Mom yammers about what shoes and accessories would best suit the dress. When Ramona leaves to find what Mom envisions, it dawns on me. Mom is only here so Ramona can tell her customers Mrs. Ashworth was in the store.

"You could've come here for your own dress fitting, you know," I say as she examines my dress.

"You're the star of the gala, my dear daughter."

"We both know people will be clamoring to speak with you at the gala. Some haven't done that since you left town."

"And, of course, I'll indulge them."

"I'm just saying, you didn't need to bring me along to fulfill your agenda. I mean, maybe it's easier when you make me your doll, but…"

Mom sighs. "Just what are you getting at?"

"You're back in town, and need to be seen everywhere. It now makes sense why you want to take over the flower arrangements and seating charts."

"There's nothing wrong with being seen, Vanessa. You should know that."

"It feels like you're purposefully making me stay away from the manor."

"Don't be ridiculous."

"Well, you come home, and make instant plans, which include me."

"Maybe it feels that way because it's been so long since we were together in Victoria Falls," Mom says, pinching the material of my dress. "But it's always been like this. Maybe you got accustomed to running the show on your own. If that's the case, I couldn't be prouder."

I grit my teeth before asking, "But what about Dax?"

She continues to fidget with my dress. "That's the boyfriend's name, correct?"

"Yes. I just don't get it. You know about him, and haven't kicked him out of the pool house. And if you're not planning on telling Dad about him…" I pause, flicking my thumb against my bracelet. "Then why aren't you letting me spend time with him?"

Mom sighs. "Is it really such a strain on you to spend quality time with your mother?"

I bite my tongue. There's always another angle.

"You know, I could ask Roger to collect him," Mom suggests. "It could be quite cute, having a coffee date with my daughter and her rugged boyfriend."

My nose scrunches as I recoil. "I don't think so."

"We could take a trip into the city," Mom says, pulling out the skirt of my dress. "I'm sure Dad would like to meet him. Does he know you plan on taking Dax as your gala date?"

My mind flashes to the moment Dad laid eyes on Dax, telling him to stay away from me. I don't want Mom to know Dad already can't stand the sight of my boyfriend.

I smooth my hands down the bodice of my dress. "Won't really be time if we want to get this fitting done today."

Mom grins at me. "That's what I thought."

I blow out a shaky breath. "Have you seen Dad yet?"

"His suite is so far away from mine. There was hardly time when he dragged himself in at some ungodly hour. I may as well still be on a video screen, waiting until midnight to connect with him."

"I wouldn't have minded missing this fitting. Then you could've met with him in the city."

"No, this fitting is a priority because there's a deadline for the gala."

"Yeah, but you're home, and Dad…"

"Would you stop fretting about your father? What's gotten into you? I thought your brother was the only one I had to worry about."

"What does that mean? What are you doing about Ash?"

Mom steps back to view me in the dress, smoothing an errant hair off her brow. "Nothing. Honestly, Vanessa, you need to stop stressing over every little detail. Mommy's here to do that for you."

She makes me try on four more dresses, only proving my point she's purposefully dragging out this experience. The dusty pink is still my favorite, but Mom can't stop raving about a similar cut in forest green.

I let her discuss the final decision with Ramona, because adding my opinion is exhausting.

Once I'm finally back in my regular clothes, Mom walks me into Fratelli's, the best Italian restaurant in town. Somehow, it slipped her mind to tell me about the reservation earlier.

"You keep working in these surprises," I murmur after we're seated.

"I told you, darling, I want to spend more mother-daughter time with you."

I lift the menu to cover my face. "Mm-hmm."

Mom orders our drinks with a server, and then clears her throat before telling me, "We're having dinner with the Prescott family this evening."

I lower my menu. "Will LJ be there?"

Mom smirks. "He's part of their family, isn't he?"

I use all my might to hide my discontent, but my mask is cracking.

"He's quite fond of you, isn't he?" Mom says, a hint of glee in her tone.

"He's practically been raised to chase me."

"And it's harder to deal with him, now you've found someone you actually want to be with?"

Unable to deny it, I nod.

Mom flexes her fingers as if ready to hatch a plan. "I could make things easier for you."

"What do you mean?"

"You've already shown no interest in dining with your family," Mom says. "I could get you out of dinner with his family."

"Why would you do that? Aren't appearances everything?"

"This is just a minor event. It won't cause a problem," she replies coyly.

"This doesn't make sense. Why would you let me spend time with Dax instead of making nice with LJ?"

"Darling." She leans in. "I care about you. I want to make things easier for you."

I swallow distastefully. This isn't my mother. My mother doesn't put my feelings first. Knots clamp and bind my back. She's not letting me off the hook. This is a new form of control, and I'm not falling for it.

I lift the menu. "No, it's fine. I want to spend time with LJ. I miss him."

Mom's arrogance shatters, shocked by my response. She composes herself quickly, but I can't help smiling, knowing I ruined her plans.

Whatever they might be.

Maybe she wants me to skip dinner so she can spin her own narrative? She could tell LJ's parents about how I'm dying for him to escort me to the gala. They'd eat it up. The Prescotts can't wait for the day their son puts a ring on my finger.

Ugh. As if.

Twenty-Three

It was the longest lunch ever. How my mother drew out the ordering process, I'll never understand. She gabbed endlessly with maître d' and sous-chef about everything and nothing. Thank goodness the sommelier was hosting a function, and the head chef was out for the day, or we never would've gotten out of there.

After a tiresome traipse through the flower market and scrutinizing too many bouquets, she finally allowed Roger to take us home. The drive was bittersweet, knowing she'll pull me away tomorrow to go over the dreaded seating chart with Mrs. Fisher.

"Hi," I call out, entering the pool house. "I can't stay long."

Dax walks out from the kitchen with a glass of water. He sets it down, looking at me curiously. "What's happening? How was today?"

"Tortuous." I move into his arms, flopping my head on his chest. "I have to go inside for dinner. It's with LJ and his family."

Dax's body constricts. "LJ?"

I pull out of the hug and meet his eyes. "I don't want to go, but my mother's up to something."

"What do you mean?"

"Well, she said I could get out of it, and it was so unlike her it made me suspicious."

Dax smirks. "She said you didn't have to go? Why didn't you call her bluff and then we could be together?"

"It'll only be an hour, two at the very max." I swing his hand, smiling. "Then it'll just be you and me."

"Well, if your family will be there I guess LJ can't be a total creep."

"I'm just there to make sure my mother doesn't lead him on. I want to make it clear LJ and I are not going to the gala together."

Dax squeezes my hand and pecks my cheek. "Okay. You do what you've got to do."

Leaving him again is like wading through quick-sand. When I freshen up for dinner, I can't help yawning through the entire process. My mother's yammering makes me sleepy during the day, and too stressed to sleep at night.

Am I the luckiest daughter in the world, or what?

Forcing myself awake, I make it downstairs for dinner.

Before I get to the dining room, Ash pulls me aside. "What's Mom playing at?"

My gut squirms. "What?"

He lowers his voice. "It's like she's trying to win me over. Or, it's an alien in her skin."

"Agreed. She said something at lunch that didn't sound like herself."

"She told me she'd get me out of business meetings with Dad," he whispers, throwing his hands up in disbelief. "Since when am I allowed to miss that stuff? She always pushed me into it because it benefited the family."

"Dad wouldn't go for that."

"That's what I said. She said she'd take care of it."

I fold my arms, watching everyone move about the dining room. "She told me I could get out of dinner tonight because she knows I don't want to be with LJ."

Ash's brow furrows. "No way. *She* wants you to be with LJ."

I jab a thumb toward the hallway. "Is it because Dad will be here? Is she trying to upset him by letting me miss an occasion with Prince LJ?"

Ash twists his lips in concentration. "Maybe? But I don't buy it. Our parents are usually a united front when it comes to advancing the family's interests. Even when Mom was away."

I press a hand into my churning stomach. "I know. I usually know our mother's angles, but this one has me stumped."

Ash puts a hand on my upper arm. "You look wrecked. You could just take the out and leave."

I shake my head. "No way. I'm not letting her win."

"It's never one battle with her. You know that."

"It's easy for you to say. You're the golden child."

Ash lets out a loud laugh, grabbing the attention of everyone around the table. He waves at them with a goofy smile. "Sorry."

Christie looks back at him, adoringly.

"I'm expected to be Dad and Grandpa's clone," Ash says harshly. "Don't tell me I have it easy."

"Well I have to agree with everything just to be included at the table. You get told everything because you're male."

Ash groans, rolling his eyes. "Whatever. I can't talk to you when you're like this. Besides, Mom and Dad will be at the same table for the first time in months. Can we just be happy for two seconds?"

"You think this will be a happy occasion?"

Ash shrugs, moving away. "It's what I've been waiting for."

I tug on my bracelet and force myself into the dining room. My brother moves to the opposite side, sitting by his girlfriend and her family. My faux smile glides into place as LJ stands by my seat, holding it out for me. His parents zealously grin at me.

I nod at LJ and thank him as I sit down.

My mother raises her wine glass. "It feels so good to have you all here."

Mrs. Prescott squeezes her husband's shoulder. "I can't believe this one pried himself away from the office in time to escort us here."

Mr. Klein chuckles. "We knew we needed to be home in time."

"I see Tom is still fashionably late," Mr. Prescott says, referring to my dad.

Mom smirks. "It's his trademark."

As if on cue, my father strides into the dining room.

"Hilda." Dad's tone sounds like he's meeting an executive he's about to fire. "So nice of you to have invited company for our reunion."

Mrs. Prescott chokes on a sip of sparkling water. She sets the glass down and dabs her chin with a linen napkin. "You two haven't seen each other yet?"

"You know my husband," Mom says, rising from her seat. "As we were just discussing, he never can break himself away from the office."

Dad pulls out Mom's chair and the two embrace with a kiss on the cheek.

From across the table, Ash watches the two and a vein pops in his neck. I don't know why he expects something more endearing to happen between our parents.

Dad pushes Mom's chair in and moves to his own seat. "I trust you had a good flight. You appear well rested."

Ash sinks in his seat. Whenever Dad speaks to Mom like she's a prospective new client, we know hostility isn't far behind.

"It's always wonderful to be home. Plus, I've had the most wonderful time catching up with Mary." Mom gestures at Christie's mom. "It feels like I've known you for so long, but can't believe this is the first time we've spoken face to face."

Mrs. Klein nods eagerly. "It's been an absolute pleasure."

Dad flicks his linen napkin like he's ready for a charging bull, and drops it to his lap. "I'm so glad you've taken the opportunity to spend time with your new friend."

"And the children, of course," Mom boasts. "I can't believe I've lost so much time with my babies. Vanessa and I caught up for lost time today. Didn't we, darling?"

"Mm-hmm."

"And, of course, I need more time with Ash," Mom continues. She reaches across, placing her hand on Dad's wrist. "You've taken up enough of his time. I think you should pull back from involving him in the company."

Dad's expression twists with perplexity. "What do you mean? He's the heir."

"He's a high schooler."

"Since when don't you agree he should be shadowing me?"

Mom's hand retreats. "I'm just saying there needs to be balance."

When dinner is served, steam billows from my brother's nostrils. Every time our parents use him as a reason to argue, it tears him up inside.

Seeing him hurt and disappointed crushes my heart. But I did warn him this would happen.

As everyone settles into eating, Mr. Prescott takes it upon himself to resume the conversation.

"You know, LJ could spend more time at the company," he says over his wine glass. "He'll be graduating soon, and if Ash doesn't have any interest."

Dad sighs. "Ash has plenty of interest."

My brother flops back in his chair, his eyes rolling. Christie places a hand on his arm, and his body reflexes ten percent.

"All we discuss is work, work, work," Mrs. Prescott cuts in. "I've been hearing such wonderful things about the gala. We trust our table will be in a prime location?"

Mom grins. "Of course, Jane. Since when are the Prescotts not on the VIP list?"

Mrs. Prescott chuckles, and moves her gaze toward me and LJ. "And are you two coordinating outfits?"

I choke. "Oh… Umm…"

"I'm having a killer tux made," LJ boasts. "But if Ness wants me to change it, I will. Anything for her."

"Oh, no… Umm, I…" Somehow I'm tongue-tied under everyone's expectations.

Mom sets her wine glass down and hums a mocking laugh. "I think Vanessa has other plans."

Mr. Prescott snorts, shaking his head. "Nonsense. These two are cute as a button together."

LJ sighs, slinging an arm over the back of my chair. "It's true. Vanessa hasn't said yes to going to the gala with me."

"Yet," Mrs. Prescott adds with urgency.

Condescension curls Mom's lips. "Are you a betting woman, Jane?"

Dad glares at Mom. "Hilda, what are you getting at?"

"I share a special bond with my daughter," Mom says, fixing the diamond-encrusted rings on her bony fingers. "Let's just say, I know what she's thinking."

With every line creasing my forehead, the ache in my head expands. Why is she doing this? It's like she's a sentence away from exposing Dax in the pool house. I thought it was in her best interest to keep my secret so I didn't blab hers.

Or…

Does she think I won't reveal what I know? It has been months, and I haven't said anything. But that was because I didn't want to hurt Dad with the news. It should come from her.

But does she really want to lord control over me by broadcasting my relationship—not only in front of our family—but the Kleins and Prescotts too?

Dad straightens in his chair, tilting his head in my direction. "Vanessa, are you planning on taking a date to the gala?"

"Oh, I should mention," LJ says, slipping his arm off my chair. "I told your father about that person I met at the tailor's. I just couldn't live with myself if I didn't warn him."

"Oh, I'm aware of what you did," I say, clutching my water glass for a much-needed sip.

"That boy is in the past now," my father interjects. "Right?"

I set the glass down and keep my eyes fixed to the stem. If I tell the truth, my dad will blow his top. If I lie, LJ's arm will be around me instead of the chair.

I steal a look at my mother. She expects me to lie, but will she call me out on it? She's practically salivating to reveal all she knows.

Maybe I should've rented a hotel room for Dax and then she wouldn't be able to keep walking in on us. The more she sees us together, the more dirt she claims to have.

With barely a thought, I place my hand on LJ's arm. "Do you want to get out of here?"

His eyes light up and his tongue may as well be hanging out of his mouth. "Now?"

I look across the table at Ash and Christie. "Do you want to go somewhere with us?"

Ash's eyebrow raises. "Us?"

I motion at LJ. "The four of us." I glance at my mother to ensure she's listening. "You know, like a double date."

Christie beams with excitement. "A double date? Aww, that'd be so cute."

I smile. "So, we're on?"

LJ straightens his tie, turning toward my father. "Only if there isn't anything important we need to discuss."

When Dad looks over at us, I make sure to cuddle closer to LJ.

Dad's eyes soften and he smiles at me warmly. "No, you kids have fun. We'd only be sitting back with a brandy, anyhow."

I place a hand on LJ's wrist. "Shall we go then?"

Mom sits tall, pivoting between me and my father. "I don't think this is such a good idea. I'm loving this time with all our families joined together."

Mrs. Klein grasps Christie's shoulder. "And it is a school night. Honey, you don't get enough sleep as it is."

Christie blushes, looking down at her lap.

"We won't stay out long," I insist, giving my father puppy eyes.

He melts, obviously grateful I won't be meeting up with the boy on the motorcycle if I have LJ on my arm.

"LJ will keep the girls safe," Mr. Prescott says. "Won't you, son?"

"Of course," LJ replies, placing a hand on the space over his heart. "Like my life depended on it."

I steady my eyes, begging them not to roll, and catch Ash staring at me.

He's not amused.

I give him a weak smile. "Coming, bro?"

Ash curls an arm around Christie's shoulders. "If you're serious about leaving the estate, then yes, I'm coming with."

I scoot my chair back. "Then let's go."

LJ chuckles, following my lead. "It's good to see you more bubbly. Where do you want to go, sweetheart?"

The pet name hits my gag reflex, but I hold steady. Ash and Christie move from the other side of the dining table, and I suggest the ice-creamery.

Christie stops by her parents, waiting for their seal of approval. They smile at her with whole-hearted trust and tell her to have a good time. They also show the same love to my brother. It must be nice to date someone who's parents aren't a complete trainwreck.

LJ puts his hand on the small of my back, leading me out of the dining room. I glance at my mother, sensing the whir of calculations spinning behind her eyes. I don't flinch from LJ's touch, instead indulging it under my mother's scrutiny.

Now, if my mother says anything about Dax, none of the parents will buy it. Why would Vanessa Ashworth choose to leave the estate with LJ Prescott if she had another boy staying in the pool house? It'd be laughed off as lunacy, and Dad would have Murphy bring Mom a double brandy.

Ash calls for his driver, obviously wanting some control over the situation. I tell LJ I want to freshen my makeup before we leave, and he moves onto the foyer without me.

Ash sidles up to me and whispers, "What happened to your boyfriend?"

I swallow hard. "Nothing."

"Then what are we doing? Since when do you want extended time with LJ?"

"Ugh. I just needed to get out of there. Did you not feel the toxicity in that room?"

Ash grunts. "I wanted to conk Mom and Dad's heads together. How hard would it've been for them to be civil? I never expected tonight to be worse than those video chat dinners we used to have."

"I just hated everyone staring at me, waiting for me to say yes to LJ, or admit who I really want to be with. I can't risk Dad finding out I'm still seeing Dax. He's just getting better, and I don't want any setbacks."

Worry softens Ash's expression. "What's wrong with him?"

"I don't really know. The doctor wanted to do further tests. But he's had such a turn around, and I won't let anything ruin it. If a silly ice-cream date with LJ gets everyone off my back, I'm happy to do it."

"Well you certainly took everyone off guard," Ash replies. "Especially LJ."

"Once we're off the estate, I'll push more distance between us. I just had to sell it back there."

Twenty-Four

Thankfully, on the journey into town, I manage to keep space between LJ and me. I could've done without seeing my brother and his girlfriend cuddled up together, but I'll take what I can get.

Christie is giddy when we enter the ice-creamery. The idea of a double date blurring how obvious it should be that LJ and I aren't a real couple.

We move along the display and LJ stands too close for comfort. "Do you know what you'll choose, sweetheart?"

My jaw tenses. "Can you lay off using that nickname?"

LJ sniggers and brushes the hair off my shoulder. "I could try, but it rolls off the tongue when I see you."

Despite the fact Dax told him I hate hearing the nickname, it's like talking to a brick wall. When the server approaches, I quickly ask for a scoop of butterscotch cream with a scoop of toffee chocolate swirl, and move to a nearby table as the other three order.

I plonk down on a chair and let my head fall into my hands. *I'm such an idiot. Being here doesn't feel worth it.*

LJ pulls out the adjacent chair. "What's wrong, sweetheart?"

Again with the nickname?

Ugh!

I lift my head and straighten up. "Nothing, I'm fine."

Ash pulls out a chair for Christie and smirks at me. "You're not bailing already, are you? You're the reason we're all here."

"I'm not bailing," I reply as he sits opposite me. "I just had a sudden headache, that's all. But it's gone now."

His smug smile doesn't budge. "Good, because I'd hate for you to fail your epic plan."

"Ice-cream is delicious," Christie says, "but I'd hardly call this epic."

I smile at her ignorance of the real plan.

"I bet it's all that talk about the gala." LJ squeezes my shoulder. "It can't be easy organizing society events when differing opinions come at you."

"It definitely isn't," Christie replies for me. "That's why Mom and I sat out this round."

"One of the smartest things you could do," I reply.

Ash's chest rises as he gives me an unimpressed look.

"What?" I blurt. "I'm being serious. If I could get away from all those women, I'd take the out too."

Christie places a hand on Ash's arm. "It's okay," she murmurs. "She wasn't being mean."

Ash's gruff temperament softens from the positive effect of Christie's touch.

A server brings over our orders and they're an array of colorful creamy goodness. LJ drives the conversation forward, no matter if anyone wants to hear or not. I slide my spoon in and around the ice-cream I don't particularly want. I've come here so often after dinner with the girls. The conversations always circle around gossip: who's dating who, and who committed a social faux-pas and needed to be taught a lesson.

If I were a cynical person, I'd say my influence is the only thing my friends think I'm good for. If someone has a grudge or a crush, I can manipulate things at school to their advantage. It doesn't matter if it is positive or negative. I do it for them.

Hence my search for karma. I'm giving over my time at St. Mark's to counteract my social crimes. The universe rewarded me by bringing Dax into my life. And what do I do? Leave him in the pool house and spend my time with LJ.

Seriously, what's wrong with me?

As LJ drones on about my father's business like he has any impact on it, Ash's eyes glaze over. No wonder Mom bargained with him about getting out of business engagements. It's obvious how much Ash doesn't want to be involved.

Everything about this night is predictable. We could've just stayed home and said all of this happened.

I side-eye LJ.

Is this a good time for him? Is he really satisfied with every aspect of his life playing out beat by beat with no surprises?

And here I am, playing into it. I sit here, letting him touch me and call me sweetheart. Why am I allowing him to think he has a shot? All because my mother said she'd help me avoid him. I'm so paranoid about what my mother has up her sleeve, I'm letting LJ believe he has the greenlight.

A throaty laugh hums out of LJ and he snakes his hand around my lower back. "I'm not boring you, am I?"

His hand anchors on my hip, making me shudder.

"No, I'm used to tuning out work talk," I reply, keeping my hands in my lap.

LJ nestles his face by mine. "Good, because this will be the rest of our lives."

Christie giggles, leaning her head on Ash's shoulder. "Aww, you two are so stinkin' cute together."

Is she really buying this?

LJ's hand plays in my hair. His face gets so close, and his breath tickles my ear. "What can I say? I just can't get enough of her."

Okay, I need the abort button.

LJ turns my face toward him, and his eyelids grow heavy. His lips pucker and edge closer to mine.

Oh my gosh! No! Someone help!

"Oh my gosh, look who's out on a date," Hope's voice booms.

LJ backs off and I snap my neck to the left, seeing Hope and her boyfriend Luke walking our way.

"Oh, hi Hope," I say, waving.

I've never seen Hope more delighted, waving to us with her phone in her hand.

"Where was our invite? This is so cute, a little double date."

Ash looks at Christie and then back at Hope. "You two can take our places."

My heart leaps into my throat. I'll drown with Hope and Luke. Ash is my life raft when I'm stuck with LJ.

Ash catches the desperation in my eyes, and sits back down. He takes Christie's hand and says, "Although, maybe you want another scoop?"

Christie shakes her head. "Ah, nope. Brain-freeze."

Ash laughs. "It won't stop you looking for a midnight snack tonight."

She blushes, smiling at him. "You know me too well."

"If you two need to get back home," I interrupt, leaning forward, "I'm happy to go back with you."

"We won't ruin your night," Christie replies.

Ash grins at me. "Yeah. Stay out with LJ as long as you want."

I give him a look that screams for an escape.

Hope nudges her boyfriend. "Get us some chairs so we can join their table."

I quickly stand before Luke takes a step. "No, really, we should be getting back."

"Oh, come on," Hope says. "Your mother can't have you on such a tight leash. Shouldn't your parents be loaded with cocktails by now?"

LJ latches onto my hand, interlacing our fingers. "Sit back down, sweetheart. Your parents know you're with me. They won't care what time I get home because they trust me."

My skin crawls. I recall staying out all night under the stars with Dax. It was so magical. Right now I feel slimy and cheap.

I rub my thumb on the heel of LJ's palm to placate him. His grip loosens and I take the opportunity to free my hand. His face drops with surprise, and I back away from the table.

"*Ash*," my voice squeaks. "I really have to get home."

Christie stands as fast as Ash. She watches me with concern, not understanding my sudden mood change.

Ash steps around the table, beckoning me over. "Bye, Hope and Luke," he says with a wave. "You guys can give LJ a ride home?"

Luke nods. "Yeah, man."

LJ's face contorts with confusion. "Okay, goodbye, I guess."

I move away without giving anyone a chance to reel me back in. The three of us make it to the sidewalk, and our black limousine awaits.

"Christie, will you give us a minute?" Ash asks.

She nods and leaves for the limousine.

With his girlfriend out of sight, Ash shoves me away. "Don't use me like that again."

I struggle to find my footing, shocked by his aggressive outburst.

"It's bad enough I'm ping-ponging between our parents," he snaps. "I don't need your games either."

I clasp my hands over my chest. "I wasn't using you."

Ash lifts a hand, turning away from me. "Save it."

I stamp my foot. "*Ash.*"

He doesn't look back and disappears into the limousine.

My stomach twists in on itself. This will be a fun ride back to Ashworth Estate.

Completely fried after a series of heinous events, I wander into the pool house, ready to crash. Dax reclines on the couch with my laptop propped against his thighs.

"Oh, hey," he says, sliding the laptop beside him. "I was just passing some time. Hope that's okay."

"Oh, yeah, it's fine," I say, plonking down.

"You seem down," he says, scooting across to me. "Were your family members being too hard to deal with?"

I hunch over, rubbing my temples.

"You're later than you said you'd be."

"We went into town."

"What? Why?"

"I didn't know what my mother was up to." My voice is jittery. "I swear she was on the cusp of telling everyone you were out here."

"Are you serious?"

"But it didn't make any sense for her to blow that. I mean, I'm keeping her secret too."

"So, what happened?"

"She kept hinting to LJ's parents that I didn't want to go to the gala with him."

"And, you don't, right?"

I pause, staring at him.

His stare is pointed. "Vanessa?"

"Of course not." I sigh. "But they wanted to know who I was going with, and I couldn't work out my mother's angle."

Dax sits back. "But if I'm going with you, does it matter if they know?"

"It didn't before my mother came back."

"Okay…" he draws out the word. "Why did you leave the manor?"

"I needed to spend time with LJ to show my mother she didn't have a hold over me."

"You're not making any sense."

I sigh, avoiding his eyes. "I had to go on a date with LJ to stop whatever my mother had planned."

His jaw drops. "You did what?"

"I had to. I couldn't risk you being kicked out."

"So you thought going on a date with LJ would solve that?"

"It wasn't a real date. I was just taking control away from my mother."

"Am I supposed to be cool with this? I thought you couldn't stand the guy."

"I can't. Can you really not see why I did this?"

"I thought you were inside, having dinner with your family. You never gave me a heads up you were leaving with him."

"I wasn't just with him, I was with my brother and his…"

"Are you trying to justify this?"

"It's not like I enjoyed any part of it."

"Man, I'm such a chump. I don't expect to spend every minute with you, but I also don't expect you to go out with another guy."

"It was fake. Okay, LJ didn't know that, but my brother did."

Dax groans. "You Ashworths and your games."

My eyes water and I blink it away. "Look, my brother already told me off, so I get it. I'm an idiot."

Dax sighs, sliding closer again. "I never said that. I just don't understand what was going through your head."

I bite the inside of my cheek. "My mother riled me up. It was an impulse reaction."

There's hesitancy as he asks, "So, where did you go?"

"To get ice-cream."

He smirks. "How quaint."

I nudge him. "It's no smoothie bar."

My purse sits beside me and vibrates against my hip. I want to ignore it, but the buzzing continues on a loop.

"What the heck?" I dig my phone out of my purse. "Why am I getting so many notifications?"

My screen is a mess with mentions, comments, and reposts. I click into the app and am taken to Hope's page. There's a photo of me and LJ at the ice-creamery. This is the moment before Hope and her boyfriend joined our table. My tongue clicks as I remember her walking over to us with her phone in her hand.

The photo is pasted beside an image of Dax and me outside the country club. Hope must've taken it when approaching us before the Saturday evening meeting.

Dax's jaw rocks and his face reddens. "Why does he look like he's about to kiss you?"

In the picture, LJ leans over me with his eyes closing and lips parting.

My grip on the phone intensifies. On top of the side-by-side images, a crude poll asks, *"Who dated her best?"* with two options: *"Prince LJ"* or *"Biker Boy."*

I grind my teeth together. She's having people vote on who I should date?

"Who does she think she is!" I shriek and reach for my laptop. "That's it!"

"What are you doing?"

My fingers furiously tap at the keys. I open up the student portal and log-on to Hope's dashboard. "Hope's about to get real honest with Mr. Riley about her crush on him."

Dax leans forward, snatching the laptop from my grip. "Sass, stop."

"Give it back," I snap.

Dax shuts the laptop and tucks it under his arm. "What will it solve?"

"Just let me do it."

He places the laptop on the armrest and grabs my shoulders. "Hope's not the one you need to focus on."

I point at my phone. "Did you not see what she did?"

"Yeah, but remember the reason you were there? You were getting back at your mother. She's the one you need to have it out with."

"Hope can't get away with this."

"Just let it go," Dax says calmly. "What does it matter what random people on the internet think? We're together, aren't we?"

I swallow roughly. "Yes."

"And your mother knows. Why don't you talk to her about staying out of your love life? Then you won't have to play these games."

"You think I'm being stupid?"

He tucks a piece of hair behind my ear. "I would never call you stupid."

I smirk. "I'll take that as a yes."

He kisses my forehead. "Just take a breath. Redirect your anger where it belongs."

I huff. "Would you talk it out with your dad?"

"I don't have to. He's already out of the picture."

"Doesn't he tell Boscoe and McCoy how to act from jail?"

"If he does, they don't act on it. Lance runs the show, and there's no talking to Lance."

I shudder at the thought. "Okay, I won't retaliate against Hope. You're right. Her posting the photo happened because I wanted to one-up my mother. I guess I need to handle this stuff differently."

He brushes my cheek. "Remember, you got me to lean on."

I smile, falling into his stormy eyes. "I am stupid. I gave up an evening with you and spent it with LJ. I need to be committed."

Dax laughs, hugging an arm around me. "That's a bit extreme. How about you don't see him again?"

"Is that an order?"

He shrugs. "It's a suggestion."

Twenty-Five

Dax must still be mad about me spending time with LJ. It's the only logical reason why I woke up in bed alone. He didn't even leave a note or text.

I thought he understood why I wanted to beat my mother's mind games. I know he doesn't like the games, but it's how things work in my family.

There's a sinking feeling in my gut.

Ash said I was playing games too.

I flick my bracelet around my wrist so hard it whips at my skin.

"Ouch."

I wrap my hand around the inflamed area and grit my teeth. Perhaps I need to give up this habit. It's starting to get painful.

Inside the manor, I head to the parlor to gaze at the view. I'm stymied by my mother, who clip-clops down the hallway. "How was your evening with LJ?"

"It was fine."

A smile cracks her pompous expression. "Had fun, did you?"

"Of course. I wouldn't have suggested it otherwise."

At that, my mother laughs. "Oh, please. Most of your days are spent doing things you don't want to do. Now, just be honest. What was that stunt about? I've seen you with the other boy. You can't tell me you wanted to be with LJ."

I twist my hands into fist, pointing my knuckles to the floor. "No. What I want is to be nothing like you."

Mom's chin drops. She utters syllables, which come out faint and unintelligible.

"I'm done being your puppet," I blurt before I lose my nerve. "I knew if I gave in, take your permission to skip out on LJ, I'd pay for it later."

Mom huffs loudly, getting her voice back. "Can't a mother do something nice for her daughter?"

"Not when she's my mother."

"Regardless, I need you by my side today."

"What for?"

"I'm meeting with Naomi Fisher to fix the seating chart."

"It doesn't need fixing. It's fine."

"And since when has fine been good enough?"

I place my hand on my chest. "Why do you need me there? It was hard enough getting between you two when you weren't here."

"We need to present a stronger united front than when I was away."

"I'm not in the mood."

"Since when is that an excuse?"

I groan. "Just go without me."

"Not an option, daughter. Now, get ready."

My mind fills with expletives. I want to scream at her. Not to mention, I can't stop thinking about where Dax has disappeared.

With the war of clashing thoughts in my head, my mother takes my stunned silence as submission. She leads me to my bedroom and forces me into her approved outfit.

So much for sticking up for myself. A headache has burrowed deep into my skull, and I find myself sitting in the country club dining room. Never has it felt harder to feign interest with Mrs. Fisher. At least her youngest daughter, Meghan, has tagged along. Not that we're given time to speak, but at least I'm not the only one rotting in boredom.

I check my phone. Still no text from Dax.

I messaged twice this morning, asking where he went. Then I sent a message, letting him know I'd left the manor and wanted to meet up with him.

Ugh. Why isn't he replying? I thought everything was resolved last night.

Did he get a call from his brother? Was he lured back to the clubhouse?

I suck in a ragged breath as my stomach turns inside out.

"What do you think, Vanessa?" my mother asks. Her tone suggests she knows I wasn't listening.

"About the Waterhouse and Hutchinson families being on the same table?" I ask, presuming we're still on the same topic as when I tuned out.

My mother beams. "Yes, darling. Thoughts?"

"They deserve to be on the same table," I say bluntly. "When they can't be bothered to buy a whole table, there are consequences."

My mother purrs with a throaty laugh. "Oh, she's a little mini-me, isn't she?"

"Yes," Mrs. Fisher mutters. "It hardly felt like you were gone at all, Hilda."

I slouch in my chair. The words flowed so effortlessly off my tongue, because they were programmed in. I know everything about the families in our circle. I know who does and does not get along, and how to leverage the information. Like a robot, I spat out exactly what my mother wanted.

I fix my posture before my mother snaps. She and Mrs. Fisher resume talking over the top of each other. My hand brushes over the outline of my phone.

I need to be better than this.

I need to get back to Dax.

"Umm, Ness," Meghan pipes up as our mother's fight over the last seats at table eight.

Desperation dominates my body as we meet eyes.

Meghan nods, knowingly. "Wanna take a walk on the grounds?"

Mrs. Fisher taps a hand over Meghan's wrist. "You don't want to strain yourself."

Meghan clicks her tongue. "I can walk, Mom."

My mother frowns. "We're not done here."

I scoot my chair back and gesture at the board. "You've taken care of the VIPs. The rest is nit-picking."

"That's true," my mother agrees.

"No, it's not," Mrs. Fisher argues. "I'm not happy with the placement of the Walters and McIntosh families."

As they go at it again, I'm quick to beckon Meghan to follow. We dash out of the dining room, making it outside toward the tennis courts.

The fresh air is heavenly. "Thanks so much for getting me out of there."

"I could see something was nagging at you. What's up?"

As we take the winding path toward the golf course, relief washes over me. I got a text from Dax.

"I just needed to go for a ride and clear my head."

I sink into my frown, lowering my phone to my side.

"Oh my gosh, Ness. What's happened?"

I throw my hair off my shoulders and fan my face. "You don't want to hear about it."

Meghan links arms with me. "Sure I do."

Miserably, I lift the phone. "I've messed things up with the guy I'm seeing."

"Oh no. Last time we talked you seemed so smitten."

"I did something really stupid last night, and it upset him. I thought he'd forgiven me, but now he wants space."

Meghan subtly peers at the phone. "What exactly did he say?"

"He needed to clear his head."

"Okay, that's not exactly a bad thing."

"But he could've talked to me about this."

"Maybe he didn't want to say anything he'd regret."

Her words give me pause. "Since when did you become a relationship expert?"

She laughs. "Since I was forced into home-school and became a rom-com addict."

I smile. "So, you've seen this situation in movies?"

"I just wouldn't call it dire."

"He thinks I play into my mother's games too much. Plus, I'm too pushy and controlling."

"You're just passionate."

A hearty laugh pours out of me. "Well, that's diplomatic. I'd hardly describe the way I act as passionate. I can be petty and impulsive when it comes to my image." I suck in a breath. "You know better than anyone. I was horrible to you in high school, and somehow, you forgave me."

"Because you're my friend and your mother turned you into a psycho."

I grin. "Thanks for dropping the diplomacy."

"Being out of the high school drama has made me more honest." She sighs. "It also gives me almost zero options of ever getting a boyfriend again."

I clasp her hands. "You deserve love. I swear, if I ever meet a real-deal prince, I'll be setting you up."

Meghan giggles, highlighting her freckles. "That would certainly clear the sins of the past."

Meghan and I dawdle around the country club grounds, only returning inside when the dining room has officially closed. Without any more excuses, Mom relents and allows Roger to take us home.

I debate going inside the manor and taking a long soak in the tub, but I don't want to risk missing Dax. Inside the pool house, I pace the plush rug, torturously waiting for his return.

I've texted him three more times. I know I shouldn't be that girl, but I hate not having contact with him. Plus, if he's anywhere near his brother, he could be in danger.

I sweep my hands under my hair and rub them against the back of my clammy neck.

I can't stand around here waiting. What if he's unconscious somewhere? What if he's come off his motorcycle and his phone is completely shattered?

I turn toward the front glass door just as I hear it slide open.

My chest lifts and my shoulders relax at the sight of Dax entering the pool house.

"Oh my gosh, Dax." I gasp, clasping the sides of my face. "Thank goodness you're back."

He slides the door behind him and walks toward me.

"I was about to get a car and search for you," I say, throwing my arms around him. "I was worried you weren't coming back."

He doesn't embrace me as intensely as I do him. One of his hands presses on the middle of my back and his other arm flops by his side.

I lift on my toes, meeting his eyes. "Dax?"

As I lean into him, a whiff of something smoky hits my nostrils. I lower onto my heels, running my hands down his leather jacket as the remnants of recently smoked cigarettes assault my senses.

I frown as my eyes prickle with building tears. "You smoked?"

His stare hardens, emphasizing every bloodshot streak. "I can't break an eight year habit overnight."

There's a lump in my throat. "But you had started wearing the patches."

"It was hard enough making up my mind to leave this morning. I hardly had space in my brain to remember the patches."

I run a hand up his arm. "If you were too anxious, you should've stayed with me."

He flinches, bumping my hand off him. "I don't need the guilt trip."

I slide my hand over my bracelet, feeling every link in the slim chain. "That's not what I was doing."

He rubs a hand over his face and huffs. "Can I just lie down?"

I step out of his way, clearing a path to the hallway. "Yeah, sure."

His pace to the bedroom is lethargic. He sits on the edge of the bed with no effort to take off his jacket or slip off his boots.

Cautiously, I sit next to him. He pulls out his phone and gets lost reading the screen. It's the first time I've ever felt invisible to him.

"Do you want to talk about what happened today?"

His eyebrows lift as he exhales hard. "Definitely not."

"Well, I had to spend all day with my mother," I reply, trying to jumpstart a conversation. "I was bored out of my mind. So I'm more than happy to talk about your stuff."

"Still planning this gala?" he murmurs, totally disinterested.

"Yeah. Mom wants to finalize everything in the next few days."

He taps hard on his phone, trying to get the cracked screen to react. "What have you got planned for tomorrow?"

"My mother wants my help, walking the decorators around the event space. But I can bail."

He pockets his phone and shrugs. "No, you should go. I have to go for a ride with Boscoe tomorrow, anyway."

I jerk back with surprise. "You do?"

"So, is the meeting with your Mom all you have planned

tomorrow?"

"Uh, no. I need to go back to St. Mark's. It's been a few days since my last shift."

"So, you've got a full day planned? You'll be away from home most of the day?"

I can't read his tone and there's something irritable about his body language. "Are you mad at me?"

His eyebrows push together. "No. Why would you say that?"

"You seem off. Like there's some kind of wall between us."

He shrugs. "I'm just tired, I guess."

"Do you want a nap? Or maybe you're dehydrated. Have you drunk any water lately?"

He clicks his tongue. "You don't need to play doctor with me."

"It was an innocent question. Are you sure I haven't done anything wrong?"

He grunts, rubbing his thumb and index finger over his temples. "No. Can you just stop?"

I move away from him. "Fine. I'll leave you alone."

He groans, dropping his hand. "That's not what I meant."

I throw my hands up with defeat. "Well there's obviously something about my presence that's annoying you."

"I'm not annoyed by you," he snaps. "I'm annoyed when I have to spend time away from you."

"Are you still mad about me leaving with LJ?"

"Ugh. No."

I pout, watching him hunch over. "Then why are you pushing me away?"

Dax stands and pushes past me. "Can't you ever let anything go?"

"*Dax.*" It puffs out of me as he paces into the bathroom, slamming the door behind him.

I jolt when the walls around me quake. I place my hands on my chest, and my nervous heart pulsates.

What should I do? Knock on the door and be yelled at? Leave the pool house and give him space? Just sit on the floor and silently wait for him to come out?

I wince from the colliding thoughts and wander into the living room. I plonk on the couch and curl my feet beside me. I cuddle a large, square pillow and rest my chin upon it.

That wasn't the attitude of someone falling in love with me. He didn't even seem to like me. I peer over at the hallway and watch the bathroom doorknob. Right now, the only conclusion I see coming, is he'll walk out of the bathroom and tell me we're through.

It's an eternity before he emerges from the bathroom. I'm rigid as he makes his way toward me.

"Can we start over?" he asks.

I look up at him, feeling helpless and small. "You yelled at me."

"I got heated. I'm sorry."

"You're mad at me for spending time with LJ?"

He looms over me with his broad frame. "No, I just have a lot going on."

"I didn't kiss him, if that's what you've been thinking."

He retches. "Ugh. Don't go there."

"Everything changed last night. Just admit you don't want to be with me anymore."

"What? Where did you get that from?"

My eyes water. "You disappeared this morning."

He sits. "I didn't want to wake you."

"Why would you leave Ashworth Estate? You're safe here."

"Yesterday, I spent all day here, waiting for you. I needed to get out."

I retch and my nostrils flare. "There it is. You are mad at me for being out all day."

He gets up and steps away. "I don't want to keep doing this."

His words cut me like a knife. On shaky legs, I stand and step toward him. "Maybe we've gone about this too fast."

His seriousness morphs into worry. "What?"

I motion between us. "This. Us. Maybe we let our feelings get too out of control."

He chews his lip, looking off to the side. "I don't feel like that."

I scrunch my fingers into my hair. "Then help me understand this. I feel like I'm going crazy."

He grabs onto my arms and yanks me close to him. I yelp when I hit his chest.

He releases one of my arms so he can hook a finger under my chin. "The only thing that's crazy is the fact I'm never letting you go."

I whimper from his pressure on my arm. "Then what's wrong?"

He releases me, and I wince and rub my arm.

"Our lives are wrong. It's wrong how being together shouldn't work." His arms fold and there's an intense flex in his jaw. "I'm doing my best, but I'm struggling to keep my brother off my back."

"I could make a call," I suggest weakly. "Maybe let the Sheriff know…"

"You need to stop trying to fix things. My life doesn't change with a bunch of words like yours does. You need to let me deal with my family on my own."

Feeling more alone in his presence than I thought possible, I hug my feeble midsection. "So, what do you want me to do? Tell me how to act so I don't upset you."

He huffs and wraps his arms around me. I keep my arms pressed against my stomach as he kisses my forehead and rests his chin atop my head.

After a long silent moment, he murmurs, "I'm not telling you how to act. You're perfect how you are. I just don't want you involved in stuff that could get you hurt."

At that, I unravel my arms and pull them around him. I lean against him, listening to the erratic thumps of his heart. I shut my eyes hard and grit my teeth. Was he pulling away from me because he's worried about his brother closing in on him?

With a voice strained with pain, he suggests, "Maybe I should go."

"No," I whisper hoarsely. "Don't leave me again."

"Until I sort things out with my brother, we'll keep arguing."

"But when will that happen?"

He pulls his arms from around me. "If I go now, it'll be soon."

I narrow my eyes, taking him in. "How can you be so sure?"

"I can give him something he wants. If I do it soon, he'll give me space."

"Wait. What will you give him?"

"I need to go. I'll explain everything when I get back."

I grab onto his hand and dig my feet into the rug. "No. Tell me what you're doing so I'll know if something goes wrong."

He leans in, pecks my lips, and whispers, "If I tell you, you won't let me go."

Fear fizzes inside me as he pulls his hand from my grip.

"Goodbye, Sassy," he says with a small smile, and disappears out the front door.

My heart swells and my eyes water from hearing that silly pet name.

And, goodbye?

For how long?

Twenty-Six

Every noise last night jolted me awake. I kept expecting to hear Dax walk into the pool house. With hope, I'd pad around the bed, desperate to feel his body lying beside me.

But he didn't come home.

Again, all my text messages went unanswered.

I have no idea if he slept at the clubhouse, his old house, or somewhere in the mountains.

Or, perhaps, he didn't sleep at all. Maybe his brother had him up all night, doing goodness knows what. Dax still hasn't told me what kind of work he does for The Scorpions. Hopefully, whatever he had to do, it's for the last time.

I clasp my hands together, and pray his plan worked.

I reach for my phone and open my ignored texts.

"Did everything go okay last night?"

I lock my phone, not expecting a reply. I saw him tapping at his phone and it barely functioned. I suppose it'll be like yesterday. He'll turn up when he's ready.

Oh my gosh, I hope he'll be in a better mood than yesterday.

That was rough.

A sudden ringing makes me almost jump out of my skin. My heartbeat slows when I realize it's the landline telephone hanging on the living room wall.

It usually doesn't ring. It's here so we can contact Murphy when we want food or drinks brought poolside. Considering Murphy knows I'm staying here, I figure he's the most likely person to call me.

I move to the phone and answer it. "Hello?"

"Oh, you are there," my mother replies.

"Hi Mom."

"Are you dressed yet? We need to head out soon."

I yawn loud enough to be heard through the receiver. "Nope. I won't be ready for ages."

"Vanessa, really?"

"Just go out without me. I'll catch up."

"I told you what time we needed to leave today. I refuse to be late."

"Then go without me."

"What about the united front we agreed on?"

"I'd hardly call my surrender an agreement."

"Look, I need to go. I've instructed Claudia on what outfit to lay out for you. I'm trusting you to get ready and be right behind me."

"Fine, whatever."

"Improve the attitude, Vanessa. I need you to be poised and charismatic today."

She hangs up on me, and it's a sweet relief. I hang up the phone and rest my back against the wall. At least I won't have to listen to her orders on the way into town.

I give it thirty minutes before venturing into the manor. I don't want Mom fussing about with Claudia and catch me before she leaves. When I make it upstairs to my wing, thankfully, it's deserted.

In my bedroom, my mother-approved outfit lays across my bed. A purse rests next to the blouse, and beneath the skirt, high heels sit on the floorboards. I dawdle over to the bed, looking over the items.

I pick up the blouse and my heart sinks. The blouse slips out of my grip and falls over my slippered feet. My eyes fall on the skirt and I grimace. I tug it off the bed, letting it fall in a clump over the shoes. I toss the bag to the floor and spring myself onto the bed. With my body sinking into the mattress, I stare up at the vaulted ceiling.

"I'm not going," I declare into the void.

My eyes close and a happy smile counteracts the dread my mother causes to my nervous system.

There's a knock at my door. "Miss Ashworth? Did you call for me?"

I sit up and smile at her. "No, I was talking to myself."

"Oh, dear." Sadness fills her eyes as she takes in the crumpled mess on the floor. "Your outfit."

"Don't worry about it," I tell her. "I'm not going out today."

"Are you sure?" she asks with concern. "Because your mother said…"

"I know what she said." I massage a hand against the base of my neck. "Can you ask Murphy to call Tonya? My body feels like a bag of knots."

Claudia smiles sweetly. "Of course, Miss Ashworth. I'll see to it now."

I thank her and she disappears into the hallway.

I flop back down on the bed and exhale calmly. Yep, a self care day is very much in order.

Tonya is a godsend. Whenever Murphy calls, her arrival is always prompt. Okay, maybe I'm her best tipping customer, but still.

Last night, Dax's health seemed to have declined. His reddened eyes, the cigarettes, and his anxiety-riddled words. And now he's with his brother.

As Tonya works her magic on my muscles, the images of Dax collapsing drift from my mind. He left to get his brother off his back. I have to trust he'll be back soon, and won't need to leave again.

"Relax," Tonya whispers.

"I'm sorry." I sigh into the headrest. "I'm just worried about someone. And there's the added headache of my mother's return."

"I'd heard she was back in town."

"She's making sure everyone in town sees her face."

"Is she running you ragged?"

"It's more like she's ruining my personal life."

"Well, I'll try my best to work out these knots and clear those negative thoughts."

I exhale hard. "Thank you. And sorry about dismissing you so early last time."

"It's no problem. I was afraid you wouldn't call me again."

"Never. I need you more than ever."

Poor Tonya. Her hands are probably cramped after working on my stress-filled back.

She's such a gem. Before she left, she lit candles in my bathroom and put new age music through the sound system. Claudia ran my bath just how I like it, and the two left me to soak, wearing a face mask.

With washed hair and a fresh face, I throw on a silk robe and toss my hair in a towel. I'll have Claudia blow-dry it later, but right now I want to crash on my bed. Even after the relaxation therapy, I'm still exhausted. I just wish all the family problems and society commitments would disappear. The only thing I want to concentrate on is my relationship with Dax. Now we feel so far apart, when all I want is to be close to him.

I turn off the music, blow out the candles, and move toward the door. When I clutch the door handle, footsteps move down the hall. The floor quakes, like heavy boots have passed by. None of the staff, my family, or Christie's family move around the manor like that.

Something deep inside sends out a warning signal.

I tie my robe tighter and pull the door open a slither. When I peek out, there isn't anyone around. I close my eyes and laugh. Claudia was probably wheeling past the laundry cart and my mind went racing. I fix the towel on my head and venture into the hallway.

I move across to my bedroom and then my breath hitches in my throat. Disappearing down the hall are two broad men with scorpions emblazoned on the back of their leather jackets. My mouth hangs open as the hallway empties again.

Did I really just see that?

Before I can blink, a hand covers my mouth and an arm pulls across my middle. My back thrusts against someone and panic courses through my body. My breathing accelerates so hard, I suck in the palm to my lips.

"You weren't supposed to be here," a voice whispers in my ear.

My heart throbs. It's Dax.

An ache burrows deep into my skull. Why is he holding me like this? When did he get here? Did he bring his crew with him?

Dax drags me backwards with his hand clasped over my mouth. As he pulls me into my bedroom, the towel falls off my head, and my damp hair cascades by my face. With the curtains drawn, the darkness is both a comfort and a threat. My heart spasms, unable to determine if I should feel relieved in Dax's arms, or terrified by this disturbing situation.

"Oh, Sassy, why are you here?" His tone is wounded as his hand slides off my mouth. "I'd never bring them here if I knew you'd be home. I thought you had plans all day."

My blood pumps so hard, I can barely keep track of what he's saying.

"You gotta hide." His whisper is raspy as he looks over his shoulder, ensuring no one is walking in on us.

"Wha… Wha… What's…"

"*Shoosh*," he hushes, panning around the room.

"Why… Why are they here?"

He turns to me, smoothing his hands down the sides of my head. "I'm so sorry." He looks to the side, targeting my antique armoire. He pushes me toward it. "In here."

He opens the door and I lean against him, losing strength in my legs as my head rushes with blood. For a moment, everything is white.

He taps my cheek. "Sass? Come on, baby, get in."

I blink my eyes open and stare at the closet-full of clothes.

"Murphy, Claudia, and the other staff are tied up downstairs," he whispers, helping me inside. "They're all okay. Just stay in here until your family comes home."

My wind whirs with thoughts, none of which help this situation make sense.

"Is there anything small in here that's worth something?" he asks.

I shake my head, not understanding. "Huh?"

He snaps his fingers, looking over his shoulder. "A piece of jewelry, or something?"

I flick my thumb against my bracelet, and a chill runs over my skin. I shudder with the realization he's asking what he can steal. With fear fracturing my reasoning, I unlatch the clasp of my bracelet.

"No," Dax whispers frantically. "Not that one. It's your favorite."

I shake my head and my whole body convulses in shivers. "Just take it."

He pushes it back. "No."

My eyes well and I hiccup a sob, dropping the bracelet in his hand.

Pain strikes his eyes, and he grunts as he pockets the bracelet.

"Okay. Just stay here," he whispers, grabbing the door. "Don't make any noise."

As the door closes, my heart pounds and I reach out to him. Dax catches my forearms and pushes them back toward me.

He shakes his head and whispers, "You're safer if I go now. I don't want anyone to see you."

With no control, I whimper. He frowns and wipes his thumb under my eye.

"I'm sorry," he whispers, closing the armoire doors.

Dax's heavy boots stomp across the hardwood, leaving my bedroom. "Cleared this wing," he calls out. "Let's move on."

Surrounded by my clothes and hugging my knees to my chest, I listen to my heavy breathing. Since Dax left, there are no other sounds in the room, but I don't budge an inch. Sickness vortexes in my stomach, my skin grows icy, and I sink further inward.

With my wet hair soaking my robe, the chattering of my teeth pulses pain throughout my jaw. I quickly lose the robe and pull on the nearest sweater and shorts. When I look down at the pink sweater with the words 'Dream Girl' in white stitching, my face crumples in tears.

It's the sweatshirt Dax made me buy at the mall.

My hand moves to tug on my bracelet, but it's not there. A sob moans out of me, and my head falls between my knees. I don't know how long I sit in this position. Time is in a vacuum until noises return to the world outside this closet.

"Vanessa!" my father's voice booms from the hallway. Urgency thunders in his footsteps as he races into my bedroom.

I squeak and fold my arms around me, remembering how it felt when The Scorpions walked past my bathroom.

"Vanessa?" Dad repeats, fear catching his voice.

I open my mouth to make my presence known, but only a whimper comes out.

It's enough. Dad nears the armoire. "Ness? Honey?"

I whimper again and Dad opens the door.

He exhales with relief. "Oh, darling, thank God." He lifts me out of the armoire and I cling to him without the energy to stand on my own.

"It's okay. You're okay," he coos, stroking my hair. "Oh, darling, you must've been so scared."

"I'm… I'm okay." My teeth chatter between the words. "They didn't hurt me."

Stress pinches his features. "They saw you?"

I quickly shake my head. "No. I saw them and hid."

Dad breathes out more relief. "Good girl. I don't know what I'd do if anything happened to you."

Dad walks me down to the first floor to join everyone else. He tells me everyone has been accounted for, even my masseuse.

I gasp. "Tonya was still here?"

Dad nods. "She was tied up with the others. An officer has driven her home."

I gag, moaning with guilt.

He hushes me, rubbing my back. "It's okay. It's not your fault."

Dad brings me into the parlor where my mother and brother stand apart. Before my brother can move, my mother rampages at me.

"Why were you still home?" my mother shouts, towering over my slouched body. "You were supposed to be on your way to meet me."

"Hilda!" Dad barks.

Mom shakes her fists. "If she had met me, she wouldn't have been here when those monsters entered our home."

Dad takes her wrist and slides an arm around Mom's back. "I know. I hate that she was here too."

Mom recoils from Dad's touch and steps closer to me. "Just explain it to me. Why were you here?"

"I… I…" My eyes dart between my parents. "I wanted some time alone."

Mom huffs, throwing her hands into the air. "And that's it? You were alone?"

Dad's tone lowers. "Why are you attacking her like she had something to do with this?"

"Because she knows I…"

"No," Mom snaps, cutting me off. "I don't know anything about this assault on our home. That's why I'm asking for answers."

"Mr. and Mrs. Ashworth," Murphy says, entering the room with Sheriff Lennon. "The sheriff would like a word."

Mom and Dad pace to meet the sheriff. I fall behind to keep within earshot. Ash moves away from the rear wall, his interest piqued.

"I wanted to let you know we've questioned the main players at The Scorpion Clubhouse," Sheriff Lennon says. "The ringleader, Lance Malone, has an alibi. He was tending bar today and submitted security footage to prove it."

"That means he sent people to work for him," Dad responds. "Wasn't that how his father operated?"

"And it took us a long time to get Vic Malone on any charges. He still hasn't seen his day in court."

Dad huffs. "So what does this mean, Sheriff?"

"We've hit a dead end."

"Dead end?" Dad's brow deeply furrows. "My staff saw their club jackets. It was them."

"Right now, we suspect it wasn't the Scorpion Motorcycle Club behind this," Sheriff Lennon explains. "We think the culprits wore knock-off jackets as a cover."

I try my best to blanken my expression. I know it was The Scorpions because Dax was with them. But I can't say anything. My heart won't let me rat out Dax.

Mom laughs nervously, a hand hovering by her mouth. "No, that can't be. It's too ludicrous."

"With all the main players accounted for, we are widening our scope," Sheriff Lennon explains.

"They can't just get away with this," Dad demands. "They must have organized someone to do the dirty work for them. Surely all those Logan's Point low-lives know each other."

"We are still investigating their network," Sheriff Lennon asserts.

"Some lower level players haven't been accounted for, but they're usually not linked to the crime aspect of the motorcycle club."

Mom scoffs. "Isn't their whole club just a front for crime?"

"I'll personally interview more persons of interest, Mrs. Ashworth," Sheriff Lennon replies. "For instance, I don't have a timeline for Lance Malone's younger brother. I've had dealings with him in the past and I believe he'll be helpful to the investigation."

"Helpful how?" Mom yelps. "By confessing?"

"I know this is distressing," the sheriff says. "We will do everything in our power to bring your family justice. In the meantime, I'll organize hourly patrols of your perimeter."

Dad holds out his hand to the sheriff. "Thank you."

When Sheriff Lennon shakes Dad's hand, Mom turns away, smirking. "Patrols will be really helpful when the damage has already been done."

Dad frowns. "Don't mind my wife, Sheriff."

Sheriff Lennon nods. "Not at all. This is quite an ordeal."

When Murphy walks the sheriff out, Dad turns to me, his eyes lingering for a beat too long.

I flinch. "What?"

"Do you know anything about this?" Dad asks quietly.

I squirm. "What do you mean?"

"I told you to stay away from that boy. You did, didn't you?"

Mom pivots around. "Are you interrogating our daughter?"

"I'm asking a simple question."

"By insinuating she had prior knowledge of this robbery?"

"No, that she had prior dealings with someone involved."

While putting an arm around me, Mom says to Dad, "Maybe it was in retaliation for you banning him from the property."

"You can't be serious, Hilda," Dad chastises. "You want to turn this around on me because our daughter was fraternizing with a Scorpion?"

"He's not like them," I insist. "He wants to get away from The

Scorpions."

Mom shushes me, rubbing my arm briskly. "It's okay, Vanessa. You don't need to defend yourself."

"How can you be so calm about this?" Dad asks Mom. "You understand what kind of havoc those thugs cause to our community. Our business."

"I'm not calm, Tom," Mom fires up. "I feel completely violated. These men came into our home and robbed us. I just don't think it's helpful to berate Vanessa about seeing a boy."

Dad's glare hardens. "You control every aspect of this girl's life. Did you put a stop to the relationship?"

Mom pushes me back, stepping in front so I'm out of Dad's view. "Vanessa doesn't have to explain anything. This has been traumatizing enough."

"Yeah, Dad," Ash says flatly, watching us from the other side of the room. "Give her a break."

Dad lifts his hands, stepping away. "I'm sorry. I'm just stressed."

Mom turns to me with a pacifying smile. "Now, just be quiet Vanessa. There's no need to get worked up."

"Worked up?" I choke. "I've barely had a chance to speak."

She brushes back my hair. "What are mother's for?"

How can she be worried about serving her own interests at a time like this? She's never fought so hard to protect me before. She could've twisted this and ridiculed me for letting Dax into my life. She could've forced me to reveal every nook of the mansion I walked him through.

She knows this robbery can be traced back to me, but she's hiding it. What good does she think will come from this?

"Sir," Murphy says, pacing into the room. "Sheriff Lennon has set a perimeter around the estate."

Dad sighs heavily. "Good, because obviously our old set up was abysmal."

Murphy hangs his head. "Agreed, sir."

"How did this happen?" Dad shouts, pounding his fist into his palm. "You're in charge of security, Murphy. Explain to me how those thugs strolled into my home."

Sorrow plagues Murphy's features. "I'm sorry, sir, I can't. They were in the building before I knew they'd entered the grounds."

Dad's nostrils flare and his neck reddens. "Unacceptable. Murphy, your time here has ended."

I gasp, wringing my hands together, my eyes darting between the two men.

Murphy nods in agreement. "I think that's for the best, sir. Over the years, I've done everything to ensure the best care for your family. Today, I failed."

Dad turns his back on Murphy, and when Murphy motions to make his exit, I react.

"Dad, no," I blurt. "You can't do this. It's not Murphy's fault."

Both men turn to me, perplexed.

"I know it's sad, Vanessa," Dad says. "I don't want to do this, but I have no choice."

"No, this is wrong," I urge. "Murphy didn't do anything wrong."

"Miss Ashworth, I appreciate this," Murphy says, "but everything that happens on this property is my responsibility."

"But it's my fault!"

With everyone's eyes boring into me, regret squirms inside me.

Dad tilts his head, scrutinizing me. "Why would you say something like that?"

Mom steps forward. "Yes, Vanessa, why would you say that?"

Sweat beads over my skin and my chest rises and falls. I pan across all their faces and glimpse my brother in the back corner. His arms are folded and his eyes are steely.

"Vanessa." There's a tremble in Dad's voice. "Explain yourself."

"She's obviously trying to save Murphy because she feels loyal to him," Mom says in an attempt to brush this off.

Dad nods at me. "Is your mother right?"

I tremble as my warring parents stare me down. One wants the truth, the other wants me to suppress it. Jitters scatter within me, contracting and expanding my stomach. My head pounds as I gag on the words I so desperately want to say.

I push myself, forcing out the words, but gag again. Attempting to take a breath, I instead hunch over, retching as my stomach gives into torture. I retch loudly, puking the contents onto the floor. It splashes on my shoes while the last of it strings out of my mouth.

My mother moans, cupping her mouth and walking away.

Dad sighs, pulling me into his arms. "Murphy, please get a washcloth?"

Murphy's already leaving in the right direction. "Right away, sir."

Dad rubs a circle on my back as I groan and wipe my mouth with my sleeve.

"Look what happens when you get worked up," Dad says softly. "I know you love Murphy. We all do. But this was a huge violation. I don't want you making yourself sick over it. You've been through enough."

I pant for breath, still hunched and doing my best not to smell the vomit on the floor.

Murphy returns with a washcloth and a housekeeper follows with a mop. Dad takes the damp cloth from Murphy, and walks me away from the mess. We sit on a bench and Dad tends to my face. The warmth of the washcloth is soothing, and my body relaxes into normal function.

I take a long breath in and out, gradually taking in the rest of the room. My mother is stretched out on an antique fainting couch, fanning her face as a housekeeper rubs her temples. My brother leaves her and moves over to me and Dad.

"Can I sit with her?" he asks Dad.

Dad smiles, standing and patting Ash's shoulder.

When Ash takes a seat, he asks if I'm okay, and I reply with a slight nod.

"What are you keeping from our parents?" Ash whispers. "Or does Mom already know?"

I swallow hard, wincing. "Please, Ash, don't push it. Did you not just see what I did all over the floor?"

"I know you wanted to spill your guts. Just with words instead."

I moan, holding my middle.

"It's your boyfriend, isn't it? The guy you didn't want me to tell Dad about. He's from that gang, just like Dad said?"

"It's not a gang," I mumble at my lap.

"But he's a bad dude?"

"No," I whisper harshly. "He's not bad."

Ash's eyebrow cocks. "He knows bad people?"

My mouth waters and the jitters spasm in my stomach again. I press my hand into my gut and moan. "*Shoosh*, Ash. I can't do this again."

Ash gets up and something scary flashes in his eyes. "I'll take that as a yes, then."

I swallow hard and force myself to stand. "Don't say anything." It comes out desperate and strained as my knees knock together. "You don't know the truth."

Ash points at me. "Then you'd better come out with it, and fast."

He turns toward the door and there's fury in his pace.

"Ash?" Dad calls. "Where are you going?"

"To check on Christie," he mutters, leaving the room.

A weak breath escapes me and I plonk back down on the bench.

"Are you okay, honey?" Dad asks.

I nod, leaning back against the wall. "Yeah." I sigh. "Just exhausted."

He smiles kindly. "Understandable. You should get some rest."

Damp with sweat, my hair sticks to the sides of my face. I swallow something disgusting stuck in my throat, and peel myself off the bench.

Twenty-Seven

Every time Claudia tried to coax me off the floor, I didn't budge. As soon as I walked into my bedroom, I pulled the throw blanket off the bed, and cocooned myself on the floor. With ugliness swarming inside, I don't deserve the comfort of a bed.

My parents sent more staff to tend to me, but when I continued in my comatose state, they eventually left me alone. All night, I shivered under the heavy blanket.

Despite being on the floorboards, I wasn't cold.

I was heartbroken.

As the morning glow mocks me with its happiness, I pick at the joints between the floorboards. My itchy eyes are half open. My chapped lips are parted, allowing my mouth to dry out further. I only stop scraping my fingernails against the floor when a twinge surges up every digit.

I twitch under the blanket, replaying the moment Dax stood over me as I hid in the closet. My stomach churns and I scrunch myself into a tighter ball.

He held his hand over my mouth.

Men from his motorcycle club walked through my home like they were invited.

And they were.

By the boy who's supposed to care about me.

Why would he bring them here? He said he was leaving to keep me safe, but he did the exact opposite. Why lie like that?

I sit up, narrowing my eyes as an idea strikes me. Was he just baiting me with adoring compliments and sweet kisses? Working me until he got a tour of the manor and found the perfect time to infiltrate?

"*Gah!*" I let it scream out of me. My fists curl so tight my manicure indents half-moon piercings into my palms. I hunch over my thighs and every muscle tenses.

I hate this.

I hate that he did this to me.

I hate that I didn't see it coming.

He was in such a bad mood the last time I saw him at the pool house. He told me he was planning on riding with Boscoe. How did I not register that meant he'd had contact with The Scorpions?

He left the pool house, saying he'd give his brother something he wanted.

My heart aches with the memory of Dax telling his brother I didn't come from a wealthy family.

How could I not piece together that I was something his brother wanted? I was the key to gaining a hefty loot.

I was used.

As I lift my head and blink the water out from my vision, my eyes mindlessly wander the floor. I glimpse the foot of the armoire and cringe. As I turn away, something catches my eye.

On second glance, a sunray beams through the window and shines against something on the floor. I get up, keeping the blanket snatched around me. I stand over the sunlit item and then lower to pick it up.

My heart fritzes when a bolt of panic and surprise hits me. Very gingerly, I hold Dax's chain with the pendant his mother gave him. As it sits in my palm, I remember the remorse stinging his eyes and his anguished apologies.

I pull the chain to my chest and gulp for air.

He didn't have a choice.

"No, it's your favorite." He was devastated when he took my bracelet.

I run my fingers over his necklace.

Did he leave this here because he felt my pain?

With my head hanging low, I clasp the chain around my neck.

The blanket cloaks around me and drags along the floor as I leave my bedroom. When I reach the first floor, staff members attempt to gain my attention, but they may as well be ghosts. I amble to the rear of the manor, and my heart draws me to the pool.

I nestle on a deck chair, gazing at the morning sun dazzling against the steady water. My heavy eyes are ready to close, but I sense I'm no longer alone.

"Christie's gone," Ash says flatly, scuffing his way to my deck chair. "Her family took her out of town and they're staying with her grandparents. Are you happy now?"

I squint at him. "You're blaming me for her leaving?"

"They left because of the robbery, caused by your boyfriend."

"That wasn't up to him. If only you'd seen his face. He was forced into it. I know it."

"You're making excuses for him?"

I clutch the fabric over my chest. "He's not a bad guy, Ash."

Ash rolls his eyes. "I'm not listening to this. And I'm not taking my eyes off you."

I scoff. "What? You're doing the whole overprotective thing with me because Christie's gone?"

"No. I'm doing it because some guy has you wrapped around his finger. His grip on you is so tight, you're still head-over-heels despite him robbing us while you were home."

"He saved me from being seen by the others."

"Ness, I don't want anything bad to happen to you. It makes me sick, you were in the manor while those guys were skulking around. Who knows what could've happened? I'll lose my mind thinking about it. I'm glad Christie's away until they lock them up." He chews his lips. "Bet you can't say the same. I know you don't like her."

"I never said I dislike her. I just never liked losing my brother."

Ash scoffs. "You left me."

"I had to leave after the mess I made." I sigh, looking away. "But I wasn't wrong about my assumptions."

"What's that supposed to mean?"

"Mom." Swallowing hurts due to the dryness of my mouth. "She had an affair. In Switzerland. She had me keep quiet about it."

Ash's mouth opens and closes, figuring out the words to respond. His thumb and index finger massage his temples as he looks down at the ground. "Why are you telling me this now?"

I shrug. "Nothing else to lose."

Ash sits beside me. "This doesn't change anything. I still don't trust your boyfriend, and I don't want you leaving the estate to meet up with him."

I gaze at the pool, frowning. "You don't have to worry. I'm getting radio silence from him."

Ash groans. "*Ness.* Are you still texting this guy? He led The Scorpions into our home."

"I know." The weight of tears builds inside me. "But he's not safe with them. I wish he was back here."

"That'll never happen. Dad will kill him."

I wipe under my eyes. "Then I'll leave with him."

Ash clicks his tongue. "And where will you go?"

"It doesn't matter if I get to be with him."

"How long have you known this guy?"

"It doesn't matter. I knew how I felt as soon as I met him."

Ash folds his arms, looking at me like I'm being ridiculous.

"And how long did it take you to tell Christie you love her?" I bite back. "You should know it doesn't matter how long you've known someone. When you know, you know."

Ash searches my eyes. "You love him?"

I rub the heel of my palm over my chest and nod. "It's love."

Ash places a hand on my back. "Do you really feel like you lost me?"

"We didn't have the same relationship when I came back. And yes, I know it's partly my fault for leaving in the first place."

"You have to know you're still a top priority in my life. I guess I didn't realize how swept up I got in Christie." A soft laugh puffs out of him. "I mean, have you met her?"

I lower my guard and mumble a laugh. "It's still so weird seeing you all loved-up. When I left, you were so adamant you'd never date."

"Like you said, 'when you know, you know.'"

"Is that your way of saying you accept my feelings for Dax?"

"Let's just say, I understand. Accepting might be a stretch."

"It wasn't his fault, Ash. His brother controls him. I've seen the abuse."

Ash's back stiffens. "You were around when they were brawling?"

"What are you not getting, Ash? It's one-sided. Dax is a victim."

Ash sighs and rubs his temples again. "I just hate that you're infatuated with a guy, who gets himself in dangerous situations."

I groan. "Why don't you just follow your girlfriend?"

"Because I'm not bailing on my family."

His words hit me in the heart.

"Dax doesn't have a family to stand by him," I whisper, holding back the urge to cry. "They're his enemy."

"Our enemy too," Ash replies, standing. "They came into our home and stole from us. That won't be forgiven."

"It wasn't Dax's choice."

Ash gives me an incredulous look. "Did he tell you that when he strolled through our hallways like he owned the place?"

"Like it even matters. We have an obscene amount of wealth. It's not like we can't replace what they took."

Ash crosses his arms. "It's not about the items. It's about the violation."

I lower my head and pick at my fingernails. "I know."

"You've been making some really dumb choices lately. I get that you don't want to be with LJ, but…"

"My feelings for Dax have nothing to do with pushing LJ away."

"You made me watch you put on a show with LJ only a few nights ago."

I push past my brother, moving toward the manor. "I can't deal with this right now."

"Where are you going?"

I keep pacing, not looking back. "To get a glass of water. Is that okay with you?"

At a furious pace, I burst into the kitchen, startling Marcella as she prepares lunch.

"Sorry," I mumble, moving to the fridge.

"Let me get that for you, miss," Marcella blurts, rushing toward a cupboard.

I pluck out a glass and pour the water. "It's fine. Just pretend I'm not here."

Marcella fidgets and stammers, with no clue how to act.

After a large chug, I gesture at her prep station. "Go back to work. I don't need you."

She slinks away. "Yes, miss."

"Miss?" Claudia enters the kitchen. "Oh, Miss Ashworth, I thought you came this way. Can I help you with anything?"

I slam the glass down on the counter. "No. I want everyone to stop trying to help me."

I pace toward the door, and Claudia moves out of the way. As I pass her, she whispers, "I saw your boyfriend."

I stop dead. "What?"

She nods. "When we were tied up."

I gasp. "Did you say anything?"

Claudia purses her lips, shaking her head.

I clasp my hands together, thankful. "Okay, but why not?"

Claudia places her hands over mine. "He wasn't like the rest of them. When they weren't looking, he told me everything would be okay. That, as long as I stayed quiet, I wouldn't get hurt."

My eyes brim with tears and I sniff hard. "He did that?"

Claudia nods. "He made sure the binds weren't too tight over my wrists. I had to tell the police I saw Scorpion jackets, like the other staff members, but it was clear he came here against his will."

I exhale my first steady breath since yesterday. "He wanted to make sure we were all okay."

Claudia smiles kindly. "He's messed up with the wrong kinds of people."

I nod. "I begged him not to go back to them."

"Maybe we should talk to the police about getting him out? We can vouch for him being a good person."

"Right now, the police think it was a copycat group. If we say anything, they'll think Dax masterminded the whole thing."

"So how do we help him?"

"If Dax's brother thinks he pulled off the robbery without any hitches, maybe Dax can break free of him."

Claudia looks around our immediate area with fretful eyes. "Do you think he'd come back here?"

An answer pops into my head and my heart pounds with hopefulness. "No, he'd hide out. And I might know where. Will you cover for me?"

Claudia gasps. "Cover for you? You shouldn't be going anywhere. Your parents want you home while the police investigate."

"I can't leave him alone. Just tell my parents I've gone to the third floor to be alone."

Claudia's eyes dart to the nearby hallway and then back to me. "But where are you really going?"

I smooth back my hair, pretending I've got it together. "I'll take a car so I can be tracked. I just need a head's start."

"No, Miss Ashworth." Her eyes water. "I don't like this. You can't go."

I lean in and kiss her cheek. "Thank you for everything you do for me. You've always made my life so easy. I know this is the hardest thing I've ever asked of you, but I need your help."

She sucks back her tears, and nods. "Okay. If you're sure."

I smile and nod. "I'm sure."

Twenty-Eight

Ash grabbed me, trying to berate sense into me, but I shoved him off. As far as he knows, I'm going to Sylvie's house. He yelled at me to stay, fearful of my lies, but I wasn't letting him slow me down.

In the garage, I snatch the Porsche 911 keys, a swipe card, and speed onto the driveway. With Murphy off the property, Claudia is tending to my parents needs and ready to be vague about my whereabouts. I just need a chance to get onto the road.

When the service gate opens, I slam my foot on the accelerator. The car whirs past a patrolling officer's car, but I hold steady behind the ultra-tinted windows. No doubt the officer will call this in to Sheriff Lennon, dismissing it as my father leaving the property.

Avoiding the main part of town, I zoom past Victoria Falls, and when I ascend Mountains Road, I breathe out with relief.

No one's tailing me.

At one of the highest points, I skid the car to a stop and race out. I run down the slope where Dax had taken me on his motorcycle. It's his favorite spot in the mountains, and if he's hiding out, he has to be here.

"Dax! Dax!"

My chest heaves and I scan every nook and cranny. The rock formation we sat on is vacant, and the majestic view is cold without him.

Unable to waste a second, I get back in the car.

Sheriff Lennon said his team hadn't spoken to Dax, meaning he wasn't at the clubhouse. Oh my gosh, I hope he got out. If he satisfied his brother with loot from my house, surely he's free to leave The Scorpions?

My heart pounds.

Maybe Lance rewarded him with being able to stay at his old house?

I step on the gas, and fly the car into Logan's Point. I don't care how much of a scene I make, revving this luxury car around the neighborhood. All I want is to see Dax.

Remembering how much Dax had to bash the front door open, I opt for the one window not boarded up. It squeaks open and I hurl myself inside.

"Dax?" I creep through the house, wary of any noises. When I get to the bedroom, and see the cabinet is still placed where I hid behind, my heart sinks.

I scrunch my eyes closed and slide down a moldy wall.

It can't be.

Is he still at the clubhouse?

With an uncontainable retch, I force myself up. On wobbly feet, I slip back through the window.

"Get out of my way!" I shout at a group, who circle the Porsche.

They jump back, and I stomp my way into the car and slam the door.

When I pull up at The Scorpions Clubhouse, a vortex of sickness thunders up from my stomach. I gulp it down, my vision blurring white.

I pull the chain out from under my sweatshirt and rub the St. Christopher pendant.

Nope. I gotta do this.

I'm not leaving him.

Tucking Dax's necklace back under my sweatshirt, and wiping my sweaty palms over my thighs, I remind myself there's a tracker in my car and law enforcement will eventually follow. My parents should be done arguing with the sheriff by now and let them get on my trail.

I walk over the chain link fence and down the cracked driveway of the clubhouse. It's eerily quiet. No raucous bar noise echo from inside. I'd swear no one was here, except there's motorcycles cluttering the garage entrance.

My heart misses a beat.

Dax's bike is here.

I swallow the bulging lump in my throat, and teeter on my toes. The bar inside is empty.

Okay, Vanessa. You've come this far.

I push on the door and it creaks open. I cringe at the noise, waiting for someone to pounce. Over my shoulder, I imagine McCoy. But thankfully, it's still only me and my nerves.

Edging my way inside, I pad across the concrete floor on tippy toes. I make my way across the bar into the rear, darkened area. Through the doorway, I pivot in indecision.

Left or right?

When I turn left, I inhale through my nose, muffling a shriek. Someone runs into me, and my heart rate accelerates, determining I'm done for.

There's a gasp, and then a female's voice. "Crap! What are you doing here?"

As the shock wears off, I double-take at Stella.

She grabs my arms and her overlined eyes widen. "Do you have a death wish?"

"I... I..." I clear my throat and strengthen my footing. "Where's Dax?"

She yanks on my arm, tugging me into a room on the right. She shuts the door behind us and glues a pointed index finger to her lips.

I look around the small space, housing a dingy twin bed and a metal chair in the corner, and gulp.

"It's Dax's room," she whispers. "We'll let him come to us."

A shiver jitters down my body. "Are you in trouble?"

"Things are manic around here," she replies. "Dax lets me hide out here whenever Hugo drags me along. But today is especially intense."

"It seemed like no one was around."

"A few are in the basement, and some are down the back. I took the opportunity to go to the bathroom while it was quiet."

I chew on my fingernail. "But Dax is here?"

Her eyes well as she nods. A sob croaks out of her, and she blurts, "I'm sorry, okay! I didn't mean for them to find out."

She latches onto me, and her urgency has my body in a chokehold.

"Wha... Wha... What are you talking about?"

"One night when Dax wasn't here, the other guys wouldn't leave me alone." Her bottom lip quivers. "I just wanted to scroll on my phone to ignore them."

My mouth stays ajar, unable to grasp what has her so upset.

"I couldn't stop staring at this post." She sniffs hard, releasing my arms. "Hugo wanted to know what had my attention. Then Lance snatched my phone."

My teeth chatter, watching the melancholy droop her face.

"It was a poll, asking who should be your boyfriend."

My heart drops to my gut, which contracts and twists. I moan, holding my stomach, sickened at the idea of Dax's brother looking at pictures of me.

"Lance said he recognized you," Stella mumbles, her eyeliner running down her cheek. "He wanted me to dish on you. I'm sorry, he scared the crap outta me."

Adrenaline races through my veins as I keep pressure on my stomach.

"Once I checked out your page and realized you were Tom Ashworth's daughter, Lance had the guys look for Dax," Stella says. "He wanted to know why he lied about you, and wanted Dax to make it up to him."

Tears fill my eyes and I trace over his pendant under my sweatshirt. "I knew he was forced into it."

Stella moans, raking her hands into her hair. "If only I'd never been on that stupid app."

I shush her. "It's okay. Don't beat yourself up."

She wipes away her tears, creating large black circles under her eyes. "Dax just looks so crushed. I hate that I did this to him."

I shudder, watching the hurt and love in her eyes. What am I supposed to say? I don't want to know if she's still hung up on him.

Instinctively, my heart leaps into my throat. Heavy boots thunder in the hallway, followed by the boisterous laughs of burly men. As I back away, three hearty knocks hammer against the closed door.

"Stella, where you at?"

Stella's chest heaves as she freezes in place. With no time to act, the handle turns and the door busts open.

My eyes lock with Lance, and a sly smile creeps across his face.

"Why, hello, Sasha." His tone is gravelly as cigarette smoke puffs out of his mouth. "Or, should I say, Vanessa?"

Behind him, McCoy and Stitch take up the rest of the hallway.

Lance takes another drag of his cigarette and then points it at Stella. "Thanks again, Stell. You keep bringing her to us."

Stella's teeth chatter as she shrinks away from him.

Lance motions to McCoy. "Get Ashworth's kid, would ya?"

I shriek, fumbling backwards onto the flimsy bed. McCoy thuds toward me, yanking me up by the arm.

Lance steps into the room, staring down Stella. "Beat it."

About to shatter into pieces, Stella scampers out of the room.

Lance nudges Stitch, ordering, "Follow her and take her to Hugo."

When Stitch leaves, Lance sets his sights on me. He grabs the front of my sweatshirt, pulling me close. The bulging veins in his neck warp the artwork inked into his skin. He takes another puff of his cigarette, and the chains around his neck jingle with his exhale.

My blood boils at the sight of his St. Christopher pendant. "Why do you wear that pendant? You hate your mother."

Lance smirks, baring his teeth. "Exactly. It's a reminder."

More footsteps pound along the hallway. My shoulders slump as Boscoe appears at the doorway, but then my emotions scatter. Dax stands alongside him.

Dax's eyes widen at the sight of me. "No!"

I whimper as Lance's hand squeezes the back of my neck.

Dax's skin is ghostly pale and dark bags hang under his eyes. There's a strain in his neck as he swallows hard, and his eyes dart between his brother's face and mine.

"Let her go," he tells Lance. There's a tremor in his stance and his shoulders droop.

Lance laughs cruelly, pulling an arm around my waist. I yelp, which delights him further.

"Don't do this," Dax pleads, gradually lifting a hand. "This wasn't part of the deal."

"Oh, I know, baby bro," Lance replies. "But I didn't grab her. She walked in on her own."

Dax's chin drops and his eyes land on me with horror.

Lance's hand slides up from my neck and into my hair. "So I guess I get my cake and eat it too."

Agony groans out of Dax as his hand snakes into his jacket and holds his side. "Just let her go."

Lance shoves me forward and I struggle to stay on my feet. For a brief moment, a swell of relief fills me as Dax steps toward me. But it's swiftly taken away when Lance snaps his fingers.

"McCoy, get some rope," Lance orders.

Boscoe drags the metal chair along the concrete floor, stopping it by me. With his meaty hand, he pushes me back into it.

McCoy approaches, licking his lips and unfurling rope around his hand. "Oh, I'll enjoy this."

Dax moves in fast. "Don't you dare touch her."

Boscoe holds out an arm, halting Dax. "Hold your roll, kid."

Uncontrollably, sobs fill my throat. I try to swallow them, but begin choking and wheezing as McCoy ties my wrists to the chair arms.

"I held back last time, McCoy," Dax threatens, nudging to pass Boscoe.

McCoy smirks. His jagged, unclipped fingernails scratch my flesh. "Malone, I treated you like the child you are. I won't be making the same mistake again."

As Boscoe keeps Dax out of the room, the other men talk over the top of each other, planning what to do with me. McCoy suggests sending a ransom video to my dad. I don't hear Lance's reply because I keep my eyes peeled over Boscoe's shoulder.

Dax isn't doing well.

His eyes glaze over, and he struggles to keep upright. As his body sways without control, I flail in my seat, attempting to get free.

When his eyes roll back, I scream. "Help him! He's falling!"

Thud. The men turn to where Dax collapses.

"What the hell's wrong with this kid," McCoy mocks.

Lance shoves McCoy away and moves over to his brother. He pulls Dax by his T-shirt and taps an open palm against his cheek. "Come on, wake up."

I thrash against my restraints. "He's sick. He needs a doctor."

Lance looks over his shoulder at me. "Sick with what?"

"Haven't you seen him collapse before?" I glare at Lance with contempt. "Keeping him here is killing him."

Lance scoffs. "Whatever." He hoists Dax up and turns in the hallway. "Keep an eye on her."

McCoy traces a finger along the part in my hair. "I'll stay with her. We'll have fun."

Lance retches. "No, not you." He then snaps his fingers at Boscoe. "You watch her instead."

McCoy slouches with disappointment, and helps Lance take Dax away.

"Dax!" I yelp, struggling against the rope.

"You hush now," Boscoe says, standing over me with his arms crossed. "Screaming ain't gonna do you no good."

My eyes water. "Please, he needs help."

Boscoe chuckles. "You're concerned about him while you're in this predicament?"

"I'm here because I love him."

Boscoe grins, wandering to the doorway and peering into the hallway. He taps his elbow like he's biding time. Well, I'm not. I continue to thrust my wrists back and forth, hoping somehow the rope unties itself.

After a good ten minutes of turning my wrists red raw, Boscoe ambles toward me, stroking his long graying beard.

"I'm giving you five minutes," Boscoe says gruffly. He smiles, showing off the gaps between his yellow teeth. "Because I like the kid."

"What?" I mumble as he walks away.

I'm alone in the room, and somehow it's more terrifying than Boscoe's overwhelming presence.

Before I can guess what'll happen next, someone races into the room.

Dax rushes over, lowers to his knees, and skids to a stop before me. His hands cup the sides of my face and wrinkles gather around his eyes.

"Oh, Sass. Why did you come here?"

He rests his forehead against mine as I reply with gushing tears. His fingers comb through my hair and my anxiety lowers from his closeness.

When his lips press against mine, they're dry and cracked. I gasp and pull away. "You're not doing well."

"It doesn't matter," he replies, moving his hands down to my binds. "Getting you out of here comes first."

"Dax," I whisper harshly. "You just collapsed. They won't do anything to me, or they lose their bargaining power. You need rest."

"I won't get that here. And you're crazy if you think I'm walking away from you."

"Boscoe said you had five minutes."

"Don't worry about him. I can handle it."

"He watches every time someone beats you. Why would he help you now?"

Dax shrugs. "Because he's never been the one that hits me."

I gulp, giving up the miniscule control I have left.

Dax pats down his jacket. "He took away my knife. McCoy is good with knots, but I'll try my best to untie you."

"Are you sure we can get out in time?"

"No, but I can't just leave you like this."

Dax hurries his fingers around the rope, trying to pull the knot apart. There's a tremor in his hand and he brushes the sweat off his forehead.

"Dax." My voice quivers. "You're so pale and you're shaking."

Dax grunts, clearing his throat. "I'm okay."

As he continues to fight against the knots, the door pushes open and Boscoe trudges into the room. My gut plummets as the burly man glares at us.

"Kid," Boscoe's gruff voice calls out. "Don't make me regret this."

Boscoe disappears again, and Dax's shoulders slouch. "The knots are too tight, anyhow. I can't get them loose."

I shiver, looking at the vacant doorway. "Is he coming back?"

Dax lifts on his knees and caresses my face. "It was just a warning. We have time."

My bottom lip betrays me with twitches. "And then what?"

Dax frowns, getting up and scratching his hand through his hair.

Fear floods my veins. "Dax?"

He turns his back on me, muttering, "Give me a minute to think."

I fidget in the seat, suppressing the sobs in my throat.

My ears prick to a clicking sound. Dax then bobs his head down, and I realize he's lighting a cigarette. When he turns back around, his frame hunches and the bags under his eyes appear gray. He unsteadily lowers to the concrete floor, and the ashy smell sends me grimacing.

Dax's hand trembles as he lifts the cigarette to his lips. He takes a long drag, and also takes his time blowing out the smoke.

"Baby," I whisper as my heart aches. "Those things are killing you."

His wrist rests on his knee, and he flicks ash onto the ground. "I don't want them, but I'm going out of my mind. They're the only thing keeping me semi-stable."

Adrenaline surges through me. "I've gotta get you out of here."

He looks at me with a guilty smirk. "You're the one tied up, Sassy."

I sit taller and thrust my fist upward in a futile attempt to break free. "But I'm walking out of here."

He returns the cigarette to his lips, getting up. He ambles over to me, his eyes running over me adoringly. "You're too much. I'd never guess such a good girl could be so feisty."

"I told you," I whisper, looking up at him. "I gave up the good girl routine."

He takes another puff and expels the smoke out the side of his mouth. His hand brushes over my hair and my skin tingles.

He angles the cigarette downward and lowers it toward my arm.

I suck in a breath, flinching in the seat. "What are you doing?"

Dax presses the ashy end of the cigarette against the rope. As it singes, the rope crackles and hisses.

"See," he says in a gravelly tone. "They come in handy sometimes."

I look and a smile curls his lips. My stomach flutters and I let myself crack a smile too.

He lowers, kneeling in front of me, and butts his cigarette on the ground. "Do you trust me?"

"Wholeheartedly."

Dax reaches inside his jacket pocket and pulls out his lighter. There's a noticeable break in the rope, but not enough to tear it apart. Dax flicks on the lighter and moves the flame toward my wrist.

I hiss, backing up in the chair.

He holds my hand as he guides the flame over the rope. "I'm right here with you. I won't hurt you."

I squeeze his hand, holding my breath as the rope catches fire.

The flame breaks through the fibers of the rope, finally splitting it in two. Swiftly, Dax lowers his head, blowing hard to extinguish the flame. Coughing hard, he closes the lighter and pulls at the rope until my hand is free.

I pull my hand up and press it against my rising chest. With relief, a soft laugh trickles out of me.

Dax leans over, kissing my free hand. His breath patters against my chest, upping my adrenaline.

He pulls away, looking into my eyes. "Ready to go again?"

I nod.

Suppressing another cough, Dax flicks on the lighter and angles the flame at my other wrist. The flame catches onto the rope and licks my skin. I yelp in pain and Dax hurriedly blows out the flame.

"I'm sorry," he blurts, cupping a hand over my tender skin. "Are you okay?"

I press my lips together, nodding. "Mm-hmm."

"Are you okay to try again?"

I gasp for breath. "Yeah. Just do it quickly."

He releases my arm and lifts the lighter back to the rope. I hold my breath, watching the flame attack the rope. With a snap, it breaks apart. Dax struggles to put out the fire, instead having to unravel it from me while still burning.

The rope falls to the ground, heating my skin as it slips past, and Dax stomps on it.

He then rushes to tend to my arm. "Are you hurt?"

I pant, heaving my chest. "I'm okay."

He clutches my hand, looking me over. "Are you sure?"

I push off the chair and fling my arms around him. "Yes. You've got me. How could I not be okay?"

As we stand, holding each other, Dax's balance wobbles.

"I got you," I whisper.

Dax doesn't reply, instead walking me out of the room. In the hallway, he leans and scuffs himself alongside the wall. I whisper encouragement, pulling him up and helping him bypass the bar.

Lance, McCoy, Hugo, and Stitch's voices echo from the bar, and I'm in no mood to serve Dax up to those wolves. A twinge of guilt cycles through me, presuming Stella is stuck with them. But I can't get her while Dax is slumped beside me.

I nudge him. "C'mon. We're so close."

But it's too late. His eyes roll back and he slips out of my arms.

His thud wasn't as heavy this time, and the bar sounds carry on. I lift his head onto my lap, coaxing him awake.

"What do you two think you're doing?" Boscoe's boots stop beside us.

I don't look up. "He needs help."

"His time was up, anyhow."

"You're not listening to me." This time I do give him eye contact. "Boscoe, if you care about him, you'll call for an ambulance."

Boscoe shifts like he's considering it, and then grunts. "Nope. The cops will wanna talk to him. I can't risk drawing more attention to the clubhouse."

"This is bigger than that. He's unconscious again, and if we don't do something, he mightn't pull through."

"He's tougher than that."

"He has been, but there's only so much fight his body can take. *Please*, Boscoe, get help."

Boscoe fidgets in indecision.

"Lance will be livid if his brother doesn't wake up," I say, desperate to put the man into action. "Or what about his dad? What will he do if he finds out you stood here and did nothing?"

Boscoe huffs, turning in the hallway. "I'll see if they've unloaded the truck yet. Maybe I can take him in that."

With Boscoe gone, I run my hand over Dax's icy face and the tears stream from my eyes. "Oh, baby, please wake up."

My tears drop onto his face. When two fall onto his eyelashes, he moans.

I lean over him, buzzing. "Dax?"

He moans again and his eyelids flutter.

I tap his cheek. "Dax? Dax?"

He coughs, turning his face to the side. His eyes lethargically open and close. When he shifts in my arms, he looks up and squints.

He coughs again. "Sassy?"

Happy tears blur my vision. "Yes, baby, I've got you."

He struggles to keep his eyes open. "What happened?"

I brush my hand through his hair. "You fell again."

"Oh."

"Do you think you can get up?" I search the hall for anyone approaching. "We really need to get out of here."

His eyes close again and he mumbles, "No. Sleepy."

I lift his shoulders, hoping he'll sit up. "No, Dax. You can't sleep right now. We've gotta go."

His shoulders slump in my arms, and when his head bobs, I lower him in defeat.

Not again. I refuse to sit here and accept this.

I hoist Dax from under his arms and drag him across the floor. Somehow, I need to get to the Porsche. Searching for strength I don't have, we curve around the hallway, and I spy a screen door ahead.

My heart palpitates.

There's a screen door at the front of the clubhouse.

With his back resting against my front, I hug my arms around him, pulling him through the doorway. As I puff my exhaustion, three sheriff's vehicles zoom down the road, sirens blaring. They stop in front of the clubhouse, encircling the Porsche. Blasted with shock, I lean against the doorframe, cradling Dax in my arms.

Officers race from their vehicles and approach the property.

Anticipation ricochets through my veins. "Help! He needs a doctor."

An officer reaches for me and I recoil. "Don't touch me! Help him. He doesn't have time to waste."

The officer pivots and lowers to check Dax. While pressing two fingers against Dax's neck, he uses his radio, asking for a medical team to arrive.

Relieved, I hold onto Dax. "Thank you."

"We'll take him from here," the officer says. "You need to get back to your parents."

My arms don't budge. "I'm not leaving him. I'll go to the hospital with him."

"We need to get you to safety."

"And I need to stay with him."

The officer relents. As other uniformed officers swarm the clubhouse, a second officer helps get Dax out of the doorway.

As the officers enter through the side of the clubhouse, Lance and the other men shout at the invaders.

"Everyone down on the ground!" Sheriff Lennon's voice booms

from inside the clubhouse. "You're all under arrest!"

As two officers prop Dax against the exterior wall, he groans sleepily.

The second officer taps Dax's shoulder. "Are you awake, son? Can you hear me?"

Dax murmurs and his eyes struggle to open.

I swoop an arm around his shoulders. "Dax? Dax, wake up."

Soon, an ambulance fires down the street with its sirens blasting.

"Sassy," Dax mumbles.

The officer leans over him. "What was that, son?"

Happiness floods my body. "He's talking to me." I brush my hand through his mop of hair. "I'm here, baby. You're going to be okay."

Twenty-Nine

"He really should've come in for treatment sooner," Dr. Harris states after Dax is wheeled into his recovery room. "His kidneys were shutting down. Another day or two without medical care, and he'd be in a coma."

I gulp for air. "Will he be okay?"

"We got to him in time," Dr. Harris says with cautious positivity. "His failing health is a result of his abnormal blood cell count. We will pump him full of fluids to flush his system, and get him on a course of medication. Once he's up for it, we'll recommend an improved diet, which will help his body pull through."

"Can I see him?" I ask eagerly.

"Just give the nurses' a few minutes to ensure the monitors are set up," Dr. Harris replies. "He'll be out, but you can sit with him."

"Thank you, Dr. Harris."

As I turn to move onto Dax's room, Sheriff Lennon approaches.

"Miss Ashworth, can I have a word?"

I bundle my sleeves over my hands. "Of course."

"First, I wanted to say, I'm sorry for the ordeal you've gone through. It must've been frightening."

"I think adrenaline got me through it."

"Before my team arrived at The Scorpions Clubhouse, we were given information by your housekeeper."

My heart jitters, and Dax's pendant swings from the heave of my chest.

"Apparently, Claudia Ramas broke down after your parents were alerted to your disappearance. When I met her on the property, she said she knew it was The Scorpions that entered the manor because your boyfriend was on the scene." Sheriff Lennon pauses for a beat. "That's Dax Malone, correct?"

I press my lips together, unsure how to answer.

"Ms. Ramas, quite passionately, declared Dax Malone's innocence."

My heart swells. "She did?"

"We're using Ms. Ramas testimony to keep Lance Malone and his associates behind bars. When Dax wakes up, we'd like to get his story to build the case."

My gut quivers. "Dr. Harris said it might take some time."

Sheriff Lennon nods. "I understand. In the meantime, I'd like to take your statement. The officers already took photos of your wrists, correct?"

I nod, pulling my bandaged wrists from my sleeves. "Yeah, before the nurse treated the broken skin and burn marks."

His breath hitches. "Burns?"

"I told the other officers everything while they were documenting my injuries," I explain. "I can't go through it all again. Not when I haven't seen Dax yet."

"It's really best if we talk while it's all fresh in your mind."

"Can't I see Dax first?"

"Okay, Miss Ashworth." Officer Lennon nods, his eyes shining with kindness. "I hope you're aware there are professionals you can talk with about the trauma you've experienced."

"Yes, thank you."

"I look forward to getting your statement. It'll help us keep Lance Malone locked up with unlawful restraint and attempted kidnapping charges. And then there's the physical assault charges." Sheriff Lennon's gaze drifts toward Dax's recovery room. "If Dax can map out everything to do with the robberies, we'll consider dropping the accomplice charges."

I clutch my chest. "So Dax would be innocent in all this?"

Sheriff Lennon smiles. "I got to know his mother well. He's a good kid who was brought into a bad situation. I'll do all I can to help him through this."

Just as I'm about to thank him again, I'm ambushed.

"Vanessa, thank goodness you're safe," my mother wails as she and Dad race down the hallway.

Sheriff Lennon excuses himself as they approach.

Mom throws her arms around me. "Come on, let's get you out of here."

I shove her off me and back away. "No, I'm not going anywhere."

"Vanessa, you scared us to death," Dad says sternly. "You're coming home."

Mom pulls at her hair. "How could you be so stupid and run into danger like that?"

I scowl at her. "Mom, I love him."

She scoffs. "You don't know the meaning of the word."

"No, you don't," I argue. "Love isn't about abandoning people."

"Vanessa, you don't love this boy," Dad interjects. "He got to you when you were vulnerable."

"You both have to stop telling me how to behave." I pant, readying myself for the next sentence. "Or you'll lose me."

"What are you saying?" Dad utters.

"I'll leave with Dax and cut you out of my life."

"You can't be serious," they both snap.

"He's the reason I'm out of that place." I tap the space over my heart. "He saved me, and I'm not leaving him."

"He's the reason you were in danger in the first place," Dad argues.

"Because I knew he wasn't safe there. I will never turn my back on him."

"This is crazy talk," Mom rasps. "This boy isn't good enough for you. You'll ruin your life with him."

"Or he'll make it the best freaking life possible. I don't care how my life plays out, as long as I get to share it with him."

"But, Vanessa," Dad says, reaching for me.

I back away, moving toward Dax's room. "But nothing."

Dax's room used to belong to the woman I found choking. I hope this means she made a full recovery and is living a healthy life. I stop by Mr. Raymond's door and find him sitting up.

"Vanessa," he says cheerily.

Happy tears spring in my eyes. "You remembered?"

He sighs, smiling. "They've pumped me with some of the good stuff. Never felt better."

"I'm so glad."

"Are you here to read to me?"

"Actually, I'm visiting somebody."

"Oh, hope they're doing okay."

I hang a thumb over my shoulder. "They're just next door."

He waves me off. "Give them my best."

I clutch my heart. In his state, he's still so caring for another person. "Thank you. You're the sweetest."

I move across to the next room and gradually make it to Dax's bedside. He's hooked up to an IV, a tube runs into nose, and he's hooked up to monitors. I clutch his tattooed hand and lower to the seat beside his bed. I watch his closed eyes as I press a kiss onto his hand.

I gently place his hand down and unclasp the chain around my neck. I set the St. Christopher's pendant by his pillow, hoping it'll bring him back to me.

"Ness?" a soft voice whispers from the doorway.

I turn and find Sylvie and Hope huddled together.

"Oh my gosh. What are you doing here? You said you'd never set foot in this place."

They step into the room, clutching hands.

"We heard about all the crazy stuff that happened," Sylvie says, wide-eyed. "Like, wow, are you okay?"

I rub my hands over Dax's and nod heavily.

Hope steps closer and presses her hand onto my shoulder. It lingers as she searches for the right words. In the silence, I look up at her and am surprised by the welling of her eyes.

"I'm so sorry you went through all this." Hope gulps when her voice cracks. She eyes Dax. "And you put yourself in danger for him?"

"I love him," I murmur.

She lifts her hand off me. "I'm sorry for getting in the middle of you two. I shouldn't have sabotaged your love life."

I sigh. "I would've done the same thing under different circumstances."

Sylvie fiddles with her necklace. "I'm prepared to put down the gossip-fueled, social-damaging weapons if you two are."

"Why do you think I've been avoiding school," I reply. "I don't want to do that stuff anymore."

Hope pats her eyes dry. "I only did the social media post because I thought if more people agreed with me, you'd finally see the light." She hides her face with her hand. "But they didn't agree with me."

I look at her sideways. "They voted for Dax?"

"You didn't see the results?" Sylvie questions.

"No. I blocked Hope so I didn't retaliate."

Hope's jaw drops. "You blocked me?"

"Believe me, I could've done a lot worse. You have Dax to thank for that."

Hope nods, knowing my reputation-damaging capabilities. "Oh, okay. Thanks."

I look Hope square in the eyes. "You should spend more time with your sister. She's shown me so much compassion."

Hope recoils in defense. "You know I love my sister."

"I'm just saying to take a leaf from her book."

Sylvie clears her throat. "So, do you forgive us, or what?"

I bite my lip, turning to the unconscious boy I love, and then back at my so-called friends. "I repeatedly asked you two to have my back, and you didn't come through."

Sylvie lets out a nervous laugh. "So, is that a no?"

"It's a *not right now*."

"I don't blame you," Hope bites her lip. "Because there's one more thing."

I tense up. "What?"

Hope claws at her long, chestnut hair. "Well, I was with Luke when I heard the news. And, umm, he was chatting with LJ."

I slouch with dread. "So LJ might be on his way over?"

Hope winces. "Yep. Sorry."

"You know, I'll consider the slate cleared if you two stick around and run interference in the halls," I reply. "I don't want to deal with LJ. Especially when Dax is in recovery."

"We can do that." Sylvie leans forward, checking out Dax. "How's he doing?"

"I don't know yet. Dr. Harris was quietly optimistic, but he also mentioned a potential coma and kidney damage."

Sylvie hisses. "*Yikes*."

"I can't believe I thought you'd be so perfect with LJ." Hope sniffles. "I've never seen you look at him the way you do this guy."

I look up at her. "His name is Dax."

She nods. "Right. Dax."

Sylvie lightly touches my arm. "We'll give you some space. And we'll watch out for LJ."

"Thank you so much."

They both wave and leave the room.

I pat my eyes dry and watch Dax sleep. As the wetness stains my fingertips, a silly thought enters my mind. He woke up when my teardrops hit his eyelashes. Could that happen again?

Before I can put the fairytale-esque theory to the test, footsteps pound into the room and irritation pings throughout my nervous system.

"LJ, stop before you even," I growl, turning in my seat. My annoyance diminishes at sight of my brother. "Oh, Ash."

Ash rushes over, wrapping his arms around me as I sit. "You're such an idiot, but I love you so dang much."

I hug him back. "Thanks, I guess."

He rubs a knuckle into my hair. "Seriously. Who walks into a biker bar?"

I swat him away from my hair, smoothing it back. "I knew he wasn't safe."

Ash nods, looking over at Dax. "So, he was worth it, huh?"

"He is more than worth it."

Ash sighs. "I'm just so glad you're okay. Can you not do anything else to scare me like that?"

"As long as Sheriff Lennon keeps Dax's brother behind bars, I won't have another reason to risk my safety."

"By the way, I saw Hope in the hall earlier. She gave me the head's up about LJ and I took care of him."

"What does that mean?"

"That you don't need to worry about yelling at him. He knows not to step foot in this hospital." Ash smirks. "Before he hung up on me, he said, 'like I'd want to go to such a diseased, flea-ridden place.'"

I laugh, unsurprised. "Certainly not the description he used when trying to become my date for the gala."

"I thought he'd be one less headache for you to deal with."

Guilt swells inside me. "I'm sorry what I did caused Christie to leave."

"It's okay. I've been on the phone with her. Her family are happy to come back now that Sheriff Lennon has the crooks behind bars." Ash leans down and kisses my head. "Love you, sis."

"Love you too."

"Vanessa?" my mother's voice enters the room.

Anger flames inside me, and I swing around to the doorway. I'm caught off guard when I find her standing beside my father.

"I've already heard this," Ash whispers. "I'll leave you to it."

Before I can reach for him, Ash walks out of the room.

I stay firmly seated in my chair, glaring at my parents. "What are you two doing here?"

Mom steps forward. "Your father knows everything."

I pivot between the two. "What?"

Mom nods, solemnly. "After you left us in the hallway, I was shattered. Coming home, my goal was to make you and Ash happy. I was overzealous about it, because I wanted you on my side when I had divorce papers drawn."

My heart aches. "That was your plan?"

Mom blinks back tears with her false lashes. "I couldn't stand the idea of you and your brother hating me."

I sigh. "I don't hate you, Mom." I turn to Dad. "When she says you know everything?"

"Switzerland and the tutor," he replies solemnly. "I had an inkling long before because of the growing distance in our relationship."

My shoulders slump as a wave of sadness drags me under. "Oh, Dad. I'm sorry."

He sighs. "It's not your fault, darling."

Gradually, all eyes fall on Dax. Mom and Dad creep closer to the bed, and Mom's the first to comment, "I know he's special to you, Vanessa."

"I love him, Mom."

"Sheriff Lennon has other witnesses who say Dax was a victim too," Dad says. "A young girl, and one of the older bikers."

My heart skips a beat. Stella and Boscoe.

Dad squeezes my shoulder. "If he fought to get you out while suffering with this illness, he must really love you. Any man who can protect my daughter like that, I can accept."

A tear rolls down my cheek. "Oh, Dad, thank you."

Mom brushes back my hair. "Take all the time you need, darling. We've told Dr. Harris, we'll take care of Dax's medical bills."

I look up at my parents, adoration in their eyes. "So, what does this mean for the two of you? You're divorcing?"

Dad puts an arm around Mom, and she leans into him. "We'll officially separate for the time being," Dad says. "We have a lot to work through, and going through a divorce with such bitterness won't be good for either of us."

"Your father agreed for me to stay on at Ashworth Estate," Mom adds.

"I can't see it being awkward," Dad says, his expression undecided on whether he should laugh or cry. "There are wings in the manor I haven't been in in years."

I exhale hard. "Whoa. Okay. I'm glad you two are finally talking and figuring this out."

"I'm sorry to have put you in the middle," Mom apologizes with anguished eyes.

"Me too," Dad says. "I know I haven't made things easy on you or Ash."

"Thank you for saying all this." I get out of the chair and open my arms. "And thank you for helping and accepting Dax."

"We know how much you love him," Mom says, wiping under her eye.

My heart squeezes and I blurt, "Dad, you have to let Murphy stay on at the manor. It's my fault those guys robbed us. I gave Dax a swipe card for the service entrance."

Dad looks over at Dax, sleeping. "And he gave it to them?"

"They threatened his safety." I gulp. "And my safety. He didn't have a choice. Have you heard what Sheriff Lennon is charging his brother with?"

"I know." Dad nods and pulls an arm around me. "So, Murphy has continually shown loyalty to you? A man who'll protect my daughter at all costs is someone I need to keep around the manor."

A tear spills from my eye. "Thank you, Dad. And what about Dax? He protects me too."

"Wait," Mom pipes up. "Are you asking for him to move in too?"

I nod, reaching out to grasp her hand.

My parents exchange a look, and return smiles in my direction.

"In a separate wing, of course," Dad says.

Exhilaration rushes through me as I hug my parents. They kiss and hug me, and I'm overwhelmed with the surge of warmth and love. They tell me to call if Dax or I need anything, and leave me to wait by his side.

With the heavy weight of my emotions, I flop my head on the bed. I watch Dax's side profile as he sleeps, and sigh. My hand runs up and down his arm, carefully not to knick any tubes attached to him. I squeeze his hand and continue to lie my head next to him.

As my breathing grows heavy, I focus on the beeps of the machines by his bed. I trace a finger around the rose on his hand and close my eyes.

"That tickles," he mutters croakily.

I shoot up to sitting, whipping my head in his direction.

He rubs his chapped lips together and squints his eyes open.

"Oh my gosh!" I squeal. "You're awake."

His eyes scrunch closed. "Ouch. My head."

"Whoops, sorry," I whisper. I get up and edge away from the bed. "I'm just going to get Dr. Harris."

He opens his eyes and gradually lifts his hand. "No, come back."

I hang a head out the door and spy Trisha in the hallway. I motion to her, calling out, "He's awake."

When her pace hurries toward me, I return to Dax's side. I scoop his hand and smile. "I'm here. I've got you."

He frowns and his puffy eyes are cloudy. "Am I dying?"

"No," I whisper, lowering to kiss his hand. "No, you're okay."

He grunts, wincing from the pain in his throat. "It felt like I was dying."

"You were just sick. But you'll get better now."

"Dr. Harris is on the way," Trisha says, bustling into the room. "Dax, how are you feeling?"

He grunts again and his voice is hoarse. "Like hell."

Trisha smiles at him. "But you're awake, and that's tremendous."

I turn to her, bursting with happiness. Before this day, I'd never heard her say a nice word about Dax. She'd cower in fear if he was brought up in conversation. Now, she's elated he's on the mend.

Dr. Harris enters the room, steadying the stethoscope around his neck.

He flashes a torch in Dax's eyes, and asks him to follow prompts like wiggling his toes and saying what day of the week it is.

Dr. Harris marks Dax's chart and a smile brightens his face. "This is an excellent start, Mr. Malone. Better than I could've hoped for."

I clutch my hands over my chest as my heart swells. "Oh, really, doctor?"

Dr. Harris looks at me, beaming. "Yes. He's still got a way to go, but I'm very impressed."

I sit back down and throw my arms around Dax.

He gradually turns his head toward me and plants a dry kiss on my forehead.

"Just take it easy, Dax," Dr. Harris says. "Don't strain yourself. Your body needs time to heal and stress will be your undoing."

Dax nods, and I say to Dr. Harris, "Don't worry, I'll be here for anything he needs."

Dr. Harris nods and moves past the bed. "I'll be back to check on you later."

Nurse Trisha follows him out, and I stroke Dax's arm. "I was so worried," I whisper gently. "But I knew you'd come back to me."

"I don't think I would've been able to without you by my side."

I lift the pendant from beside his pillow. "I think this helped too."

Life comes back to his eyes. "You found it."

"It gave me hope again."

"Your bracelet..." He tries to sit up. "It's at the clubhouse... I..."

I press on his shoulder, lying him back down. "You need to rest. The bracelet means nothing if you don't get better."

"But my brother..."

I smile. "Your brother is locked up. Baby, you're free."

His chin drops. "What?"

I nod eagerly. "It's over. Sheriff Lennon has him in custody, ready to throw away the key."

"You're serious?"

"Yes!"

He blows out a breath. "Wow."

I caress his cheek. "You're going to be fine."

He swallows roughly. "You know, I really thought I'd get better on my own."

"I know you did. Now you can get treatment, and my family will make sure you get the very best."

"I don't want to take advantage of you."

I laugh nervously. "You're not. I'm doing this because I love you."

A sparkle lights his eyes and his smile curves. "I love you too."

I lower myself to press a gentle kiss on his lips. He doesn't have the strength to kiss me back, but the fact he's present is all I need.

"I'll also make sure you're on a healthy diet. I'm going to help you through this no matter what."

"That cigarette I used to free you, was the last I'll ever smoke. I swear."

I tear up, nodding.

He gasps and jolts his head up, forcing me to recoil in alarm. His eyes widen and he searches for my arm.

"Your wrist. You got burned. Is it okay?" he asks in panic.

I place a hand on his chest, feeling the drumming of his heart. I shush him gently, smiling as I lift my bandaged wrist.

"I'm okay. Remember what the doctor said, no stress. You can lie down."

His head falls back onto the pillow out of necessity.

I run a finger over the bandage that encases the burn mark. "It still stings, but it'll heal."

"I hate that I burned you."

"Baby, you saved me."

"But I ruined your precious skin."

I grin. "I don't know. Maybe you marked me for the better."

He tilts his head, the sparkle livening his eyes. "There's something deliciously bad in you, Vanessa Ashworth."

I run a finger under his bottom lip. "That's Sassy to you."

Epilogue

Seven Weeks Later...

From what I'm told, the gala for St. Mark's Hospital was a roaring success. Of course, my mother wanted me there, front and center, but no one was prying me from Dax's side. How could I possibly schmooze benefactors when the guy I'm in love with was still in recovery?

I wrote a speech for the event and my mother read it on my behalf. Let's be real, this is how it always should've gone down. My mother loves the spotlight and taking in the adulation. But when I told her I was quitting the society events committee, her vicious side came out to play.

It didn't matter how she tried to deal with me, I wasn't backing down. Besides, she promised our family that she isn't leaving town

308

again. She's here to lead the committee, and she loves doing it. Somewhere down the line, we can re-evaluate my involvement, but right now, I'm done with that world.

While Dax remained in recovery, Dad asked me to join him at the office. Even though it was an invitation made out of guilt, I gladly took him up on it. Usually, work stories bore me, but hearing him describe how the finance, marketing, distribution, and human resources departments work under his leadership had me hooked. When I met the head of the finance department, I volunteered my help with crunching some numbers. It was nice that he wasn't annoyed by the boss's kid hanging around.

It was at the office I told Dad about my thoughts on school. I can't believe the amount of eye contact he gave as I told him I wanted a year off before attending college. He even smiled when I said I wanted to choose my college. I guess he thought it was better than me saying I wasn't going at all. Mom's thrilled to have me around for another year. I'm sure I'll be dodging more social engagements she signs me up for with little notice.

With that all being said, I've never seen my brother more relaxed. The fact I've rewritten the rules the family set for me is giving him hope. He'll be able to do whatever he wants after high school, instead of becoming the second Thomas Ashworth clone.

Now, I'm testing my parents on giving me freedom without interference. Dax and I are traveling interstate on his motorcycle. While Dax was recovering, he agreed to let my father's PI track down his mother. I'm so glad he was still being closely monitored in hospital because during the wait, his anxiety spiked. I almost called off the search when Dr. Harris found another irregularity with his kidneys. Luckily, a new course of antibiotics worked swiftly.

Nothing was more beautiful than seeing his pure joy when we were given his mother's address. As soon as Dax was given the all-clear from Dr. Harris, I had Murphy pack our supplies and we hit the road.

And now, the moment of truth.

Dax parks the motorcycle in front of a small sandstone home. I slide off the bike, and smile at him after we remove our helmets. Dax leans against the bike, exhaling slowly.

I place my hand on his chest, nicking his pendant. "Are you ready?"

He scoops up my hand, rubbing it tenderly. His fingers move down my wrist and find the sensitive bump of my burn mark.

I bite into my lip, smiling at the love heart tattooed into my skin which encircles the mark.

"I still can't believe my girl got some ink," he says.

I giggle. "My parents are gonna flip."

Dax shrugs. "They let you come this far. What's one more change to the perfect Vanessa Ashworth?"

"I don't think they expected me to get a tattoo on this trip. By the way, how is yours healing?"

Dax pulls up the sleeve of his leather jacket, and I can't help grinning. The tattoo artist did such a phenomenal job. Where once lay a horrible scorpion that shackled him to a miserable existence, now is a landscape scene based on the magical spot where Dax and I had our first kiss under the stars.

"I love it so much," I say, tracing a finger over his forearm.

"Me too. I don't feel like I have to wait until I'm eighty to be free."

I rise on my toes and peck his lips. "You're free now, baby."

Dax smiles and clutches my hand. "Shall we go in?"

I nod, squeezing his hand.

As we approach the front door, the door knob turns. We step onto the porch, and the door opens.

"Is that…" a voice sounds, but it's dark inside the house so we can't see the face.

Dax's ears prick. "Mom?"

Suddenly, a woman rushes out of the house. I drop his hand in time for the two to embrace.

Dax's mother's body trembles in his arms. "But… But, how?"

"It's okay, Mom," Dax says, his eyes growing watery. "It's over. They're both locked up. You can come home."

His mom pulls out of the hug, placing her hands on the side of his face. Her mouth hangs open as she stares at him with questioning eyes.

Dax smiles. "It's really okay. They can't hurt us anymore."

Tears stream from her face. "I've missed you so much. Every day, I regret not taking you with me."

Dax sniffs hard, pushing to keep his smile. "Don't be sad. We can be together now."

She motions to the house. "I have a home here. It's not much, but you can move in."

Dax rubs behind his neck, nervous embarrassment causing him to fidget. "Umm, I might have something better in mind." He gestures to me. "Mom, this is Vanessa."

She places a hand on her chest. "Oh, I'm so sorry for ignoring you. I was just so caught up in seeing him."

"Don't be sorry," I reply. "This is a big moment."

"I'm Jessie," she introduces.

I take her hand. "Nice to meet you."

"Mom, Vanessa has a huge home," Dax says, "and her family have agreed to let us stay with them."

"Why would they do that?" she asks, skeptical. "They don't even know me."

"But they know Dax," I pipe up. "And I love him. I love your son, and I know it'll make him so happy to have you back. Will you please come home with us?"

Happy tears spring into her eyes as she looks at Dax. "Is this true?"

Dax nods. "Can we go inside and catch up? We have a ton to tell you about, and I want to know everything that's been happening with you."

Jessie hugs him once again. "All that's been happening in my life is waiting for you. I love you so much, Dax. Thank you for finding me."

"You can thank my pushy girlfriend for that," Dax jokes.

They pull out of the hug, and Jessie quickly wraps her arms around me. "Thank you, Vanessa. I can't believe my son found such a wonderful girl."

I hug her back. "You're welcome. I'd do anything for him, and you too."

Jessie welcomes us into her home, but before we follow, Dax pulls me into a kiss.

"Thank you, Sassy," he whispers an inch from my lips. "Don't stop being your never-quit self."

I grasp his pendant and kiss him back. "I love you so much. I can't wait for the rest of our lives."

Scan the QR code to get a FREE chapter from Dax's perspective.

This chapter runs parallel with chapter 25 of *Shy Girls Can't Date Bad Boys*.

See Dax's point of view when his brother threatens Vaness's safety if Dax doesn't agree to work with him on one last job.

Also, stay subscribed for updates on the upcoming romance starring Meghan Fisher!

Thank you for Reading

If you enjoy this book, please consider leaving a review! Reviews help other readers discover new books. Just a few short sentences about why you liked the book is truly appreciated.

You can leave a review on Amazon, as well as websites like Goodreads and Book Bub.

www.goodreads.com
www.bookbub.com
www.amazon.com
www.hcpbooks.com

Thank you, again!

About the Author

Milly Rose is an animal-loving romance enthusiast with a swoon-inducing book formula. Shy girl + hot guy + first kisses. Her YA sweet romance books will have you falling in love every instalment. Milly Rose is the quintessential shy girl, who you can contact via her mailing list and reply to her monthly email blasts! Milly spends her days vying for her cat's affection, dreaming up her next book boyfriend, and writing a fun meet-cute under candlelight with a lovely brewed cup of tea.

Join Milly Rose's Mailing List Here

By joining the newsletter list you get a free ebook, exclusive deals, and are first to know about new releases.

Follow the Author

Follow author **Milly Rose** in the following places:

Website
www.hcpbooks.com

Amazon
www.amazon.com/Milly-Rose

BookBub
www.bookbub.com/authors/Milly-Rose

GoodReads
www.goodreads.com/MillyRose

Follow along on Instagram & TikTok
@shy.author.milly.rose